THE FONTRE

CHRONICLES OF LASHAI | BOOK TWO

JULIEN JAMAR

Pisteuo Publications

For Laura and Ryan
The best siblings a girl could ask for

And for Christina
I love you too much for even me to describe

Halanah
Forest of Fondair
Northern Borderlands
Kiatri Realm
Inner Kingdom
Southern Borderland
Perene-Valla
N

1

THE DECISION

A sixteen-year-old girl curled her legs against her chest in the blackness of the castle larder. The Fontre had rounded up Kiatri from all over the region the morning before, and since the castle lacked a proper prison, they herded their captives into this cramped, shelf-lined storage room. Thick walls and a heavy door created a secure holding cell. Sophie had already tested the door and walls for any weak spots four times since they threw them in.

Around sixty other Kiatri captives were with her. They were pressed against each other, awaiting the return of the black-clad Fontre warriors. *At least we're in a room full of food,* Sophie thought at first. *They don't intend to starve us to death down here.*

There was no way to determine the passing of time, which added to Sophie's anxiety. Within a few hours, they grew hungry. Sophie guessed it was the normal time for the evening meal. She had suggested they feel around for any food easily shared. People pressed against the shelves turned and began a search for edibles. The discovery and munching of plums, chunks of cheese and a barrel of crackers passed the time for a while. Now the hours and minutes dragged, with nothing to do but wait for hunger again.

A Troikord scullery maid named Tanna hunkered next to Sophie, each absorbed in her own thoughts. They said very little, but Sophie drew comfort from the girl's presence.

"When do you think they'll come back?" whispered Tanna after a lengthy silence. Her voice shook so badly that Sophie focused hard to understand the question. She wasn't usually prone to touching, but she wrapped her arm around the girl's shoulders. Tanna ignited Sophie's protective instincts.

"It'll be alright, Tanna. Someone is out there right now thinking of a way out of this situation." Even as she said it she figured it wasn't true. The Kiatri had been peacekeepers for so many years they'd forgotten how to fight back.

They heard someone fiddling with the lock outside the door, and everyone in the small space shrank away from it instinctively.

"Tanna?" the man's voice, whispering, was barely audible through the heavy wooden door.

"Tipps! What are you doing here? How did you know where we were?" Tanna cried.

"They made Cook show them this place and he told me they'd brought you down here. They've locked the door with some sort of seal, but take heart, my love. I'm working out a way to break the lock."

Sophie smiled into the darkness. "What did I tell you? He'll have a plan in no time." She gave Tanna's shoulders an extra tight squeeze and prayed Tipps would hurry. Her legs were falling asleep and the floor was bruising her bottom.

"You, boy!" A booming voice in the corridor made Sophie's stomach flip-flop. It was too deep and cruel to belong to a Kiatri. Tipps was caught by a Fontre. "What are you doing down here?"

"I – I was getting some jam for the Castle cook, sir. They're out of pinkberry and it's the Chief of Gate's favorite."

They heard Tipps' muffled explanation through the door and every captive held their breath.

"By all means, let's get your jam," growled the Fontre. The

lock clicked and the door creaked open. A tall, skinny Kiatri was thrust into the wedge of light. "Get in there. Maybe we'll take you with us too." The Fontre stepped into the doorway, his broad shadow blocking most of the light from the hall. Sophie cast about for a way to escape while the door stood ajar. She slipped her arm off Tanna's shoulder and scooted along the floor an inch to the right. The Fontre's black eyes met her blue ones and she froze.

"Going somewhere?" he asked in a low, harsh voice. He looked younger than some of the soldiers who'd rounded them up, but growing up with the ageless Kiatri hadn't given Sophie a good sense of age based on looks. All the Fontre looked older than most Kiatri men, who could be hundreds of years their senior.

The man's gaze flickered to Tanna. This was the first time Sophie had seen the girl in the light and she knew why the Fontre stared. Tanna was beautiful. Her fine, blonde hair curled around her face, accentuating her wide eyes and dark lashes. Tipps noticed the Fontre's attention and his jaw tensed.

"Sir, if I may, the preserves are on the second shelf down." Tipps tried to draw the man's attention away from the girls, gripping his arm and pointing at the shelves on the opposite wall. Three men crammed against those shelves attempted to lean away to give the Fontre a clearer view. "If you're planning to keep me here, would you mind terribly taking them to Cook for me?"

Sophie' stared at Tipps, in complete awe of his nerve.

The warrior in black paid Tipps less attention than he would a fly. He brushed his hand from his arm and took another step toward the girls. "Get up, girl," he said to Tanna. She pushed into the shelf at her back. The light from the corridor threw the angles of the Fontre's face into sharp relief; as if he was chiselled from stone. "I said, get up!" he shouted grabbing Tanna's arm and wrenching her from the floor so fiercely the girl cried out in pain. Sophie sat still, staring at them with a mixture of horror and rage.

"No, please don't!" Tipps threw his entire weight into the man's arm. "Sir, if you please, I was going to ask if I could take the place of one of the women. Would you allow me to go to the Inner Kingdom with you instead?"

"I thought you came for preserves," the Fontre growled. He grabbed Tipps' shoulder and shoved him into the shelves of jam. One shelf broke and sent jars of preserves and pickles smashing to the floor. Sophie jumped up to avoid the juice that seeped across the floor.

Tipps lay, covered in jam and shards of pottery, gripping his head where it had struck the shelf. The men who'd ducked aside now reached to help him up. The Fontre grinned at Tanna. Sophie saw one of his front teeth was broken off almost at the gum. "Think I'll make a special request of Lord Devilan. I want you as my personal companion when we get back to the Inner Kingdom."

Tanna burst into tears, and Sophie scrambled to her feet. "Stop it!" she yelled, though she instantly regretted it. The look the Fontre speared her with withered her resolve.

Another figure stepped into the light from the doorway. "Racalf," barked the newcomer. "Let them out."

The man in the larder stood to attention and his mouth snapped shut. Sophie watched with huge eyes as he released Tanna and marched from the cramped space without another word. Tanna fell towards Sophie, who threw out an arm to catch her.

Their unlikely savior nodded to the group. "You're free to go." And he also turned and marched away, his heavy boots creating an echoing cacophony that hurt Sophie's ears.

"We're free?" Tanna sobbed. It took Sophie a long moment to realize she was shaking from the inside out, and that Tanna was in danger of slipping from her grasp. Everyone in the larder looked at each other, as though waiting for someone else to make the first motion to leave. This small, seemingly insignificant act irritated Sophie so much she managed to pull herself together.

"We should get out before they change their minds," she said to the paralyzed group. Several snapped into action, pulling each other up from the floor and filtering out the door.

Sophie propped Tanna up onto her feet, checking to make sure the girl was steady enough to stand. "Tipps." Sophie dropped to her knees in the mess of food and pottery. She twisted up her long black hair and tied it in a knot on top of her head to keep it from getting preserves or pickle juice in it. "Tipps, are you alright?"

"Tanna," he whimpered, opening his eyes a crack.

"She's still here. She's fine, and the Fontre have gone. They said we're free, but I'm not sure if it's a trap. Can you stand? We should get out of here and find a good place to hide till we're sure."

"Tanna? Where is she?" Sophie pulled Tipps up and he threw his arms around the small, shaking Tanna. "There you are. I'm here. You're safe. We're okay," Tipps said, sounding as if he was reassuring himself as much as the girl in his arms.

"Right, and we should get out of here," Sophie said more forcefully. The larder had completely emptied, but a few Kiatri lingered in the corridor, waiting for everyone to get to safety.

"Come on, honey, we're safe now. Let's get away from here and get you a cup of hot tea or something," said Tipps in a soothing voice. Tanna had taken several deep breaths by then and calmed enough to pull away and nod.

"You could have been killed! How could you risk yourself like that?" Tanna demanded as Sophie shunted them out the door.

"I just figured I would rather be taken as slave than to watch you being carted off somewhere with those swine." Tipps kept his voice low, which made Sophie smile. The Kiatri were not rebellious by nature, but if they were to hint at rebellion, it would always be done quietly.

Sophie shook her head and squared her shoulders, her mind wandering to her handmade bow and arrows, wrenched from her when she was taken from her favorite hunting spot the morning before. She marched down the hall, only slightly less rigid than the men who'd imprisoned her. *I'll get my bow and arrows back. And no Fontre will ever get the drop on me again.*

∼

ELIAN AND HOLLIS stood side by side waiting for the Kiatri Council to let them enter. Elian glared at the ornately-carved wooden door. He noted this chamber was at the opposite end of the castle from the original Council Chambers that Cassai, Hollis and he had been led to that morning.

He understood the reason for the relocation. The Kiatri didn't want to meet in a chamber that looked as if it had been struck by lightning and an earthquake simultaneously. This room, much farther away from the scene of Cassai and his earth-shattering kiss, had escaped irreparable damage. Elian looked at the ceiling and reminded himself to breathe. Cassai was gone, taken by his cruel brother, and what happened to her was temporarily out of Elian's control. Just temporary, he reminded himself. They would save her from Devilan.

"Will you speak first?" He broke the awkward silence.

Hollis nodded, his hazel eyes focused on the door. "I think I should. I don't know if you've made the right impression to get through to them. Though you are Fontre, I'll paint you in as positive a light as possible," Hollis promised.

Elian grinned. Considering that in the last two hours he had threatened to kill Hollis, and then spent the remainder of the time planning a war strategy with him, they were getting on surprisingly well.

"Stick to the plans we laid out. Only use that final part as a last resort," Hollis said, nodding to the parchments they'd scribbled their points of persuasion on. "Ready?" Hollis' hand kept twitching toward his back as if to reach for an arrow.

"Are you? You seem nervous."

"I'm fine."

"I wish Cassai was here. She's better at this."

Hollis nodded. "Yes, Cassai could talk anyone into anything. But —"

"But she's being tortured by my brother at the moment," Elian said bitterly. Hollis looked surprised at Elian's bluntness. "You're the only one who can be painfully honest?"

"I was going to say — we'll do our best to represent her in her absence. But I suppose what you said is also true." Hollis glared at the door. "Can you tell if he's hurt her?"

Elian shook his head. The connection between Cassai and him hadn't given him the slightest twinge since his brother Devilan had taken her captive that morning. "Not physically, yet. He'll be cautious. The Fontre were hasty and uninformed about the Namarielle once, and it's almost cost them their most coveted conquest. They won't make that mistake again. They only have one Namarielle left to work with. But there are more ways than physical pain to torment someone. My brother is proficient in all of them."

"Do you think he'll ... force himself on her?" Hollis asked.

Elian chuckled. "You may have noticed it's damaging to life and property to make any sort of sexual advance on a Namarielle," he said, pointing out the cracked stones and ceiling, all damage caused by their one kiss earlier that day. "My brother's a fool, not an idiot."

"I guess that's something."

To their great relief the door finally creaked open. Elian expected the chief of gates, but a taller, more serious-looking man opened it.

"You may enter," he said solemnly.

Hollis stepped inside, followed by Elian and the tall Kiatri. An oval table almost filled the room, and around it sat the councilmen. The door shut, and to Elian's shock, the councilmen began to applaud.

Hollis inclined his head graciously and directed the accolades toward Elian. The men looked at him and continued clapping. Two actually got their feet. Tears streamed from the eyes of another. Elian fought the urge to tell them to stop because the applause should have gone to Cassai. She was responsible for freeing their loved ones.

"My daughter was among the captives," the weeping man said.

"And I," another said, "was locked in that wretched larder myself. Thank you, son."

Elian glanced at Hollis, who looked as uncomfortable as Elian felt. The Kiatri tried to smile at the men. "We're not the ones who freed you, but we come on her behalf," Hollis said, bringing the room to silence. Wooden chairs scraped against marble floors as the Council sat once again. "The woman who sacrificed herself for us came here for another purpose. We intend to see it through, if possible," Hollis continued.

The Chief of Gates sat directly opposite them at the large round table. He nodded at two empty seats. "Please, sit. We'll hear your plan."

"Cassai came to the city because there's rebellion stirring against the Fontre. Throughout the Borderlands factions are sprinkled who are willing to organize a fight for our freedom. They call themselves The Keepers of the Kingdom. But they aren't enough to fight alone. The Keepers number in the hundreds, the Fontre at least twenty thousand."

A surprised murmur rippled through the room. "Revolution? The Kiatri are not warriors, Hollis," one man protested. "What do you expect us to do? Fight the Fontre with our goat-keeping skills?"

"The prisoners the Fontre brought can help with that. One was a colonel in the Dukain Wars and a proficient trainer. He's willing to train you to fight. I know it's not the Kiatri's normal course, but −" The sound of protest had grown so loud Hollis could not continue.

"Madness!" one shouted.

"That's suicide!"

"We're keepers of the peace!" The tall one, who had not taken his seat, boomed.

Elian held up a hand. "What peace do you keep?" he demanded and the room fell silent. "The Kiatri were respected under the Namarielle. Every province in Lashai heeded your words of wisdom, from the Light Ones of the North to the most esteemed regions of Dukai. Now you settle skirmishes among your own people. Scuffling for the last bits of meat or measures of grain. The Fontre have already made fighters of you." Elian stopped at the look on Hollis' face; he wasn't sticking to the plan. The Councilmen's glares showed his grave error. Reminding them of their current poverty was tantamount to a slap in the face, considering his kin caused it.

"What Elian means is this," Hollis interrupted. "Things will worsen as long as we cling to our old ways. The Kiatri are a strong, noble race. The Fontre know this and perhaps they even fear us a little." Hollis' approach, though not that different from Elian's, was having a better effect. "This time, something was offered of greater value than slaves, but they'll be back for what they planned to take. They've taxed us into starvation and now they plan to enslave us."

Elian watched their faces. Some looked convinced, others skeptical. These men weren't revolutionaries; they were old and settled in the ways they'd observed for hundreds of years. Now Hollis had had his say, Elian was supposed to map out their attack strategy. But they needed these men entirely convinced before any strategy could work.

"Did you know they're breeding you?" he asked softly. Every eye, old and young, stared at him. The Chief of Gates' mouth went slack. Elian braced himself to continue. He knew how to frighten people. After all, he was raised by the Fontre. "The people they took last time, sixteen years ago; they conduct experiments on them. Your longevity is a mystery to the Fontre. It's something

9

they've long desired. Their lifespans are short, partly because they're such violent people, and partly because of the poisons they use to grow crops and breed livestock. They say these concoctions don't affect their superior bodies, but I believe otherwise.

"Rather than stop their corrupted way of life, they look for ways to sustain it. Your blood-lines factor into that plan." Elian swallowed and looked around. He didn't want to continue. The dread on their faces made this tactic harder than he'd originally thought. So, instead of looking at them, he focused on a mural on the back wall: A little girl laughing as she ran through a meadow of wildflowers. "Some of the girls they took are made to serve in their temples."

"Wait!" one of the men shouted across the table. "What does that mean?"

Elian stared at the painting. "The temples are how the Fontre reproduce." He paused, letting this sink in. Focusing on the laughing, innocent girl wasn't helping his resolve, so he averted his eyes to a different scene. On the right wall was a painting of a man fighting a dragon; the Kiatri patriarch and namesake. Better. "They believe they can create a crossbreed with your people and increase their years. The experiments haven't worked well, so they need more of your women."

"What do you mean — the experiments haven't worked well? Why do they need more?" A wizened man in the corner asked. Elian guessed him to be about five hundred judging by the wrinkles on his face.

"I think the girls are dying. Either in bearing the children or in the attempt to impregnate them. Fontre men aren't known to be gentlemen."

Chaos erupted.

Everyone at the table was shouting. Two men lunged for Elian and knocked him from his chair. He let them pin him to the floor and pound him with angry fists, because it was likely Elian had just described the fate of the man's daughter or granddaughter. It was also what he, Elian, probably would have done had the situation been reversed.

"Enough!" shouted Hollis, hauling the enraged Kiatri off Elian and pushing them back toward their seats still spitting curses at the Fontre. "There could be a way to stop it if you'll just listen!"

The Chief of Gates pounded the table with his fist. "Order!" he screamed.

Everyone stopped. Hollis grasped Elian's forearm and helped him painfully to his feet. Those who'd risen took their seats, still looking murderous. Good, Elian thought, the information had the effect he'd hoped for. Hollis shot him a glance that said he wondered if Elian was brilliant or insane. Elian didn't feel either. He felt despicable.

"Revolution is our only option. Reasoning and diplomacy aren't going to work. You already know that, so if you will listen to him for a moment, Elian can lay out our strategy."

The Chief of Gates had recovered his dignity and he pinned Elian with a calculating frown. "Very well, we're listening, young man. Lay out your plan of attack, if you must, and we'll proceed from there."

Elian dipped his head. "Thank you."

"I don't promise to agree, only to listen and decide."

"Understood. We know the Kiatri aren't trained for war, but you have a guest here, Marcus. He was a captive of the Fontre when they arrived."

"Yes. He's receiving medical attention from our healers," said the tall Kiatri who had finally taken a seat.

"Marcus was a Captain in the Namarielle Armies. He fought in the Dukain Wars, even the Great Battle for Hutten."

"And lost, apparently, as Hutten was demolished shortly thereafter," the Chief muttered.

"True, they lost that particular battle, but they won many prior to that bloodbath, and several of the victories were thanks to

Marcus' leadership. He's a good man, and a good Captain. We want him to stay and train your men to fight, if he'll agree."

"What about weapons? We're destitute, as you so lightly pointed out. How can we build an army with no armory?" A Kiatri who looked the youngest of the council asked.

"We have weapons," murmured the Chief. Only Hollis and the younger man looked surprised.

"What?"

"The Kiatri were once warriors. The man for whom our entire race is named was one of the bravest warriors in recorded history. But the longer we lived, the wiser we became. Eventually, we learned to seek peace rather than war. Boys and girls were taught to keep gardens and goats. All the weapons in our lands were gathered and sealed in the mouth of the mountain."

Hollis looked stunned. "That's an old legend, Your Honor. My mother used to tell it to me as a lad, as a bedtime tale. There's no room full of armor and gold in the mountain."

The Chief glared at Hollis. "I was there when the room was built, young man. I saw them seal it with my own eyes when I was no older than a whelp like you."

Hollis' jaw stiffened. At eighty years old, Hollis was treated as a grown man in the outside world. In the Kiatri Realm, he was considered a child. Elian grinned, but avoided eye-contact with Hollis.

"So, you have access to weapons, then?" Elian asked. The Chief nodded. "Very good. You'll need them and all the recruits you can get. We must leave you as soon as possible, I'm afraid. Cassai is in mortal danger and if the worst should happen, our strategy will mean nothing. The plan is for Marcus to stay and train your men. We'll meet him at the Westerling Field at Nuelletide."

The mention of the forbidden Namarielle holiday had a marked effect on the room. Tears filled the eyes of council members and the Kiatri who'd wept upon their arrival shook his head and started to cry again.

"May the Weaver allow us to celebrate Nuelletide in peace once more," he sobbed into an ancient handkerchief.

The Chief stood up and took a deep breath. "We will deliberate, young man, and inform you of our decision shortly. Meanwhile, we would ask you to wait in the holding room. Tipps will bring you tea while we discuss your plan." The man pulled a long purple cord and a boy entered, tall as Elian, but clearly young.

"Take them to the holding room and see to their needs," the Chief ordered. The boy smiled and gestured Elian and Hollis to follow him.

THEORIS TWISTED his long fingers at the Mountain entrance to the Realm of the Fey. He'd sent the message over a half an hour ago. Surely someone was coming up to speak with him. He sighed and tried to swallow his hurt feelings. He was no longer welcome in his homeland, yet he must appear when summoned and give The Queen information at her whim. It was insulting.

"Well hello, Theoris," A large fairy finally materialized. Theoris cringed at the sight of him. So Dahlia had sent Goliard, his former Captain of the Guard. Delightful.

"Hello Captain," Theoris said as rudely as he dared. "The Queen sent for me?"

Goliard grinned and cracked his knuckles. "Indeed she did. Have you discovered anything of interest about the girl?"

"They're meeting with the Kiatri Council today. They want help to overthrow the Fontre regime." Theoris sniffed.

Goliard took a step toward Theoris. "Is that all you've learned after a full fortnight of being with them?"

"I – well, there isn't much to know. They're part of a group of

Borderlings. They just want Lashai back," Theoris answered, stepping away.

"What have you learned about the girl?" the Captain growled, obviously enjoying the effect he had on his old subordinate.

"N – nothing beyond what I've just told you."

Goliard closed the distance between them and grabbed a fistful of Theoris' jacket. "What are you holding back, Theoris? You know how much I'll enjoy taking what I want."

Pain ripped through Theoris' body, as if Goliard had stabbed him with a dozen knives in a dozen places. The Captain released him and Theoris dropped to his knees, every ounce of strength drained. He gasped for breath. The pain finally lifted, but Theoris stayed on the ground.

"They haven't told me anything," he whimpered. "They don't like me."

"Then find out by other means, you worthless worm!" Goliard shouted. "Did she discover the book yet?"

"I don't know!" Pain again. This time it burned like red irons pressed into his skin. Theoris drew his knees into his chest and ground his teeth, trying not to give the Captain satisfaction by crying out.

"Ah, the poor exiled fairy. Do you miss your family?" Goliard taunted him. The burning ceased. Goliard stooped and murmured in a voice Theoris knew was meant to be soothing. "Tell me about the girl. Is she Namarielle? Has she read the book?"

Theoris sat still, looking at the ground and sniffling. "I've been told nothing."

"Very well," the Captain gave in. "The queen wants the Lost Book back. She wants you to take it somehow. If the girl's too stupid to look at it, Dahlia will find some other means of obtaining the information."

Theoris looked up, astonished. "She – she wants it back? Didn't she give it as a gift?"

"A gift? Are you mad? It's no dishonor for the Fairy Queen to reclaim something she gave a mortal. What's wrong with you Theoris, besides the obvious lack of intellect? You're still a fairy aren't you? You're at least capable of taking one thing from a small, unarmed, female human?"

Theoris swallowed hard. "Yes, sir," he mumbled.

"Get up." The Captain caught Theoris under his arms and heaved him roughly to his feet. "I'll send you another message soon. If you don't have the book by the time we meet, I'll pay your mum and brother a little visit, shall I?"

As instantly as he'd appeared, he was gone.

Theoris stood where the Captain had planted him, arms wrapped around his torso as though trying to keep from flying apart. His body ached. He couldn't stop shaking. He turned his face toward the Kiatri villages again. All he had to do was get that book back, and perhaps he'd never have to endure another visit from Captain Goliard.

"THEY'VE DELIBERATED for over an hour. How long do they need?" Elian fumed and paced.

"The youngest member of that Council is at least two hundred years old," Hollis said, pushing back in his chair and looking bored. "Coming to a hasty decision to satisfy your impatience is probably not their priority." Although he hadn't mentioned it, Elian could tell Hollis didn't appreciate Elian's deviation from their original approach.

"Do you think it worked?" Elian asked.

"Whether it did or not, you wearing a hole in that rug won't be any use. Settle yourself. I'm weary of watching you." Hollis leaned forward and rested his elbows on his knees. "An intelligent but risky move. You've succeeded in making them angry. I believe they're considering joining our cause, but I wouldn't sleep unarmed tonight if I were you."

Elian smiled. "I never sleep unarmed. Your concern for my safety makes me uncomfortable."

"Maybe I'm just finding a way to thank you for letting me paint you in a positive light," Hollis replied dryly. "Or did you forget that was our strategy?"

"Our strategy was to convince them by any means necessary," Elian said. "Besides, you know I was telling the truth. I thought you'd be proud. Devastating but honest. That's your creed isn't it?"

"Don't start with that again."

Elian sank into a chair and closed his eyes. "If only Cassai had been there," he continued. "I could have struck her with something equally horrifying about my past, or the truth about what's in store for her when they reach the Inner Kingdom. She could use toughening up."

Hollis rubbed his temples. "Shut up, Fontre. You're giving me a headache."

Elian resisted the urge to lash out. Arguing over their differing treatment of Cassai wouldn't accomplish anything now.

The door opened at last. "Gentlemen, we've reached our decision. The Council requests that you return to the chamber," the tall Kiatri said, leaving the room without looking at them.

Elian glanced at Hollis, who pushed himself up and started for the door with no reassurances in word or demeanor.

"The Council has deliberated your proposal," the Chief of Gates said as soon as they sat down. "Given the current circumstances, we believe you may be correct. Fighting a war with these barbarians is the wisest course of action. Ask your friend Marcus if he's prepared to train and organize troops. I'll open the mouth of the mountain and retrieve the hidden weapons."

Hollis nodded. "If there were any other way —" he began, but the Chief waved his hand, warning him it was not a good idea to speak.

"This is our decision. We'll announce it this evening at our 'victory celebration'," the Chief remarked bitterly. "You are dismissed."

Moments later, Hollis and Elian found themselves in the hallway shaking their heads in disbelief. "It was you that tipped the scales in favor of the plan," Hollis admitted.

"I'm sure they would never have let me enter this realm without your help," Elian responded, his voice empty of feeling.

"Very well. I guess our score's even." Hollis remarked offhandedly.

Elian's features darkened at this. "Not quite even, Hollis Farrell. I've yet to betray you and sell your loved ones to those who will torment and kill them." While he kept his voice as nonchalant as Hollis had, no one could mistake the animosity behind them.

However, Hollis didn't look abashed by this statement. "On the other hand, your people have already raped and killed the majority of my loved ones."

Seeing no end in sight to that argument, Elian rolled his eyes and let the subject drop.

2

THE FEAST

S ophie rocked back and forth on the balls of her feet outside Elian's bedchamber, waiting for her uncle to reappear in the doorway. Would he refuse to meet her and even listen to her request? She'd slung her handmade bow over one shoulder and the sheath of arrows on her back. She hated to admit how badly she wanted to impress Elian with her skill. It made the other Kiatri angry to see her with unconcealed weapons, and she enjoyed watching them squirm.

The door creaked open and Hollis walked out. "Come in," he muttered. He looked very unhappy, but she was beginning to think he always looked that way.

They walked through the entryway to a sparse sitting area with a fire. It was like Hollis' own guest room, except there were only two straight-backed chairs in front the grate. No cozy lounges, or even a rug, brightened the corner. She supposed the Kiatri weren't inclined to be overly gracious to a Fontre; even one who posed no threat.

A large man with wavy blond hair stood glaring into the fire, feet set apart and arms crossed, looking as if his mind was many miles away. He turned to face her and she caught her breath. His right cheek was bruised and swollen, there was a cut under his eye, and his lip was swollen and looked as if it had only just stopped bleeding. His clothing was travel-worn, dirty and ripped. She almost cringed at all the dark brown spots; obviously not mud. His eyes struck her most. She was used to the ancient eyes of the Kiatri, but his were bright blue and old beyond his years. They looked more sorrowful than ten Kiatri men who'd lost everything in the Great Raid. The Fontre warriors who'd yanked her from her house were dark, menacing and evil. There was only light and good about this man.

"Good afternoon. I assume you're Sophie?" The Fontre spoke in a deep, kind voice that sounded terribly hoarse, as if he'd screamed or cried too much today.

"Yes, sir," she answered.

"I am Elian. I'm glad to make your acquaintance." He smiled.

She watched him for a moment, wondering what to ask him first. So many questions bombarded her brain she wished she could have a week-long interview with him. "Is it true you're the Fontre that came to our house that day?" she asked. Elian's eyes flickered behind her to Hollis, then back to her.

"Yes. I was the boy. The man was my father."

"Uncle Hollis said you spared my life. And wanted to save the others as well."

Elian's face was inscrutable. His jaw tightened and his lips pressed shut. He drew in a breath and looked at Hollis again. "I thought you said she had questions about our journey."

"No, I do. I'm sorry. I just ... I've thought about you many times growing up. I always wanted to meet you and thank you. I'm sorry to bring it up now. Thank you. That's all," she said, wishing she'd shown more restraint.

"It's fine and normal that you should be curious about that day," Elian reassured her. "Please sit. I'm happy you survived the

Fontre both that day and this. I wish I could have spared you the pain of growing up without a mother and father. If I could have saved your family, I would have."

Sophie was so moved by this speech she couldn't think of a single appropriate reply. Finally, she just nodded and tried to hide her glistening eyes. She didn't want him to see her crying.

"Hollis said you had something in particular you wanted to know about our journey," Elian added, seeming to notice her predicament. "I'm sure you're concerned about his safety. Your uncle's under no obligation to me, and I'll do whatever I can to bring him back to you." Elian gestured to the nearest chair and Sophie clenched her hands to stop them trembling and sat.

Hollis walked past her and took the other chair. Elian seemed three times larger standing while she sat. Her argument for joining them felt less and less viable.

"Thank you for that. I just ... I was wondering about something else." Her hands folded and unfolded nervously in her lap. It had been a long time since she'd been this unsure of herself. Elian's blue eyes pierced hers and she looked away at the fire. "I want to go with you," she blurted.

Elian looked so shocked she tried not to feel insulted. Such a request had clearly never crossed his mind. He looked at Hollis, who stared resolutely at the floor. "Did you know what she was going to ask?" he demanded, all his bruises standing out brilliantly in his white face.

Hollis didn't look perturbed in the least. He tried to settle himself comfortably on the supremely inhospitable chair and crossed his arms. "You might at least listen to her before you explode. She might have a good point."

"She might have a good point?" Elian repeated slowly, his voice growing louder and raspier with every word. "I'm not convinced I should take you on this quest, let alone a child!"

Sophie's courage, which had returned to her bit by bit, came back in full force. "A child?" she demanded, desperate to force Elian to look at her. "I'm sixteen, and can take care of myself."

Elian glowered and she wished she hadn't spoken. He seemed to grow bigger when angry. "I'll escort you back to your home in Dulon and answer any questions you may have about the Fontre, or The Great Raid, or anything else you wish. On this matter, however, I'll not speak again. It's out of the question."

"Elian, if it were Cassai sitting there, you'd give her the courtesy of being heard. You could at least pay Sophie that much respect." Hollis spoke quietly and calmly.

Sophie wondered how he managed to summon the nerve when Elian looked fierce enough to destroy him with his bare hands. All the muscles in Elian's jaw and forehead seemed to be twitching at once.

"If you really believe that, you don't know me, Hollis Farrell. You think I'd listen to this kind of foolishness from Cassai?"

Hollis stood.

"Are you suggesting, Fontre, that because I want my niece to be heard and treated with dignity, I don't care for her safety?"

"This discussion has ended," Elian growled back, not looking the least intimidated by her uncle's wrath. She looked from one to the other, her insides feeling they would bubble over with excitement.

"It isn't safe for me here," she interrupted.

Elian looked at her again. "It's safer here with the threat of the Fontre coming back some day in the distant future than chasing after them," he countered.

"So I should just sit in our little hovel and wait for them to return and take me to their Temples? Is that it?" she demanded. Elian looked surprised by her boldness but not impressed.

"You aren't coming. I'm sorry if your uncle told you differently. Now, if you'll both excuse me, I haven't slept in a long while, and they expect us to be at their wretched celebration feast in a few hours." Elian looked back at the fire as he dismissed them.

Sophie, not daring to say another word, stood and walked to the door with as much dignity as she could muster. She could feel Hollis close behind her.

"Sophie," Elian said her name quietly.

Her heart jerked in surprise and she turned to face him.

"That look on your face – I know it well. I've seen it from Cassai when she's feeling stifled and rebellious. You're obviously strong and independent and that's admirable. However, if you mean to disobey me and I get the least wind of it, I'll lock you up myself and not let anyone release you until we're well out of range. Do you understand?"

Her eyes widened. She turned to Hollis, expecting him to defend her, but he was already in the hallway and showed no sign of re-entering the room.

"Yes," she breathed.

Elian thawed slightly. "I'm sorry to be harsh. It's been a very long day," he said. He looked close to falling over where he stood.

"Yes, I know it has," Sophie assured him, aching at the look on his face. "I apologize for troubling you."

He shook his head. "No need. I'll see you at the feast."

She nodded and left the room.

Hollis had waited for her outside. His hands were clasped behind his back and he was staring intently at a tapestry knocked slightly askew in the earthquake that morning.

"Right then," he said calmly. "That's Elian."

She grinned. "I think he's wonderful."

"He's spoken for, if that's what you mean," Hollis reminded her coolly.

Warmth rushed to her cheeks. "No, that's not what I meant. I mean, I've never heard of a Fontre who was...kind."

Hollis rolled his eyes. "Yes, his kindness, that's what stands out most about him."

"You don't like him?"

"He's Fontre," Hollis said as if that settled the matter.

"Did you hear him threaten to lock me up if I follow you?"

"I heard something like that. I wouldn't test him, if that's your next question."

"But would you stick up for me? Would you tell him to let me stay?"

"No." Her eyebrows rose in surprise at the finality of his answer. "I was no match for Elian when he was seven years old and charged into our house with his father. He could have overpowered me even then and killed us all. I'm not the least inclined to start a fight with the full-grown version of him." Sophie could tell this admission had cost her uncle greatly and let the matter drop.

ELIAN WOKE that evening to Tipps gently shaking his shoulder. The Kiatri page had come to take Elian to the banquet hall. He was surprised to find he'd slept. His anxious thoughts had weighed on him so heavily that he'd lain down without the slightest thought of getting real rest. Rising, he took a long breath. His body felt better than in weeks. Sleep. He hadn't realized how much good it did.

"I brought you a clean set of clothing, sir," said Tipps kindly. Elian smiled at the pristine white shirt, trousers and sturdy-looking jacket. "There are undergarments in that cupboard. I'll draw you a bath, shall I?"

"Thank you, Tipps. I'm sure you'd prefer to be elsewhere. I'll fend for myself."

"No sir, I prefer to be here," Tipps insisted. He walked to the screened-off corner of the room concealing a washtub with a white towel folded over the side. "I'll heat some water."

"Much as I appreciate the gesture —." Elian felt guilty that he'd been assigned a servant.

"My betrothed and I were among the hostages," Tipps interrupted. "One of the Fontre *Koninjka* had an eye on her and the Weaver only knows what would have happened if it wasn't for you."

Elian could only shake his head, speechless at the gratitude in the Kiatri's voice. "It's my fault she was taken in the first place, Tipps," he reminded the servant. "The *Genraal Majure* is my brother and wouldn't have come if he'd not been anticipating my arrival."

Tipps smiled and tipped his head respectfully. "All the same, I have my Tanna back safe, and you shall have a hot bath. Let me help you out of those ... er, clothes."

Then Elian smiled too. His appearance must be startlingly ragged after so many days in the elements. "Yes, something fresh would be welcome."

THE KIATRI HAD DECORATED the great hall lavishly considering their impoverished state. Garlands of mountain laurel and lunamere buds festooned every available wall, trellis and fireplace. Elian also saw that some cracks in the wall were camouflaged with greenery. Cracks caused by our kiss, he thought painfully. The hall was filled with large round tables draped in hand-woven linens. The tables groaned beneath the weight of the most delicious looking food Elian had ever seen.

Tipps navigated Elian through the grand room to a table. It was filled with his companions. Hollis and Sophie sat on each side of the chair assigned to Elian. Theoris sat on Hollis' other side, his pointed face even paler than usual. His bright yellow hair was spiky as ever. Also sitting at this table were the Chief of Gates, the Head of Council, and Frederick and Cornelius. Frederick rose as Elian approached and wrapped him in a hug.

"So this is what you look like under all that grime!" he boomed cheerfully, clapping the shepherd's back.

Elian grinned. "Yes, I'm not sure why a bath was insisted upon, but Tipps was adamant." He nodded at Hollis and sat down. Sophie smiled, looking nervous. "Good evening, Sophie," he said, forcing cheerfulness into his voice.

"Yes – um – good evening," she stammered, not looking up from her plate.

He felt a twinge of guilt. "So, tell me about delicacies of the mountains."

"Well, the plums are good. They're just in season. They only stay for a few weeks so we dry them and eat them all winter, but they're best fresh."

He smiled. "I apologize for my behavior earlier. I'm afraid I came across too hard," he said quietly.

She flushed. "I got a little carried away. I should have realized how ridiculous I'd sound to a seasoned warrior."

An uncomfortable silence followed. Elian covered his awkwardness by filling his plate with the delicacies overflowing from the center of the table. He grabbed two grainy-looking rolls from the bowl and surrounded them with goats' cheese, plums and roasted hare.

"Theoris, you're looking ... ill," he observed.

Theoris jumped at his name. "It was a delightful day, thank you," he said at a much higher pitch than normal. "How was yours?"

Elian raised his eyebrows at this response, but couldn't think of a reply.

Hollis glowered at the fairy and Theoris shrank away and stuffed a huge bite of roll in his mouth out of pure nerves. "Mff ... sorry," he mumbled around the food. "Of course your day was dreadful. They told me all about it."

Elian nodded. "Hopefully, it'll be set right soon."

"Poor Cassai," Theoris moaned. The fairy looked so concerned Elian wished he could reach him and pat his back.

"We're going after her, Theoris. It'll be alright," he assured him.

"I don't suppose you'd ... I mean, could I possibly ...?"

"Would you like to come?" Elian finished his thought. Hollis glared at the meat on his fork. Elian grinned.

"If I did, I'd be no trouble, I swear. I'll be more vigilant at hunting and learn to play my flute properly so I can offer musical solace on sad evenings. Not, of course, that we'll have reason for sadness."

"Perfect," Hollis interjected. "We'll be glad to have you along, fairy." Theoris looked stunned and pleased by this. From the cruel tone in Hollis' voice, Elian sensed the fairy wouldn't be pleased long. "In fact it might work out very well. You know the entrance to the Fairy Kingdom from the Mountain, do you not?" finished Hollis.

"Um – well, yes. I mean, of course I do," Theoris stammered.

"Excellent. You can lead us there at first light. Elian and I have business with the Queen. Your assistance in the Realm will be invaluable."

Theoris stared at Hollis. His mouth sagged, but he seemed completely unaware of it. "But – well, I'm banned from the realm. You know that."

"Perhaps we can talk Dahlia into making an exception. Just this once." Hollis thumped him hard on the back. Theoris looked ill.

Elian couldn't help smiling again, though he tried to suppress it.

～

KRISPEN SNIFFED the air and bore west, amazed at the sharpening of his sense of smell. But his eyesight had gone all strange. Colors weren't as they should be and light reflected off things funny. But he could smell; could smell the trail of the pack, and he could smell Isabel. She was still alive.

He felt alien squeezing in his stomach when he remembered he'd left Cassai and Elian, the only family he'd ever known. But it was better this way. They might be in danger from him. What if he killed someone? What if he hurt Cassai? He shuddered. Yes. This was best. He'd done it right at last. Even Elian would never have guessed that he, Krispen, would have the courage to leave in the middle of the night.

He sniffed again. How he'd get Isabel free when he caught up with the pack ... well, he'd worry about that when the time came. It was growing dark, but he kept running. Then it happened, not all at once like he thought it would, but slowly, he began to change. Crushing pain stopped him in his tracks. It felt like every bone in his body was being broken one by one. Inky darkness shadowed his mind for a moment, easing the pain, making him feel feral and numb, but a light fought against the dark and won out in the end. Brutal clarity returned. He was Krispen, the shepherd ... agony. He sank to the hard packed earth, drew his knees against his chest and pressed his face into them.

His skin burned as long, coarse hair sprouted from every pore. His gums inflamed as large pointed teeth sliced through them. Just when he thought he couldn't bear another moment, the pain slowly began to lift. He lay his cheek against the cool ground, panting for a long time.

Burning thirst.

Water. He must have water. No. It wasn't water he craved. Blood. He must find blood. One thought overwhelmed all others. Isabel. Isabel tiny and helpless, surrounded by wolves thirsting for blood. He sprang to his four paws and sniffed the air. Every smell of the forest was identified and set aside instantly. All that remained was Isabel's scent. He started running, fast. Much faster than was possible when he was human.

He sniffed as he bolted and smelled the pack underneath him. They were underground. A strange urge overtook him. Dig! His senses screamed at him and he started digging. Faster and more ferociously than he'd ever done anything in his life. Krispen's claws threw the earth aside.

In an impossibly short time the hole was big enough for him to fit into. He kept digging. A tunnel was forming, and then, to his surprise, he was not clawing earth. He had dug through to a hole already underground. He gouged and scraped until he could see all of it, then he slid his canine body through.

Despite the changes in his eyesight above ground, he could see clearly here. The underground darkness illuminated his path better than the moonlight. It wasn't a cave, it was a tunnel. Reeling from this new revelation, he tried to get his bearings. Forks led to other passageways. They led everywhere. Off the tunnel he had jumped into, at least six more were visible. He sniffed again. The scent was stronger. He chose a tunnel to his right and streaked toward the pack: toward his stolen lamb.

THE DELECTABLE FEAST held little appeal for Elian. He was constantly interrupted by grateful Kiatri, each wanting to shake his hand. He also suspected he held a certain fascination for them, being the only Fontre they'd met who showed them kindness. He smiled, nodded and shook hands until exhausted. At last, the Chief of Gates looked at the Head of the Council and sighed.

"I suppose you expect me to be the one to address them?" he said, his voice weak with weariness.

"It's down to you. I don't give speeches anymore, you know." rasped the Head of Council. "At twelve hundred years old, I'm allowed a bit of a retirement, wouldn't you say?" he addressed this question to Hollis and Elian. Both nodded.

The Chief of Gates looked resigned and made his way to the platform at the front of the room.

"My friends and fellow countrymen," the stately Kiatri called to the crowd. "I require a moment of your attention." The room began to fall silent. "This feast is not only a celebration of our captives being set free," he paused for the deafening cheer, then waved his hands for quiet, "but also to inform you of a Council ruling.

"Our guests have sacrificed much to be here and even more for the dreaded Koninjka to free our kinsmen. We were informed this morning that the price was much heavier than we thought. The woman who sacrificed her life for ours was named Cassai, and she, I'm told, is the last of the purest and oldest bloodline of the Ancient Namarielle."

These words were greeted with so much surprised chatter it took several minutes before order was restored.

"Please, please listen. You all know the burden the Namarielle bloodline carries. They are the life source of our beloved land. We've speculated how Lashai lasted so long after the Midnight Revolution, where, we were told, they had all been slaughtered. The Fontre lied. We don't need their magic for the land to survive. In fact, their methods are poison to our soil and our animals. Therefore, we have decided to organize forces and ... and go to war!" At the mutinous outcry to this statement the Chief of Gates called for silence.

"Please understand," he shouted. "We did not make this decision lightly. One of our guests has fought in many battles. He's offered to help ready us."

"No!" screamed a large man with an enormous red beard. "We Kiatri are peacekeepers. We will not follow in the treacherous and bloody ways of ... another who has forsaken us." He looked directly at Hollis, who glared at his plate.

"I know it's not our way to fight. But I believe that on occasion the keeping of the peace requires it. Do you truly think the Fontre have any interest in diplomacy?" Utter silence. "The time has come to take our stand. Stand with us, and you'll give freedom to your children and grandchildren. A man called Marcus will be teaching us methods of battle. We'll give him one week to recover his strength, for the Fontre badly abused him before he came here. The first training session begins at dawn one week from tomorrow. We expect every able-bodied man or woman who can be spared from their households to sign up for this training." The Chief nodded curtly and stepped down. He didn't stop at their table again, but made his way through the buzzing crowd and exited the room. The roar of the crowd rose to the greatest heard all night.

"Well, we should get some sleep," Theoris shouted over the din. "Fairies rarely need sleep you know, but perhaps tonight – " Theoris didn't finish his thought, but hurried out of the hall after the Chief.

"Are you going to bed?" Sophie asked Elian.

"I have little hope of sleep tonight," he admitted tensely. "While Cassai is in my brother's hands, I'd be surprised to relax enough to sleep again."

"I suppose you mean to leave first thing?"

"Yes. We'll travel to the mountain at first light. Will you see us off?"

She blushed again. "I – yes. I'll bring you breakfast and supplies for your trip."

Elian's chair scraped against the flagstones as he rose. "Until the morning." He nodded politely.

"Yes, good night," she replied and left the table without a word to her uncle, who scowled darkly at their exchange.

∼

KRISPEN RAN toward the scent of Isabel with a speed he'd never thought possible. The underground tunnels seemed to go on forever. He wondered if perhaps they ran under the entire Forest of Fondair. Another thing changing in him was his mind. Usually he could only think of one thing at a time. Normally that thing was either how much he loved his sheep, or how much he loved Nanna, Elian and Cassai ... mostly Cassai. Now different parts of his brain worked at once. He focused most on his lost lamb, Isabel, while also worrying about his friends. The part of his consciousness that he was vehemently pushing back was his desire for fresh blood and meat.

The scent grew stronger and he heard a ghastly ruckus from somewhere not far away. Growling and snarling and snapping of jaws mixed with the pitiful cries of his lamb. Krispen burst toward the awful sounds with renewed urgency.

The young wolf emerged into a giant cavern. He shook his furry head, trying to make sense of the scene before him. In the farthest corner, an alcove looked as if dug out recently. Isabel huddled against the darkest corner of the hole, bleating pitifully. Bars of thick branches stretched from floor to ceiling, imprisoning her.

Against the opposite wall, heavy chains bound the legs of four furious werewolves. They fought their bonds as if they were one. They snapped at the chains and snarled against the hooks set in the floor. Their eyes were wide and red, and foam dripped from their jowls.

Krispen stared at them for one moment, then darted toward the cage that held Isabel captive. He paced back and forth in front, looking for a way through the bars. Isabel pressed herself as hard as she could against the back of her prison and bleated louder. Krispen's heart jerked. She was trembling with fear of him. Him. Her protector and savior on many occasions.

New resolve filled Krispen. He clamped one bar in his mouth and yanked as hard as he could. He felt his teeth were ripping out, but the branch didn't budge. His glance flew to the mad wolves surrounding them and he tried again. Nothing. He scratched the floor, but the ground was solid. Despair ripped through him and he tried to force Isabel to look at him; to understand he meant her no harm. Then, against the frenzy engulfing them all, he stretched himself in front of her prison to wait for day and transformation back into human form.

3

THE FAIRY CELL

W hen Elian rose next morning, the sky was a purple haze between darkness and dawn. He went to the window and looked out at the surrounding mountains. In the creeping light of dawn, the streaks of sun breaking through the mist, turning patches of the valley green while the rest remained steely purple took Elian's breath away for a moment. There was a soft knock at the door.

"Come in."

Tipps backed into the room carrying a breakfast tray.

"Morning, sir," he said brightly.

"Morning, Tipps. Thank you for this." Elian indicated the breakfast tray. A thick roll stuffed with eggs, sausage and mushrooms sat on a porcelain plate tipped with gold. Fresh plums swam in a bowl of something purple and sweet and a steaming cup of coffee sat beside it.

"I've also got your clothes for the journey. Hollis wished me to tell you he'll be ready in a few minutes. I made your breakfast into a sandwich so you can eat quickly if you wish."

Elian tipped his head in thanks and took a large bite from the sandwich. Too soon, breakfasts would consist of nothing but dried fruit or meat. "Have you eaten?"

"I have, thank you, sir. Can I help with your clothes?"

"Thank you, Tipps. I'm alright. A full hot breakfast was more than I hoped for before this trip." He stuffed two more bites into his mouth and washed it down with the hot coffee.

A few minutes later, dressed and satisfied, Elian waited outside the door of Hollis' bedchamber.

He heard the Kiatri moving around and wished he'd hurry. With nothing else to occupy his mind, his thoughts went to Cassai. She would have loved the breakfast this morning, and would be happy to see him dressed in a bright crisp tunic and trousers. His traveling coat had been cleaned, the sheep fleece lining white and soft as new and the leather treated with something Tipps said would make it waterproof for the coming winter.

Hollis' door opened and he emerged looking very unrested, but all of his gear strapped to his body.

"Morning," he mumbled.

"Is Sophie meeting us? We should be leaving to get Theoris this moment."

"She's coming, I'm sure. There's Theoris now."

"He looks terrible," Elian commented as the fairy stumbled toward them from the end of the corridor. Half his yellow hair lay flat against his head and the other half stood straight up in its usual spikes, making him look like a porcupine with half its quills plucked.

"Are we ready?" he whispered, balancing gingerly as if trying to stop his head toppling from his shoulders.

"We're waiting for Sophie," Hollis said, not bothering to lower his voice. "She said she'd see us off."

Theoris cringed. "Oh, I say, could you speak more quietly?" the fairy pleaded. "I shouldn't have taken that bottle of wine to my room last night." His eyes were rimmed with red, his clothes rumpled and badly assembled. The new trousers provided by the Kiatri were too big for his slim waist, so he'd gathered them in bunches and belted them too high.. He'd fastened the buttons on his shirt wrongly, making his collar stick up on one side and he'd only stuffed the shirt tails into his trousers in two places. "I can't get the hang of all these layers," he mumbled.

Tipps smiled. "I can sort you out, sir. Give me a moment." The Kiatri rushed to fix Theoris' buttons, and Hollis cast Elian a glance.

"Ah! Here's Sophie," Hollis announced more loudly. Sophie, laden with a heavy-looking basket and large burlap bag, appeared at the end of the corridor and waved.

They started toward her. Theoris, still holding his head, followed them out into the courtyard.

"Breakfast is in the basket, and the bag has food that will travel well," she explained in a whisper, holding out a large basket to Elian and an even larger bag to Hollis.

"Thank you, Sophie," Elian said.

Hollis gave her a pained look and set the bag down. "I wish I didn't have to leave you so soon."

She smiled and threw her arms around his neck. "We'll meet again, Uncle. Soon, hopefully. I'll pray for you," she added as she pulled away.

"If the Weaver would listen to anyone it would surely be to you," Hollis whispered.

"I'll bring him back to you," said Elian, taking her hand and squeezing it. Her eyes shone with tears.

"Promise?"

"Promise." And Elian turned to follow Hollis.

Elian heard Theoris muttering hasty thanks for the food and his hurrying to catch up.

The cold morning air hit them all in the face when they walked through the two giant front doors of the castle. The courtyard was empty save for two guards waiting to open the gate. The shrubs and greenery of the courtyard garden were frosted over, but the fountain at its center still bubbled cheerfully.

"Do you believe this trip to see the fey is worth the delay?" Elian asked as they strode to the gate.

"If it goes well, it could mean the difference between victory and defeat," said Hollis.

"Yes," Theoris groaned. "In the unlikely event that it goes well."

With these discouraging words, the companions departed through the hazy light of dawn. None of them turned to look back, or they might have noticed sporadic flickers in the shadows, almost as if a wisp of a person was following them into the mountains.

CASSAI FELT as if every muscle and joint was jarred out of place. Her broken wrist ached beneath its wrappings and she stared resolutely at the upholstery ahead of her not occupied by Devilan. She'd spent the previous day entirely in his silent company. He'd observed her as if she was a bug he'd pinned to a board.

The night sleeping on the ground in the Forest had done nothing to ease her pain. She'd grown accustomed to sleeping on hard packed dirt in her journey to the mountains, but that was in the company of Elian, Hollis, Theoris and Krispen. Sleeping between Dershom and Devilan himself made rest impossible.

Devilan smiled at her and stretched his arm across the seat beside him looking rested and at ease. Cassai glared at him as darkly as she dared. "Are you uncomfortable? Is your arm hurting?"

"I'm fine," she answered.

"Very well, shall we begin?" He leaned forward, resting his elbows on his knees. Even if Cassai hadn't been trained all her life

36

to fear and despise the Fontre, she would have feared and despised this man. He had the usual sharp, high cheekbones and dark features of the Fontre and just enough of Elian in him to be a constant, stabbing reminder of everything she'd lost.

"Begin?"

"I have questions. Do you remember our arrangement?"

She glared at him and didn't answer.

"What will happen if you don't answer the questions to my satisfaction?"

Her eyes flickered to his for a fraction of a second, and then she looked out the window. The image of the carriage box Devilan had shown her was burned into her brain. It was too short and narrow to sit comfortably, with edges and sharp points poking from every angle.

"I'll ride in your torture chamber on wheels," she replied, steadying her voice. Anger boosted her courage.

"Well done." His grin turned her spine to ice. "Now, first question. Are you afraid of me?"

Cassai frowned. This question struck her as the sort Cobbs might ask when he was tormenting her as a younger girl. "Why? Is my fear some sort of necessity?"

The look Devilan gave her was decidedly unCobbsish. She shivered at the cold, calculating steel in his eyes. "It answers several questions without my having to ask. Answer me."

"Yes."

"Good. That's a start." He pulled a curved knife from a sheath in his belt. Cassai swallowed hard, but he used the tip to clean his fingernails. "We had an interrogator in our ranks named Kirkus who used to waste a lot of time and energy extracting useless information from his victims and, by the time he got to the things we needed, they were used up and unable to cooperate. We finally found a better use for his skills." He put the knife down and smiled at her. "I begin differently. I build a profile of you; discover your fears, because fear is the only real motivator of humanity."

"There are other motivators," Cassai pointed out.

Devilan laughed, "Ah, so you are of my brother's making after all. I assume you refer to love."

Cassai looked out the window rather than answer.

"Consider this, little Namarielle; what is love, really, besides fear? To give in to love is to experience one of the deepest and basest fears known to mortals; the fear of loneliness."

His black eyes fixed on hers so intently Cassai knew he would require an answer this time. Something squirmed inside of her. "Love is deeper than fear of loneliness." Her heart raced at her boldness. "True love has its own power. Power you'll never understand."

"I understand much more than you realize. You needn't experience something foul to recognize its stench. But enough about me. You fear me, as you said. Why? What is in me that you fear? Pain?"

"Everyone fears pain."

"Not everyone. My brother has almost no fear for pain. There were times in his training I even thought he enjoyed it. You're a different matter. Pain and cruelty, you fear both, don't you?"

Cassai stroked the bandage on her right wrist absentmindedly. It hurt more deeply when she thought about this. "I don't want to be in pain, if that's what you mean. I'm not sure fear is the right word for that." Cassai looked out the window.

"We'll come back to that when you understand yourself more clearly. Tell me about your parents."

Cassai blinked and continued to fix her gaze on the passing landscape. His voice unnerved her, it was too similar to Elian's. *Pretend you're talking to him.* With a deep breath she sat up straighter. "I don't remember much."

"Why does your memory fail you?" Devilan asked.

"Because I was four when they died," she said.

"Have you always known your identity: always remembered your significance to the Kingdom of Lashai?"

She finally looked at him. "No." She wished he would stop.

"How could you forget you are a member of the ancient, essential bloodline of Namarielle?"

"I started to remember ... a few weeks ago." She wished she could lie; wished she could weave a story to tell him, but she couldn't. Nanna had trained her well, and Nanna despised deception of any kind.

"Interesting," he smiled again and looked out his own window. Unbidden tears pooled in her eyes, threatening to fall and humiliate her further. "My brother made you forget, didn't he? He removed your childhood memories."

Her throat stung like she'd swallowed a bee. "You'd murdered every one of my kinsmen in one night. I was a child. He did it so I wouldn't say something about my past and be discovered and killed."

"He's Fontre. He was saving his own skin," Devilan said.

"If your plan is to turn me against Elian, I'm afraid you'll be disappointed."

"Not to turn you against him; to see him in the proper context. Elian is a trained Fontre warrior. Fontre don't learn swordplay, we learn the artistry of war. We're cunning and deception is easy. You defend him because he told you he loved you, but what he didn't tell you is this; it's impossible for a Fontre to love. Love is burned out of us before we're even born. It isn't his fault, just the way of things."

"Because of the potions your mothers take in those wretched Temples?" Cassai asked, enjoying the surprised look that crossed his face for a split second.

"He's told you many things, hasn't he?"

"Yes, he has."

"What else did he tell you about his mother?" Devilan asked.

"That Fontre brothers aren't usually related by blood, but you are. Your mother didn't take the pills or potions she was supposed to. He didn't know for sure, but thought it was true because he can feel emotions."

"He said something similar to me once. It was the worst beating I ever gave him." Devilan smiled. Cassai felt ill. She remembered the night the Fontre Draught had made Elian relive a horrible beating from his brother. Was it the one Devilan now enjoyed?

"I don't think she took them with you either," she said, trying to repay him in some way for relishing Elian's pain.

"Why would you believe that?" His voice was low, and dangerous. She knew she'd touched a prickly subject.

"I remember the night of the Revolution very clearly. It visits me in my dreams time and again and there's one thing I can't ignore." A day's ride in that horrible carriage would be worth it for this shot at her tormenter.

"Speak plainly, little Namarielle."

Ignoring the warnings screaming inside her head, Cassai sat back and quoted a verse she'd learned years ago.

"Fear not the enmity that comes
From some old grudge long past,
Nor malice from a rumor that
Doth in a dark light cast.
No hatred born of fear or pain
Will hold such dire cost,
As hatred and the bitter wrath
Of those who've loved ... and lost."

Devilan frowned. *He's trying to conjure a witty reply.* Her heart fluttered with a strange mixture of peace and fear. "I remember the way you looked at him that night; how you tried to spare him the pain of watching me die. You even tried to comfort him. You can go on all you like about Fontre being unable to feel, but I know the truth. You loved your brother once."

Fire flashed into Devilan's eyes and his nostrils flared. His hand rose so quickly that if she'd blinked she wouldn't have seen it. The palm of his hand collided with her cheek and her head smacked against the window. Her face stung as though on fire and her head pounded, but Cassai couldn't help the small smile that creased her lips. She'd guessed correctly.

~

HOLLIS, Elian and Theoris paused outside the Troikord, facing the largest mountain of the Kiatri Realm, Mount Korin. Hollis felt their pull as if the mountains physically detained him. It had been years since he'd seen these peaks and it would, no doubt be many more before he did again.

"We should eat here. I can't guarantee we'll be allowed comforts like food in the fairy realm," Hollis said.

Elian glanced sideways at him. "Right."

Theoris perched on a rock nearby and hugged his knees, misery and dread etched in every feature. He reminded Hollis of a gangly, depressed bird.

Hollis settled on a fallen log and Elian sat beside him. The Kiatri passed Theoris a plum, which the fairy turned over in his hand, a blank expression in his pea green eyes. Hollis decided against goading him. He wondered, for the first time, how the outcast would be received when they arrived, or if the Queen might block him from entering.

"Do you know the Fairy Queen well?" Elian asked after they'd each taken fruit and boiled eggs from Sophie's basket.

Hollis and Theoris exchanged looks, each remembering the unpleasant moments in their last exchange with the queen. "Better than I care to," Hollis replied.

Elian, confused by this answer, turned to ask something else, when suddenly, his eyes shut tightly and an intense look of pain shot across his face.

"Elian," Theoris said, stirring a little. "Are you ill?" There was no reply. "What's happening to him?"

41

"I don't −" Hollis stopped midsentence. Elian's eyes opened a crack, and he looked stuck in a trance. Hollis remembered that look. "He took medicine a few days ago. It makes him −" He was cut off by a sickening snap. Theoris jerked and Hollis glared at the Fontre. Hollis knew one of Elian's bones had broken, but couldn't tell which.

Elian's eyes stayed partly open, but he didn't cry out. He whispered something Hollis couldn't understand and another snap followed.

"Oh I say! Look at his hand!" Theoris yelped.

Hollis' eyes went to Elian's right hand; outstretched as if offering it to someone. It was oddly misshapen; a bump rose on the back.

"I see it, fairy. I have no idea what to do," Hollis said through gritted teeth. Elian's head jerked to the side and his breath caught, but still he didn't cry out. Hollis reached out to steady him, and when he straightened, Elian's cheek burned with a handprint. His lips were pressed together tightly.

"Elian?" said Hollis. The younger man made no sign of hearing.

Another snap. Theoris yelped and hid his face in his long fingers.

"Yes, Father," Elian whispered.

Theoris' fingers cracked open. He mouthed the horrified question, "Father?" Hollis' pained expression mirrored Elian's.

"His childhood was unpleasant to say the least." Hollis took a deep breath. "Elian!" he shouted. No response except the snapping of another bone. Elian clasped his broken hand to his chest. His whole body trembled, his breathing heavy and uneven. Hollis finally recalled the thing which drew him back last time, but still he hesitated.

Theoris had plugged both ears with his fingers and rocked back and forth murmuring something in the language of the Fey. Hollis recognized the rhythm as a fairy child's song; something Theoris' mother doubtless sang to him when he was small.

"Elian!" Hollis screamed one last time, as loudly as he could. No response, except Elian released his broken hand, squeezed his eyes shut and held it out again. "Stop! Don't give it back to him!" Hollis screamed, as if Elian could hear and follow instructions. The next snap was louder and Elian swallowed a whimper. His hand dangled from a broken wrist.

"Stop it!" Theoris screamed, apparently unable to block the sound. "Please make it stop."

Hollis stood in front of Elian, raised his hand, and brought the back of it down on Elian's face as hard as he could.

"What on earth?" Theoris gasped.

Hollis didn't answer; his gaze fixed on the Fontre. The blow didn't knock Elian from his seat, but his head had whipped to the side. He opened his eyes and Hollis breathed a sigh of relief. It worked. Elian's eyes were clear and focused.

Elian drew several shaking breaths before looking up at Hollis. "Thank you," he said and pulled his broken arm against his chest.

"I should've acted sooner," Hollis replied, his voice unsteady. He sat down. "Your hand and wrist."

Elian righted himself. "Never mind. It would have been worse if you hadn't stopped it."

"Worse?" squeaked Theoris, lowering his hands.

Elian moved his tongue over his cracked lips and shut his eyes again. "Is there anything there to drink?"

"Yes," Hollis jumped to the basket, eager be moving. "Water skins and blackberry wine. The wine would be best," he said more to himself as he pulled out the bottle.

"Just water," Elian requested in a whisper that sounded as if he was very far away.

Hollis pulled the cork from a water skin and offered it.

"The wine would numb the pain," Theoris said.

Elian took the water with a grateful nod. "It might, but I don't drink alcohol."

Hollis rolled his eyes toward the dull blue sky. "Of course you don't," he grumbled.

"I'd take a drink then," Theoris said. Hollis shot him a look and the fairy's mouth snapped shut as if his jaws had sealed by magic.

"I don't suppose you could trouble yourself to explain - that," Hollis said, dropping his gaze to Elian's right arm.

"Ffastian," Elian said and took a long drink of water before continuing. "One of his punishments."

"Who's Ffastian?" Theoris asked.

"The High King," answered Hollis. "His given name is Ffastian."

Theoris shuddered. "He broke your hand as a punishment?"

"He broke every bone in my arm and my hand. Fingers as well. A training session in which I didn't perform properly." Elian's face contorted as if the conversation hurt.

"You said Father. The High King was your father?" Theoris asked, looking near vomiting. Elian nodded.

"Perform properly?" Hollis repeated. "Meaning you were supposed to kill someone and you refused?"

Elian raked his uninjured left hand through his golden hair, causing it to stick up everywhere. "Close. I wouldn't torture one of the *danaai* into obeying his sick commands."

"*Danaai?*" Theoris asked.

"Unqualified warriors. He was six years old," Elian said, his voice flat.

"What was the command?" Hollis asked, handing Elian a piece of bread smeared with goats' cheese.

Elian took the bread and scowled at the ground. "It doesn't matter. And what I *did* didn't matter. Ffastian forced the boy anyway, in the end," he said in a tone that said he'd finished describing the memory.

Hollis looked at him with narrowed eyes for a long time. "You're not responsible, you know?" he assured Elian quietly. "For everything Ffastian and your brother do."

Elian sighed "I know." He pulled his damaged arm away from his body and examined it.

Hollis cleared his throat uncomfortably, and Elian looked at him with eyebrows raised. "I'm afraid the fairy healers may have to help you with that. I've never had much success setting broken bones."

"No need," Elian said grimly, holding his right hand in his left and bracing himself. Theoris yelped when Elian forced the bone in the middle of his hand back in place. He closed his eyes and breathed deeply, dealing with the pain. "I've had plenty of practice," he finished in a strained voice. "Could you find me a few straight sticks?"

Theoris sprang from the log where he was sitting. "I'll find them." The fairy left so quickly Hollis wondered if he'd learned the fairy vanishing spell.

The Kiatri shuddered and took another bite of bread. It tasted like ash.

STANDING at the mountain entrance to the Fairy Realm, Elian rocked impatiently back and forth on his heels. Theoris had fidgeted for over half an hour, pretending he couldn't remember the exact place to enter the Fairy Realm. Elian knew he was stalling and couldn't bring himself to force the fairy to pinpoint the spot. He looked at his splinted and wrapped hand. Theoris had performed the first successful magic attempt Elian had ever seen from the fey. A spell to relieve throbbing.

Suddenly, pain burned through his cheek and jaw. He went rigid as a statue and Hollis shot him a concerned glance.

"Elian?"

"He hit her," Elian replied, his voice a ragged whisper.

"What?"

"He hit her face. And she − I don't know − struck her head on something."

Hollis stared at him in sickened shock. "I'll kill him for you," he promised instantly.

Elian rubbed his cheek and nodded. "Thank you, Hollis Farrell. I'll let you. Theoris, are we in the correct spot at last?"

"I − well, it seems it may have been a few more degrees to the −" he cut off abruptly because, when he looked back at Hollis, the Kiatri had nocked an arrow in his bowstring so swiftly and smoothly the fairy missed the gesture until the tip was pressed against his neck. "That is − yes, this is the place," he choked, trying to back away.

Elian laid his left hand on Hollis' bow, lowering it. "Very good. Sorry this is difficult for you, but we'll do what we can to protect you in the Realm of the Fey." Elian knew as well as Theoris that such a promise was empty. The three of them were no match for an entire kingdom of fairies.

Hollis wrinkled his forehead thoughtfully. "The queen and I parted on much less than friendly terms. However this visit goes, it won't be smooth. If she imprisons me, or tortures me into insanity, or exiles me to the Woods of Terryn, or all three, get yourself out by any means necessary. I know your proclivity toward selfless heroics, but just - don't."

Elian's eyebrows rose. "Is that likely?"

"It isn't unlikely," Hollis muttered.

"Well then," Elian started, swallowing an enormous lump of doubt rising in his throat. "Shall we?"

Theoris sighed, squeezed his eyes shut as if bracing for one of his limbs to be severed, and chanted softly in the language of the Fey.

~

SOPHIE HAD KEPT enough distance between herself and her uncle's companions to remain undetected. Now she crouched motionless and alert, listening to the tall, beautiful fairy chant in his native tongue. A thrill at engaging in something forbidden trickled up and down her spine. They were going to see the fairies. *She* was going to step, for the first time, into the mystical land of the Fair Folk. She knew from stories that her Uncle Hollis had consorted with the fey many times, even before the Great Raid.

She started and almost lost her balance as the three men disappeared. Snatching her supply bag and slinging the strap over her shoulder, she darted from the copse and ran full tilt into the air where her uncle had just dissolved.

One moment she felt solid ground, the next she fell through nothingness, landing with a thud on a grassy slope. She sat up painfully. Flowers she'd never seen grew everywhere in sprays of red, orange and purple. The sweet scent filled her lungs in her first gasping breath. She felt lightheaded and happy. She managed push herself up on the velvety grass and look around. There was no sign of her uncle, or Elian and Theoris.

She smiled to herself and picked one of the flowers, inhaling deeply, and then sneezing. Its perfume burned as if she'd just breathed fire into her nostrils. "Mustn't touch, mustn't touch, mustn't touch," sang voices all around her, but she couldn't see anyone.

"Hello?" she whispered. Her throat felt sore.

"Mustn't speak, mustn't speak, mustn't speak," the voices chanted now.

She stood on wobbly legs and looked out over the sloping field. Behind her was a wood, which she knew from reading fairy stories wasn't safe to enter. A little ways in front of her, was a large stand of trees, and flowers and gardens. She wondered if it was where the fey lived. And surrounding that was the sea.

She squinted at three dark dots growing larger as they came toward her. In a moment she realized they were fey. She opened her mouth to call out to them, but no sound would come from her throat now. As they drew closer, dread began to fill her. Their impossibly perfect features were set in grim lines and focused solely on her. She contemplated running, thought better of it. This was their realm. There was nowhere to run.

4

THE TEST

"Here, boy! Get up," Edgewater growled, fumbling with a heavy-looking key. Krispen stirred, as did the rest of his pack. He ached all over from the night as a wolf. He stretched his sore arms and legs, turning instinctively to check on Isabel. She was curled up in the back of her makeshift cage, asleep but restless. Krispen reached as far as he could through the bars and brushed her soft wool.

He jerked toward a scuffling behind him. The other men stirred and tried to stand, not remembering their bonds. One pulled at the chain and, when it didn't yield, he appeared to go mad. He yanked mindlessly at the manacles, screaming and clawing, and bit his own leg with razor sharp teeth.

Edgewater rushed to the man and gave him a hard kick in the ribs. When the man crumbled to the ground, Edgewater kicked him once more for good measure. "Craifen! Get hold of yourself. I've got the key right here that'll loose ya'." Edgewater dangled the key in front of the man's red eyes. Craifen was unable to focus. He twisted away from Edgewater and continued to struggle, his face turning redder with his efforts.

Krispen watched the proceedings and felt the blood drain from his face. He shrank back against the cage, both arms thrown wide, blocking as much of his lamb as possible. "It'll be alright, Isabel."

Edgewater attempted to unlock Craifen's manacles with the other man still flailing and thrashing. Finally, Edgewater drove a fist into the smaller man's stomach. Craifen doubled over with pain and stopped fighting. "Shut yer trap and let me get this unlocked, you bloody idiot!" Edge screamed at him. The key turned and the manacles fell away. Craifen stumbled across the room. His wolf teeth returned to normal and he no longer had claws.

He kept a hand on his stomach and grumbled, but Edgewater ignored him. His focus was on Krispen. The boy began to shake.

"Oh come on, kid, don't look at me like that," Edge said, his voice very soft. "We're not a bad lot really. You'll like it here ... eventually." The giant man didn't approach the trembling boy, but continued to unlock his other two men.

"Where are we?" Krispen asked in a very small voice.

Edgewater had just unlocked the last and smallest of the pack and he pushed the key into his pocket. "Someplace the rest of the world don't know about, and you have to swear never to tell 'em, neither. You swear?"

Krispen shook his head. "I can't swear anything. I tell Elian everything."

"Elian!" Edgewater guffawed and the rest of his pack joined him. "That soft-fisted Fontre turned sheepherder, you mean?" Raucous laughter bounced off every corner of the cavern and Krispen curled up, clapping his hands over his ears to block it out. Isabel bleated pitifully. Edgewater stopped laughing and smacked Haliberk, the man beside him. "Shut up, idiot!"

"Hey!" said Haliberk. Edgewater cocked his fist and Haliberk cringed away.

"What're you makin' fun of the kid for? Can't you see we've terrified him?" Edgewater shouted. Craifen and Jakas sobered instantly.

Krispen looked up when the laughter ended, his eyes shining with tears. "Did you feed her? She's really hungry."

"We let her graze on what she could find last night. To be real honest, boy, there ain't much in this forest for anyone to eat nowadays. We did our best by her. As you can see, I locked up my boys to keep 'em off her when they turned."

Krispen's eyes darted back and forth to the newly freed men. "You tied everyone up?"

The older man nodded. "Knew you'd want your lamby in one piece when you came, is all. We ain't monsters, but o' course we had to get you somehow. You understand that, don't ya'?"

Krispen bit his trembling lip. "Will you let me have her?" His voice was barely a squeak.

"Of course, of course, kid. I want you to have her. I just need you to agree to a few things first, is all." Edge approached Krispen softly and the boy didn't recoil as much as before. "Here's what we need from you: just your promise to stay with the pack. You'll soon feel drawn to us as a firebug's drawn to campfires, so that ain't a problem. Also, we need some information."

"I don't know any information. And I don't want to stay here. I want Cassai." Tears streamed down the boy's face.

"I know, I know." Edgewater drew close enough to kneel in front of the shepherd boy and pat his knee comfortingly. "You don't want us yet, but you will. And the information, it's as easy as talkin'. Tha's all. Just talkin' with us. You must be hungry," Edgewater crooned. Krispen squeezed his eyes shut, but nodded. "There's a good lad. Let's get us some breakfast and we'll explain everything."

~

ELIAN CAME to his senses lying on his back in darkness so thick if he held his hand up he couldn't see it. He first thought days and nights in the Fairy Realm were the opposite of Lashai. He pushed himself off the floor, forgetting his broken arm. He ground his teeth in agony and switched to his good hand. He smelled earth and stones and the sharp green scent of vegetation. *We're underground.* His heart began to race.

"Hollis?" he whispered. His throat felt thick and drawing breath was a struggle.

"Yes, I'm here. I wondered when you'd wake. I feared perhaps she'd laid some sort of curse on you when we entered." Hollis' voice came from his right.

"Theoris?" Elian asked.

"They took him."

The cold and damp all around seeped up Elian's spine at those words. "What do you mean, took him? Where are we?"

"We're in the dungeons of the fey," Hollis muttered.

Elian sighed and sat back on the cold ground. "So, you're as unpopular as you warned," he muttered. "Did we land in their prison, or were we dragged?"

"Not dragged. Fair folk don't waste energy if they don't have to. We came into the realm in this very cell."

"Did they say anything when they took Theoris?"

Hollis didn't answer immediately. Finally, he cleared his throat. "They said the Queen has a surprise for us."

Elian looked toward him, though he couldn't see his shape. "A surprise?"

"Yes, I'm sure it'll be delightful," said Hollis.

Elian attempted to stand again. Feeling steadier, he started feeling for the walls. "There has to be a way out," he murmured.

"Don't touch the walls," Hollis warned. "They're covered in poisoned thorns and nettles."

Elian jerked his hand back. "Of course they are."

From somewhere on the other side of the room they heard footsteps. Elian assumed they'd halted outside the door.

"Don't speak unless you have no choice, and don't anger them whatever you do," Hollis whispered hastily as a key jiggled in a lock, and shaft of light sliced into the cell. Light glowed from an orb carried by a fey entering.

"Hollis Farrell," he barked.

"What?" Hollis barked back. Elian grinned.

The light glowed brighter and a guard appeared. His features were smooth as glass and he shimmered with every movement. When he smiled, Elian frowned. He couldn't remember a smile except his brother's holding more contempt and cruelty. "We seem to be seeing a lot of you lately. Did you come back for the wedding?" sneered the fairy.

Elian's eyes darted to Hollis. So they knew each other. "Yes, I just wanted to wish you every happiness with your unwilling bride, Goliard," Hollis replied.

"I'm deeply touched. I'll send Lily down so you can pass your sentiments to her in person," returned Goliard. Hollis glared at him. The fairy turned toward Elian. "Captive of yours, Hollis?" he asked. "You're bringing your Fontre prey here to be tortured now, instead of doing it yourself? Interesting approach."

"He's not a prisoner. We wish to see the Queen."

"The Queen has no interest in seeing you. She wants the girl, and the book. Theoris' information so far has been highly disappointing. Please tell me he's lying when he says you've lost them both. So careless."

Hollis smiled a very unpleasant smile and crossed his arms.

Goliard glared and turned his attention to Elian. "You tell me, Fontre, or I will make you," he threatened.

Elian stepped into the clearer light and Goliard saw his full height and breadth for the first time. He rapidly wiped the surprise from his face. "I'll tell you nothing," Elian replied. He wondered if it was wise to anger the fey by refusing to give information he fully intended to reveal in time, but Goliard grated his nerves.

The guard grinned. "I'll enjoy making you tell me."

"I don't think that would be enjoyable for anyone," Elian

replied, his tone light. He appraised the fairy guard. Two leather straps dangled from Goliard's belt next to a sheathed sword and a slim silver dagger. Elian recognized the dagger as the one he kept in his boot. So they'd stripped him of weapons while he was unconscious. "Are you the only guard they sent?"

"I'm not just any guard," said Goliard, correctly interpreting Elian's question. He stood almost as tall as Elian, and obviously felt equal to the Fontre. "I am Goliard, Captain of the Queen's Guard. We've taken precautions, Fontre; we're not fools. You have no weapons and −" The end of his threat was cut short. Elian had sprung and buried his good fist in Goliard's stomach. Hollis instantly joined the fight.

In seconds, Goliard was on his knees, his hands bound by his own leather thongs, Elian pressed his silver dagger to the fairy's throat while Hollis held him from behind. "And I'm not just any Fontre. And I haven't had a good day. Now, when did you say we could speak to the Queen?"

"You think this wise, Fontre?" Goliard demanded breathlessly, trying to pull away from the knife. "Antagonizing the Queen's guard when you seek a favor?"

"I don't seek a favor," said Elian through gritted teeth. "I'm going to ask her to help me free the only hope for our world, and probably yours. Now stop wasting my time with threats and get up." Hollis pulled Goliard to his feet.

"You should release me."

"And why's that?" said Hollis.

"Because I have something you want."

"If you're again referring to your unfortunate bride, there's nothing I can do for Lily now. I tried to free her from your sister's clutches long ago. You may have noticed I was unsuccessful."

"Not Lily, something else of greater value to you."

Elian sighed. "We've no time to play games with fairies. What is the leverage you hold?"

Goliard smiled and expelled a low whistle. Two more guards

materialized, holding someone between them who was putting up a furious fight.

"I believe this belongs to you?" the Captain aimed at Hollis. The Kiatri's eyes slid shut. A swish of black hair flew away from her face and revealed an outraged Sophie. Elian made a sound between a growl and a sigh.

"I knew I should have locked you up," he muttered.

~

"DRIVER, tell the men we'll stop here awhile," Devilan called through the window above his head. The carriage clanked to a halt. "Get out and stretch your legs," Devilan ordered.

Cassai stumbled from the carriage and felt relief all over her body. She almost wished they could travel the road on foot. She sensed Devilan behind her. He said nothing, but took her arm and led her to a brook. "Drink. We don't stop again until nightfall."

Cassai knelt at the stream and scooped handfuls of the cold, clear water, sipping as slowly as possible. When she could delay no longer, she straightened and saw the Koninjka also drinking their fill.

Her stomach growled, but no one was pulling food from the packhorses, and she remembered that most Fontre only ate twice a day. Devilan conferred with Dershom about where they would make camp for the night and then returned to her side. "Back into the carriage."

Cassai returned to her father's carriage with a familiar pang of loss. She sat in her seat, and Devilan climbed in after her. As the carriage lurched forward she looked out the window and wished they could ride to the Inner Kingdom in silence.

"Let's discuss your future in this kingdom," Devilan said.

"My future?"

"Yes. We're making arrangements now. I need information from your book for the final details."

Cassai felt cold all over. "What arrangements?"

"For our wedding. Namarielle weddings have a number of stipulations. Ignoring those details could prove fatal to you, and, we've determined, would also be fatal to the kingdom."

Cassai could barely hear Devilan's words in her misery. *Our wedding. The rest of my life, married to Devilan.*

"Why you?" she asked.

"What do you mean?"

"Why are you marrying me and not the High King?"

Devilan's eyebrows rose. "Would you prefer to wed Ffastian?"

"Of course not. But isn't the point of this to have a Namarielle on the throne?"

Devilan sighed and looked as unhappy as she felt about their upcoming nuptials. "I will step away from my duties as *Genraal Majure* and be ruler of Lashai in title. The High King will remain in control, of course. The kingdom is rightfully his."

Cassai snorted. "I forgot how 'rightfully' he rules the kingdom. So, by title, we'll be rulers, but he still gives the orders."

"Of course he gives the orders."

Cassai rolled her eyes and looked out the window. She wondered if the specifications of Lashai's rulers would be satisfied with Devilan's proposed arrangements. She ached to get her fingers on the Lost Book of Times, but she'd already told Devilan she wouldn't read it until she reached the Inner Kingdom and she still felt this was the safest course. Even so, it would be nice to know if she could somehow foil the plans of the man opposite, and the man awaiting their arrival.

THE PACK LED KRISPEN, carrying Isabel, up another entry to the forest. It took several minutes for his eyes to adjust to the morning light. It took so long, he began to fear they wouldn't adjust at all. He also noticed the others squinting.

"My eyes hurt," he said to Edgewater.

"Aye, they will for a bit, lad. Let 'em water, and keep 'em open as wide as you can. You'll get used to it."

They foraged through the underbrush for food while their stomachs grumbled and their tempers grew short. Finally, the one called Jakas walked back to the pack with a large feathered mass slung over his shoulder.

"Found a hakgaard," he muttered. Krispen looked at the bird and then at Edgewater.

"Mostly feather and bone," the man grumbled. "Right then, clean it. Craifen, build us a fire. I'll draw some water from the Kai." Haliberk carried two blackened pots strung on his back with twine. He untied the largest and handed it to Edgewater.

"Why we cookin' it?" Craifen asked. "Can't we just eat, Edge? We're starving."

Krispen's stomach rumbled and roiled. The thought of eating the bird raw made him flinch, but the hollowness inside yearned to be filled so badly he thought he might manage it. He curled his arms around Isabel and looked up at Edgewater, whose gaze was pinned on him.

"I don't think the kid can handle that just yet," he said with surprising gentleness.

Craifen and Jakas exchanged confused looks. "The kid? We're doin' stuff for him now? It ain't enough we kept his stupid lamby alive?"

Edgewater's back bowed and both men jumped back. "Cookin' it. Right. We'll git on that," they said..

Edgewater plopped down by the riverbank and patted the ground beside him. "Sit yerself, kid. Tell me 'bout yer life."

Krispen lowered himself carefully next to the giant man and buried his face in Isabel's wool. "I just want to go home."

He felt Edgewater's huge hand on his back and forced himself to sit still. "S'okay. S'okay to want yer family righ' now. You'll lose carin' about them soon enough."

Krispen took a deep breath, the way Nanna had taught him when he got too emotional to think straight. "I don't want to stop caring."

"They don' need the likes of you about anymore. Werewolves is dangerous creatures. We go odd in the brain and can't think like we used to. Trust me, I've changed plenty."

"How long have you been a werewolf?"

Edgewater thought, screwing up his face. "Comin' up on abou' sixty years, I guess. Wow. Don't seem possible."

"You never miss your family?"

"Don't have no family anymore, kid. None at all." Despite his previous bravado, Edgewater sounded mournful. "My bes' friend in this whole world don't even wanna be 'round me no more. S'alright. I got me pack. That's all I need now."

"There's not as many of you as I thought."

"Used to be more. Less because of our encounters with your Fontre pal and - Hollis." He seemed reluctant to say Hollis' name and Krispen wondered why.

"Sorry," Krispen said because he thought he should.

"Where d'you think they'd go now? They were goin' to the mountains, but Craifen checked there and they'd gone. They have some other idea in mind?"

Krispen shook his head. "I don't know. I just know Cassai wanted to see the Kiatri. She met Hollis and got really excited, thinking maybe he could help. I don't know if he did or not. If they left already, I guess not."

"So, they don't have no more plans after? Nothin'?"

Krispen shrugged. "Don't know."

"You think on it, then, won't ya? The boys would really like to know somethin' pretty quick. They don't hear nothin' it may just start to be upsetting." Krispen couldn't always follow what was going on, but his few unhappy years before Elian rescued him taught him a few things. He always knew when the woman who kept him was at the edge of her patience; her voice went all low and shaky. Edgewater's voice had done this just now. It made Krispen want to run and hide.

"I'll try and remember something."

"Do that. I like you, kid. But they don't." Edgewater pointed a crooked finger at Craifen, who had just burned himself fanning the campfire.

~

"WILL they trade Sophie for their Captain of the Guard?" Elian asked Hollis, pressing the knife harder against Goliard's throat. The fairy's eyebrows shot up. "Because I'm wondering if they wouldn't mind if I just slit your throat now."

Goliard frowned. "Release me or I'll see to it she stays here for eternity. We'll torment her every —" His sentence was cut off by the blade, pushed so hard into his skin it would slice him to speak further.

"Others might torture her, but you won't have the pleasure." Elian hissed. "I wish to speak to the Queen," he told the guards who held Sophie. "Arrange that."

The fairies glanced at each other. "Yes, sir," one stammered. "Do you want her?" he asked, holding Sophie forward.

"We do. Leave her here and leave the light. I'm not fond of sitting in the dark." Hollis smiled. They set Sophie carefully on her feet and pressed a small glowing sphere into her hands. The fairies backed away from their captive leader. "What if the Queen won't agree to a meeting?"

Elian scowled. "How much does she care for her Captain of the Guard?"

"We'll do our best," the other fairy assured him and both hurried into the dark hall.

Elian removed the dagger from Goliard's neck and slipped it back into his boot. "Thank you for entering into negotiations," he said. Blinding pain seized him. He staggered back. Hundreds of white hot knives ripped through him. "Hollis," he managed to groan. Through bleary eyes he saw Hollis' understanding nod. Without a word, the Kiatri reached down and hefted a heavy stone from the floor.

"My pleasure," Hollis said, slamming the rock into Goliard's temple, knocking the fairy unconscious.

The pain evaporated. Elian took a deep breath. "Thanks."

"So, taking friendly advice just isn't your way?"

"You didn't seem fussed about angering them. Besides, every minute we spend here playing their games, Cassai draws closer to the Inner Kingdom and beyond our reach. They'll toy with us for months if we let them," Elian said.

"Yes, I'm well-acquainted with fairies' tendency to play with their food," Hollis reminded him.

"What are their names? Do you know them?" Elian asked.

"The tallest is Finnis, and he's not at all fond of Goliard. The other is Herelle. He's scared of everyone, so he does what he's told by the loudest voice."

Elian nodded, and then his gaze turned to Sophie, who glared back. "I seem to recall saying you weren't invited."

Her gleaming eyes defied him. "I can help you."

Hollis crossed his arms. "Yes, you've been a tremendous help. Thank you for handling the situation so deftly."

Sophie flinched as if stung. "Fine. I'm sorry. What else can I do?"

"If we get out of here, and that's a very big 'if', you can turn back to the mountains and go home," Elian answered. "Our journey is too dangerous."

"Why?" She bristled. "Because I'm a girl?"

"No," Elian answered. "Because you're a child."

Sophie's mouth opened to reply but no sound emerged. Her face burned red and her fists clenched so hard her knuckles were white.

Footsteps sounded down the hall and the group fell silent.

Finnis and Herelle reappeared, each holding a new glowing sphere.

"We – um - spoke with the Queen," said Herelle, shifting his feet. "She'd like a w-word with you in her chambers."

"Fantastic," Hollis muttered, moving toward them.

"N—not Hollis or the girl, just the Fontre," the guard stammered. "If that's agreeable."

"She expects me to leave my companions in her dungeons while we chat? No, that's not agreeable. They come with me."

"Please sir," the guard begged. "I'm only following orders." His eyes moved to Goliard.

Elian regarded him. His stomach twisted to see them cower from him. He felt too Fontre for his liking, but he swallowed the pity. Getting to Cassai was his only concern. "What will she do if you disobey?"

The two guards exchanged nervous glances. "P-probably turn us over to Melkana. Or-," The fairy looked at Goliard. "Something worse."

Elian didn't know who Melkana was, but could tell from the look on Hollis' face that being at his mercy was punishment indeed. Elian nodded.

"I assume Melkana is a torturer?" he asked. They nodded. "You see what I did to your Captain when he tried to torture me. Draw your own conclusions on what I'll do to you if you try to keep my companions here."

In the utter silence that followed, Elian heard the tallest swallow. "Of course, there aren't really enough of us to stop them leaving."

Elian smiled. "Thank you," he said as if they'd consented willingly. "I'll require one more thing before I agree to meet her."

"Just one?" the one on the right muttered.

"Where's Theoris? You're going to let him go."

❧

KRISPEN DRAPED Isabel across his shoulders. She was getting bigger, but he knew it would be a while before she had the stamina to keep up the pace set by Edgewater.

"Where're we headed, Edge?" growled Craifen.

"Lord Devilan's heading to the Inner Kingdom. I need a word with 'im."

"What word? We don' know nothing about that girl or the other shepherd."

"I got words to say to him, is all. I don't explain myself to you lot." Edgewater dropped back and walked next to Krispen and Isabel. "So, boy, talk to me abou' Cassai. What's her deal? What makes her so special that Devilan cares if she's delivered alive?"

Krispen's heart began to race. "I don't know what you want from her, or what that other guy wants. Cassai's just normal. She's a normal girl who's really nice."

"Don't know how much contact you've had with girls, kid, but I can tell you, niceness ain't that normal," Edgewater informed him.

Krispen flushed. "I'm not telling you anything about them if you're just going to turn them straight over to...that one guy you keep saying."

"Devilan? Oh, don't fuss about that, kid. Devilan's Elian's own flesh and blood, see? Can't think he'd want to do no harm to his own brother, now would he? Do that make sense?"

Krispen readjusted Isabel on his shoulders and tried to think fast. He'd never been successful at this. "The boys in town were mean to me. There was one that was meaner than most and he was their leader. Elian saved me. Cassai and Nanna healed me up. That's all. I can't tell you nothing. We took care of our sheep and minded our own business." Tears raced down Krispen's cheeks and he turned his face away, hoping Edgewater wouldn't notice. If he did, he didn't comment. Edgewater patted his shoulder in a friendly way, and walked silently along beside the shepherd boy.

CASSAI SAT CLOSE to the fire, trying to fight the bone-chilling cold.

"Are you hungry?" Devilan asked quietly. He approached so silently the sound of his voice made her jump.

"Yes. A little," she said. He offered a piece of bread and a bowl of something that smelled strongly of onion and salt and some kind of fowl. She looked at the food for a moment, wondering if it was poisoned; wondering if they could poison a Namarielle.

Devilan nodded, understanding her hesitation. He sat next to her and took a bite of her bread. Then he took the bowl and lifted it to his lips, sipping. With a look in his black eyes she couldn't read, he held the bowl out. "I suggest you accept. I won't offer again," he said, his voice still quiet. Cassai forced herself not to shrink away.

"Thank you." She accepted the food. Devilan rolled his eyes.

"Thank you?" he repeated. "What a polite little prisoner you are." His gaze raked her up and down and settled on her face. "You make an intriguing profile, little Namarielle. I know that you are, in some ways, of my brother's making. I assumed you were weak. Then you act as you did this afternoon, surprising, strong: foolish, but strong. I suppose that shouldn't surprise me. Elian is strong too, in some ways."

"All people have both weakness and strength," she replied, taking a bite of the crusty bread. She recognized the strong flavor of goat's milk. So they'd stolen the food from the Kiatri. She sighed and took another bite.

"The Fontre are not mortals as other races would like to believe. We train the weaknesses of humanity from our young in their infancy. Not only with potions and enchantments but with traditions."

Cassai longed to be elsewhere. She didn't want to hear the "traditions" the Fontre employed to train children to be hardened killers by the time they reached their seventh birthday. Elian had intentionally skirted this issue so she wouldn't think about it. She expected no such compassion from Devilan, and she wasn't disappointed.

"When infants cry, they're taken outside the camp, wrapped in a blanket called a *Farsah*. It's designed to hold the infant securely, with a hook on the back. The hook's fastened to a tree and the babe is left until it has submitted to its father's will. It stops crying, and doesn't cry again. Then the infants are taken back to camp and their needs are met. They understand they will be seen to at the proper time. They learn not to be demanding and that crying is the least likely way to get what they want. Other mortals underestimate the intellect of babes."

Cassai swallowed the bread, which had gone very dry. She took a sip of soup to prevent herself choking. Devilan looked at her, expecting some reply.

"You think that barbaric?" he guessed. She didn't look at him, but nodded and took another bite of bread. "Consider, then: Fontre camps are usually out in the Wild. They travel miles surrounded by fierce creatures and enemies. If a pack of wolves sought our camp at night, what would they be drawn to?"

"I don't know." Cassai looked away. A shepherdess knew what wolves were drawn to, but she wanted the conversation to end.

"Of course you do. They're drawn to smells, sights and noises. Smells you can mask, sights you can camouflage, but what if, after all that effort, one babe begins to cry? Where will that wolf look first? In the bed of the infant. You think us cruel, but we're keeping our young alive. Is it kinder to let them be torn to pieces by a wolf?"

Cassai stared at his stone-like face. "So because I wouldn't tie a baby in a tree and let him scream and cry, not caring for him, I want him to be devoured by wolves? Is that your real question, or did I miss a point somewhere?"

"You've missed the point entirely," said Devilan calmly. He

gestured to one of his Koninjka, who silently joined them. "Summon Racalf. I need him." The Koninjka bowed his head and marched away. "There are three types of weakness that love engenders in mortals, none of which I possess, despite what you believe. Firstly, the weakness men portray when pain's inflicted on them. Second, the weakness of my brother, who falls to pieces when pain's inflicted on someone he loves. The last, I believe, is you." A Fontre Koninjka was being marched to their corner of the camp.

Without understanding its source, terror grew in Cassai's mind. This was punishment for her earlier comments about Devilan and love, she was sure. Her cheek throbbed where he'd struck her, as if her body had already worked out what her brain couldn't.

"This is Racalf. He's an officer of my elite Koninjka." Devilan explained unnecessarily as the Fontre stood at attention. Two Koninjka stood on either side of Racalf, awaiting orders. "He's done nothing wrong, but he's newest to our ranks, and will therefore serve as my example."

Cassai's skin felt too tight for her body. Devilan got to his feet. "Take off your glove and give me your right hand," the *Genraal* ordered. Racalf silently obeyed. Cassai couldn't tear her eyes from his face. No fear, no objection, just obedience. She shuddered.

Devilan drew the long curved knife from its sheath. "Don't," Cassai whispered, unable to stop herself.

Devilan turned at the sound. "Yes, I thought as much. You're the third kind. You suffer when anything suffers. Animals, people you don't know, even your enemies." Racalf's face was inscrutable as Devilan took his hand, pressed his blade against two fingers, and without a word, sliced cleanly through them, snapping through the joint with a jarring crunch and letting them fall to the ground.

One of the severed fingers rolled toward Cassai and she jerked as far from it as possible. Racalf remained silent, agony in his eyes. Devilan nodded at the other two. "Bandage his hand so he can return to his duties." There was no coldness in his voice, no anger ... nothing. It was as if he had given orders to build up the fire, or pitch their tents.

Cassai's throat burned with unshed tears. Devilan watched the men march away and settled on the ground beside her. "Look at me, Cassai," he said.

Cassai looked up.

"Now tell me, which weakness do you think is mine?"

Cassai looked away and curled her legs into her chest, wishing she could protect herself from his gaze. "It isn't a weakness to hurt for others. But you don't seem to have any of the three."

"Had my brother been with us, I would have chosen him as my example. Tell me then, do I love him?" Even without looking at him, Cassai felt his glare.

"No," she said because it was safest. "You obviously don't love at all." She just barely stopped herself from adding, "anymore".

5

THE QUEEN

K rispen walked as slowly as he dared behind the pack. His arms shook as he carried Isabel, but not from the weight of the lamb. Edgewater wanted to know things; wanted him to know things. But Krispen had no idea what his friends were doing, or where they were going. He thought they were still in the mountains, but this information wasn't received well. A tear rolled from his chin and landed on Isabel's nose. The lamb nudged him affectionately.

Edgewater looked back and Krispen froze. "Yer fallin' behind, kid." Edgewater motioned Craifen to take the lead and dropped back to walk beside Krispen again. "Thought of anything I may find helpful?"

Krispen blinked rapidly, hoping the older man hadn't noticed the tears. "Maybe if you told me what yer wanting to know," he said.

"I need to know more about me opponents, is all. Why's Devilan so interested in the girl? I mean, the shepherd's his kin, but the girl...she ain't nothin'. Why waste so much time lookin' for a nobody?"

"I don't know about Cassai. I told you that."

"Hollis Farrell's protecting her too. That ain't normal. He don't care about no one no more."

"Hollis is real nice," Krispen stammered.

Edgewater roared with laughter, startling Isabel, and making Krispen shrink away.

"I wanna go. Please, I just wanna go back to Cassai." Krispen's chin trembled and tears pooled in his eyes.

Edgewater glared at him. "You ain't goin' nowhere, kid. Yer one of us now and you stay. I didn't want to have to do nothin' to prove that to you, but if you force my hand-," Edgewater let the sentence hang in the air. Krispen pulled Isabel tighter against his chest. "Boys! Stop here a moment."

The others halted and turned back.

"Why are we stopping?" Krispen whimpered.

Edgewater dropped his gear and motioned the other pack members to do the same. "I'm sorry, kid. I tried to get on without this kind of thing, but yer makin' it real hard." Edgewater cracked his knuckles and the other two men grinned at each other.

Krispen took a step away. "Don't hurt Isabel."

"You do as yer told, or I swear, roasted lamb's what's for supper."

Krispen took another step back. Edgewater's giant fist connected with the boy's jaw. Krispen lost his footing; tiny lights popped across his field of vision. He rolled onto his side, wrapping Isabel in his protective arms.

"Finally," growled Craifen, kicking Krispen's ribs.

The last thing Krispen saw before squeezing his eyes shut against the pain, was a deer watching from between the distant trees, its head cocked to the side, as if it recognized Krispen.

CASSAI CURLED in front of the campfire that evening, hugging her knees. The air was unnaturally chilly. She assumed the

68

weather was accommodating her current mood. It had been hours since supper and the Koninjka settled into the night shift, but she had no wish to sleep. Every time she shut her eyes her mind replayed Racalf's fingers being sliced from his hand. The agony on his face was burned into her mind's eye.

"I thought you'd gone to sleep," Devilan's voice made her stomach lurch. She curled up tighter, but didn't answer. He sat down next to her. "Are you still hungry?"

"I'm fine."

"That's no answer."

"I just wanted a moment of peace," she said.

Devilan nodded and poked at the campfire with a stick. "Good lord, woman. You look a mess." He ruffled her hair then his hand lifted her chin. "Your face is dirty and what do you even call this business with your hair? It's tangled and...there are leaves actually stuck in it."

"Please leave me alone," she growled.

"I thought women cared about their appearance. Isn't that sort of a priority?"

Shock overwhelmed disgust and she lifted herself to stare at him. "Do your female prisoners usually make their looks a priority?"

"My female prisoners are usually headed for the Temples, so... yes." Her eyes grew large and she wanted to hit him so badly it hurt. He rolled his eyes. "Stay here. I'll be right back."

Her one moment of solitude shattered, she glared at the fire, seething.

By the time he'd returned she was so angry she stood and rounded on him. "How dare you expect me to care about my appearance and keep myself looking nice for you? What business is it of yours how I look or if I've got leaves in my hair? You are a pig, and I will not marry you if I can find some way around it, and I'm sure I can. I'm sure there's something in that book about marrying a Namarielle against their will. I'll find it, I'll get away from you and your High King and your thugs one way or the other."

Devilan waited for her to finish, his arms crossed over his chest. He was holding two objects, but Cassai couldn't tell what they were. "If you've done with that, come sit down."

"What?"

Devilan walked to a fallen log. He sat on it and patted the ground in front of him. "Sit down."

"Why?"

He sighed and held up the objects. One was a small brown bottle of something, and the other a wooden handled hairbrush. "It's not the right kind of brush for curled hair, but I didn't buy it for you, so it'll have to do."

"I don't understand." But she had started to understand his intention and it repelled her.

"A feeling you're quite familiar with, I've no doubt. Come here and sit down on the ground. Surely you do understand at least that much, and I suspect you understand the rest as well." When she still didn't walk to him, he gave her a stern look. "I can force you to do whatever I like. I'd rather not waste my men's time just now, particularly for such a trifling request. Sit down."

Cassai forced her legs to move toward him. "Why does it bother you what my hair looks like?" she demanded as she settled on the ground in front of his knees.

"You ought to care, and you don't. That bothers me. You are the last of the most ancient and most powerful bloodline this world has ever known. You should never go anywhere or do anything looking like a street urchin, even if it's sitting in front of a fire surrounded by your enemies. How can you take so little pride in who you are?" She heard him unstop the bottle and felt his fingers run through her hair. She squeezed her eyes shut. "Relax, and don't hunch your shoulders like that. The oil is to help untangle it."

"I can brush my own hair."

70

"Your wrist is broken."

"It's been set. You're supposed to continue moderate activity with broken bones. It strengthens them." Relaying this medical information oddly made her feel calmer.

Devilan chuckled. "They said you had the qualities of a healer. Hold this." He handed her the small brown bottle. It had a rose painted on it.

"Who did you steal this from?" she asked, contempt dripping from every word.

"I didn't steal it. I purchased it from a street merchant in the Troikord." Devilan corrected her calmly. He'd started pulling the brush through her hair, separating a section at a time.

"Why?"

"Why what?" He asked, sounding as though he were concentrating.

"Why did you buy hair oil and that brush?" The brush caught a tangle and the top of her scalp stung as several hairs ripped out. "Ow."

"Sorry." Though he didn't sound sorry. "And none of your business."

"Are you the only one allowed to ask questions?"

"You can ask as many questions as you like. That doesn't mean I'll answer."

"Ha! What if I tried that?"

He yanked her hair again. "I'm afraid you don't have that option."

Cassai's eyes watered and she wondered if she'd have any hair left when he'd finished.

"Do you have any more questions for me?" he asked. She could tell he was smiling from the tone of his voice.

"No," she said.

"Good, then this will likely be less painful for us both." He worked in silence for a long time and Cassai found herself calming down in spite of the circumstances. He was surprisingly gentle when he wasn't annoyed. "This takes ages," he said after a while.

"Yes it does," she agreed.

"We should plait it. Then you'll be able to sleep on the ground and not get it so tangled." She felt it separate between his fingers.

"Are you braiding my hair?" She turned to look at him and he startled as if he hadn't realized who he was talking to.

"What?"

"I didn't realize…I can braid it myself if you want."

He looked at her face for a moment as if he was coming back to the present. "I'll do it," he said softly. "Turn around. I won't pull it again." He turned her head back to face the fire, and fell silent once more.

Cassai curled her legs against her chest as she had before and waited for him to finish. She burned with curiosity about him now. How did such a monstrous man learn to plait hair? Surely his childhood hadn't included any more maternal influences than Elian's, and she knew Elian never knew his mother. Where had Devilan's mind gone when he went quiet?

"Hold this," he said at last, handing her the end of a long thick plait. "I'm going to get something to tie it off."

She pinched the end and waited. He returned with a thin leather strip. He sat back down on the log behind her and wound it carefully around the end.

"We should get some sleep. I hope to make better progress tomorrow." He put a hand under her arm and lifted her off the ground. "Do you like it here by the fire?"

"Yes. Watching the flames is nice." Cassai didn't say that it reminded her of home, thinking Devilan would probably douse all fires in the kingdom of Lashai if he knew that intimate detail.

He nodded. "I'll get you a blanket then. You can sleep where you like, tonight, Cassai."

∿

KRISPEN ROLLED over on his back, trying to find a comfortable place to lay. Every position hurt a different place on his body. Tears rolled from his eyes and clutched Isabel to his chest wishing for Cassai and her healing touch.

Edgewater had let the pack carry on with beating him until he felt broken all over. His clothes were ripped in places and the skin under the rips was raw or bleeding. Though he'd curled up and cried out that he didn't know nothing, no one had believed him or even cared. They just liked hurting someone, he decided. Like the town boys, some people were just mean.

"Ye'll heal soon enough, kid," Edgewater had said when he finally called them off. "Our kind always does, ye know."

And they left him there to rest while they'd built a fire and told horrible stories that he tried not to hear and finally settled down to sleep.

Something soft and furry nuzzled against Krispen's neck. A wet nose touched his chin. He thought it was Isabel, but she was asleep on his other side. He craned his neck painfully to see what it was. A white rabbit looked straight at him, like it wanted to tell him something. He couldn't understand. When he looked up again, there was that deer he'd seen earlier, standing over him, looking him in the eye, with its own great brown eyes shining at him.

"What is it?" he asked weakly.

The deer lowered its head and nudged him, as the rabbit had. Isabel came off his chest and looked at the deer, seeming to understand better than Krispen. Now Isabel looked at him and nudged him.

"Can't walk," he whispered, finally understanding they wanted him to move. "Hurts too much."

All three animals nudged him again. The deer flapped its velvet ears when Krispen pushed himself up painfully. He looked around to make sure the pack was all asleep. Though they usually posted a sentry, tonight, they were all in a deep sleep.

"Y'want me to come with you?" he whispered to the deer, whose ears flapped harder than ever. "Okay, I'll have to limp along, but I'll come if you need help or something." He stumbled off into the woods, the deer in the lead, Isabel and the rabbit bounding after him.

He limped as quietly as he could, terrified the other men would hear and come after him. He'd just turned his face to make sure they weren't followed when he ran into someone and yelped in surprise.

"Steady there, my lad. Quiet now," said a soft, comforting voice.

Krispen turned and saw a man clad all in brown clothes. He had a grizzled beard and eyes that twinkled even in the dark forest night. "Who're you?"

"You can call me Hermit if you like."

"Do you need help? I thought maybe these animals wanted help or somethin'."

"Actually, I had them fetch you. Come along with me, my boy. Let me help you for now." The Hermit put a gentle arm around Krispen and led him away from the pack to safety.

THEORIS' look of relief as his captors thrust him out into the narrow tunnel to join Elian, Hollis and Sophie, made Elian feel slightly better about his Fontre-like approach. He could only guess what they'd done to his friend, but one obvious sign of damage was that Theoris could barely walk alone. Elian lent him his shoulder.

"Thank you," said Theoris in a hoarse whisper.

"Are you alright?"

"I am now. Thanks to you."

"Your voice sounds - never mind." Elian looked away, but pulled his friend up a little tighter.

"I've been screaming a bit," Theoris admitted. Elian felt rather than saw the blush creep onto the fairy's pale face.

"I'm so sorry. I didn't wake until a few minutes ago. I'll do whatever I can to get us all out of here in one piece."

The fairy swallowed so hard Elian felt his neck muscles contract and relax. "You're taking me with you again?"

"Of course we're taking you. Do you think I could leave anyone I liked at all in this wretched place? Let alone a friend."

Theoris sighed and Elian thought he heard him repeat the word "friend" when he exhaled. Sympathy for Theoris almost overwhelmed the Fontre.

The anxious fey guards under Elian's command led them up a steep staircase dug straight from the earth and pounded down by fairy footprints. A tiny patch of sunlight shone in the distance, giving Elian the resolve he needed to drag Theoris up the narrow steps. At last they reached the exit. Theoris and Hollis drew breaths so deeply full of relief that Elian guessed they'd never expected to breathe fresh air again.

"We're in a hurry," he told the guards.

"Yes, sir," said Finnis in a trembling voice. "It's just down this path." He gestured toward a massive cathedral of branches, leaves and flowering vines. Elian nodded and they continued toward the Palace.

Hollis glanced at him.

"What does she want with me?" Elian lowered his voice to a whisper.

"To toy with you, undoubtedly. Also, she's probably hoping for information. The Queen possesses insatiable curiosity, as her mother did. A peaceful Fontre is a peculiarity she'll be dying to explore. And she'll want to know your weaknesses, so she can exploit them."

"I'll bear that in mind." Elian wrapped his arm more firmly around Theoris and they limped across the threshold together.

As they entered the giant structure, Elian glanced around, but the beauty which entranced Cassai in her first visit had the opposite effect on him. He found it overwhelming, disturbing and too lovely to be natural; though the room itself was woven from nothing but nature. It made his eyes water and set him on edge.

"Where is she?" he demanded.

"Her chambers are down that staircase and to the left. You cannot miss it, sir," Finnis replied.

The entire group walked toward the stairs, but the guards blocked them. "They should stay. She wishes to see you alone. We begged her to free them too, as a compromise." Finnis shuddered at the look Elian gave him. Hollis nodded, apparently he'd expected this.

"Allow it, Elian," he muttered under his breath.

Elian nodded, unwrapped himself from Theoris, and headed toward the stairs alone. His companions looked nervous, not for themselves, but for him.

Pain cut through his scalp. His jaw tightened and his hand went to his head. He frowned. It happened again. His eyes met Hollis' and the Kiatri's features went very dark.

"Cassai again?"

Elian nodded and rubbed his head, though it had stopped burning. "He's...I can't tell exactly, hurting her head."

"Her head?"

The pain had subsided, but Elian saw his confusion mirrored in Hollis' face. "Like he's pulling her hair out?"

Hollis' eyebrows narrowed. "My offer still stands. We'll see to him."

Elian nodded and tried to refocus. He had to get the Queen's help. He must get to Cassai. He turned back to the stone steps and descended two at a time. Why did he feel such an overwhelming urge to recite the Fontre mantra? His undamaged hand was shaking when he reached the last step and sucked in a breath before entering the jasmine archway that led to the Queen. That he had just made a mockery of her guards and knocked their captain unconscious didn't seem a promising start.

"Please come in!" said a higher pitched, more girly voice than he expected. He stepped through the arch into a room filled with red roses and fairy lights. In the middle stood a fairy no taller than five feet with silky black hair that fell below her waist and the impish smile of a naughty child.

He dipped his head. "Your Majesty," he said respectfully.

Her laugh was like the tinkling of crystal - before it shattered against sharp rocks. "No need to be so formal here on our own," she said sweetly. Too sweetly. Elian's mouth tasted bitter. "Please sit. I'd love for you to be comfortable." Elian looked at the proffered chair, so soft it looked like a town girl's powder puff.

"Was there something you wanted from me?" he asked, staying put.

"My goodness!" she said softly. "How very like your brother you are!"

Elian took a deep, steadying breath and looked back at her. "I'm not sure what you mean by that."

"You look like him, move like him. So sure of yourself. So distractingly good looking."

Elian felt as if she'd siphoned the blood from his veins and replaced it with ice. So Hollis had been wrong. She wouldn't be trying to discover his weaknesses; she knew them already.

Dahlia moved toward him – glided was a better word, he decided. Her feet didn't seem to touch the ground.

"You know my brother then?" he asked quietly.

"Oh yes! I've been in his company twice. He's never come here, but we have our ways of connecting with each other," the Queen said, smiling and perching lightly on a couch with so many pillows on it Elian wondered where she found room to sit. "We met in the Forest years ago when he was searching for the Lost Book. Then just recently, when he was searching for you," she explained. The eyes of fairies were hard to look at directly. The unnatural blue in Dahlia's made Elian's own eyes ache.

"He wasn't happy to learn you'd had the Lost Book all along," said Elian. "Next time he finds a way to 'communicate' with you, I'd advise against it."

Dahlia giggled. "I don't fear him in the least," she assured him. Elian believed her. "Sit next to me. I want to know all about you and your strange love affair with a Namarielle."

"I have little time to talk. I need to catch my brother and Cassai before they reach the Southern Borderlands."

"Oh, no need to cut our visit short over that. Devilan and his company are about to be delayed by an enormous crack in the road. I don't know what caused it exactly, but Fondair was shaken to its core yesterday."

Elian looked down. He didn't want to reveal what caused Lashai to break into pieces. "The caravan's stopped?" he asked.

"It should be shortly. It will be some time before they're up and going again. Meanwhile, I'm sure we can think of something to do," Dahlia rose smoothly from the couch and let her hips sway as she walked toward him. All the hair on Elian's arms prickled as she approached.

"I need your help." He took a step backwards.

"Perhaps." Dahlia breathed, coming even closer. "I want to talk first." Her dazzling blue eyes lowered suggestively. Elian balled his hands into fists.

"I should be clear. If you allowed this audience for anything other than making plans to free Cassai from my brother, we're wasting our time."

Dahlia laughed. "How refreshing. I never encounter hesitance when I request anything. It makes you even more alluring. Did you know that?" The queen's voice went low and husky. She stood only inches from Elian.

"I'll be going if there's nothing else." He turned, stopped by Dahlia's hand on his arm. From her fingers, warmth spread to every part of his body. He tried to breathe, but his lungs constricted.

"I've never been with a Fontre. It's something," she took another step toward him, "I've always been curious about."

Elian wrapped his hand around her wrist. "Well then," he said, forcing her hand back to her side, "I recommend the Inner Kingdom. I imagine the novelty of a fairy in their Temples, especially the Queen, would give you all the Fontre attention you could possibly crave."

Her eyes darkened, and so did their surroundings. She backed to the couch without replying. She lowered herself against the cushions, her whole body trembling with agitation.

"You spoke with Cassai," Elian said. "From what I understand, you held her here for days. Surely you gathered from your conversations that her survival is critical and I've gone to great lengths to assure it. Also, I'm sure you know that I love her."

"She mentioned it," Dahlia said in a clipped tone. "So, you came here, at the foolish suggestion of Hollis no doubt, to use me as some sort of genie who will grant your wishes. I don't know why he failed to mention that I require payment. I don't grant requests."

"Tell me your price."

"One price has already been denied. What makes you think I'll renegotiate?"

Elian studied her for a moment. "Do you want Cassai alive and whole?"

"She was very much alive at my last report," Dahlia snipped.

"Breathing perhaps. Devilan won't kill her. Rescuing her with her soul intact is a harder issue."

The queen glared at him at length. Elian stood still as a pillar in the great halls of the North and waited for her answer. "Her," she said at last.

"Her?"

"Yes, I want her. I want the Lost Book of Times back and her with it." She pursed her blood red lips.

Elian considered this for a moment, wondering what she'd say if he refused her second request. The look in her eyes when she claimed to want Cassai made Elian's skin crawl. "I can't do that."

She rolled her eyes. "You won't, but you certainly can."

"The Book I can deliver. I don't care if I never see it again; but Cassai isn't my property to barter."

Her eyes narrowed and the room grew darker still. "The Book is useless without a Namarielle."

"I'll ask her if she'll bring the book and read some of it to you. I know she enjoyed her visit here." The two looked at each other for an uncomfortably long time.

"If she refuses, you will replace her."

Elian's left eyebrow raised. "What good will I do you?"

Dahlia cocked her head to one side. "What happened to your hand?" she asked softly, ignoring the question.

"What does that have to do with —?"

"Answer me."

"Ffastian broke it years ago." Elian mumbled, hoping she would accept this and move on.

"It's freshly injured."

Elian shifted his weight. "It's a long story; one that has no relevance to our discussion."

Dahlia smiled and the room didn't lighten one shade. "You've threatened my guards, disabled Goliard and then asked me to put my armies in danger for good measure — humor me."

"Fair enough. The memory revisited me because of a particularly nasty medicine of the Fontre's making."

"Memory? Forgive my ignorance, but I've never known memory to break bone."

Elian tried to read the fairy's expression. He didn't want to guess what she expected to gain from this information. "The

80

draught's powers strengthen over time, making you relive the worst of your memories. In this case −" He held up his hand.

"How interesting." Deep hunger crept into Dahlia's eyes. Elian's heart began to race. "Do you still have this medicine?"

"I do." Her lily-white hand stretched out in a silent demand impossible to misunderstand. Elian reached into his jacket and withdrew the almost empty pouch. "It's poisonous to any race but the Fontre," he warned her, pressing it into the eager palm. Dahlia's fingers closed over it; her sharp nails reminded him of talons. "It will kill any fairy that ingests it."

"What are the ingredients?"

"I don't know. I've never cared to find the recipe."

"Melkana could use something like this..." she whispered to herself. Elian's jaw set hard at the way her sapphire eyes sparkled. After a few moments, she came back to the present. "Come, sit here. I'll repair your injured hand. I know you'll need the use of both if you intend to battle against your brother."

"That's not necessary. The bones are set and splinted as well as possible."

The darkness in the room lifted as she gave him her first genuine smile. Again she stretched her hand out expectantly. He considered refusing but, assuming it was useless, finally nodded and sat next to her, placing his poorly bandaged hand in hers. She slowly unwound the torn cloth. "This cloth is old and filthy. I can clearly see you've ripped it from your tunic. We'll have your clothes replaced before you leave. How many bones did you say he broke?"

"I didn't say." Elian glared at his hand. It was swollen and dark purple bruises had formed wherever one of the bones cracked.

Dahlia laid her other hand gently on the middle bone. A knot of pain pulsed where her fingers touched. Elian pressed his lips together, trying to displace it. The pain deepened and spread to his fingers, and finally his wrist. Dahlia looked at his face for the first time; the pain increased significantly. All his neck muscles tightened and his nostrils flared as breathing became harder and harder, but he didn't break eye contact.

The room began to swirl as if made of colorful smoke. When he could focus again, he almost screamed.

Cassai lay at his feet, dead, stabbed to death. Goliard stood over her, mocking Elian with a sneer. "Too late, Fontre. You got here too late." Elian sank to his knees. It wasn't true. How could the fey have gotten to her?

"Taiya! Speak to me!" he cried, feeling as if his heart would burst.

The room swirled and it was Sophie on the floor, an arrow through her heart. "Wha —?" The smoke returned and when it cleared, Krispen lay before him instead, beaten to death. Huge claw-marks slashed his chest. "Krispen?" Elian looked everywhere for Dahlia. "Where are you? Why are you doing this? How?" he screamed, but there was no answer.

Krispen was gone. Collin had replaced him, lying face-down, whipped, and bleeding out. "Collin, hold on. I'll stop it. I'll stop the bleeding!" Elian pressed against one wound only for three more to stream with blood.

"It's alright, Elian," Collin gasped. "Just let me go home to Anaya."

"I can't do that," Elian protested, but Collin was gone. Hollis lay in his place, his throat ripped out by Edgewater. "Hollis, I can't — I'm so sorry —"

Elian was back in the Queen's chamber. The pain had lessened; dissolving from the middle and radiating out as when it began. He looked at her, and she smiled an evil smile.

"That's better, isn't it?"

Elian's body quaked when she released him. He felt cold, but beads of sweat dotted his forehead. "What was that?" he whispered.

Her eyes glowed as she leaned so close he could smell tea and honeysuckle on her breath. "Nothing here is free, my dear Fontre. Speaking of payment, I'd like to keep a sample of this." She indicated the leather pouch lying on the cushion she'd recently vacated.

Elian frowned at her and finally managed to calm his breathing. "What do you intend to do with it?"

"Our terms are set?" she demanded, ignoring his question.

"You'll bring me the book. If Cassai doesn't want to come, you'll surrender yourself to me?"

He glared at her. "Yes," he said, silently vowing never to ask Cassai to return to this place no matter what it cost.

"The Book will remain in my realm and be under the protection of my people from now on." The Queen studied him for a long while. "You won't even ask Cassai if she'll come, will you?"

Elian returned her intense stare. "Of course I won't."

"You will stay at least seven days. I won't negotiate that."

A muscle jerked in Elian's jaw. "What could you want with me for seven days?"

She grinned coyly. "Oh, don't worry. I'll think of something."

6

THE DELAY

Hollis watched with increasing irritation as Theoris drummed his fingers on the marble steps. The fairy had sunk to the step where Elian left him, and hadn't tried to stand since. He drummed again. Sophie kept stealing glances at Hollis as though waiting for him to boil over.

"What do you think they're talking about?" Sophie asked. Hollis assumed this was an attempt to redirect his attention.

Hollis glared. "Nothing good." He wished he'd insisted on accompanying Elian. After all, he knew Dahlia, knew her tricks and ploys.

"I say, they have been down there a while, haven't they? Do you think perhaps she's managed to best him?" Theoris fretted. His fingers hit the marble again.

"She hasn't bested him, fairy. Settle yourself. Can't you just keep your hands at your sides?" Hollis snapped. Theoris, stricken, pressed his arms against his sides. Hollis sighed. Theoris had the worst of this plan, by far; Hollis knew he should show some compassion. The fairy looked as though he might fall over and, when he thought no one was watching him, a look of excruciating pain creased his face. He ironed it out a second later. Hollis felt another stab of guilt. "Ignore me, Theoris. I'm anxious too. What did they do to you down there?"

"Oh, it was nothing," the fairy looked away so Hollis couldn't see his expression, but he couldn't keep the pain from his voice. "They're upset at Cassai being taken by the Fontre. They sort of ... took it out on me." Theoris shifted his leg and Hollis spotted a rent in the trousers Theoris had received from the Kiatri. It was hard to rip Kiatri spun wool.

"Let me see that," Hollis said stepping closer.

"It's a mere scratch. Nothing to fuss over."

"Sit still and let me look. I have something that can help you, surely," Hollis tried to sound caring, but the order came out harsh. Theoris gripped the steps at each side and let Hollis pull the ripped fabric from the wound. From the fairy's ankle to his knee stretched a cut so deep that in a few places, Hollis could see his bone. "By the Weaver, Theoris! Why did you not tell Elian?"

"I - I didn't wish to trouble him. He didn't seem to be in the mood for trifling with wounds." Theoris leaned away from Hollis' wrath, making the Kiatri feel worse.

Hollis looked at Sophie, who stared wide-eyed at Theoris' leg. "Sophie," Hollis said, "Bring me that satchel." Hollis' leather bag lay at Sophie's feet, but she was rooted to the spot. "Sophie!" he barked. She jerked and looked at him with unfocused eyes, her face white as the marble on which they stood. "The bag at your feet. I need it."

"The bag? Oh, right. Yes."

"You aren't telling me that the mighty huntress who makes her own weapons and flaunts them at her kin faints at the sight of a little blood."

"Of course not." She snatched the bag from the floor and thrust it at him, looking furious. *I shouldn't have goaded her about her weaknesses,* he thought vaguely.

"Steady on, Hollis. It's a very different matter to hunt an animal than to dress such a wound on a man, or in this case, a fairy," Theoris said soothingly, focusing his purple eyes on Sophie, rather than Hollis. Beads of sweat formed on Theoris' brow and he pressed his lips together so tightly they'd all but disappeared.

Hollis rolled his eyes, but managed to hitch up the corners of his mouth into what he hoped was an encouraging smile. "Thank you, Sophie." He dug his hand into his bag, seeking a small pouch of soothing herbs. "Here we are. Not as good as Cassai's concoction, but I didn't have bee pollen at my disposal, or the flower of *Nundain*."

Hollis put the dried leaves in his mouth to get moisture into them. They tasted dusty and bitter, but the cooling sensation that spread through his tongue and throat reassured him. Still potent. He spit them out, making Sophie grimace in disgust. Hollis ignored her.

"Deep breath, Theoris. This will sting, but only for a moment." Every muscle and tendon in the fairy's leg tightened as Hollis applied the spit-sodden leaves as gently as possible.

"Uncle, I think...I think they burned him too," Sophie observed. "Look at the skin around the cut."

Hollis studied the wound more closely. Angry red blisters surrounded it. Bile rose in his throat. "Tell me what they did," he whispered, his voice so full of fury that Theoris looked, if possible, even more uncomfortable.

Sophie sat down next to the fairy and awkwardly patted him on the shoulder. "It'll be alright now, Theoris. Uncle Hollis knows what he's doing. Tell us what happened." Comforting as she was trying to be, Hollis saw her shoulders heave up and down, her cheeks flooding with color. Sophie was seething with rage. He grinned and almost felt sorry for the fey.

"The slice was for the unfortunate information." Theoris' face started to relax. "Oh, I say, that is better. What did you use?"

"Just some herbs my father used to mix for pain. Go on."

"Right you are. Well, as you know, I'd nothing to offer. I knew they were taking Cassai to the Inner Kingdom, but apparently the

Queen already knew that would be Devilan's plan. They asked me about the boy, Krispen. Of course, we've had no news of him." Theoris' voice trailed off, and Hollis felt another twinge of fear. Whatever had happened to Krispen, Hollis feared the once sweet shepherd boy would be beyond recognition if they ever saw him again.

"So they pressed a hot iron to your wound because you knew nothing?" Theoris was silent, but Hollis nodded understanding. He felt his head might catch fire from pure fury. "Alright." he stood and brushed off his knees, though there was no dust in the throne room.

"So what's the plan?" Sophie asked eagerly as he started toward the door that led down to the queen's quarters.

"I'm going to tell Elian what they-," Hollis stopped midsentence.

In the doorway he was headed toward there appeared the only being in the world more beautiful than the Fairy Queen herself. Lily, Dahlia's sister, saw him at the same moment and started so badly she turned and almost fled.

"Wait!" Hollis called. "Don't go. Lily, just … please wait." Hollis forced air into his restricted airways. Lily hesitated for so long, he thought she'd really leave, but she slowly turned back.

"Does my sister know you're here?" she whispered. The sound of her voice hurt Hollis so deeply his eyes watered.

"She – she does. Yes. I'm sorry she did nothing to prepare you. I'm not surprised, just sorry." Hollis looked away from her face. His insides felt as if a giant hand had clutched them and was squeezing the life from him mercilessly. "Are you … well?"

"I'm…I guess so," she said without conviction. "Theoris, how lovely to have you back." She noticed the others in the room.

"My lady, how good it is to see you!" Theoris said, giving her a weak but affectionate smile. He started to rise, but cried out in pain and sank back to the step.

"Are you alright?" Lily started toward Theoris and Hollis

followed with his gaze. Each move she made caused the giant hand to tighten more.

Sophie stood as Lily approached and glanced at Hollis apprehensively. "Don't touch him," she ordered. Lily froze and her eyes flicked from Sophie to Hollis.

"No, Sophie, it's alright," Hollis said, walking back to the steps. "Lily means him no harm." Tears sprang to Lily's eyes when Hollis said her name and he instantly regretted it. "I don't think she's capable of harm," he added, hoping that would evaporate the tears.

"I can help him if he's hurt," Lily assured Sophie.

"Well, that's nice. You people have quite a system, don't you?" Sophie snapped. "One tortures – another mends. How kind of you to provide such a service."

Hollis swallowed hard and whispered. "Sophie, she isn't like them. Just let her be."

Sophie chewed her bottom lip, either biting back a clever reply, or considering what he'd said, Hollis couldn't tell which. She finally nodded and dropped back on the step with a belligerent thud.

Lily approached Theoris and held out a hand. He took the offered hand and kissed it. "I cannot express how lovely it is to see you, Your Highness."

She smiled so brilliantly, Hollis had to look away. "You dear thing. What have they done to you?" She went smoothly to her knees in front of him and he released her hand so she could examine his wound. "Oh, Theoris! Close your eyes, love. I'll see what I can do."

Theoris squeezed his eyes tight shut. Lily touched his leg and her mouth began to move. The whispered words rose to a chant. The language of the fey flowed from her too quickly for Hollis to translate.

The wound sealed itself slowly from top to bottom and the

blisters began to dry up. Then the rawness faded until at last, Theoris smiled and opened his eyes. Lily smiled. "Better?"

"So much better. Thank you."

Lily glanced at Hollis. "Why did they do that? What happened?"

Hollis opened his mouth to reply, but before he could utter a word, there was a clatter at the entrance. "Lily! Step away from him!" shouted Goliard. He stood in the archway, red-faced, his broad chest heaving up and down, his fairy guard surrounding him.

Lily winced as if slapped.

"Shut up, Goliard. Let her be," Hollis growled.

Goliard's blazing eyes pinned Hollis in place and all thought vanished in the searing pain that followed. Hollis felt his knees give way. Every muscle in his body was being shredded by jagged glass.

"Stop it! Please stop, Goliard. I found them here by accident!" Lily cried, running to the Captain of the Guard. Through vision blurred by agony Hollis watched the fairy regard his fiancé. His pain lifted slowly, leaving Hollis aching everywhere. He drew a painful breath and stood up.

Goliard touched Lily's smooth white cheek. "Found them by accident?" he sneered.

"I came up and they were here. I'm so sorry." The pleading in her voice burned Hollis worse than Goliard. He clenched his fists.

"Did he touch you?" Goliard demanded, jerking his head toward Hollis.

"No, of course not. He was as taken back as I was." Lily trembled so hard Hollis feared she would collapse.

"What a harmonious couple you make," the Kiatri commented dryly. "What are you planning to do now, Goliard? Strike her for discovering we were here? Torture Theoris a bit more? How charming you are to your future wife." Out of the corner of his eye, Hollis saw Theoris shrink at the sound of his name. Silently the fairy's eyes begged Hollis to leave him out of their exchange.

"Open your mouth again, Kiatri, and I will seal it for eternity. It's for your safety she pleads, not her own. I would never hurt her." Goliard glowered at him, then lifted Lily's face to his and kissed her. Hollis froze. He forced himself not to react; not to fly across the room and rip Goliard's throat out. At first the kiss was as harsh as the Captain of the Guard himself, but it softened and deepened, and Lily did nothing to put him off. *For our benefit, not hers,* Hollis silently assured himself.

"Well," the voice of the Fairy Queen from the opposite side of the room startled everyone. "How nice to see you two being affectionate for once," Dahlia said.

The Queen and Elian stood in the doorway, looking resolved.

Goliard released Lily and stood to attention. "Apologies, your Highness. I couldn't help myself. Lily looks particularly pretty when she's just stopped crying." He smirked at Lily, who blushed and looked at the floor. The guards surrounding them snickered.

A muscle worked in Hollis' jaw. He instinctively felt for the bow and arrows he no longer possessed. The futile gesture drew another chuckle from Goliard.

"Crying? No one has been distressing you up here I hope, sister?" Dahlia asked.

"No," Lily answered so quietly Hollis could barely hear her.

"What a relief," Dahlia replied. "Now then, Goliard, ready your men."

"My men? Ready them for what?" Goliard asked, clearly surprised. Hollis looked at Elian, who smiled grimly at the Captain of the Guard.

"Battle. We're going to the mortal world," said Dahlia as if such an order was merely routine. "I've offered our assistance to this Fontre and his companions."

~

DEVILAN WATCHED her thoughtfully as the carriage jostled forward the next day. "Did you sleep?"

"Not really."

"The ground is too hard?"

"No, I'm used to sleeping on hard ground. I can't...I have a hard time getting comfortable."

He gave her a look that reminded her of Elian when he was searching for the truth. "Nothing to do with the ground though. I see."

Cassai looked out the window. He was starting early today. All she'd had for breakfast was thin gruel, apparently the usual Fontre fare. Being expected to take Devilan's abuse on top of that was a bit much. Her stomach growled in agreement.

"You're still hungry?" Devilan said, looking satisfied he had his answer. "I asked you if you were hungry before bed last night."

Cassai frowned. "I don't sleep well in the company of those who'd enjoy killing me, or tearing me apart piece by piece. It makes me restless. Also, my scalp hurt from my hair being brushed and braided by a lunatic."

Devilan grinned. "I have something you can eat if you're hungry. My company have no interest in killing you, or ripping you to pieces, in fact, quite the contrary. And I'm sorry about your hair. In my defense, I'm pretty sure it hadn't had a brush through it for several weeks and I think a family of birds had been nesting there. I had to evict them to make any real progress."

"It was thoroughly brushed the day we were to meet with the council."

"I do remember it looking very nice that day," Devilan conceded. He reached into a bag at his side and pulled out a parcel. "Bread and cheese. Not really breakfast fare, but they're yours if you want them."

Cassai stared at him. Weighing her desires to eat, or to fly at him and hurt him as much as possible. "Since when are bread and cheese not breakfast fare?" she asked, accepting the roll smeared with sharp goat cheese.

"If you're still hungry after meals, you just need to say so." Devilan said instead of answering.

"I don't understand why you're suddenly pretending to be human."

He shook his head and drew a deep breath. "If I told you that, my pretending wouldn't be as effective. Now, are you feeling reasonably compliant? I'm curious about something." She nodded. "Why do you carry a Fontre blade?"

She stopped mid-chew.

"Did my brother give you his sword? I didn't think any but a Fontre could wield our blades without doing serious damage to their soul."

"Your brother didn't give it to me; he thought it was destroyed. I kept it as a small child having no idea of its powers or history and it just sort of...called to me."

Devilan's eyebrows raised. "Have you used it?"

Cassai shrugged. "Not really. I held it for a few seconds after a fight with Edgewater."

"You fought Edgewater?"

"Mostly Elian and Hollis did, I got in the way a lot. I was what they were after thanks to you."

Devilan didn't seem to be listening anymore. He stared at her, deep in thought. "What did the sword do when you held it after the fight?"

"It sort of tingled up my arm and then it did nothing. Hollis and Elian both watched me like they expected me to change before their very eyes or something."

"Yes," Devilan murmured. "I'm sure they did. Fontre swords are not to be trifled with. Very interesting. I don't think, Cassai, that even a normal Namarielle could hold one with no effect whatsoever." He was back to studying her. "I wonder if it's because you're the last. The concentrated powers fall to you," he mused quietly. "Your emotions control the weather. Is it every time?"

"Yes."

"Alright. And if you're physically hurt or in danger, do you notice a change in your natural surroundings?"

"What are you getting at?"

"Last night, when I pulled your hair, did the trees react?" Devilan still looked deep in thought and as though part of his mind was somewhere else solving a puzzle.

"I didn't notice," she replied.

He huffed out a frustrated sigh. "I didn't either. I wasn't watching. Give me your hand."

"Why?"

"By the Weaver, why do I always have to ask things twice with you?" he snapped, grabbing her hand and laying it palm up in his. Her heart started racing and she pulled uselessly against him, but his grip was iron and he paid no notice. He was engrossed in the mystery. "No, better with the other. Give me your other hand."

"Devilan, please don't. What do you want to know? I can probably just tell you."

He ignored this and took her broken wrist instead. She braced herself as he worked his fingers deep enough to feel the bones under the bandages. "Where's the break?"

"M-my wrist," she said, shaking. He looked up at the tone in her voice.

"Just give me one moment. I'll not do any more damage to it." His fingers found the joint between her two bones and she cried out. His head jerked to the window. The trees of Fondair swayed against each other as if a great wind had suddenly whipped through them. "Incredible," he whispered. Raindrops began to pelt against the carriage window and he looked back at her.

Tears spilled from her eyes and she shrank away from him, holding her wrist against her chest and glaring at him.

He was shaking too, but she could see it was pure excitement.

93

"It takes so very little," he said. "You wouldn't have lasted a moment being raised by a Fontre."

"Well, I wasn't raised by a Fontre," she returned, furious with herself for crying.

He stared at her as though he were lost in thought again. "Clearly. I can't believe the trees do that in response to you."

"I could have told you they would...if you'd asked," she whispered, wiping the tears from her eyes and rubbing her throbbing wrist.

Devilan looked frustrated at her, but she didn't know why he should be. "The pain is nothing. It's not an injury. It's weakness leaving your body. Let it come and let it go. I honestly don't understand people's gross overreactions to insignificant pain."

He looked like he was going to say something else when the carriage swayed dangerously and rattled to a stop. Devilan threw open his door.

"What is it?" he shouted.

Dershom appeared in the opening. "There's a giant crack in the earth just ahead. Trees are felled everywhere and the road is impassable," he explained, pointing to the shattered ground.

"Make it passable. Have the men move the trees and branches. I'll have a look down the road and see how far the breach extends."

"Yes, my Lord," Dershom bowed and disappeared.

Devilan ducked out of the carriage and Cassai spent a few minutes alone wishing she was anywhere else in the world.

The carriage door opened, but she didn't look at whoever lowered into the seat beside her. "You're to come with me," said an unfamiliar voice higher than Devilan's or Dershom's. She looked into the cruel, angry eyes of Racalf just before he grasped her arm with his uninjured hand.

"Where are we going?" she asked.

"You're to come with me," he repeated and stepped out of the carriage, pulling her after him. Cassai managed to find her

94

feet just in time. She had no doubt if she fell she would be dragged.

"I'm sorry about your hand," she said as he jerked her along. His grip tightened painfully, but Racalf didn't speak again. Cassai bit the inside of her cheek to keep from crying out. The trees began to sway again in response.

The Fontre drew her to the broken road and thrust her toward Devilan, who stood glaring at the breach.

"Back to your duties," he barked at Racalf, who nodded and vanished into a sea of black leather uniforms. Devilan grinned down at Cassai. She tried not to look at him. "I believe he rather holds it against you."

"Can they repair it?" Cassai tried not to squirm. He'd taken hold of her arm and his grip was as painful as Racalf's. "I'm not trying to escape or anything. Could you let up a bit?"

He noticed the pain in her eyes and dug his fingers deeper. "This is causing us delay we cannot afford," he growled. "We're supposed to be at the Castle the day after tomorrow."

Cassai bit her cheek harder. The salty taste of blood filled her mouth, but she didn't care. Oddly enough, it had a numbing effect on the pain in her arm.

"All this because you kissed him?" Devilan muttered.

"If I recall correctly," Elian's voice slammed into the two of them, "I kissed her."

Devilan pivoted toward the sound, dragging her with him. She blinked, wondering if she was dreaming. Elian stood between two trees, smiling a devilish smile.

Devilan cleared his throat to cover his shock. "Is there no limit to your stupidity, brother?"

"I wouldn't think so. I'm pretty sure it's hereditary," Elian returned. Devilan glowered.

"I've always admired your humor in the face of crushing defeat. What will you do now that you've managed to catch up with us?"

"Let go of her arm," Elian said. "You're hurting her."

"Oh, it's nothing serious," Devilan replied, jerking his fingers up. Cassai cried out. "See? It could be worse." The forest began to rumble.

Elian's nostrils flared. "Give her to me, and we'll leave right now. No one will be hurt. You can return to your master and tell him your earlier suspicions were correct. We're all dead. Or you can spare your honor and tell him you killed us. Either way, you'll leave us in peace. That's my offer." He delivered this with so much assuredness Cassai felt a spark of hope bloom in her breast.

"Your offer?" scoffed Devilan. "Thank you for your generosity. Is there anything else you'd like? Use of the royal carriage? The High King to come and personally apologize for any inconvenience we may have caused?" Devilan's raised voice drew the attention of the Koninjka working on the road. Dershom dropped a giant log to approach the group.

"Just Cassai. But thank you for asking." Elian caught her eye and gave her a wink.

"I assume that idiot Kiatri's hiding somewhere in the trees. Ready to strike with his one bow and arrow, is he? Brilliant, brother. I'm lamenting my decision not to have you plan all my attack strategies."

Cassai's heart sank. *Why would Elian attempt a rescue like this? Has worrying about me driven him completely mad?*

Elian grinned. "You won't release her then? I recommend you think this through. You may come to regret your decision."

"Ah, I doubt that. Even if you've rallied a few pathetic Kiatri, you cannot hope to defeat my Koninjka, but I'll enjoy watching you try."

"No, I don't think you'll enjoy it at all," Elian assured him, his right arm rose, bent at the elbow. His fingers curled into a fist and Cassai thought she must have blinked. In a shudder of dead leaves the world surrounding them filled with grimly determined, other-worldly beings. Devilan's eyes grew wide and his lips parted, although he said nothing. Goliard stood on Elian's right. He grinned at Devilan and drew a long, curved fairy blade.

"The fey army? How did you —?" Devilan murmured, shaking his head in disbelief.

"You needn't worry about how. If it makes you feel better, you were right about one thing," Elian began.

Dershom had come to stand on Cassai's other side when an arrow whizzed past her and sank deep into the back of his neck. The man froze, dazed for a long moment. He looked at Devilan. His lips moved uselessly as if he wanted to speak a final word, but of course, he had no use of his voice any longer. "Hollis is in the trees behind you," Elian finished.

Dershom sank to his knees, clutching at Cassai's dress, splattering her with blood in a final attempt to stay upright. Then he crumpled at her feet, and died.

7

THE LIGHT ONES

Collin stood at the Gates of Halanah and glanced uneasily at his uncle, Julius. "Why did I volunteer for this?" he whispered. The ornately wrought golden gates loomed above. He felt so tiny and insignificant beneath them that his resolve was slipping away.

"It's in your blood to push back. It's a cause worth fighting for. And ... Anaya." Julius' voice cracked.

Collin's eyes slid shut and he swallowed so hard it hurt. Or maybe the pain was from the tears he refused to allow. Anaya. The Fontre had not only whipped him almost to death, they had murdered his little sister. There was nothing left for him but war after that.

"Yes, alright," he snapped. Her name spoken aloud clouded his mind. He needed to stay focused and have all his wits for what he was about to attempt.

"Right," said Julius quietly, with too much understanding in his voice. It grated Collin's nerves to be coddled. Six weeks of hard travel had changed him. He'd grown a little taller, a little stronger, and his curly hair now fell past his chin. His uncle wanted him to cut it, but he refused. He'd heard that the Light

Ones let their hair grow because it wasn't the nuisance to them it would be for the hard-working Borderlings.

Most of the Light Ones, especially their dignitaries, spent their days in study and rigorous debate. He'd read that when the Senate held session over some new law or petition, they spent days in their Capital building, reclining on their cushions and eating food served by slaves. Collin thought it odd that people who claimed to be so enlightened justified owning slaves.

"Go on. Pull the cord," Julius prompted him, gesturing to the thick purple rope hanging through the bars of the gate.

Collin gave the cord a hard yank – perhaps too hard. The gong sounded so loudly he jumped and backed away from the giant structure. His ears rang as an impossibly tall man dressed in a white robe glided toward the gate.

"Who calls at the Gates of Halanah?" the man asked in a regal tone.

"Collin, son of Malton, of the Eastern Borderlands," Collin answered, trying to mimic the man's formality. He straightened his back to draw attention from his knocking knees. The heavy lock lifted and metal scraped against cobblestone as the gates swung inward.

"Collin, son of Malton, is this your father who accompanies you?" The man dropped his clear blue eyes to Julius, who, in spite of his considerable height and breadth, the gatekeeper dwarfed.

"No sir," Collin mumbled – never had he sounded more like a Borderling. "He's – he's my uncle. My father is dead."

The man's scowl melted slightly. "I'm sorry to hear that, young man. It is my hope that your father now roams the halls of the Kingdom of Arora."

Collin pressed his lips together and tried to think of some reply. He suddenly forgot everything Elian had taught them about the Light Ones and their religion. "Er, thank you," he mumbled.

"What business brings you to my beautiful gate when the sun is barely at his zenith?"

Collin looked at his uncle for help. Julius smiled encouragingly, but said nothing. "I was ... I hoped I could speak with your Senate about something really important." The words tumbled from Collin before he could think them through. The man at the gate smiled; an indulgent smile he might give to a child. Collin bit his tongue to keep from saying what he was thinking.

"Enter then, Collin of the Eastern Borderlands. We will hear your petition forthwith." Collin, hopeful this meant something good, remembered just in time not to shove his hands into his pockets as they stepped into the border city of the Light Ones.

"I am Acamus, and I am the Gatekeeper of Halanah." Acamus said "Gatekeeper of Halanah" in an even loftier voice than before. As though the title was its own sentence.

Julius gingerly placed a hand on Collin's shoulder. The boy winced. Despite their best efforts, a few cuts across his back and shoulders wouldn't heal. He suspected the Fontre's poisoned whips.

"Please follow me. We will arrange a place for you to wash and eat. You are surely exhausted after a journey from the East. You'll have been on the road for a fortnight, I would imagine," Acamus said.

"Six weeks. We took it slowly," Julius answered.

Collin let his uncle describe their journey while he took in the City of Halanah. Green trees grew everywhere and flowering vines trailed up the sides of tall stone buildings. The air smelled of flowers. Unnaturally tall children and young people his age lounged in a large open structure housing a giant pool. The slabs of stone looked as if they had been hewn centuries ago. Steam rose from the water and a sign at the arched entrance read, "Public Bathhouse".

Collin squinted at a tall boy he guessed to be around sixteen ascending the pool steps. The boy was naked. Collin blushed and looked away. Acamus and his uncle were ahead and when he rushed to catch up, Collin tripped on a cobblestone and fell to his knees.

"Oh, careful!" a girl cried from the doorway of her house. She ran to him, helping him back to his feet. Collin blushed deeper still.

"Thank you," he muttered, wishing a fissure would open in the road and swallow him whole.

The girl's hair was the color of honey and her eyes matched the hue exactly. Her slim shoulders were draped in a pure white gown tied just above her waist with a thin golden cord. A chain hung from her neck, also gold, with an emerald butterfly dangling from it. She was short compared to the towering Lightlings surrounding them. Collin hoped this didn't mean she was years younger than him. The creamy skin on her shoulders made the boy's heart pound unhelpfully in his chest. "I'm Laurelle. Are you injured?"

"Um, no. Just – well –" Collin grinned and then wished he hadn't. Surely this angelic girl had boys grinning like idiots at her constantly. He tried to cover his embarrassment by clearing his throat. "My pride is injured, but the rest of me is alright."

"Oh. No need to feel ashamed. The stones are uneven at that part of the road. What's your name?" Her speech wasn't as pretentious as Amacus' and Collin gave her a genuine smile, which she returned.

"Collin, from the Borderlands," he answered. *Of course you come from the Borderlands, idiot! You think she'd mistake you for a Lightling?*

"Collin, your curls are the loveliest I've ever seen!"

Collin's legs went watery. "Um, thank you. Your hair is ... very shiny," he stammered. She laughed and threw an arm around his shoulders. He caught his breath at the pressure on his wounds, but she didn't notice and he didn't complain.

"What a dear you are! Come, let's follow your father and Acamus. You can tell me all about yourself on the way. What part of the Border do you hail from?" she asked easily, letting her hand rest on his waist as they walked.

"The East. My village is Plahn," he answered, feeling foolish. Why should she care what his village was called? She lived in this vast, perfect city, with every building carved from gleaming white marble.

Laurelle, it so happened, was interested in everything. She peppered him with questions and waited in rapture for every answer. She was almost as easy to talk to as Cassai. The pinching ache around his heart, present since Anaya's death, eased slightly.

"The man I'm with is my uncle, not my father," he told her as they approached a building many stories high, supported by pillars taller than most buildings in Plahn.

"Oh. I have an uncle too. My mother's brother. He disapproves of my father because he's ..." She leaned in close to Collin and pressed her lips closer to his ear than was necessary. "He's not of the Halanic Race. He's from ... well, he came from the mountains."

"A Kiatri?" Collin yelped in surprise. No wonder she wasn't as tall as her fellow Light Ones. Laurelle giggled and pressed a finger to her lips.

"Shh... it's a huge disgrace to Momma's family and she lets no one speak of it. Of course, anyone looking at father would know."

"So ... how old are you?" he asked.

"How old do you think I am?" she countered, her eyes dancing.

Collin looked at her hard. "Fourteen?"

"Sixteen."

The tension left Collin's shoulders. "Me too."

"This is our Hall of Hospitality." Laurelle beamed, waving her free arm at the towering building Acamus and Julius had already entered. "You'll love it here. It's the most comfortable place in the world. Are you hungry? Of course you are. I'm sorry. Foolish questions are my downfall. Momma says I never learned to think before speaking. I just say whatever comes to my mind. I wish I were one of the intellectuals, you know?"

The Hall of Hospitality was a grand building, with ten steps leading to a wide marble porch. On every side an even row of columns supported the gleaming building, most with a dark green ivy covering.

As they walked the steps together, Collin smiled and dared to wrap his own arm around her shoulders. "You seem sufficiently intelligent," he assured her. "I feel like a complete idiot just having a conversation with you."

She laughed and Collin had to remind himself to keep breathing in and out. "You're the nicest boy I've ever met. Where do you study in Plahn? Do they have professors of the scripts? Are there clapboard houses, like I've read about, where the children sit at desks?"

"We called them schoolmasters, but yes, the houses are made of wood. And the buildings have large rooms with desks."

"It would be uncomfortable to sit like that to study. Why don't they sit on pillows and cushions? Hours of reading with your bottom on hard wooden planks seems illogical."

"Agreed," he said nodding and grinning. "I'll suggest cushions when I return." Another laugh echoed off the ribbed, vaulted ceilings. Collin's head buzzed.

"Collin? Who's this?" Julius asked kindly. His eyebrows rose slightly when his glance fell to Collin's hand on the girl's shoulder and hers at Collin's waist.

"Uncle, this is Laurelle," Collin stammered, feeling his chest tighten again. His hand dropped, and Laurelle stood away from him. "This is my Uncle Julius."

"How very nice to meet you," Julius said extending a hand. Laurelle nodded and placed her hand in his.

"Thank you, sir. It is my unparalleled pleasure to make your acquaintance," she said. Julius raised her hand and kissed it lightly. It was Collin's turn to look surprised.

"The pleasure is all mine. Please excuse us now. Our journey was … arduous," Julius explained. Collin stared at the white marble column on his right, trying to hide his amusement at his uncle using a word like "arduous".

"Please allow us to offer you respite from your journey." Amacus waved a long-fingered hand at a doorway draped in a light curtain. "This room is at your disposal. At the noon hour we will bring you tea, and after that, the washing ceremony. I will fetch fresh garments for you," he offered, smiling. Then he bent down and kissed a speechless Julius on both cheeks before gliding gracefully away. Laurelle also stood on tip-toe to kiss Collin on both cheeks.

"I'll bring the tea if you like."

His cheeks blazed where her lips had brushed. "Er – right. I'd like that. Thanks," he mumbled and ducked under his uncle's arm into the chamber.

Julius let the curtain fall. "Well, your life-long dream is coming true."

Collin rolled one of the strings on his jacket between his fingers and didn't answer.

"What do you think?" Julius prodded.

"She's wonderful," he finally responded, dropping his green canvass satchel on a large bed. The bag was almost swallowed in the depth of blankets and the down-filled mattress below. "I just don't know if she likes me the same way."

Julius rolled his eyes heavenward and exhaled. "I meant – seeing the White City. Finally being with the Light Ones of the North. You've been hoping for a chance like this since Elian showed you all those picture books as a lad. Now all you think about is a girl."

Collin opened his mouth to cover his mistake, but closed it again and sank into the billowy bed. "Never mind," he said, feeling the softness in every aching muscle. "I'm just tired from our *arduous* journey I suppose," he poked at his uncle.

Julius smiled, but didn't rise to the goad. "She's beautiful, but tell me your impression of the city."

"The buildings are unbelievable. They look like they've stood for centuries. But they're so physical here. Did you see the bathhouse? Boys and girls were in there together completely naked!"

Julius laughed, but seemed as uncomfortable as Collin. "I missed that. I guess you know why they call themselves *The Photastole?*"

"The Enlightened?" Collin translated. "I guess because knowledge and learning is important to them."

"Yes. They consider themselves above most laws, even the laws of moral character. Too enlightened to worry about such mortal issues as modesty." Julius smiled at his nephew as he shrugged off his jacket and sat on the edge of the bed to remove his boots. The mattress was so low to the ground he was grunting and sweating with the effort by the time the shoes pulled free.

Collin pushed himself up on his elbows. "They're not immortals, are they?" he asked, trying to remember Elian's old lessons.

"No. They have similar life spans to a Lashaian. They simply disregard the physical world sometimes, in search of ... I don't know ... higher awareness or something. It wears me out to think of it. Let's rest a bit before tea." With that, Julius flopped backward on the bed, folded his hands over his stomach and was snoring within moments.

Collin watched him for a while and then realized his dust-filled clothes were soiling the snowy bedding. Weariness melted away and he pulled himself up, glanced at Julius long enough to decide he was truly sleeping, then slipped through the curtain to explore the Hall.

"Over here," chimed the voice he hoped to hear. Laurelle stood against a pillar, beckoning him. There were three boys with her, one with her smaller stature, and two that towered over them. Collin bit his lower lip nervously and started toward the group.

"I guess I wasn't as tired as I thought," he muttered as he approached.

"Oh, join us then." Laurelle beamed in delight and Collin's

nerves eased. The shorter boy grinned and Collin saw a resemblance. Though the boy was taller than Laurelle, they had the same large green eyes, the same perfectly straight nose. Collin's hand went automatically to his own freckled nose, slightly crooked; Cobbs had broken it years ago.

"I'm Marcole," said the boy pleasantly, extending a hand in greeting. "Friends call me Marc."

"Collin," offered the Borderling, taking the hand and glancing nervously at the others. His experience with older boys had been mostly unpleasant.

"Nihl," said one, with black straight hair that hung past his shoulders.

"Jacque," said the other Lightling whose ginger locks curled around his ears like Collin's and he had stubble on his chin. He beamed at Collin when he shook his hand.

"Nihl and Jacque are brothers and friends of mine and Marc's. He's my brother," Laurelle said.

Collin grinned, "Yes, I see that."

"Elle said you're from the Borderlands," Marcole said.

"Yes."

"Are things as violent there as they say? I heard that the hostile Fontre have infiltrated the very air surrounding the Inner Kingdom."

Collin's back twinged at the mention of the Fontre. "Fontre are rare in my village, I've met them a couple of times." Collin's insides burned. He didn't want to talk about Fontre.

"Really?" Jacque beamed. "What are they like? I've heard some of them file their teeth to sharp points so if they lose a weapon in battle, they can tear into opponents like animals." His tone held nothing of the usual formality of the Light Ones. Collin liked him instantly.

He shrugged. "I don't know about their teeth, but their whips definitely bite."

Jacque's eyebrows shot up at the word whips, but Marcole's tone dropped in awe. "Do they dress all in black?"

A cloud reclaimed Collin. The black clad soldiers that sprang into his nightmares every time he closed his eyes were not worthy of the fascination he heard when Marcole spoke of them.

"The ones I met were. I'd rather not talk about them, if that's alright."

"Of course it is," Laurelle cried, giving her brother a withering glare. "Come. Let's find you something decent to wear, and food. We're going to the park for a bit of entertainment. The theatrical society is performing one of my favorite plays in a couple of hours." The light that danced into her eyes filled Collin with excitement.

"We should go to the Bathhouse first," Nihl suggested, wrinkling his nose. "He smells like he hasn't had a decent wash in weeks."

Collin's insides roiled. "Um – sorry about that. It's – the journey –" His clumsy explanation was cut short by Laurelle, who slipped her arm through his.

"Ignore Nihl. He always says what he thinks and what he thinks is usually unpleasant." She raised her chin huffily and refused to acknowledge Nihl for the remainder of the walk.

Collin realized with dread that they were heading back toward the bathhouse they'd passed on the way. He halted in the lane when it came into view. "No. I'm not – I mean I can't –"

"Oh, it's a lovely clean bath, Collin. The *malderones* keep it beautifully."

Collin's mind wrestled with the familiar, yet unfamiliar word, taking his mind off the pool for a moment. "Slaves," he muttered, remembering the word from Elian's stories.

"What?" Laurelle asked, leaning closer to hear him.

"No, it was nothing. I was trying to remember what *madlerones* were."

"Oh, yes, the pool slaves? They keep it clear and perfect. The bath fills from an underground spring that's always warm. You'll love it."

"Right, but —"

"Don't worry," Jacque said, correctly interpreting Collin's flushed face and stammer. "There are private areas too." He wrapped his long arm across Collin's shoulders and propelled him toward the arched entrance to the steam-filled structure.

Collin kept his gaze pinned to the floor as they passed the giant central pool. The air felt wet and hot when they entered and smelled of warm jasmine flowers. It had been so long since Collin smelled flowers it made him lightheaded. Or maybe that came from so many bare bodies flashing past him. Jacque glanced sideways and grinned jovially.

"You'll get used to it," he assured Collin.

Collin swallowed as a naked girl darted by with another girl in pursuit. Both were giggling and trailing gauzy white towels behind them.

"I doubt that," said Collin concentrating on the pink marble floor.

"Let's take him in the arbor pool. It's cooler and much quieter," Laurelle suggested from behind the group. They agreed and headed away from the center toward several archways shrouded in thin black curtains.

"I think you should wait for us out here," Jacque said to Laurelle, turning them toward a particular arch.

"But who will perform his washing ceremony?" demanded the girl, appalled at being left out.

Marcole's glance darted from Collin to Laurelle. Nihl rolled his eyes.

"We can see to him, Elle," said Marcole in a pacifying voice. "Jacque has a point. Collin's new here and more comfortable with the barbarism of the Borderlands. Give him time to acclimate, that's only polite."

Collin thought it rather rich of Marc to suggest his people were barbaric, while nude bodies swirled around him.

He winced when the weight of Jacque's arm increased on his back, moving him toward the silky curtain. "We'll hardly be a moment," Marcole assured Laurelle as the curtain slipped down behind them.

Instant cool hit Collin's face and the relative quiet of the place soothed his raw nerves. Only two Lightlings bathed here, at the far end of the room, talking so softly he couldn't understand them. The sunlight streaming into the main bath filtered through a canopy of something leafy and purple.

"Over here. I'll get a cleanser for you," Jacque said clapping him painfully on the back and heading toward a tall, ornate cabinet.

Collin looked nervously at the other two boys.

"I can wash myself. I don't need a ritual or anything," he mumbled.

"Oh, it's no trouble. The washing ceremony is a time-honored custom," Marcole explained as if that settled the matter.

"It won't bother anyone if you don't want it, though," added Nihl.

"Fresh soap, a robe and a new tunic. Unless you're particularly attached to your travel clothes," Jacque added politely. He handed Collin the folded linens. A small cake of something that smelled like lavender perched on top.

Collin stared at the stack of pure white and shook his head slowly. "I'm not attached to these clothes, no. But could you give me a moment?" All three boys looked surprised, but turned their heads respectfully away as Collin loosened the fastenings on his coarse brown jacket and trousers. He hesitated before pulling his undershirt over his head. A groan escaped him when the shirt stuck to the sores on his back and peeled away with his clothing. Three pairs of eyes jerked back to him in alarm.

"What happened?" Jacque asked, looking around as though

someone had assaulted Collin from behind. Collin chuckled despite the pain. The very idea of someone accosting him at this perfumed bathhouse was laughable.

"Nothing," he replied, trying not to flinch as he eased the shirt from his arms.

"What in the name of Amastole happened to your back?" Jacque asked, swivelling Collin by his shoulders to inspect his wounds.

Collin suppressed the instinct to pull away. "A gift from the Fontre."

"The Fontre did that? Do they know you came here? Were they in pursuit?" Nihl demanded, taking a step toward Collin, his voice rising so the people across the room looked over at them.

Collin glared defiantly at Nihl and didn't budge. Years of enduring Cobbs' torment left him with little fear for these tall, skinny creatures who spoke in lofty tones and performed ceremonial bathing rituals. "They did it weeks ago in my village. They wanted information I wouldn't give. No one followed us," he assured them. He looked at Jacque because he liked him most and, of the three boys, it seemed most likely Jacque would believe him.

"They did that to you weeks ago and it hasn't healed better than this?" Jacque whispered. He looked angry, but not at Collin.

Collin shrugged. "They put some kind of poison on their whips. Some stripes healed, but the worst stayed. We tried medicine, but nothing worked. No cure."

"Well, that's despicable!" Marcole spat under his breath. "We'll see about that. There are healers here who've studied every healing art under the sky. Maybe Askelpos, or Tyrnius ... someone will be able to do something for this." Collin's opinion of Laurelle's brother took a giant leap upward.

"So why are you here? Why come to the White City?" Nihl's quiet question sounded thick with accusation. He hadn't moved and his closeness made Collin angrier than he'd felt in weeks. The smaller boy took a deep breath and stepped back.

"I came to ask for help," he admitted. "The Fontre are taking over the Borderlands. They've stolen our crops and herds and nearly starved us to death. We're gathering forces to revolt. I'm here to speak to your Senate about joining us."

Jacque exchanged a look with his brother. "War?"

"Yes."

"You probably won't get far around here, suggesting war," Marcole said, putting a hand on Nihl, who finally backed off.

"You want to go to war against the most powerful war machine in existence?" Jacque clarified.

Collin looked at the pool and wished he could dive in and disappear. "Yes," he murmured finally.

A smile grew on Jacque's face. "You're a beast. I'm in. I'll go to war with you."

Nihl elbowed his brother in the ribcage. "And?"

"And what?" Collin snapped.

"And what actually happened to you? I get it: starving, stolen livelihoods, blah blah blah. But you're just a kid. What makes a kid bold enough to rally an army against the invincible Fontre?" Nihl still looked serious, but not as unpleasant. He indicated Collin should sit on the poolside while he and the others took seats.

Collin let his filthy feet dangle in the water and breathed. "Nothing. Just some other stuff." He glared at the water, avoiding their gazes.

"That's okay, mate. You don't have to tell us everything now," Jacque said.

Nihl pressed his lips together and nodded.

"We'll help you if we can, Collin," Marcole promised.

"Right, let's get you all cleaned and sorted, shall we?" Jacque peeled his clothes off, and lowered himself into the pool.

Marc and Nihl stripped and followed him. Collin shook his head, wondering if this day could get any stranger and slipped into the pool after them, still in his underwear. Jacque noticed and gave him a wink, retrieving the soap from the marble steps with one long stretch.

"We usually recite the Washing Poem, and use special oil in your hair. But it's kind of ... a girl always does it," Marc explained, swimming over.

Collin shrank back. "Honestly, I just want to wash off the road and put on clean clothes. I don't need poems or - anything." He snatched the soap from Jacque and swam a short distance away.

"Really? No recitations at all? I can quote the entire first stanza of 'Torrid Tales for Dark Nights,'" Jacque offered, wiggling his eyebrows.

Collin raised his own eyebrows and sank up to his chin in the dark water. "Please stay away from me."

"Are you almost done in there?" Impatience dripped from Laurelle's every word. She hadn't moved from the gauzy doorway.

"Give us a few more minutes," Marcole called, trying not to laugh. "He's not cooperating and I'm trying to remember the words to the second verse of the ceremonial poem."

8

THE FEYSONG

The ground beneath Cassai felt mushy; or maybe her legs were that way. Whichever it was, falling over seemed inevitable. It took Devilan a moment to register that his *Kolonel*, second in command of the Koninjka, lay dead at his feet. He drew his sword without taking his eyes off Dershom. His other hand dropped from Cassai's arm. Blood rushed painfully back to her fingers and she stumbled forward, almost falling before her legs became firm once more.

"*Aantasken!!*" Devilan screamed. Like many bodies operating with a single mind, the Koninjka simultaneously ceased their work on the road, drew swords and advanced on the fairies. Cassai watched in horror as the solid, stony warriors marched toward the gauzelike soldiers from another world.

"*Assallaire!*" Elian screamed in the language of the fey.

Wings — it sounded as if thousands of wings were flapping everywhere. Cassai squinted at the fey, wondering if they grew wings in battle, but none appeared. The fairy soldiers opened their mouths wide, too wide, their faces stretched grotesquely and ethereal voices began to sing. The woods went black, as if someone had blown out the sun in one puff.

Cassai's head filled with visions from neither her past nor present. Skeletal, wraithlike animals galloped all around her through the trees, but they weren't in Fondair any longer. The trees were slender and smooth. Thick green foliage flourished all around, a green that the Forest of Fondair hadn't seen in a decade. Yet the shape of the trees was oddly familiar; the bright, poisonous shade of green toyed with her memory. She finally realized she was standing in the center of the Woods of Terryn: cursed forest of the Fairy Realm.

A misshapen stag inclined its head to look at her. She screamed. Its neck was long and hairy, its face human. Hollis' face stared back, as if he'd transformed into the disfigured creature.

The roar of a lion ripped Cassai's attention from the Hollis-stag. The regal beast poised on a high rock surrounded by more ghastly animals. When its gaze met hers, her heart clenched. The lion was Elian.

The air filled with screeching ravens. They flew at her and when she looked closely, every one of them had the cold, calculating gaze of a Koninjka.

"Stop it!" she yelled. "Get away from me!" She squeezed her eyes shut and clapped her hands over her ears, trying to drown out the wings, the roaring, the *Feysong* ... everything. She felt her own power, the Namarielle's power, working, fighting the fairy's magic. She took a deep breath and let it leak out of her lungs a trickle at a time. The song continued, but the wild images were gone.

A hand grasped her arm, too small to be Devilan's, pulling her upright, and she dared to open her eyes. Hollis' real face looked back. A dim blue light had filled the forest, casting his features in a ghostly glow. The blue light emanated from the fairy's own skin.

Silent Koninjka battled the fey, who fought viciously, their mouths still open, singing their eerie dirge as their weapons clashed against the enchanted Fontre blades. Cassai couldn't tell who was winning.

"Another emotion besides fear would really be helpful about now," Hollis yelled at her over the uproar.

"I don't –," she started, but he'd released her and nocked an arrow in his bowstring.

"Get angry!" he screamed, pivoting to shoot his arrow between the shoulders of a Fontre locked in combat with Theoris.

Cassai tried to make sense of this request in the midst of the chaos. A young woman appeared at her other side. She had black hair that fell below her waist. Though she wore the armor of the fey, her stature and features were distinctly Kiatri. Cassai looked from her to Hollis.

"Stay on that side! Shoot any Fontre that approaches us!" Hollis ordered the girl.

She nodded and pulled an arrow from a quiver at her back. "Yes, Uncle," she shouted above the battle's clamor. *Uncle?* Cassai thought. *This is Sophie.*

The girl let the arrow fly. It sank into the breastplate of a Fontre heading toward them. The Koninjka grimaced, pulled the arrow from his leather armor, and continued forward. The next arrow found the only weakness in the Fontre's armor and the warrior dropped to his knees, Sophie's arrow sticking from his neck. The sparse life left in the eyes of the Fontre dissolved. His back went rigid and he clunked to the ground. Cassai's insides squirmed.

Sophie didn't spare him a moment's glance, but reloaded her bow and pivoted to end another life. Hollis and Sophie protected Cassai from every side. They aimed deftly at attackers and moved to shoot before the last had fallen. They whirled around her, performing their deadly dance.

Anger, Cassai reminded herself. *Get angry.* Her chest heaved as she focussed her energy. She wished she had a sword; anything to defend herself with. She couldn't think clearly enough to consider why the protective cage Hollis and Sophie were weaving around her made something pinch in her chest, but she should grasp it, she decided. Anything to move her past crippling fear.

Hollis had betrayed her, hadn't he? How dare he show up now and pretend to care about saving her life? How dare Elian trust him again? Elian. Her thoughts instantly muddled; her attempt at anger derailed. Fear was back.

She squinted between trees and bodies for Elian. Theoris brandished a long fairy blade which glowed with the green of his eyes. It sparked each time it clashed with the Koninjka's sword. Cassai noticed he wasn't singing as his fellow fairies were. He fought, looking desperate, more terrified than she'd ever seen him.

Goliard smiled, glaring down at a black clad warrior. The Fontre knelt on the forest floor, clutching his head, then neck, then ribcage, his mouth set in a silent scream of agony. Cassai shuddered. She couldn't decide which combatant she disliked most.

She turned again, scanning the broken road turned battlefield until she saw him. Elian and Devilan – locked in a struggle fuelled by naked rage. Devilan's back was to her, but Elian's face was red, even in the blue light. Every vein in his forehead stood out; every stroke of his blade fell with a passion unlike any Cassai had ever witnessed. Devilan parried a particularly hard strike and drew both their blades upward. He brought his knee into Elian's side and the younger man grimaced, but didn't yield. Cassai caught her breath. Pain seared through her side. Elian's rib was broken no doubt. Devilan brought his knee up again.

Elian sank to one knee and Devilan flicked the sword from his hand. Cassai screamed and started toward the pair, barely avoiding Hollis as he stepped right to aim at an oncoming foe. She cast around for something she might use as a weapon. Dershom lay on his face in the dirt and she fell to her knees beside him. The hilt of his sword was visible beneath his stomach. She grabbed it, and yanked as hard as she could. The sword slid free. She heard Hollis yell for her to stop. To stay back. *Get to Elian* was the only thought her mind registered.

She stumbled to her feet, dragging the heavy sword. Before she could reach them, someone grasped her from behind, restraining her arms. "Have you lost your mind?" Hollis screamed.

"Let me go!" She tried to pull away as Devilan raised his sword. Elian's face lifted to his brother's, an odd look of triumph in his blue eyes.

Cassai stopped struggling against Hollis and watched. Devilan's arm was swinging toward Elian in a deadly arch. A flash of silver in Elian's right hand streamed upward. The silver disappeared, sunk deep into Devilan's side. Devilan's sword dropped and he screamed in rage and agony. Elian pulled the dagger out and stood. Devilan stepped backward, pressing a hand to his side. The fairy light made the blood glow bluish as it oozed between his fingers. Elian snatched his and his brother's swords and brandished a weapon in each hand as he faced Devilan.

"Call them off!" he yelled above the fairy's battle refrain.

Devilan spat at him. Elian leapt toward him. Devilan fell backward, tripping on a tree root and tumbling gracelessly to the forest floor. He gained his knees to find both swords crossed at his throat.

"Call them off," Elian repeated.

Devilan glared at his brother with such dark malice that Cassai shivered. *"Maffraikal,"* he whispered hoarsely.

The fury of the battle increased and Cassai's heart slammed hard against her chest. The fairies faltered at the renewed ferocity.

There was flicker of light and daylight streamed through the trees again, illuminating the gore of the battlefield. Fallen Koninjka lay everywhere. One fairy lay on the ground among them, still alive, but writhing and holding his side. Some Koninjka were missing limbs. Many still had fey weapons, burning brightly, sticking from their chests or necks.

Cassai's gaze was fixed on Elian so it seemed that the black warrior exploded from the ground at her feet. She stumbled back. Racalf glared at her and raised his sword.

"You're dead," he screamed and lunged forward. She threw Dershom's blade up to protect herself. Racalf laughed at the gesture, but only for a moment. His raised sword had left his chest vulnerable and Cassai thrust Dershom's sword forward with all her strength. She felt the sword push through something solid. Every muscle and joint in her body recoiled at the squelching sound that followed. She looked up into Racalf's wide eyes.

For a moment he looked confused, and then he squeezed his eyes shut and crumpled to the ground, taking her stolen sword with him.

"Dead," she whispered in horror. Thunder cracked somewhere, or maybe it came from inside her. A grunt of pain in the distance cleared her head before she had time to decipher it.

Elian. Forgetting to reclaim her weapon, she lifted her foot over Racalf's body, swallowing the pain of killing him.

Racalf was doubled over at her feet; his arms wrapped around Dershom's sword as though embracing it. The sounds of clanging metal and the harshly breathing men filled every part of Cassai.

Elian and Devilan had not budged an inch. "I should kill you," Elian snarled. The cold metal of the two swords had sliced a fine line on either side of Devilan's neck.

"Kill me then, boy," Devilan said, quietly. Cassai took another step toward the brothers, sure she'd misheard. "You're a fool, Elian." Metal scraped metal and the blades cut deeper. Devilan's eyes widened in surprise and pain.

"We're even now. I owe you nothing," Elian assured him. Both blades swung away from Devilan's neck and, in one swift motion, Elian brought the two hilts together and crashed them down into his brother's skull. A soft thud. Devilan's face went slack and he sank to the ground, unconscious. Cassai wasn't sure what she'd expected to happen. Perhaps that all the machine-like warriors would stop fighting as one and stand motionless before their opponents, or the Koninjka would notice their fallen leader and turn on Elian. Instead, the fighting continued as if nothing had happened.

Cassai moved to run to Elian, but a hand strong as granite gripped her wrist and jerked her back, a hand missing two fingers. Cassai jerked her wrist, but Racalf's bloody face glared into hers. He bared his teeth, his own blood gurgling between them. He clutched her jacket, ripping it as he pulled himself to his knees and knocked her off her feet.

"Dead!" He spat at her. His arm swung up and she caught a glimpse of a jagged rock in his left hand before he brought it down against her temple. Lights popped before her eyes and pain ripped through her skull. Then everything went black and she felt nothing.

9

THE RIVER

All pain lifted, and she felt so light and happy. Cassai looked around, wondering at all the light. Where could she be? Where in Lashai was there so much light and so little pain? A river splashed somewhere close by. Oddly, the sound didn't come from the ground below, but above her head. Cassai peered through the tree canopy into the endless blue sky. The splashing came from up there somewhere.

I should find it, she decided, but as soon as she decided to leave, something drew her back, pulled her toward the ground. She hadn't realized she was floating. She wavered somewhere between the ground and the tree tops. The scene below was horrific. She wanted to get away from it. She felt the tiniest twinge in her chest and a faint memory of too much blood and agony.

"It's our old friend," said a voice so familiar and beloved that it banished all other thought.

"Elian!" There he stood, or hovered, beside her. There was no wound on him. His clothes were purest white, so bright that at any other time the glare would have hurt her eyes. There were no lines on his face, no worried crease in his forehead. He looked utterly peaceful. He smiled at her and her heart fluttered. She was surprised it would still do that, here in this – was it an afterlife?

"I recognize him," Elian said, pointing into the distance and she turned to look.

Another man walked toward them. "Hermit!" she cried in surprise.

The hermit smiled, but stopped long before he reached them. He stood somewhere in the midst of the dead brown trees, his hands folded as though waiting for something. Cassai took a step toward him, but he shook his head, and directed her gaze downward toward the ground and the scene she didn't want to look at. Here there was light and joy, below held nothing but horror and hurt. He looked back up, smiled with too much understanding, and then looked down again. Reluctantly, she allowed her gaze to drift over the ground. The misty darkness began to lift and forms solidified one by one.

"I don't want to see," she whispered to Elian. She felt his comforting arms encircle her. "Do you hear the river? It's the River of Light. The path to the Land of Havilah. I know it."

"Are you sure you're ready to follow the River, Taiya? Something else draws me downward instead of up. Perhaps it isn't time yet. Not our turn to go."

"Hollis," Cassai said, though it wasn't an answer.

Hollis acted so strangely, she couldn't help but point at him. He crouched over a body in the midst of a battle. Cassai realized with a jolt that the body was hers; her face covered in blood. She looked down and saw her front was clean and fresh, as if her dress and jacket were new.

"We were fighting, I think. Were we killed? What is Hollis doing with that silver vial?" Her hand instinctively touched her neck where the chain had always hung. It was missing. Below, Hollis dripped liquid into her mouth. He yelled something and shook her shoulders roughly. "He isn't being very gentle, is he?"

She heard the amusement in Elian's voice. "Well, he was never subtle. He's running toward me now. He'll probably shoot me in the head just to make sure I'm truly dead."

Cassai felt she was falling slowly downward, feet first. As they drew closer to Hollis, she understood what he was screaming at Elian.

"Breathe! Breathe, you stupid son of the Fontre!" Hollis pounded Elian's chest with one fist. He stopped suddenly, as if he'd felt something. Reaching into Elian's jacket, he pulled out the pouch of all that remained of the Fontre Draught. Elian groaned.

"Just when I thought the visions couldn't get worse," he mumbled.

"No, Hollis, don't!" Cassai shouted, knowing he couldn't hear.

Hollis considered the pouch a long time, and then sniffed it. Understanding dawned and he ripped the pouch open. Cassai felt Elian's chest heave up and back down in a sigh. But then Hollis turned the bag upside down, dumping its contents into the dirt around him. He pushed himself up and stamped on the remnants, swirling them around until no visible signs of the poison remained.

Cassai looked at Elian in surprise. He was smiling, ever so slightly. "Thank you, Hollis."

Hollis pried Elian's lips apart and tipped the silver vial, allowing the last few drops to trickle into Elian's mouth. "You cannot leave me in this mess," he bellowed, his voice hoarse. Cassai realized, to her utter shock, that he was crying. He shuffled around to face Elian on the ground, gripping the shepherd's jacket. "Elian," he said more softly. "Come back, please. For Cassai. She won't live unless you do. She can't. You have to come back."

"One would even think he cared about me." Elian tried to sound light, but Cassai could tell he was moved by the Kiatri's plea.

Thunder cracked. Cassai jerked in surprise, and Elian's grip tightened. "What was that?"

"It was Lashai," Elian observed. The trees began to sway. The ground beneath them shook and trembled. It would have unbalanced them had they been moveable in this state.

"Hollis is weeping over you. Look at him. I never knew he could cry." She felt sadness for the first time. In her heart she knew what must be done, but she dreaded it. "We can't follow the River yet. I feel those wretched drops healing me even now." Disappointment gripped her. Elian gave her a hard squeeze.

"So this is what it feels like not to hurt," he observed softly. "I can't remember the last time nothing hurt. How could that fool waste those precious drops on me? He should have used the Fontre Draught."

"I'm glad he didn't. I'm glad it's gone forever. But how I wish we didn't have to go back."

"Since we have to, let's go now, before any further damage is done." The landscape around them buckled and heaved. The Koninjka looked stricken and scanned all around for the cause of the shift. Devilan had recovered from the blow Elian had dealt him, and he stood unsteady on the shaking ground, yelling orders to his men. The fairies turned to Goliard, who looked toward Hollis and the prone shape of Elian beneath him.

"Is he dead?" Goliard shouted.

"Shut up, fairy! I'm working on it."

Hollis turned just in time to see Devilan approaching his brother. The Elian standing beside Cassai shuddered. "Leave me alone," he muttered under his breath.

Cassai wondered: *if Devilan stabbed his brother through the heart, what would happen to them both? Would there no longer be a chance to return? Would they watch Lashai rip itself apart before their eyes?*

"Get back!" Hollis warned, training an arrow on Devilan's chest.

"Elian?" Devilan's voice was low and harsh. "No! Elian, you cannot be dead." Devilan's head swivelled toward Cassai. He glanced at Hollis, his face so pale he looked as if he might pass out again. "Is she dead too?"

Hollis lowered his bow and shook his head. "I don't know. I've done what I can."

Devilan's chest rose and fell and his hands started shaking. "We're all doomed if they're gone." He dropped to his knees beside Elian. He pressed two fingers into Elian's neck, feeling for his pulse. The Elian beside Cassai pulled his neck away instinctively. "There's a pulse, but I can barely feel it. Check the girl's," he ordered, but there was no one to obey. His men were still fighting the fey, though it was impossible to tell if anyone had the upper hand the way the earth tilted and shook. Hollis just glared at him.

"Get away from him," he raised the bow once more, aiming his arrow at Devilan's face. Devilan stood on the unsteady ground, giving Hollis a dark glare.

"What good are your arrows now, Hollis Farrell? If that girl is dead, Lashai won't be around long enough to −" He cut off, the point of Hollis' arrow pushed into his Adam's apple.

"Get away from him," Hollis growled again, more slowly. "Elian may spare your worthless life, but I will not. I'll give you to the count of three to call off your men before I shoot you dead."

"And if he doesn't, I will." Devilan turned to find Sophie a few feet away, her own arrow aimed at his neck.

The *Genraal* looked back and forth between them for a long moment and then turned toward the battle. "*Rukkzaine!*" Each soldier, to the man, stood at attention wherever they fought, and sheathed their swords.

"Tell them it's over," Hollis said wearily to Goliard when a few of the fey warriors continued fighting their disarmed opponents.

Goliard raised his fist in the air. "*Assaizze!*" The fey stopped immediately, and began to gather around Goliard.

"Get the book." Elian had let go of Cassai's hand and leaned toward his brother, but he couldn't reach him, and even if he were able, it wasn't possible to grasp something from the mortal world in this place.

"We have to go back now," she whispered. Immediately she felt swirling wind, and the crushing weight of blackness pressed against her eyes.

~

EVERY INCH of Cassai's body ached. The hard ground beneath her still rumbled, and she lay flat against it. Deep in her mind she felt cheated, but couldn't remember why. What had she just been dreaming? The harder she tried to remember, the faster it drifted away. She decided she should try to move some body part. Fingers, maybe that wouldn't hurt too much. Most of the pain was in her head and, now she thought of it, her legs. And both wrists screamed. Memories slipped back into her head one by one. Racalf had grabbed her unbroken wrist and damaged it. Had he tried to kill her? She remembered the rock and her head throbbed more sharply.

"*Nordian!*" she cursed under her breath. She realized that he lay very near, almost as if he was on top of her, and someone had shifted him. The ground stopped writhing and the trees calmed.

"I said I'm fine, Hollis. Let go." She heard Elian's voice, but couldn't see him. "Where's Cassai?"

She pushed herself up painfully, trying to spot him. As soon as her head peeked out from behind Racalf she saw a shocked and elated Hollis, and a pain-stricken, furious Elian.

"I'm here! Hollis, Elian. I'm over here."

Hollis hesitated a moment, as if afraid to look at her. Why should he be afraid?

"Cassai? By the Weaver! You're alive."

"Yes, Hollis, I'm alright. Elian? Are you injured?" Neither answered as they leapt to their feet and charged across the uneven ground toward her. Sophie, who'd been standing next to Hollis ran as well. Both men reached her at the same time. Both looked at her with so much relief it made her eyes hurt. Sophie's face was streaked with tears. Elian's hand brushed her left temple.

"You're bleeding. What happened? Did he stab you?" He threw a glare at Racalf's corpse.

"He smacked her with a jagged rock, and she killed him. I thought you were both dead!" Hollis said.

Elian and Cassai looked at Hollis' white face. "I – I remember," said Elian quietly. "I was fighting Devilan, and I knocked him out. I saw you fall, and I–."

"Crumpled like a squashed tin." Hollis finished.

"Where's Devilan?" Elian jerked his head around, looking for his brother.

"Gone. They left the carriages and horses. What's left of them took off over the ruined road."

"The fey?"

"Vanished. Goliard looked very unhappy."

"Where's Theoris? Tell me they didn't take him prisoner."

"Good question. I haven't seen him since the battle started." Hollis pushed himself up and peered through the trees. "Sophie, look that way, I'll go to the other side of that stand of trees." Sophie nodded and took off, calling Theoris' name.

"He's here!" Hollis shouted from a hundred yards away. Cassai tried to get up, but Elian held her down.

"Don't. Hollis will help him. The more you move, the more you bleed."

Cassai was vaguely aware that he was holding a piece of cloth against her forehead. She felt no pain in her head, which she thought was probably not a good sign.

"Oh, I say, did I pass out again?" Theoris' voice in the distance made her smile.

"Yes, fairy. As usual, you're completely useless in battle. I think you should lean on me now," Hollis was saying. His words were harsh as usual, but his voice was soft, much kinder than Cassai expected. "Everyone is up this way."

"Did we save her?" Theoris cried.

"Yes. She's safe for now."

"Thank the Weaver!"

The two men stumbled into sight, Theoris leaning heavily on Hollis, his left leg dragging at an odd angle. Dark blood oozed from above his knee.

"Oh no! What happened to him?" Sophie gasped, coming from the other direction.

"The leg's broken clean through. I can see the bone there." Hollis pointed, out of breath from bearing the fairy's weight.

"Oh dear, that's his femur. Very painful break," Cassai said.

"Lucky shot," Theoris managed weakly. "One of those Koninjka fellows caught me there just as I was about to deal a killing blow."

Hollis rolled his eyes and lowered Theoris onto a fallen log. "Of course you were. I'm going to pull your leg out straight. Apologies in advance." Theoris screamed so loudly when Hollis pulled his leg that Cassai felt it deep in her chest. "I don't think it's set right. Elian, I need you."

"Oh stop a moment, please. Can anyone see my bag? I've something that will help with the pain." The companions searched around, and Cassai remembered she'd been dragged from the carriage. "The last carriage in the line," she said. "If we can get to it, my bag should be in the seat."

"I'll get it," Sophie said, jumping to her feet and heading back to the road.

Elian went to Theoris. "I need to splint it. Find me two straight sticks. Are there bandages in your bag?" he asked Cassai.

"Yes, and a sewing kit. I think that wound may need stitches."

"Don't get up," Elian ordered her. Blood seeped through the cloth on her head and start to trickle into her eyes. Elian sighed.

"We have to get out of here. She needs real help, but there's nothing near here."

"I can help." At the voice behind them, they all swung their heads. Cassai's vision, blurry as it was from blood loss, must have been playing tricks.

"Krispen?" she murmured.

The tall boy nodded his curly head, tears streaming down his face. "I'm sorry I left. I'm so sorry!"

Elian sprang to the boy and grabbed him in a furious hug. "I thought we'd never see you again."

"I'm sorry," Krispen buried his face in Elian's jacket and his shoulders shook with sobs.

Cassai tried to push herself up to get to them, but her wrist gave out and shot pain through her arm. She cried out and Hollis was instantly at her side. "Please don't try to get up. Come on, back down you go."

"Is she alright, Hollis?" Elian asked, flexing his own wrist as if he'd just felt her pain.

"No," Hollis barked.

"I feel...dizzy," her legs buckled and Hollis caught her and lowered her to the ground, but kept an arm around her waist.

"I know a place to take her for help." Krispen pulled away from Elian and wiped his eyes.

Hollis looked at him hard, and Cassai felt him start to shake. "How can we trust him?" he demanded.

"Are you serious?" Elian turned to frown at the Kiatri. "What do you mean, Krispen? Does this place have medical supplies?"

"It has better than that. Someone lives there who can do all the medicine stuff. Like Nanna, or maybe better." Krispen scratched his head nervously.

Elian nodded. "Alright. We'll have to fix Theoris enough so he can walk."

"Oh, just leave me here," Theoris exclaimed dramatically. "I'm useless to you all. Always getting myself banged up and never contributing to the cause."

"Shut up, fairy, or we'll take you up on that," Hollis muttered.

"Come on, Theoris. Brace up and hold onto something." Elian knelt next to the fairy and put a hand on either side of his broken leg.

"Wait a minute," Hollis said, letting go of Cassai to dig through a pouch at his belt. He withdrew a long, thick piece of leather. "Put this between his teeth. Believe it or not, it helps."

Elian reached for the leather and handed it to Theoris. The fairy gave Hollis a grateful smile and clenched it between his teeth. Elian took a deep breath and pulled down hard, twisting the fairy's leg until the bone was set. Sophie then rushed back into the trees, swinging Cassai's satchel.

"I got it. Oh my word!" she exclaimed, throwing her hand over her mouth at the sight of the fairy in agony.

"Bring it here," Elian ordered, holding Theoris' leg steady with some effort. Theoris couldn't stay still; his eyes were wild and beads of sweat rolled down his forehead.

Sophie shoved the bag at Elian and dropped down next to Cassai covering her ears to block out the sound.

"Elian! Please hurry up," Sophie yelped.

"Done. We can get him where we need to go. Krispen, lead the way." Elian pulled Theoris up and kept the fairy steady with his shoulder.

"I'll get him," Hollis offered, rising to his feet. "I'm closer to his height. I think Cassai needs to be carried."

Elian nodded and walked back to Cassai. "Easy now, Taiya. You're going to be alright." One arm wrapped around her torso and the other behind her knees. He lifted her as if she weighted nothing and cradled her against his chest.

"I'll bleed on your jacket," she said weakly. She felt a quick, searing pain in her side. "And your broken ribs."

Elian squeezed her and hurried to follow Krispen. "Your blood can only improve this jacket. The rib is nothing."

"I can feel how it hurts you with every step."

"Yes, but I like the pain. Reminds me that I'm still alive." He smirked at her.

"You came for me. You shouldn't have done that," she murmured.

"Ah, you know me. Wise choices were never my strength."

She smiled and rested her cheek against his chest. She could hear his heart thumping beneath his tunic. "I love you."

He kissed her head and Lashai rumbled in protest, but neither of them cared. "I love you too. Hold on a bit longer. We'll get you somewhere safe."

"Through here. It's kind of a drop, but I'll go in first and lower her down from below." Krispen had come to a large, cleverly camouflaged hole in the ground. Hollis nocked an arrow in his bowstring before Cassai could summon the strength to protest.

"What's this, Krispen? You can't take her down there."

"It's a shorter way. This isn't the place we're going. I only know how to get there from here."

Elian looked at Hollis. "What is it, Hollis?"

"It's the tunnels."

"What tunnels?"

"Their tunnels: the werewolf pack's. It's how they get through Fondair and Lashai so easily and quickly: how they vanish from sight. He's leading us to the pack. Stand away from him."

Krispen paled, but Elian stepped between the boy and Hollis' arrow. "You know I'm not going to stand aside and let you shoot him."

"I'm not taking you to them. I'm taking you to someplace safe for Cassai," Krispen whimpered.

"He's turned. I swear to you, he is one of them now. Where's Isabel, Krispen? What happened to the lamb?" Hollis fumed.

Krispen's enormous brown eyes filled with tears. "She's there.

She's where I'm taking you all. I promise. This is just the only way I know to get there. I would never take Cassai to them. Never."

Elian looked at Cassai. She looked from Hollis to Krispen, and then at Elian. "I trust him."

Elian nodded and put a hand up. "Lower your arrow, Hollis. We're going."

The Kiatri glared at him. "This is suicide," Hollis said, but he slung his bow across his body and sheathed his arrow.

Krispen dropped into the hole. "It's not deep here," he called up. "Lower her down."

Cassai felt Elian lower to his knees. "Ready?" he asked.

She nodded and felt herself lowered slowly and cautiously. Krispen wrapped his arms around her from beneath and Elian let go. She fell into Krispen's arms, and into the blackness of the underground tunnels.

"DID you have a nice afternoon with her?" Julius had woken up when Collin came in through their curtained doorway.

Collin hesitated for a moment, wondering if he was in trouble for leaving and giving his uncle no explanation. "Um, yes." he stammered. "I wasn't sure if you were angry. I left while you were sleeping. I just wanted to explore a bit."

Julius gave Collin a smile that looked a bit forced. "I'm not angry. I was just a bit concerned. She seemed a nice enough girl."

Collin smiled sheepishly. "She's great."

"You look very...Lightling."

Collin glanced down at his Lightling garb and his cheeks turned hot. "Yeah. They got me new clothes. I have some for you too, if you want something fresh. Did you eat already?"

Julius shook his head and nodded toward a boy hovering in the corner. "I was offered something, but I waited."

Collin looked at the boy. "Hi, I'm Collin." The boy's eyes

widened; they were such a dark shade of brown, almost black. His dark skin shone as if he'd been rubbed with oil.

"I will be happy to get you tea, sir," he said, looking at the floor, not at Collin.

"What's your name?"

"It's too hard to say, sir. Here, I'm called Timothy."

Collin turned his eyes to Julius, who shrugged. "Thank you, Timothy. We'd love some tea."

A brilliant smile lit the boy's face. "I won't be a moment, sir." Timothy vanished through another curtained doorway toward the back of the room.

Collin frowned. "What in the name of −?"

"I don't know. He was there when I woke up. He said you'd gone out and he'd been assigned to us for the duration of our stay."

"He's a slave, right? We have a slave assigned to us," Collin said, pacing to relieve his agitation.

"I don't know what to do about it. What if we say something and they think he didn't do well for us and punish the boy?"

"This is my least favorite thing that's happened since we got here, and I just took a bath with three strangers who stripped totally naked in front of me like it was nothing." Collin grumbled, lowering himself to the bed and resting his head in his hands.

"What?" his uncle said.

"Don't ask. It's a long story."

"That girl you were with?"

"Some of her friends," Collin rubbed his temples, feeling the little energy he had left draining away.

"Girls?" Julius asked hesitantly.

Collin glared up at him. "No, her brother and a couple of others. Why? Is that better?"

"I don't know. I guess not. This place may prove too much for me. Amicus said something about bathing after tea. I hope I'm not in for a similar experience."

"Oh, it'll probably be even better. Apparently, there's usually a washing ceremony."

"A what?"

"Performed by a woman."

The look on Julius' face made Collin forget his anger. He roared with laughter, and was still laughing when Timothy returned with a tea tray. The sight of the slave boy sobered him, but Julius still looked so pale Collin couldn't help but grin at him.

"Are you feeling unwell, sir? I could bring you a tincture from the kitchens," Timothy offered, looking concerned at Julius' discomfort.

"No, I'm alright, son, just tired from traveling."

"Oh, certainly, sir. Master Amicus told me to take you directly to the Bath to refresh yourself when you've finished eating."

Julius shot Collin such an alarmed look, the boy doubled over with laughter again, while his uncle glowered from across the room.

10

THE HERMIT

E lian felt the dark like a physical thing; like a thick fur pressed against his face. He pulled in a breath and felt less oxygen in his lungs than before. Krispen had pulled Cassai out of the way and Elian moved toward the earthy wall. He heard Hollis and Sophie arguing overhead.

Hollis dropped into the darkness and Sophie followed right after him, landing soft as a cat on the tunnel floor.

"I told you to wait for me to see it was safe," Hollis chided. "Who's going to help Theoris down?" The fairy dropped a long stick down as Hollis looked up, and it hit him squarely between the eyes.

Elian resisted the urge to laugh aloud and rushed to help lower the injured fairy through the hole. "We've got you, Theoris. Just fall into us." Both Hollis and Elian caught their friend and lowered him to the ground.

"It's a bit dark and damp down here, isn't it? What an odd way the wolves choose to move around."

"Yes, as well-known as they are for their intellectual prowess, you'd think —" Hollis began, but Sophie put up a hand to stop him.

"Krispen, let's get moving," Sophie said, shouldering her own pack and Cassai's.

"We walk this way, but must keep very quiet. It's supposed to be a secret," Krispen whispered.

"What's supposed to be a secret?" Cassai asked as she was transferred from Krispen's arms back to Elian's. He realized too late that her wrist was broken and he had twisted it against his chest. He felt acutely the pain that shot through her.

He hurried to press a hand over her mouth and muffled her scream between his fingers. "I'm so sorry. I'm sorry. Are you alright?" Elian whispered. She nodded, but tears streamed from her eyes onto his hand. "Hang on, Taiya. We'll get you there. Krispen, hurry up."

He heard Krispen stop farther ahead. "I'm hurrying," he insisted. "It's not very far. Just keep coming."

"What if he's leading us to his pack?" Hollis hissed under his breath. "There's no way to be sure."

"It would take more than a werewolf pack to turn Krispen against Cassai," Elian assured him. "Trust me. He has her interests at heart at the very least." Even in the darkness, he felt the skeptical look Hollis gave him.

He felt the pain shooting through Cassai's wrist with every step they took. They shuffled through the darkness for what felt like an hour before he saw a pinprick of light ahead.

"We're here. We're going to be okay!" Krispen exclaimed.

Elian felt Hollis relax on the other side of Cassai. "I think you were right," he breathed. Elian tried not to show his own relief.

The air grew fresher and cooler. Elian walked faster.

"It's easier to climb out than to get in," said Krispen. "Do you want me to take her?"

"I've got her. I don't want to shift her any more with her arm as it is."

Finally, light and air. Elian gulped in the cool fresh air as he climbed out into the forest again. Cassai was almost unconscious in his arms. Krispen continued through the trees. There was no path Elian could see, so he slowed down, trying not to catch his foot and pitch forward, landing them both in dirt and leaves. "Still with me?" he whispered to Cassai. She smiled.

"Still here."

"We're almost there," he assured her. She leaned her head against his chest.

"Safe?"

He squeezed her gently. "Safe."

A tiny stone structure came into view and Elian stopped dead.

A low stone wall surrounded a lush green meadow. Vibrant flowers waved and winked in and out of the tall grass. A cottage nestled at the center of this haven and Elian stared at the scene, blinking twice to make sure his eyes were working.

"Krispen. Where are we?" Elian looked at his shepherd boy, bewildered.

"Help. He likes to help wounded animals and stuff, and he helped me when the pack beat me up. So, I thought he'd help you too."

"You'll want to see this," Elian whispered in Cassai's ear.

Cassai turned her head outward and then her eyes widened in shock. "What on earth?"

Krispen looked uneasy. "Is this alright?"

"Of course, it's fine, Krispen," Cassai assured him weakly. "We're just a bit confused. Are we still in Fondair?"

"Yes. I mean, I think so. Maybe I should ask him. He calls it Haven House." Krispen turned and walked toward the cottage, glancing uncertainly back at the others. Elian followed him. The boy stopped at a gate, whispered something to the latch, and it popped open. When they drew closer to the green meadow, Elian saw several breeds of animals playing in the grass, or asleep beneath the shade of a giant valarca tree. Some he recognized: a family of rabbits, a deer, a snowy white lamb resting under the tree. Other animals that had only thrived in olden times, so Elian had never encountered them. A dozen flying insects with large colorful wings, patterned like cathedral windows, hovered over a flowering bush by the cottage door.

"Butterflies," Cassai murmured. Of course she'd know their name.

The weathered door opened and a man stepped out, smiling at the group. He wore coarse brown trousers and a heavy woolen cloak. Elian started in surprise.

Cassai gasped. "Hermit!"

"Who have you brought to me, Krispen? A haggard looking group, indeed." The Hermit took in the group, but when his gaze found Cassai's, he reacted in violent surprise. "It cannot be!"

"These are my friends, sir. They're in trouble so I thought you might help." Krispen twisted the hem of his rough wool shirt nervously, but the Hermit didn't seem to be listening.

The man had dropped to one knee in front of Elian and Cassai. "Your Highness, this is the greatest honor of my lifetime. That I should live to see the daughter of Patrice and Annabelle, alive and grown. The last Namarielle. I am entirely at your disposal."

Cassai looked up at Elian, who winked at her.

"Forgive our appearance, sir. We've just come from battle." Elian took a step toward the aged man.

The Hermit grimaced. "Battle. A disgusting exercise. What does it really accomplish?"

"Well in this case, it freed the last living Namarielle from the hands of the Fontre," Elian said, grinning at the ancient man. He reminded Elian too much of Nanna to take this rant seriously. "Did you...were you there, by any chance. I have a strange feeling of seeing you at the scene."

From the depth of The Hermit's gaze, from eyes of light brown, flecked with green, Elian suspected he only vocalized a tenth of his thoughts.

After a long moment, the old man shook his head. "I have no such recollection. Krispen says you're in trouble. We should get you inside and see to your wounds." He smiled so kindly Elian felt his muscles relax. "Please, come in and rest. You all look about to fall over." He limped toward his cottage, his long stick clacking on the orderly flagstones leading to the cottage. "Food and drink and medicine, that's what makes the world go round. I must apologize in advance. I'm not used to doctoring those who stand upright. My specialty is more with the four legged variety. Except, of course, for our friend, Krispen. But he's a special case."

Elian looked at Krispen, but the boy wasn't paying attention. He'd knelt and opened his arms. The snowy lamb beneath the tree bounded toward him, bleating joyfully. Elian smiled. So Isabel was alive and very well fed by the looks of her.

As they continued down the path, a doe approached the Hermit and pressed her head into his hand. "Well hello, my dear Challa. Aren't you looking beautiful this evening?" The deer melted into the man's caress. "Everyone, this is Challa. She came a week or so ago with an arrow sticking out of her chest. Some fool shot her in the forest, but somehow bungled it. Not much of a hunter, I'd imagine."

At these words, Theoris flushed scarlet. "Oh, I say. I thought she looked familiar."

Hollis shook his head in disbelief and his eyes sparkled with humor. "A terrible hunter indeed. How on earth −?"

"Animals find Haven House. They all have their ways. I do whatever I can for them. And Isabel, she hasn't rested a moment since you left, Krispen." The Hermit scooped up a brown spotted rabbit from the doorstep and put her in Theoris' arms while he fiddled with the doorknob. "Apologies for the door. It sticks." The door gave way and the Hermit heaved it open. They entered a small kitchen, with carvings and runes etched into every square inch of wall.

Cassai gasped. "A *Lozere!*"

"Indeed," replied the Hermit, following, and shutting the heavy door with a thud. "An unusual one. Most have no keeper, but this one has me." He indicated spindly-legged chairs around a table and an overstuffed couch in the sitting room just off to the left. "Please rest. I'll see to you one at a time. Whose wounds are the gravest?"

"Please see to Cassai first," Elian said. He walked to the couch and lowered Cassai on the cushions, propping her head with a soft yellow pillow.

"Oh, don't. I'll get blood on something," Cassai protested.

"Yes, she's lost lots of blood," Sophie agreed. "And then, Theoris. His poor leg."

"No need to worry about blood, Your Highness. That pillow has endured much worse than cradling the wounded head of a queen." The Hermit hurried to a cabinet by the table and produced a large wooden case with a broken lock.

Hollis' face looked more peaceful than Elian had ever seen it as he moved around the Lozere, silently touching a rune here and there. The Hermit approached Hollis quietly with his cane sinking into the thick gray carpet.

"Beautiful, aren't they? I wish I could take credit for them."

Hollis nodded. "I've heard of this place for decades. I never thought I'd see it with my own eyes."

"I'll happily show you more later. For now, I must see to your friends."

"Certainly, please don't let me delay you. Cassai has waited too long already."

The Hermit chuckled to himself as he headed back to the tiny living room. "You are well loved in this group, Your Majesty."

She smiled. "Please, call me Cassai."

The Hermit's eyes crinkled at the edges when he smiled. "I'm afraid I cannot do that." He began with her head wound and pressed into it a cloth that smelled strongly of lavender and something else that Elian couldn't place.

"Oh, that feels so much better. Lavender and...what is the other oil?"

"Clove, peppermint and olive oil."

"I also have an ointment in my bag that will set the wound and keep it from getting infected, almeris."

"Ah! I see Nanna has not been idle with your training."

"You know Nanna?" Cassai looked so shocked and delighted at this, it made the Hermit laugh aloud.

"Indeed I did and, good lord, what a woman she was. I knew every member of the royal court." He stroked her cheek, his eyes full of love and sorrow. "You look exactly like your mother. Beautiful, just as she was, and stubborn as a mule, no doubt."

Elian rolled his eyes. "Yes."

Cassai smiled, her eyes sparkling with excitement. "Please tell me what you remember about them."

"I certainly will, but there will be time enough for stories and catching up. First, let's get you doctored. I think both your wrists may be broken. The right one certainly is. And your head needs more than this cloth and ointment." He wiped his hands on a white towel and went to a chest of drawers surrounded by books nestled in a corner. "We must stitch it, I'm afraid. The wound is too deep to mend without some help." He withdrew a small leather pouch Elian recognized as a sewing kit. "I apologize, my dear girl. This will be painful."

"It's alright," Cassai dug out her little blue bottle. "Almeris also lessens pain." She set her jaw and Elian flinched when the needle pierced her sensitive skin.

"Ah! I forgot your connection," the Hermit apologized to Elian.

"How do you know about that?" Elian asked.

"I know much about you and your people. Much more than I care to, in fact."

"So the connection is from my people?"

The Hermit shrugged. "The connection is as old as Lashai itself. It's nothing to do with bloodline."

"What does it have to do with?" Cassai asked through her teeth as the needle threaded through her forehead again.

"Love. And sacrifice. Quite a lot of both. More than most experience their whole life, between you two. You risked your life to save hers that night; sacrificed your own family, your own creed. Everything you did was against a Fontre's nature. And of course, it was wonderful."

Elian and Cassai looked at each other. "I see. So, there's no way to break the connection?"

"Break it? Why should you wish to break it?"

"We're sure it connects us even in death. I wish I could change it so I'm not risking her life every time I risk my own. From here we're heading to war."

The Hermit shook his head. "I don't know how to sever a bond such as this. Too ancient, much too powerful. Perhaps if you could somehow reverse your love? Despise each other?"

At this, Cassai smiled at Elian, and his heart pounded painfully in his chest. "So it's impossible then," he muttered.

"Yes. Quite." The Hermit had finished stitching and moved down to Cassai's right wrist. "We'll set the bones and get you nicely wrapped up, Your Majesty."

"I can set her bones, if you'll see to Theoris. He lost a lot of blood too," Elian offered.

"Of course, my boy. Feel free." Hermit pushed himself up and headed to the fairy seated at the table, face pale and shining with a sheen of sweat. "Let's get you to a cot. You should be lying down with your leg elevated." The Hermit put an arm around Theoris and helped him hobble down a narrow hallway into another set of rooms.

Elian focused on Cassai's arm, feeling for the exact location of the break. "If you'd avoid breaking this again for a while so it can actually heal, that would be fantastic."

Cassai rolled her eyes. "Oh, I'm so sorry. I suppose I should have just evaporated during that fight. I'd hardly have been missed."

Elian grinned and shook his head. "Beautiful and stubborn. That's about right."

"Not beautiful enough for your brother though, apparently. I don't take good enough care of my hair," she said.

The grin died on Elian's face. *"Nordian,"* he muttered under his breath. "Did he pull your hair?"

"He...brushed it," she grimaced at the memory.

He took a deep breath and tried not to overreact to this. "I'm sorry."

"It could've been worse. It's okay."

"I want to kill him."

She smiled at him. "I guess I'll marry you instead then."

His eyes widened. "That easy, huh? Alright, here comes the twisting." She squeezed her eyes tight shut and he set the bone as quickly as possible and with a more advanced splint than he was used to. "Real medicine...Krispen got that right," he said to himself, examining the device. He moved to her other hand. "This one's broken too. By the Weaver, what is it about you and your arms?" She glared at him while he set the second bone.

"People just feel free to jerk me about. I'm not good at fighting them off."

Elian's eyebrows rose. "I think there's at least one dead Koninjka who'd disagree." Cassai bit her lower lip and looked away. He felt a sharp twinge. "It's alright, Cassai. He would have killed you...he tried very hard to do so."

Hollis came into the room carrying two glasses of ice-cold water. "Drink. There's some sort of chewy biscuits in the kitchen with chocolate pieces baked in. Are you hungry?"

Elian took the water for them both. "Of course she's hungry. Have you ever known her turn down food?"

"I – I'm actually not that hungry. I feel a little ill."

Elian saw his own alarm mirrored in Hollis' face. "Right. That's fine. Maybe just drink your water and rest awhile. We'll have cookies when you feel better."

"They do sound really good. I'm just so tired."

Hollis put a hand on her shoulder. "May I have a moment?" he asked Elian.

The shepherd nodded and headed for the kitchen. Sophie was sitting at the table, looking very pale herself. A glass of water and plate of cookies sat on the table, forgotten. Elian glanced back at the couch where Hollis was kneeling to speak to Cassai in a low whisper.

To distract himself, he picked up Sophie's water glass and handed it to her. "Drink, Sophie. You need the water." He nudged the plate of cookies closer, snatching one for himself.

"Oh, yes. I guess I should." Her gaze was pinned to the window. Just outside, Krispen was playing with Isabel under the valarca tree, which looked like it had been there for at least three hundred years. She ignored the food and drink.

"Hey, Sophie," Elian snapped his fingers at her.

Sophie jerked. "What?"

"Water. Food. Please take a drink and eat something."

"I'm..." Her eyes filled with tears, and Elian wrapped an arm around her.

"It's okay. You're okay." She broke down and sobbed into his shoulder for a long while. "It's good to let it go."

The girl pulled away, wiping her eyes, her cheeks so flushed Elian wondered if it wasn't mostly from embarrassment. "No, it's fine. I'm fine."

Elian grinned and wiped away one last tear that was about to drip from her chin. "You're fine. Drink some water, won't you please?"

She sucked in a deep breath and drank until she'd almost drained the glass. "Oh, that's better. I should have done that before falling to pieces like an idiot."

Elian chuckled. "Right, Idiot. How are you feeling? Any wounds that need attention? Or just any wounds in general. You're not a good judge of what needs attention."

She shrugged and drank the last of the water. "No, I'm alright. The nice thing about bow and arrows is you don't come close enough to get stabbed...ideally." She grabbed a cookie and took a small bite. "Oh my word!" she exclaimed and shoved the rest into her mouth. She ate the next two without comment.

"So, you're not hungry?" Elian quipped.

"Shut up. What do you think they're talking about?" She nodded toward Hollis and Cassai.

"My guess is he's apologizing profusely, but that's just a stab in the dark. Can I see your hands, please?" He noticed where the leather had frayed on her fingerless gloves there was blood seeping through.

Sophie put her hands in his without looking concerned in the least. "Why should he apologize?" She looked genuinely surprised. "I'm going to mend those gloves; I like them."

"I'll let him tell you, if he feels the need." Elian worked the gloves off and examined her hands. Bleeding knuckles and blistered fingers. "I'll get you some ointment for these."

Sophie rolled her eyes. "What is that? Some sort of male secrecy code?"

"Just human decency code. I don't think it's specific to our gender. It's his story to tell."

Sophie huffed, grabbed the plate of cookies and headed into the living room. Elian grinned and followed her. Cassai and Hollis looked like they were finished.

"You're kinder than you should be. You know that?" Hollis looked sad, but content. He took Cassai's bandaged hand gingerly and started to kiss it, but remembered in time not to. "Sorry," he muttered. "I guess I can't do that."

Cassai smiled at him. "That's okay." She reached up and pulled him into a hug. "It's alright, Hollis. Really." Hollis hugged her back gently, and Elian saw tears in his eyes. Cassai's gaze swivelled to Elian. "What will Devilan do now I've broken our agreement? Will he go back to the Kiatri and punish them?"

Elian rummaged through the medical bag until he found an ointment to sooth Sophie's hands. Sophie had already dropped onto a cushion in front of the couch. A cloud of white hair rose from the cushion. "I don't know. He knows a rebellion is brewing in the Borderlands. Possibly he'll want to get back to the Inner Kingdom before the fighting begins, or he may see it as so insignificant it's not worth his time."

"Then we must be sure it's significant enough to be worth it."

"Agreed. We'll take a few days here first. I think we could all use the rest," Elian said, his mind returning to his own bargain with the Fairy Queen.

"You suddenly look sad. Are you alright?" Cassai asked.

"Fine. Just tired. I thought you were going to shut your eyes a moment. Sophie, I've got medicine for your hands." Elian held up the ointment, but Sophie looked supremely unconcerned.

"Actually, I think I'd like to eat something," Cassai said.

Hollis jumped up. "I'll get you something. You should eat if you can."

"Do you want one of these?" Sophie held out the plate she had mostly demolished. There were two cookies left.

"COLLIN, ARE YOU COMING?" Collin heard Laurelle whisper loudly through the curtain that separated their bedchamber from the hallway.

"Yes, on my way. You don't have to whisper, by the way. Uncle is still out with Amicus. I'll be there straight away; I'm still working out my shoes."

"The sandals? Oh, have your boy lace those. They're too tricky."

Collin cringed as Timothy started toward him. "Don't. It's fine. I can get them." Timothy looked as if Collin had slapped him, and retreated to his corner. Collin put up a hand. "It's fine. You're in no trouble. I just…I'm not used to… Actually, your help would be great. Thank you." The boy's dark eyes lit up and he rushed to fix the straps.

"I do these. Don't worry any more over them. I'll always do them," Timothy offered, looking so happy that Collin felt guiltier than before.

"Thank you. Sorry," Collin mumbled as the boy's deft fingers wove the leather straps halfway up his calves.

Laurelle poked her head in. "Ready now?"

"Sure. Where did you say we were going?"

"To see The Spectacle. They only do it a couple of times a year. You're just the luckiest to be here now." She beamed as he stood up. "You look just like any Lightling now."

"Except missing a few inches," he said, grinning and holding one hand over his head to indicate the height of Nihl or Jacque.

Laurelle waved the comment off. "Oh, Lightlings don't worry about such petty prejudices."

Collin cocked his head in the direction of Timothy, who stood beaming in his usual corner. "Right."

"What? The *malderones*? Does that bother you?"

"Slavery? Yes. That definitely bothers me."

Laurelle looked genuinely shocked. "How is that fair? We saved him. The life of Riverfolk is desperately bleak. He would've probably starved to death if not for the *malderone* system."

"But maybe he wouldn't have. And did you ever ask him if he wanted to be taken from his family?"

"Anyone would want to be taken from that life. Would you want to live in a mud hut on the river, fishing for all your food, or begging? Trust me, he's much better off. As for his family, if he had any, they were probably brought here as well. He may see them regularly."

Collin frowned. Laurelle had been so kind, he wanted to think of a way to disagree with her without being disagreeable. "I don't think people should be treated as property. That's all I'm saying."

She smiled. "What a kind boy you are."

Collin looked at his sandals and shoved his hands into his pockets. "Right. Thanks. Ready to go?"

"Oh yes! We don't want to miss it." Laurelle grabbed his hands in hers and pulled him outside. Her hand was so soft against his rough skin he could barely think straight.

"Finally," Jacque fell into step on Collin's other side with Nihl and Marcole just behind. "I thought you were chickening out."

"He had a bit of trouble with his sandals," Laurelle said cheerfully.

"Ugh! I hate them. I'll get you some moccasins. They do something to the leather that makes it feel like you're walking in a cloud."

"Oh, that's alright. I'll get used to these," Collin said, blushing. His new friends' generosity overwhelmed him.

Jacque ruffled Collin's hair. "Nah, we'll go to market tomorrow and you can pick out your own things."

"Is the arena open tomorrow?" Laurelle asked.

"Elle, you're not going," Marcole glowered at her.

"I never said I was. I just wondered." Laurelle looked over her shoulder at Nihl, who winked at her. She giggled guiltily and pulled Collin along faster.

The friends walked along a cobblestone street, explaining everything they passed for Collin's benefit.

"Down that hill is the Elythium, where all the smart people go to get smarter," Laurelle said, waving toward a massive building surrounded by a maze of smaller buildings. "We'll take you to eat there while you're here. Their chef is amazing."

"Maybe," said Jacque quietly.

Laurelle flushed, looking as if she understood Jacque's remark. Collin looked back and forth between them, but neither said anything else. He couldn't help feeling left out of something, but tried to ignore it.

"Here."

"This is The Spectacle?" Collin asked.

They'd arrived at a park lit by a thousand colorful paper lanterns strung up in the trees. Blankets in every color imaginable were lain out on the bright green grass. Children playing a game of touch and go wove throughout the area. Other groups ducked behind tree trunks and grown-ups while one Lightling child stood under a tree, eyes covered, counting aloud. *Malderones* were everywhere, serving platters of food and tending smaller children.

"Oh, The Spectacle hasn't begun yet. But isn't this fun?" bubbled Laurelle, watching for Collin's reaction.

Collin smiled and felt so happy he wondered if it was even decent. "It's brilliant," he breathed.

Jacque grinned and propelled him toward a blanket near the center. "We're set up over here."

"Are your parents here?" Collin asked as they settled on a blanket, which Laurelle informed him was called a quilt. Hundreds of bright patches of fabric were sewn together to make a pattern which Collin couldn't distinguish with all the bodies sitting on it.

"They're somewhere. At our age, it's a bit weird to show up with your parents," Nihl explained, as if this was something Collin should have known.

Collin bit back a retort, and settled for wrapping an arm around Laurelle. She nestled against his side. "I'm so glad you came."

"Me too," was the only response he could think of. Her warm body pressed against his made breathing difficult, even less being capable of putting together coherent sentences.

Jacque pointed across the park and over a small body of water. "Watch across the pond."

A loud pop made Collin jump, and a pinprick of light streamed up into the starry sky. The second, louder pop accompanied a cloud of red and blue lights exploding into the sky.

"Pyrotechnics," said Marcole with a wide grin.

"Pyro – what?" Collin asked.

Jacque rolled his eyes at Marcole and elbowed Collin in the ribs in a friendly way. "Fireworks."

Another burst followed the first, and then another, until the sky was filled with exploding red, green and yellow stars. "Wow," Collin whispered.

Laurelle beamed at him. "Like it?"

"It's incredible! I've never seen anything like it in my life."

The fireworks lasted ages, and Collin gasped and exclaimed with his companions.

He was enjoying himself more than he'd ever thought possible, when Laurelle accidentally ran her hand across his back over the worst of the stripes that never healed. Eye-watering pain shot through him and he cried out. Both Laurelle and Jacque jumped.

"Oh my goodness, I'm sorry. Did I hurt you?"

"No." Collin grimaced and sat forward, trying to breathe until the pain dulled.

"His back is all ripped up," Jacque murmured.

"I'm fine. Don't worry, Elle, you didn't know."

Laurelle bit her bottom lip. "How did your back get ripped up?"

Collin shot Jacque a look that made the taller boy stare intently at his shoes. "Something happened a few weeks ago, before I came here. It was nothing. I'm okay."

Laurelle looked from Collin to Jacque and then settled back. "Tell me."

Collin pulled his knees into his chest and rested his chin on them. This posture stretched his wounded back painfully, but he ignored it, knowing the pain would fade eventually. "It's a really long story."

"Do you have some other pressing engagement to get to?" Jacque demanded.

"What's happening?" Marcole shuffled up beside them, handing Collin a paper bag full of popped corn. "I got you butter, because I had no idea how you like your popcorn."

Collin took a bite of the crunchy, salty snack and smiled. "Wow, that's so good. Thanks."

"Collin was about to tell the horrible-cuts-across-his-back story for us." Jacque grabbed a handful of popcorn from Collin's bag.

"Oh, good. Out with it, then. Tell us everything," Marc said.

Collin looked into the faces of his new friends and calculated his chances of them still wanting to socialize with him if they knew he was marked by the Fontre and scarred beyond repair inside and out. Jacque's face was serious for the first time Collin had seen, and Laurelle hadn't taken her eyes off him since she'd asked for the story.

"I ... so I guess I'll start with − my mum and dad died in a fire a few years ago. So I live with my uncle, Julius. And I had a sister." Collin hurried through these painful details and covered the huskiness in his voice by taking more popcorn. He wished he hadn't. His throat felt thick, making it hard to swallow.

"I worked for a friend of my uncle's at his printing press. His name was Phineas, and he used to print books, and a paper every week about town issues. Then he started including subtle jabs at Fontre law, or stories of families suffering because they'd been visited by the Southern Guard ... or just, whatever. You know, he was fed up with all of it. One day, I went to work and the Guard came for him. There's this guy in town named Cobbs who's just...so evil he joined the Guard to torment his own townspeople. So Cobbs came in to help arrest Phineas, and Phineas made me hide when he saw them coming. I watched from an alcove hidden behind a bookshelf while they dragged him away."

Collin clenched his hands. He could smell the wood, the ink and oil; he could hear Phineas' crying out when they struck him to the ground. "So they took him, and we never heard from him again. I ran out the back door. Didn't stop running until I got home. That was when I realized I'd left my bag, and I guess it wouldn't have mattered, but I always carried a book my father gave me and it was in my bag.

"I left it for a while, but I finally worked up the courage to sneak back into the shop. The day I went back, Cobbs saw me. He grabbed me as I came out and dragged me to the Southern Guard's station house. A Fontre was there that day too. *Genraal Majure* of the whole Fontre *Koninjka*. He asked me all these questions about the town and my friends. I...I couldn't tell him much. So he had me whipped in the square. And..." Collin's throat burned too hot to continue. He didn't want to cry in front of these strange, beautiful people who thought he was worthy of friendship. To make matters worse, Jacque rested an arm across his shoulders. The friendly contact almost undid his last ounce of control.

"You don't have to tell us it all, mate, if you don't want. We get it. It was bad."

Laurelle let her head drop against his shoulder again. The friends sat silent while the fireworks' sparks faded into the smoky black sky.

Marc finally broke the silence. "They took your little sister?" he guessed in a whisper.

Collin's head drooped between his knees. "Killed her," he choked.

"Oh no!" Laurelle gasped. "I'm so, so sorry, Collin."

"Sorry to spoil the evening. I didn't ... I wasn't going to say anything."

Jacque's arm tightened around Collin's shoulder. "Hey, don't do that. Tell us what we can do to help."

Jacque's compassion touched Collin to his core. "This," he said quietly. The boy's arm felt wet and he realized Laurelle was crying silently into his sleeve. He straightened up and pulled Laurelle against him. "Don't cry. I'm okay."

He could hear the smile in Jacque's voice. "Well, that was easier than I thought it would be."

Collin managed to lift the corners of his mouth. "And —"

"Ah! I knew it. There's always an 'and'." Jacque popped another handful of Collin's popcorn into his mouth, relieved to lighten the mood.

"I need to speak to the Senate and ask for their help in this war we're planning against the Fontre."

"Oh, we're all over that," Marc assured him.

"We love going to Senate hearings," Nihl finally spoke up.

"Really?" Collin asked.

"Nothing interesting ever happens around here, mate. A Senate hearing's as good a show as any," Jacque assured him.

Collin managed a hoarse laugh. "Well, great. At least I can make your life more interesting."

11

THE SHOW

Hollis felt restlessness growing inside. Cassai and Elian were out walking a trail they'd walked every day since they came. Theoris sat in the kitchen talking with Sophie. The two were laughing at a story of Theoris' from his childhood. Hollis didn't feel up to feigning cheerfulness, so he wandered the small hall of Haven House, his fingers running over runes carved centuries ago.

One door hadn't been opened since their arrival and Hollis paused there now, wondering if it was too intrusive to enter without permission. He looked back toward the kitchen. The occupants seemed preoccupied and there was no sign of the Hermit or Krispen. A strange tingling ran up his arm when he touched the doorknob. He ignored it, twisted the knob and pushed in.

He felt an unpleasant swooping in his stomach when he saw the Hermit sitting at an enormous loom in the center of the room. "I beg your pardon. I shouldn't have intruded."

"You're welcome to come in, dear boy," said the man.

Hollis shoved his hands into his pockets and walked in. The

door creaked closed behind him. "Developing an interest in tapestry?" Hollis asked.

"I've always enjoyed weaving. The depth of importance in every single strand of thread fascinates me."

Hollis approached the giant loom, feeling hesitant. He had the uncomfortable sensation of snooping in someone's private affairs. He couldn't stare overlong at the pattern without the wrongness growing. The Hermit watched him, understanding in his ancient eyes.

"It isn't private. You're welcome to look."

"I see no weavings in your home." Hollis let his eyes drift over the pattern. "Do you do this often?"

"When my employer has a particular job for me, otherwise I leave it to him." The Hermit's hands were back at the loom. He worked constantly while they talked, and so quickly Hollis couldn't follow the movement without going dizzy. Though he was deeply curious about who employed such a man, the Hermit offered no further information, and he didn't think he should ask.

The Hermit looked back at him, but seamlessly continued his work. "You're restless in my valley. Your companions need time and rest, and you're ready to move on, even though you've nowhere to hurry off to." This wasn't a question. Hollis watched the shuttle shoot across the warp threads, again and again, back and forth with mesmerizing speed.

"Haven House is lovely. I'm never comfortable sitting still."

"Being left with your own thoughts is disconcerting to you." Another non-question.

Hollis sighed. "Yes. When you've done the things I've done, solitude is not friendly."

The old man's hands and feet stopped moving; stopped working the loom. The room went silent. "You've suffered so much, Hollis. It is no sin to suffer."

"I've caused suffering as well."

"You have indeed. Black threads are woven throughout your

life's tapestry, some there to form you, some unnecessary, because of the darkness you've brought on others."

Hard as the Hermit's words were to bear, Hollis didn't resent them. They were true, blunt and to the point. No malice intended. Hollis always appreciated that sort of honesty. One point annoyed him though.

"I've never understood why people say suffering is good for you, or necessary in some way. Suffering only does harm."

"Ah! You are one of those who suffer and never learn from it," said the Hermit, shaking his head. "And so you step on a thorn, and rather than remove it from your foot so it heals properly, you let it stay and fester. And you thrash the bush that grew it and throw thorns all about for others to step on."

Hollis frowned. "Thank you. I wasn't feeling guilty enough as it is."

The Hermit rolled his eyes at the sarcasm. "Guilt can be a good thing, if it is earned and productive. However, you make a good point. Guilt that someone else lays upon you is merely a burden and much too heavy to bear."

A long silence hung between them. The Hermit seemed perfectly at ease with this uncomfortable conversation, but Hollis shoved his hands in his pockets and rocked on his heels.

"Will you tell that to Elian?" Hollis said at last. "Those words would do him good. He carries too much guilt for things he bears no responsibility for."

"Poor Elian," the Hermit said so sympathetically that Hollis felt his heart melt even more toward the man. "That is a painful life indeed. What guilt does he bear that doesn't belong to him?"

"Every evil committed by every Fontre since the day he was born. He feels he should have stopped it, but of course that simply isn't possible. There's just too much wrong in them to fix ... and he was only a boy. Can you help him?" Hollis asked.

The Hermit's green-flecked eyes bored into Hollis until he felt the ancient man was staring at his soul. "Possibly... if you ask me to."

"Why should I have to ask?"

"Of course I could, my boy. But, there are all sorts of powers at work in this world. There is unique power in the requests made on our behalf by those who love us. Your request will give me access to that power."

Hollis blinked, confused, but nodded anyway. "Very well. I ask it of you for him. Help to ease his pain, if it's possible."

The Hermit smiled his life-giving smile. "And now you, Hollis Farrell, you will be helped more than you know. Caring for another's burden does not only change them ... it changes those who care."

"Very well then, thank you. I'll bid you good day."

"But you have received no help ... nothing to ease your pain. Have you no request for your own welfare?"

Hollis turned back to the tapestry rather than meet the Hermit's searching gaze. "I'm beyond your help, I'm afraid." He expected the Hermit to argue this point, but though he looked sorrowful, the Hermit said nothing. "I don't suppose you could ... just end it. Could you?"

"End what, dear boy?"

"End the cruelty of the Fontre. Stop the mad war we're marching to. You know it means nothing but bloodshed and heartache for all involved. I know you have power beyond the normal. Use it for that."

The Hermit shook his head. "I'm afraid what you're asking cannot be done. I wish it could."

"You're telling me the powers of the Fontre are beyond yours?" Hollis demanded. "Too strong for your reach ... to this little glen?"

"The powers of the Fontre are powers I rarely meddle with because the consequences can be disastrous."

"More disastrous than this war? What power is that,

pray tell?"

"Free will, Hollis Farrell. I can take a man's will if I wish, but I don't. That was not the point of mankind's creation. You wouldn't enjoy a world like that, no matter how you think you would. You have my sacred word on it. There are sins that must be allowed. Some darkness is necessary."

"Really? Free will?"

"Indeed. Would you have choice eradicated?" the Hermit asked kindly.

"I would free this world of evil if I had the power to do it ... not just sit by and let innocents be destroyed and good men slain. Is that wrong of me, Hermit?" replied Hollis, not managing to conceal the bitterness in his question.

"The point you make has, of course, been made before. It might surprise you to know by whom it was made. No one believes they're the villain. Men believe their evil actions are justified, just as you do. Also, with no choices, there is no love, kindness, or true joy. Would you also do away with those, Hollis?"

Hollis clenched his fists in his pockets. "Possibly. I don't see they've done much good."

"Then you would do this world a great disservice."

Hollis merely nodded and turned to leave the weaving room. The loom began to move again, clacking and whirring as he opened the door. He turned a final time to look at the Hermit, but the man was busy with the shuttle and pedals, almost as if Hollis had never been there.

ELIAN BREATHED in the morning air gratefully. It might be the last clean air he'd breathe for a long while. Here, where everything was green and flowers bloomed, and animals feasted on the foliage, he felt almost whole and at peace.

"The Hermit says breakfast is ready." Cassai's voice made him smile.

"Come here." He reached out and she came to him. He pointed out a field of buttercups. "Look at that pink. How long will it be before we see such a color again?"

"You're going sad on me again," she said. "Don't do that. It's hard enough preparing to leave."

Elian's lips brushed the top of her head. The ancient valarca tree rumbled from the trunk up in response. He sighed. "I wish I could imprint this place on my eyes forever."

"We have work to do."

"I know."

"You're the one who said we needed to go."

"I know."

"So...breakfast? We could still do with a bit of that before heading to our doom." She swept an arm toward the cottage, her eyes sparkling.

"Breakfast sounds wonderful." He allowed her to lead him back toward the cottage.

Hollis sat at the table, staring into a cup of strong coffee. "If I believed in Havilah I would hope it included this drink at every meal."

"You should certainly believe in Havilah," said the Hermit, giving him a stern look. "And it is a delightful beverage indeed." He smiled and set a steaming mug in front of Cassai.

"No thank you, sir, I like the chocolate."

"Of course you do. It is Elian who prefers the bite of the roasted beans." The hermit slid the cup to Elian and bustled to the stovetop where a pot of chocolate was bubbling.

Elian sipped the steaming liquid and inhaled gratefully. "Thank you, Hermit. I'm sorry to leave this place."

"This place is sorry that you're leaving it," answered the older man, placing a hot platter piled high with pancakes and sizzling sausages. "Here's the syrup." He clunked a heavy jar beside the platter, and the three pounced on it.

"Where are the others?"

"Coming any moment, I think. I sent Sophie to fetch Theoris. Krispen is just heading in from tending to the animals. That boy makes me happy."

"Yes, he makes everyone happy," said Cassai.

Elian felt heavy with the news he hadn't shared yet. Even Cassai had no idea he was about to leave them again. Krispen opened the front door, his cheeks rosy with the cool morning air, his expanding frame filling up almost the entire opening.

"Everyone is fed and watered," he said to the Hermit.

"Thank you, my dear boy. I wish you wouldn't leave me. Do promise to return whenever you're able."

"I will," said the boy, lowering himself into a chair, eyeing the food hungrily.

"If you've taken all the sausages I'll shoot you all where you sit," Sophie promised, stomping in from the hallway.

"Ha! We aren't scared of a little Kiatri whelp," Elian said, grinning at the glare she shot him.

"Jerk," she punched him as she passed.

"Ow," Cassai yelped, rubbing her own arm.

"Oops, sorry, Cassai. I forgot your thing with him," said Sophie.

"Yes, so you should be nice. As far as we know, no one will feel it if I hurt you," Elian said, flicking her ear playfully, but hard enough to make her wince and clap a hand to her ear.

"Oh, leave her alone. Here," Cassai said, pushing the heavy platter of breakfast food in Sophie's direction. "Coffee or hot chocolate?"

Sophie closed her eyes and inhaled so deeply her chest rose and fell three times before she replied. "Both."

The corners of the Hermit's eyes crinkled and he grabbed a

large mug. "Coming up directly. And there's more of everything should you need it."

"How do you get the meat?" asked Sophie suddenly.

"Meat?" asked the Hermit.

"For the sausages?"

The Hermit looked appalled. "My dear girl, I thought you knew me better than that. Of course it's not meat. I have a special recipe I developed years ago." Sophie wrinkled her nose and eyed the sausages suspiciously.

"Good morning, Theoris," Cassai said cheerfully to the very rumpled fairy hobbling the room on the crutch Hollis had made him.

"Is it?" Theoris asked. His spiky hair listed heavily to the left.

"I thought the fey didn't need much sleep. You seem to need it often," Hollis observed.

"It's your mortal world that does it to me. I don't know why you all think it so important to stay in constant motion." Theoris lowered himself painfully into a chair and groaned.

Hollis shrugged. "No reason, really. Just Fontre always trying to kill or abduct us, werewolves attacking us and the general hospitality of Fondair. We should sit in one place for a while and invite them all to tea."

"Have some coffee, Theoris," said the Hermit, smiling and pressing a warm mug into the fairy's long-fingered hands.

"Thank you, my good sir. You are one of the few truly pleasant things about this world."

The Hermit chuckled.

Elian set his coffee down and looked intently at the table. "I can't go with you all now," he announced at last.

Everyone at the table paused. Cassai sat, a fluffy roll suspended near her open mouth.

"What did you say?" she asked.

"I've made a promise and I must keep it. If I don't, none of us will be safe."

"The fey?" Hollis guessed, looking grim.

"Yes."

"What do the fey have to do with anything?" Cassai asked, still holding her roll aloft.

"The Queen made you pledge something? I knew she would never send in her armies without payment," Hollis growled.

Theoris glowered at Elian. "Whatever she's said to you, you know you cannot trust her."

"It isn't a large debt, Theoris, considering what the fey armies sacrificed for us." Elian wrapped a hand around Cassai's and slowly lowered the roll to her plate. He smiled at her and squeezed her hand. "I'll join you at the Westerling field in less than a fortnight."

"A fortnight?" yelped Hollis. "What is this price she demanded?"

"Me."

Elian hadn't realized Cassai could look even more shocked. "What on earth?"

"It's nothing. She just wants to ask me questions, like she did when you visited her."

"Ask you questions? Rubbish. She's got something nasty in store and you know it." Hollis fumed. Elian glared at him and shot a pointed look at Cassai.

"I'm sure it'll be nothing," he insisted again.

Hollis pushed away from the table. "Stop coddling her. She knows what this means as well as any of us," he growled.

"Yes, stop coddling me, and you −" Cassai glared at Hollis, "stop talking about me as if I'm not here."

"I'm well aware you're here. Stand up for yourself for once and I won't have to bother."

Cassai pushed up from the table, her face crimson. "You're angry with me now?"

Elian put a hand on her arm. "He's just angry in general, Cassai. It's nothing to do with you."

"Don't speak for me, I'm angry at her," Hollis barked.

Cassai jerked away from Elian's touch. "Why didn't you tell me where you were heading? You let me think you were coming to the Westerling Field. I thought you were leading this army. Now you're going to the Fairy Realm to be with −" Angry tears choked the rest of her words. Out the window, Elian saw dark clouds gather in the sky.

"I'm sorry. I know I should have told you. I don't know what she wants. She didn't tell me anything specific. I'm sure whatever it is, it won't be pleasant."

"I'm going with you," said Krispen quietly.

"I'll meet you at the Westerling Field, Krispen. Stay and look after Cassai." The clouds broke and outside, animals pelted in every direction to escape the sudden storm. In the kitchen, Cassai stood glaring, fists clenched, eyes snapping. Hot tears raced down her cheeks.

"I don't need looking after!" she shouted at Elian.

"Not like that," Elian put up his hands in surrender. The Hermit's possessions had lifted from their places and looked like they might start hurtling around the room. Everyone at the table sat like stones, not wanting to send Cassai into a deeper rage. "Not like a child; like someone being hunted by vicious killers."

The Hermit dared approach Cassai, resting one hand softly on her shoulder. She took a deep breath and books lowered slowly onto their shelves. The platter of food clattered as it landed on the table. Cassai looked as shocked as anyone at the effect of her anger. "Oh my word," she whispered. Rain ceased pelting the window. "I'm sorry."

The Hermit patted her affectionately. "Quite alright, my dear. Frankly, a bit of a squall is good for you sometimes. Not healthy to keep it all bottled in."

Elian stood frozen, unsure whether he should touch her again. Her eyes softened when she met his gaze. "It's okay. I do wish you'd told me. But old habits are hard to break. I understand," she said softly.

"I was waiting for the right moment, and then I was just enjoying this peaceful place."

"I'm going," Krispen said again, his voice shaking; tears streamed from his eyes.

"If anyone goes, it should be me," Hollis offered. "I know the fey better than you."

"If you go, she'll never let you leave," Elian said. "I don't think I can break us out of that dungeon again."

"How could you have made such a promise?" demanded Cassai, much more calmly but still clearly upset. "What if she doesn't release *you*? What if she wants things you can't give her? I should go instead. I know she wants me to and I doubt she'll dare torture a Namarielle. You go to the Westerling Field and meet the Keepers."

"I promised her I would return with the Lost Book. But I appreciate the offer."

"But you don't have the Lost Book," Cassai pointed out. "What do you think she'll say to that?"

"Probably nothing good," Elian admitted.

Krispen stood up and wiped his face with a napkin. "Cassai will have Hollis, Sophie and Theoris to keep her safe. You won't have anyone. I'm staying with you."

Elian felt the deepest affection for his shepherd boy, and an even deeper terror of what the fey might do with him. "I don't know what I'm headed toward. Whatever the Queen says or does, I've agreed to cooperate. You can't interfere with that, Krispen. No matter how much you may wish to."

"I know. I won't get in the way. I'll just...be there."

Elian nodded and stood to leave. "Alright. Hollis or Theoris, do you know of any entrance to the Fairy Realm near here? I can go back toward the mountains if I must."

Hollis and Theoris exchanged a look. "There's a spot I discovered yesterday. I don't feel I should allow you but...I suppose you'll find an entrance one way or another," Theoris said, his face extremely pale.

Elian nodded.

"Wait." The Hermit also stood. "Let me pack food and drink. No doubt the Queen will find any reason she can to bind you to their realm. Let's not give her more cause."

"I say, Elian, this feels like a terrible mistake." Theoris had paled.

The Hermit took Elian's satchel and carried it to his larder. When he came back into the room, it bulged with cakes, dried fruits and vegetables, and a parcel of biscuits. "Can they drink the water there?" he asked Hollis.

"I wouldn't," the man replied. He hadn't taken his eyes off Elian. "Theoris and I will refill the skins at the pump, Hermit."

"Take the canteens. They hold more." The man passed three large containers to Hollis and slipped another pouch into the satchel. "Coffee. Just in case."

"Thank you, Hermit. Thank you for everything."

"I've one last thing for you, Elian. If you can wait a moment," the Hermit said, going toward his cluttered desk.

"We'll meet you out there," Hollis said, holding the door for Theoris. The fairy pulled himself up by his crutch and clunked his way out the door.

Elian nodded and touched Cassai's cheek. "Want to walk with me for a moment?"

She gave him a sad smile. "Yes."

"I'll be right there." Cassai left as well, and Elian waited for the Weaver to dig through a stack of papers which fluttered to the floor as he dismissed them.

"I know it's here somewhere. Ah ha! Here we go." The Hermit resurfaced with a scrap of paper that looked several years old. "Find him. He can help you and Cassai with your situation. If he's still alive, he'll be in the Inner Kingdom somewhere."

Elian took the scrap and read the faded name, "Banaker?"

"I believe his first name is Gideon, but I wouldn't swear to it."

"Thank you."

"You're most welcome, my dear boy. The Weaver guard you and keep you. Don't get lost in that cursed Fairy Realm. Don't forget your people here who love you."

Elian smiled and nodded politely, slipping the precious piece of information into his jacket pocket. "I won't forget. I can't," he shrugged. "I'm Fontre. I don't forget anything."

The Hermit's eyes crinkled at the edges again in his ancient, knowing smile and he placed a weathered hand on Elian's cheek. "A particularly nasty curse indeed, my boy."

They walked out the door, and Elian turned and took the stone-lined path Cassai had grown so fond of. The path itself was well worn and lined with ferns and pink flowered mimosas. He found her under a particularly tall mimosa tree. Its fluffy pink flowers perfumed the air.

"Don't go," she begged.

Elian pulled her against him and pressed his lips against her wild brown curls. "You smell so good," he murmured.

She began to shake. Soft rain began to patter around them. "Please don't go."

"Hey," Elian said pulling her far enough away to look at her face. "Don't do that, please. You know I can't hold up under that kind of pressure." He cradled her face in his hands and wiped the tears from her cheeks with his thumbs. "I'll be alright."

"I don't know if I can stand being away from you again. Especially like this, when I don't know what's happening to you, and I can't help. Plus...leaving me alone with Hollis and Theoris. How can you do that to me?" She gave him a weak grin.

Elian chuckled dryly and hugged her tight. "I'm sorry about that. You don't deserve such a lot. Perhaps Sophie will have a civilizing effect on her uncle, eh?"

"What do you really think Dahlia plans to do with you?"

"Ah," Elian waved a hand carelessly, "torture and torment with a side of death. The usual."

"Elian," Cassai scowled.

"You said to stop coddling you," he chucked a fist playfully under her chin. "She says she's curious about me, about the Fontre, about you. I'm sure she wants all the information I can give her."

"And you don't have the book. What do you think she'll do about that?"

Elian looked into the distance, but wasn't seeing the trees or the pond. "I'm sure it will be addressed in some way."

"I hate her," said Cassai.

"She's not my favorite, either. But she paid me a great service, and I intend to pay her back."

"Why do you have to be so noble? Couldn't you, just once, let someone else take the licking while you stand on the side-lines?"

Elian grinned. "Never much enjoyed the side-lines; I always preferred the licking. I hate leaving you though. I promise I'll see you again as soon as humanly possible. Will you do me a small kindness?"

Cassai nodded. "I'll do anything for you."

"I want to say goodbye to you here. Don't accompany me to the entrance of the Fairy Land. I know the Queen has some knowledge of mortals entering, but I don't know how much. If she sees you at the opening, she may not resist the urge to take you as well."

Cassai laced her fingers through his, and inhaled deeply, letting his scent fill her up. "Yes, I can do that."

Elian kissed the tips of his free fingers and touched her cheek as he had done for years. "I love you so much, Taiya."

Cassai swallowed hard. Then kissed her own fingers and laid them against his scruffy cheek. "I couldn't love anyone more than I love you, Elian."

Elian gave her one last, fierce hug, then released her and

retraced their steps down the path. Elian saw Hollis and Theoris standing in the clearing waiting for him. Krispen was patting his lamb goodbye, but he wasn't crying. His grim determination was more painful to Elian than his tears would have been.

~

COLLIN STROLLED to the Hall of Reasoning with his new friends. Jacque's arm rested comfortably across his shoulders. The taller boy had informed Collin that he was just the right height for an armrest.

"Don't forget, they're just a group of pompous windbags," Marcole said as they approached the massive stone structure. "They say they value intellect above everything, but really they were all just popular enough to be elected and they're bored out of their minds. Make your case full of drama and angst. They'll lap it up. Nothing interesting ever happens in Halanah."

"I don't have a lot of drama in me, Marc. How do I do that?" Collin asked.

"Tell them about the whipping and Phineas. Tell them about your sister," Marc advised, sounding more delicate than before.

Collin froze. "What? You mean ... are you saying...I don't understand. So that's drama then, is it? I thought drama was nonsense made up for entertainment. So...use my little sister's death as just...nonsense...entertainment?"

Marcole was shaking his head frantically. "That is not what I meant. I swear, Collin, I'm so sorry. I meant...Oh Zeno. No. Jacque?" He looked at the taller boy for rescue Collin glared at him too. Jacque wrapped his arm back around Collin's shoulder.

"Come here a minute, Collin," he said, leading Collin away from the group. "You go on and get seats. We'll be along." Collin went because he liked Jacque best, but even this gesture made him clench his hands.

"Let me go, Jacque."

"Promise you won't fly off and attack Marc."

Collin laughed and felt angrier than before. "You think Marc is afraid of me? That boy's built like a bloody ox."

"He's not afraid of you. He feels bad, Collin. So he won't fight back no matter what you do to him. He knows perfectly well he said a stupid thing, but didn't mean it the way it came out."

"Drama and angst, really?"

"I know. I said it was stupid."

"Fine. It's fine." Collin groaned and buried his head in his hands. "What am I supposed to say to these people? They're never going to listen to me."

"Then what do you have to lose? If they aren't listening anyway, say whatever you want. Say what you said to us about the Southern Guard's raids and the Fontre coming in now. I would mention them whipping you without any sort of trial. I would tell them about Cobbs. That's just me though. Say whatever. The senate has to sit there. You might as well get your story in."

"This is really important. If I fail at this..." Collin shook his head. Jacque's arm tensed on his shoulder.

"You'll be alright. We've got you. I'll see what I can do if it seems to be going badly, okay?"

"You will?"

"Yeah. I'll do whatever I can for you, mate. I know these nutters. Maybe one of us can talk some sense into them. Are you alright now? Ready to go in?"

"I'm alright."

"Good with Marc?"

"Yeah, I know he's trying to help."

"We're all just trying to help."

"Okay. Let's go in then."

They'd entered the crowded hall. People pressed against them on all sides. Collin allowed himself to be led to a pile of cushions on the floor in the eastern corner of the room. The others were already there, smiling anxiously at him; except Nihl, who looked like he didn't care whether Collin lived or died. Collin returned their smiles and sat next to Laurelle.

From this vantage point they could see and hear the members of the senate.

The Senate was composed of the most beautiful Light Ones Collin had seen since entering the city. Lady Ella, whom he'd heard about from Elian, sat in the center of the room on a cushion like his. While other Lightlings reclined, surrounded with food and drink, none of the Senate brought refreshments.

"Lady Ella doesn't allow them to eat and drink while in session so things keep moving swiftly. If they get too comfortable, business drags on forever," Laurelle said in his ear. She leaned against him looking more comfortable, making him grin again.

A man in the center hit a gong for silence. The chatter died down, but didn't cease until Lady Ella called out names in the order they were to be heard. Collin's heart raced when he heard his own name midway through the list.

A Lightling from farther North was first. He stood tall and spoke in a commanding baritone, so Collin and his friends could hear him well, even across the room. The Senate gave him their full attention while he complained about the availability of *malderones* in his province and that there was never enough imported wheat and wine. "We've had to start our own crops and as you know, wine grapes don't grow well in our region."

A stunning girl sat next to Lady Ella, scribbling on a long scroll as quickly as she could. The girl's skin was a lighter brown, but just as shiny as Timothy's. However, Timothy's garments were well worn and this girl was dressed in pure white linen, her silky black hair arranged in delicate curls piled on top of her head.

"Lady Ella's handmaiden," Laurelle whispered in his ear. "I've heard she treats her *malderones* really well; even gives them pocket money." Collin rolled his eyes at the admiration in her voice.

"Well, that's magnificent of her," he said under his breath.

The man from the Northern Province settled back onto his

cushions, looking satisfied. Collin hadn't heard the decision of the Senate, but assumed an increase in the slave and wine quota.

Another lady stood, tall and speaking with the affected air of the gatesman Collin had begun to get used to.

Laurelle kept up a quiet commentary about each person and their grievances. Some of them spoke exclusively in the Lightling tongue and Laurelle translated. Collin enjoyed this immensely.

"That's Tybia, Lady Ella's cousin. She always speaks at the meetings because she feels jilted by the senate. So many rumors about her —" Laurelle's eyes sparkled with humor as the lady in question registered various complaints.

"Your turn's next. Are you prepared?"

Collin took a deep breath. "No. But I guess I have to be."

"Finally!" Laurelle huffed when Tybia threw her gauze shawl around her skinny neck and marched from the hall. "She's always complaining about the things her taxes pay for and blah blah blah...but the street sweepers are *malderones*. Her taxes certainly don't pay for them, because nobody pays them. Unless you count clothes and food."

Marcole poked Collin in the back.

"It's you."

Collin jumped ungracefully to his feet. The senators turned their undivided attention to him. His palms started to sweat. "Right. So...I was going to ask —" Collin's mind had gone blank.

"Hello, Collin." The soft voice of Lady Ella filled him with calm. "You and your uncle travelled quite a distance to speak to us." She waved her hand toward a pillar near the hall's east exit. Julius was leaning against it looking completely calm. Collin breathed easier when his uncle gave him a nod.

"Yes. Sorry. I'm not used to public speaking." A murmur of encouragement rose from the room, and the spectators smiled at him warmly. "I belong to a group of men in the Borderlands planning a rebellion."

"Rebellion?" asked a man sitting to Lady Ella's right. "What can you hope to accomplish with such an immature display?"

"We're not a group of children throwing a tantrum … we're organizing to fight back against the Fontre. We're taking back the Inner Kingdom."

"Are you? What is your plan, Collin of the Borderlands? March to the Gates of the Inner Kingdom and demand they return the city to you?" This drew a wispy laugh from the crowd, and Collin's hands started to shake.

"Of course not. We plan to take it by force."

"Force?" Lady Ella blanched. "You mean war?"

Collin chewed on his bottom lip and looked at Laurelle. She smiled and nodded. "Yes." He looked around the room. Heads shook in disbelief. A low buzz filled the hall as if someone had released a swarm of wasps.

"We see no value in killing people just to get what we wish. We would be much more likely to enter into peace talks with the Fontre. We could send a committee with you to negotiate. There are reasonable Fontre. Let us confer about this matter," Lady Ella said.

"There are no reasonable Fontre!" Collin shouted. The polite tones everyone argued with here were grating him.

"Of course there are, dear boy. The Fontre are intellectuals, scientists and historians. What would you have us do? Wipe out such an advanced race just to suit your whims, or lower your taxes?" this was the same man who called him immature.

"Lower my taxes?" Collin repeated. Blood rushed to his face.

"It's not taxes and rationing. That was just the start." Laurelle had risen to her feet and slipped her cool hand into Collin's trembling one. She squeezed gently. A warning or encouragement? He couldn't tell. "They've been brutal in Collin's village. They've even taken his friends away for disagreeing with the Fontre's unjust laws. Isn't that so, Collin?" Collin nodded and kept his lips pressed tightly closed.

"Tragic as that is, the Enlightened do not rush off to war every time some villager gets apprehended for lawbreaking." The man beside Lady Ella waved his hand dismissively at the two young people.

Laurelle's cheeks flushed. "We believe in freedom of speech here, do we not?" The senate frowned and muttered to each other, but didn't give a clear answer to this.

Marcole stood. Collin waited for him to speak, but Marcole put a gentle hand on Collin's shoulder and leaned close to his ear. "Show them your back."

Collin's glared at his friend. "No."

Marc broke eye contact to address the senate. "The Fontre terrorize and starve their villages, and all of the Borderlands. No one knows what they've done to the people inside the Great Wall. Were it a simple matter of taxes or regulations, perhaps a committee would suffice, but this is a matter of innocent children slaughtered. Not lawbreakers."

Collin went stiff as a corpse. "Don't," Collin muttered, gripping Marc's arm. "It's alright. I'll think of something else."

"I'm sorry," Marcole whispered, and Collin's throat burned, anticipating Marc's next move. "They killed his little sister. She was only nine years old and did nothing to deserve it."

Moisture pooled at the rim of Collin's eyelids and the room went wobbly. He felt lightheaded. His back throbbed. He wanted to run and attack Marc, and burn down this Hall. Instead he stood, frozen, as if his feet were embedded in the marble tiles.

Marcole nodded to Nihl, who stood up silently. "The Fontre don't fine people for disobedience," Marc continued, "or even incarcerate them."

Collin felt the tension Marcole was building, felt his shirt lifted from his back. He thought about pulling away from them, but knew if he did, if he didn't seem to be in on it, everyone would be confused and all of this argument would be for nothing.

He just had to go along.

Nihl tugged the tunic over the boy's head. His arms lifted as his shirt pulled off. Nihl turned him to show the senate his wounds. Collin looked at the floor, shaking all over.

"The Fontre came looking for one of their own, a friend of Collin's from the village, and when the boy refused to betray his friend, they whipped his back beyond repair."

Collin heard gasps. The buzzing changed from disapproval to anger. "Despicable." He heard Lady Ella's sympathetic voice unmixing from the drone. "I'm so sorry, dear boy. We have physicians who can see to you. Marcole, take him to Askelpos."

"I don't want to be taken to Askelpos," said Collin. "Give me back my shirt." He glared at Nihl. Marcole shook his head.

Jacque stood too, Collin wondered if he was surprised at the turn of events. At least he looked upset.

"Sorry, mate," Jacque muttered. "Take him out of here. I'm going to keep trying to convince them." Jacque looked at his brother, who nodded. Marcole took Collin's arm.

He swallowed hard. "This is wrong," he whispered to Jacque.

Collin ground his teeth as he was led from the hall by Nihl and Marcole. Marc took his time, making sure when they passed the senate Collin's scarred back was in full view. Collin shook with anger as the crowd craned their necks to catch a glimpse of the unhealed stripes. He heard Jacque arguing with Lady Ella, but his ears weren't working properly and he couldn't comprehend what they were saying.

Sweet, fresh air hit his face as he exited under the hall's last archway. The fragrant garden surrounding the Hall of Reasoning was balm to his chaffed feelings. He inhaled deeply. A marble fountain stood in the middle of the garden carved with mermaids swimming around a king, holding a trident aloft.

Collin paused by the fountain, and stared at a stone mermaid's vacant expression as water flowed from the king's trident into her outstretched hands. He envied the mermaid's lack of emotion.

"Collin?" Laurelle's voice felt like being cut by glass.

"Leave me alone," he growled at her. "I said my sister wasn't entertainment for your stupid masses. I wasn't going to use her as a tool to draw sympathy."

"I know. I didn't know they were going to do that." Tears ran down the girl's rose petal cheeks. "I'm so sorry."

"It felt pretty well-orchestrated to me."

"Get off her," Nihl shouted, shoving Collin away from Laurelle. "She didn't know, alright? We planned it. We thought it might work if the situation wasn't...if it seemed to be going badly."

"Seemed to be going badly?" Collin shrieked. "Of course it went badly. Those people are so bloody full of themselves. I'm sure when the Fontre march in, they'll welcome them with open arms."

Nihl cocked a fist, but Collin didn't move. "Keep talking, Collin. I'll shut that pretty mouth of yours."

"Nihl, stop it." Laurelle put her hand on the taller boy's arm.

"And using my sister wasn't enough for you? Stripping me and parading me out like that? Stroke of brilliance. I hope they liked the show." Collin felt his throat tightening too much. He was not going to break in front of them. He wasn't.

"Alright, enough," Marc said softly, putting his hands up and getting between Collin and Nihl. "Enough Nihl."

Nihl's face relaxed and he took several breaths before patting Laurelle's hand. "Sorry. Something about that kid makes me want to hit him. Just once and then I'd like him."

"Oh please hit me," Collin said. "I'd actually prefer it to what you just did."

"Hey, no one's hitting anyone." Marc handed him his shirt. "I know. Okay? I'm sorry. We told the story you came to tell," he insisted. "We can't convince them that war will accomplish peace. They're too high and mighty for that. You're right; we gave them a show. They're all such idiots. Your back and your dead sister are your only weapons against their vacuous brains."

Collin turned away from them and slipped the tunic over his head, slowly lowering it over his sore back.

"I'm sorry, mate." Marcole's pleading cut straight through Collin's resolve to hate him.

"Collin." Julius was standing under the archway behind him. The tears Collin had been holding back broke free at the sound of his uncle's voice. He clenched his fists and glared into the water, trying to compose himself.

"I screwed that up, didn't I?" he choked.

Julius walked to the fountain and they all stepped back to let him wrap his arms around his humiliated nephew. Collin pushed his forehead into his uncle's boulder-like chest as hard as he could. "Of course not; you didn't screw up," Julius whispered. "The truth of war is ugly, and this place hides ugliness. It's nice... for a while."

"We did it!" Jacque roared from the steps and charged into the group beaming. "Oh, hey Collin, are you alright? Are you crying?" he leaned, breathless, against the fountain wall on his other side.

"No," Collin pulled away from his uncle. "Did you know about all that?"

"That they were gonna' strip you? Nah, I'da had them take your pants off too if I'd planned it. If you're going to give people a show, Collin, give them a real show." Jacque's eyes sparkled, but he didn't look like he really thought anything was funny about the situation.

Collin looked at him for a second and burst out laughing. "I'll keep that in mind for next time."

"And sell tickets," Jacque added, winking at him.

He nodded. "And sell tickets. I could use the money."

"I got you a private interview, mate." Jacque's smile was so infectious Collin couldn't help but return it.

"Thanks, Jacque."

"Sure. Are you good with tomorrow morning? Lady Ella can see you in her private office. That never happens."

"That's brilliant, Jacque!" Laurelle cried. "Lady Ella will listen to you. She *has* to."

Marcole nodded. "She's the one you want to convince. The only senator with an ounce of actual sense."

Collin rolled his eyes. "Don't hold back, Marc. What do you really think of the Senate?"

"Have you done with him then?" Julius cut across their banter in a tone that made Collin jump. His uncle stood frowning at them, arms folded across his chest.

"Yes sir," said Jacque. "Are you taking him?"

"I am. He's barely slept, eaten almost nothing today, and he's just had a much bigger ordeal than he's letting on at the moment. You can see him again once he's had a break."

"Um...okay. I guess I'll see you. Maybe," Collin mumbled.

"Right. We'll come by later then, if it's alright with Julius," Marc said looking doubtfully at Julius posture which hadn't changed. "I'm really sorry about the senate nightmare, Julius. Honestly. We'll take better care of him in the future."

"I would appreciate that. I'd say he's been through enough. Wouldn't you?" Julius' words weren't harsh, but the group all looked as though he'd been brandishing a whip at them.

"I definitely agree, sir. I'm so sorry," Marc managed.

Julius nodded, put a hand on Collin's arm and led him out of the garden.

"They mean well," Collin said quietly.

"I know they do. That's why I said you could see them again. But good intentions are not the same as good actions."

Collin grinned at him. "You can be really scary when you want to be."

Julius shook his head, looking very tired again. "I think someone should just line them all up and give them a good beating."

"Not Laurelle!"

He smiled. "No, not Laurelle. She's about as sweet as they come. Why she wastes her time with those boys is completely beyond reason."

12

THE FONTRE AND THE FEY

E lian, Krispen, and Hollis walked slowly toward a looming, craggy rock, covered in gray lichen.

"There's a crack you can only see when you get there. Head straight into it, chanting the *fey aria* and you'll be in the Fairy Realm," said Theoris.

"She swore she'd release me to the Westerling Field the day before Nuelltide," Elian said, straightening his pack and staring at the crack.

"That's still two weeks away. What she's going to do to you between now and then is anyone's guess," muttered Hollis.

Elian shrugged. "Don't let Cassai worry about me too much, will you?"

Hollis rolled his eyes. "Right. That'll be easy."

Elian turned toward Krispen. "Are you ready?"

"Yes."

He held out at hand to Hollis. "May the Weaver guard and guide you, Hollis Farrell."

Hollis shook Elian's hand firmly. "And you. Take care of him, Krispen."

The young man nodded soberly. Hollis looked at Elian one last time, then shook his head and walked toward the Hermit's cottage.

Theoris looked sheepish. "Well, good luck." He turned to rush after Hollis.

"Hold my arm, Krispen, and walk slowly. Hopefully, they'll take us both." Elian felt Krispen' hand grasp his forearm and they started slowly toward the crack in the giant rock. *"Audmette je compagnon al di Lioux di Fae,"* murmured Elian as they advanced. He repeated the words to the *aria* Hollis had hummed. The crack grew closer and showed no sign of widening, but Elian sang the words again and kept walking. One moment they were walking toward the rock, the next they went through, as though passing under a cold waterfall. His foot caught on a root looping up from the trunk of a pale green tree. Elian fell forward, but Krispen caught him and pulled him back to his feet.

"Where are we?" Krispen asked, looking around uneasily.

"The Woods of Terryn." Elian's voice shook and his hand went to his sword. At the piercing cry of a bird overhead, Elian brandished his weapon and moved to hide as much of Krispen as possible. "Gwythaints! Cover your ears, and follow me."

Krispen pushed his fingers into his ears and they started forward, keeping their eyes open for a path. Elian plugged one of his ears to block out the birdsong, but he didn't sheath his sword to block the other. The qwythaint's screams made his head ache within moments.

Neither spoke as they stumbled through the underbrush. Finally, they came to a path and Elian stopped to look at the sun. "Their sun rises in the West and sets in the East. The Palace is East, so we should take the path...this way," he yelled, pointing. Krispen nodded and followed Elian, still blocking his ears. Elian's headache pulsed stronger with each passing moment.

They emerged from the woods onto a sand dune towering over them ominously. Elian glanced back at Krispen. He reached up and tugged the man's arm down, unstopping one ear. "It's safe now. The climb will be brutal, but the Woods are the most treacherous part of this realm."

They started the long climb, their feet sinking into the sand with every step, making their progress slow and exhausting. Elian's legs burned as they crested the edge of the dune and looked down to take their bearings. A long formation of sand dunes stretched to the south and again to the north. Directly to the east Elian could see the Akkadian Sea, which Cassai had fallen so deeply in love with during her stay. "We go toward the sea. We'll be able to see the Queen's Castle from there."

"Yes sir." Krispen chewed his lip as he looked down at the long beach. "Are you sure we'll find it?"

"I think so. If not, the fey will find us. They know when someone enters. The aria Hollis taught me is a request that goes directly to the Queen. She decides whether or not to grant admittance to anyone who sings it."

Krispen eyes grew round. "If you say so."

Elian grinned and shrugged his pack from his shoulders. "If you're tired of walking, there's a better way down." He sat on the pack, grasping the handles as he would a toboggan in winter back home. "Just like a long snowy mountainside. Shall we?"

Krispen gave him an uneasy smile and took off his own satchel. "I guess so."

"Enjoy it while you can, my friend. I think it's the only bit of pleasure we'll be allowed for a long while." Elian pushed against the sand and gathered his feet onto his pack. The two slid down the dune and, despite the considerable danger they were surely headed to, Elian couldn't help but whoop as they gathered speed.

❧

"READY?" Hollis asked Cassai as she buckled the strap on her satchel. They were in the kitchen, packing the last bit of food and herbs into their bags. The others were waiting for them outside.

She sighed and threw the strap across her shoulder. "Ready as I'll ever be."

Hollis patted her back. "He'll be alright, Cassai. None know better than you how tough he is."

"Wouldn't it be nice, just for a change of pace, if he actually had time to *heal* between acts of heroism?" She pulled herself up and started for the door.

"That's rather rich coming from a girl with two not-yet-healed broken wrists, already setting out through Fondair...to start a war."

Cassai paused with her hand on the doorknob, looking at her carefully-wrapped wrist. "That's different," she said, though with no logical reason. She opened the door, and walked into the cold morning air.

The companions gathered near the gate. The Hermit bowed to Cassai as she joined them. Hollis come to stand behind her, but she didn't turn to look at him.

"And so, my children, you're heading on your way. I wish I could offer you further safety, but I can do very little to protect you once you leave this valley." The Hermit smiled sadly at the group.

"Thank you for your hospitality. It's been a truly wonderful week of rest," said Cassai.

"Yes, thank you so much," Sophie echoed. The men nodded.

"You ladies keep these fellows in line, won't you?" The Hermit directed at Cassai and Sophie. He reached out a hand and placed it gently on Theoris' forehead. "The mortal world is a hard one for someone like you. May you find peace, happiness and connection in this perilous, alien land." Theoris smiled blearily, clasped the Hermit's hand a moment, and then stepped aside. The Hermit turned to Sophie. "May your strength of body match your strength of spirit. May you win victory over your foes and joy in your journey to freedom."

Sophie stood on tiptoe and kissed his withered cheek. "Thank you, you dear, dear man. I wish we could stay with you forever."

He chuckled softly and touched the place she'd kissed. "I wish the same. But unfortunately this place is too sheltered for you to be content for long. To you, Hollis the Wanderer, I hope you find rest, peace and home at last."

Hollis bowed his head respectfully. "Thank you, Hermit."

He turned last to Cassai, and cradled her face in his withered hands, reminding her forcibly of Elian's goodbye. Her stomach twisted. "My Queen, the rightful ruler of this broken land, for you I wish safety and –" The Hermit's voice cracked, and he cleared his throat to cover it, "– justice. May the Weaver grant you justice for the loved ones lost to you without cause. A thousand shall fall at thy right hand, and ten thousand at thy left, but they will not touch you." Tears welled up in his gray eyes and he turned away. "Safe journey my friends," he muttered and walked into Haven House without another word.

COLLIN PACED OUTSIDE the private chambers of Lady Ella, his fists clenched so tightly his fingernails dug into his palms, leaving tiny crescent-shaped wounds. Jacque and Laurelle, who'd collected him that morning, sat in a domed windowsill, waiting for the interview time.

A man taller than even most Lightlings emerged from the doorway. "Are you Collin?" The boy nodded mutely, craning his neck to see the man's long face. "The Lady will see you now. You should speak only when spoken to. You should address The Senator as Lady Ella or My Lady. Sit on the red cushion and only take one sugar cube in your tea. Do you understand these instructions?" The man's lofty voice echoed off the frescoed walls, and Collin nodded again, feeling his tongue grow obtrusively large in his mouth, making speech impossible. "You will wait here," he ordered Jacque and Laurelle.

They nodded, also mute. Collin felt a little better that he wasn't the only one overwhelmed by this man's presence.

"Enter." The man stepped aside and Collin forced his feet to move. He took a deep, steadying breath and passed the arched doorway into the well-lit room. The handmaid Collin had seen the day before sat cross-legged on a cushion in the corner behind the doorway. She didn't make eye contact. The room opened expansively to his left, and he turned in that direction.

"Collin, please come in and be comfortable," the Lady called from an archway to his right. Guided by her voice, he entered a cozy alcove full of cushions. Lighted lamps hung from the ceiling, casting golden light on Lady Ella reclining comfortably against a pillow- lined wall. Murals covered every unoccupied inch of wall.

Collin hesitated at the archway, looking for the red cushion. Cluttered as the space was with purples, blues and greens, he couldn't find the one he sought.

"My Lady," he said, nodding respectfully, stalling.

"It doesn't matter where you sit," said the Lady sweetly. "Ignore Nathaniel. He's overzealous about regulations. Please be seated anywhere and let's discuss your plight."

Her welcoming tone put Collin more at ease. He finally spotted red and, weirdly the sight of it calmed him. He moved into the alcove and made for the red cushion directly opposite the senator. She waited for him to sit. He still hadn't mastered the relaxed way these people reclined. He missed regular chairs.

"Thank you for agreeing to meet me. I ... I just wanted to see if there was something that could be done to aid the Keepers in our village."

"They are the ones planning war against the Fontre?"

"Yes, ma'am, er — My Lady." Collin wasn't sure what to do with his hands, so he folded them in his lap like a child in school.

"There will be an enormous loss of life in such an undertaking.

I can't in good conscience send any of my people with you to war. I'm sorry. Our armies have long been dissolved and we've given our time to more academic pursuits."

"Surely you still have some men-at-arms? How do your cities stay safe?"

"We have security forces of sorts. Nothing like the force needed to breech the Inner Kingdom or challenge the Fontre. I'm not sure such a force exists."

"Well, anyway," Collin wiped his sweating palms on his pants as he rose to leave. "I'm sorry I've wasted your time."

"Not at all. You misunderstand me." The Lady held out a creamy white hand towards Collin's cushion. "I would like to help you, just not in the way you're asking."

"How can you help?"

"Enlightenment, Collin, is more powerful than any skill in swordplay. I am hoping to help you reach an understanding with your enemies. Understanding is the first step to resolving your conflicts."

Collin looked skeptically at her. "Resolving my conflicts?"

"Of course. I have someone I wish you to meet." Lady Ella reached behind her, grasped a thick silk cord and tugged it. Somewhere in her cavernous chamber a bell rang. Collin squinted through the alcove's opening.

A man stepped into the arched entrance, clothed in the linen tunic and brown pants of the Light Ones, but he was of average height and powerfully built. Softened as his features were, he was unmistakably Fontre. "Collin, this is Kirkus. He's lived peacefully in Halanah for three years now."

Kirkus smiled. Collin's back lanced with pain so severe he cried out. "Are you alright?" asked the Fontre.

Collin shrank away from the man. "I – yes. Um –"

"Oh, you poor boy! I'm sorry we've startled you. I'm hoping you and he can sit and discuss your differences. Kirkus has a son about your age. They are chefs in our kitchens. The things they can do with poultry are legendary." Lady Ella smiled and rose gracefully from her cushions, extending a hand to Collin.

Collin felt a rush of cold, then hot, in such quick succession that he started to shake. He held out a trembling brown hand and grasped Lady Ella's cool white one. She helped him to his feet, and he tried to make his legs solid enough to hold him up. He would not collapse before a Fontre if he could help it.

"Collin, could you do with a cup of tea? Just to talk. Nothing formal." Kirkus' voice, though low and gruff, also held something Collin wondered at coming from a Fontre. Feeling.

Collin clenched his hands again. "Did Jacque and Laurelle know about this?" he asked Lady Ella quietly.

"Oh, not at all, dear boy. They know Kirkus and his son, of course, but they know nothing of this meeting."

The man's dark eyes returned to Collin's and the boy straightened his aching back. "So? Tea?"

"Um...okay."

"Your friends can come, if you're afraid to meet alone." The Fontre's tone held no guile.

"I'm not afraid of you," he said, but his shaking voice betrayed him. Kirkus held out a hand that wasn't quite as smooth and clear of scars as his face.

"Then shall we?"

Collin's jaw stiffened. "Right."

ELIAN TOLD Krispen all he knew of the Fairy Realm as they walked along the seashore. His time had been so short on the last visit, he didn't have much to relate except what he'd read in books to Cassai and to Collin.

"The Woods of Terryn are dangerous. The creatures held there are dark and cruel as the skorpelak or molrats of Fondair, but the trees themselves are also deadly. They shift and speak to each other in their own way. They mislead travellers and can even force them into the dens of dangerous beings, or off cliffs."

"The gwythaints we heard crying —"

"Birds of prey."

"I thought birds of prey ate rodents."

"Most do, but gwythaints aren't exactly like hawks or owls. They're trained for battle. With unmatched tracking skills, they remember smells and sounds, and can spot a living being from more than a mile in the air. Their beaks are sharp enough to cut through armor. They can even pierce chain mail if they get a direct hit. Even their cry can be deadly." Elian rubbed the side of his head, which hadn't stopped pounding, although the gwythaints were miles away now.

Krispen shuddered. "Why would the fairies want such birds flying around their realm?"

"The fairies are an odd mixture of hoarders and thieves, sometimes even protectors. I don't know what makes an object or creature worthy of their ownership, but when they've decided something is theirs, you can employ no logical reasoning to dissuade them. The gwythaints have been under their protection and bound by their ownership for over a thousand years."

Krispen shrugged his bag up his shoulder. "Remember when Cassai tried to get you to take us to the sea?" he asked, eager to change the subject.

Elian grinned. "She tried to talk me into taking us to the sea at least a hundred times a year."

"Why didn't you?"

"Too many enemies in between. At least she got to see this one." Elian picked up his pace. The closer they drew to the Queen's palace, the larger the giant knot in his chest grew. "I don't know what they'll do to you, Krispen. It's me the Queen is most interested in, but because you're my companion, you're probably in danger."

"I knew that already." Krispen looked steadily forward,

betraying nothing. Elian wondered if he was really as fearless as he looked. "Why does the queen want you so badly?"

"I'm a strange phenomenon. Fontre aren't supposed to care about people."

"Why do you?"

"I don't know."

"Do you think the Queen knows?"

"Possibly."

"Will she tell you?"

Elian squinted into the distance. "Only if she thinks the knowledge will get her whatever she wants. She isn't famous for granting favors. The Queen's Palace is there."

Krispen stared in the direction of Elian's pointing finger. "Where?"

"There in the distance. Do you see the garden?"

"I see a garden."

"That's the entrance."

"How could anyone know that?" Krispen' eyes narrowed. Elian guessed he was trying to spot the difference between the Palace and its floral surroundings.

"Hollis showed it to me. That's the only reason I know." The knot had grown so large, Elian was finding breathing difficult. He rummaged through his sack for the food the Hermit had given them. He didn't know when they'd have a chance to eat again. He smiled at Krispen and handed him a roll filled with cheese. "Shall we get this over with?"

Krispen made eye contact for the first time. His soft brown eyes had filled with resolve. "Yes." He took the roll with a nod.

Elian's affection for his shepherd boy swelled. They walked to the Queen's Palace eating in silence.

Two fairy guards greeted them at the flowering archway by Elian recognized as men who'd fought the Fontre with them. He was secretly relieved to see no sign of Goliard.

"I am Elian of the Borderlands. The Queen is expecting me,"

he said. Neither guard made any sign of recognition. The one on the right nodded coldly and turned to allow them entrance to the courtyard. Elian and Krispen entered the giant grassy chamber followed by the guard.

"I'll announce you to The Queen. Wait here."

Elian nodded and the fairy left through the archway at the other end of the courtyard. The grass carpet at their feet muffled his footsteps, but Elian could hear him descend the stone stairway that he himself had gone down on their last visit.

"Elian!" cried a voice from another archway ahead. There was no mistaking the high girly tone and false cheerfulness of the Queen of the Fey. "How very good to see you again."

Elian forced the corners of his mouth upward. "You remember Krispen, I'm sure." The Queen gave Krispen a smile as sickly sweet as her greeting.

"How could I forget him? I didn't realize you were bringing him."

"He insisted."

Dahlia's eyes widened as she fluttered toward them, her hand outstretched. "Of course he did. How are you, Krispen?"

"I'm okay," Krispen said. At this moment, the guard who'd disappeared down the stairs came back into view.

The Queen ignored him and stopped in front of Elian, who bowed, and pressed his lips against Dahlia's hand. "Where did you come into the Realm?" she asked as Krispen bowed as well.

Elian straightened and suppressed the urge to roll his eyes. There was little chance the Queen didn't know exactly where they'd come into her kingdom. "The Wood."

She feigned surprise. "Really? What a terrible welcome for you."

"Better than the dungeons," Elian countered.

Her laugh tinkled and echoed through the courtyard, dying off somewhere between Elian's brain and his throbbing eardrums.

"Indeed. Though not much of an improvement. You have my stolen property?"

Elian shook his head. "I wasn't able to get the book from my brother. We took Cassai to safety, which was my primary concern."

The room darkened and the light turned reddish. "Interesting. I suppose you'll make that up to me in some way while you're here?"

Elian nodded.

"Very good then. We were promised your company for seven days, but I'm afraid I'll have to extend that a bit. Are you hungry? It's my tea time."

"I'm not hungry, thank you."

The Queen's face showed plainly her understanding. "I must insist you try our fare while you're here." Elian swallowed, but nodded. The Queen snapped her fingers and two fairy guards appeared at her side seemingly from thin air. "Please show the young man to his guest quarters and tell Goliard to see to him."

Elian's eyes cut to Krispen. "It's my fault he came," he said hastily.

"No matter. We'll take good care of him while you're here." Dahlia's sweet smile turned Elian's stomach.

Elian glared at the guard who grinned as he took Krispen by the arm. "This way to your guest quarters, sir," he sneered. Krispen' face remained stony.

"I told you I would come and do whatever you wanted as payment for your army. I didn't offer my shepherd boy to the mercies of your Captain," Elian growled at Dahlia.

"I don't remember anything in our agreement about you bringing him along. I'll let you see him tonight if that makes you feel better. Shall we?" She offered Elian her arm. He took it and walked reluctantly to the stairwell, throwing a glance over his shoulder for a last look at Krispen before he disappeared.

"We'll start down here and take it slowly."

"Fine," agreed Elian, too distracted with concern for Krispen for the words to make an impression.

They walked into the Queen's now familiar bedchamber. His eyes were drawn to a glass dome sitting on a table by her bed. A tiny light flickered from within.

"Do you like my pet?" she asked.

"The light? Is it living?" he asked, peering more closely at the glass without walking closer to the bed.

"A dandelion fairy. I trapped her in the mortal world long ago. She's been my companion now for decades."

Elian's stomach churned. "I see."

There was a tea tray laid out on a small table between her two overstuffed couches.

"Tea?"

"If I have no choice."

"You don't." She smiled at him coyly and began to pour. "Sugar?"

"No, thank you."

"You don't take your tea with sugar? So, a few Fontre traits clung to you. In what other ways are you like them I wonder?" She pushed a dainty cup and saucer into his hand. "What sort of cake would you like?"

Elian breathed a sigh. The tea smelled like flowers. "Do you have any with honey in them?"

She smiled brightly and chose a golden brown cake with a thin layer of lavender icing. "One of my favorites."

He waited politely while she served her own tea and cake. When she tipped the teacup to her lips, he did the same. The tea tasted like a spring day and the cake melted in his mouth. He closed his eyes and tried to enjoy them.

"Good?" she asked quietly.

"Yes."

"We'll talk a little then. As long as you like. I don't want your stay here to be unpleasant, but I can certainly arrange it, if you're uncooperative." Elian nodded understanding, but when he said nothing, she huffed out a breath and continued. "So answer my question. In what other ways are you like your race?"

"I don't forget anything." He replied. "And I'm a strong fighter." He took another sip of tea.

"And?"

Elian looked at her, measuring his words carefully, knowing she had the power to extract from him whatever she wanted to know. "I was trained by Devilan," he said finally. "I can put up with a lot."

"A lot of pain?"

"A lot of everything: pain, hunger, sleeplessness. I can go longer than most without breaking under pressure. Of course, I break eventually."

"What is it that makes you break?"

"I assume we'll find out soon enough."

"Perhaps not." The Queen took a dainty nibble of her cake and put it back on the plate. "It doesn't have to be that way between us, you know. There are other options." Her gaze flitted to the bed.

Elian's jaw stiffened. "That isn't one of them."

The Queen's chin rose. "You said you would be cooperative."

"You said you wanted to be with a true Fontre. You know very well I don't fit that description."

"I would settle for you," she smirked, but he looked down at his tea and didn't respond. She sipped from her own cup and set it down with a clatter that jangled his nerves. "The other way then."

"Sorry to be a disappointment. It's one of the few things I'm really good at," he smiled wryly.

Dahlia glared at him and stood up abruptly. She went to a cupboard tucked away in a dark corner. "Thank you for the gift from the last time you were here. I've been testing it on various creatures, but you were correct, of course, it just kills them slowly and painfully. You should see what it does to a fey."

Elian's brows furrowed. "What did you do?"

"We isolated the ingredients so we could produce more. There's one particular herb I still can't find, but Melkana grows a decent substitute. I think it will suffice." She started back toward him, holding a small brown bottle and a syringe filled with dark liquid. "You usually drink it, don't you?"

Elian's eyes went from the bottle to the woman holding it. "You're replicating the Fontre Draught? Why? It's only effective on the Fontre."

"And here I just happen to have a Fontre before me. Besides, effective might mean something different to the two of us. To you, it means healing someone quickly, the tortures they relive being an unfortunate side effect. Interesting of course, but not necessarily the only reason for its use."

She sat opposite him and slid the teacup from his hand. He surrendered it willingly and, when she reached for his arm, he surrendered that as well.

"I should have guessed. You don't care if they live," he said.

She rolled his sleeve up to his elbow. He felt a momentary sting as the needle pierced his skin, and she twisted it around, seeking a vein. He didn't turn away or move a muscle as the needle found its mark and she pushed down on the plunger. The solution burned his arm as she injected it. He set his jaw against the pain.

The fairy's eyes twinkled. "Why should I care if they live?"

"ARE YOU HUNGRY?" asked Kirkus cheerfully as he walked Collin into the long galley kitchen of the Elythium. Huge copper pots and pans hung on hooks on the walls, and stood in stacks on top of gleaming counters. Everything was painted buttery yellow. Collin had a hard time picturing a Fontre cooking in such a bright, cheerful place.

"No, sir," Collin replied.

"No need for the sir. I'm only a chef." Kirkus grinned and headed to a large kettle sitting on an iron stovetop. "Coffee, tea or wine?"

"Tea, if that's an option."

Kirkus nodded and opened a door beneath the stove to add another log. He took hold of a built-in bellows and compressed it twice. Collin heard the fire roar to life. "That'll set the kettle boiling in a few moments. Milk and sugar?"

"Yes."

"You're back! I've got ducks marinating for dinner in the cold-room." Called a voice from around the corner at the opposite end.

"Good lad. Come here a moment, Sacha. I want you to meet someone."

A young Fontre rounded the corner and started toward his father. Collin forced himself to keep breathing. He had no doubt that either of these men was capable of killing him and then getting on with their day. "This is Collin. He's a Borderling." Kirkus started to wipe his hands on his linen breeches, but Sacha threw an apron at him.

"Da! Those are new. What if the soot doesn't come out?" The boy demanded. Kirkus shook his head and dutifully wiped his hands on the apron. The boy, who was taller and more slender than his father, turned to face Collin. He had the chiselled look of all Fontre. Black curls stuck out under the white bandana he'd tied around his head, but his dark face was aglow with a genuine smile and his eyes were shockingly blue. "Borderling, right? Good to meet you." He held out his hand and Collin gripped it.

"Collin," he said.

"Yeah, Marc told me you were about. I was hoping to at least get a glimpse of you. How'd you meet Da?"

Collin's head reeled. The cleverness of the Fontre was legendary, and Kirkus himself was possibly in on the ruse, but it was hard to imagine this smiling boy killing anyone or anything.

Also, he was sure "Da" was a term of affection for Sacha's father. He smiled uneasily. "Lady Ella introduced us to, er – enlighten me."

"Oh, right. The senate hearing. Marc told me about that too. Sounds like you've had a rough go of it, yeah?"

Collin swallowed. "Yeah."

The kettle whistled and both boys jumped. "I got that, Da," said Sacha, grabbing a thick towel to remove the kettle from the heat. "Making tea?" he guessed grabbing a teapot.

"Collin takes his with milk and sugar." Kirkus clapped Collin on the shoulder genially and started toward the end of the galley. "I'll get the ducks on the spit if you two want to get to know each other."

Sacha spent a few moments brewing the tea and Collin watched him closely. This day wasn't turning out as he'd expected. What would Uncle Julius say when he related this new development?

"How much sugar?" Sacha broke into his thoughts.

Collin's mouth watered as he found his caution slipping away. "Two scoops."

"My kind of man," said Sacha, spooning two generous heaps into one large mug, then the same into another. "Let's take it out of here. We can sit at a table like civilized people if you like."

"Sure," Collin agreed. *Civilized people.* He shook his head. His back gave another twinge as he followed Sacha to their table.

13

THE FIRST TO FALL

Cassai stopped dead in the middle of the trail. Hollis called a halt and backed up. "Cassai?"

"She just...injected him with something. It burns like mad." Cassai rubbed her arm. Hollis frowned.

"Okay." He put an arm around her shoulders.

"What would she inject him with? Do you think it's something poisonous?"

"How do you feel? If you don't feel poisoned, he probably isn't either."

"I don't know. At least, I can't really tell right now."

"If you could try not to think about it too much, it'll be more bearable."

"Right. That'll be easy. I'll just think of sunshine and roses."

Hollis looked away from her. "I'm so sorry, Cassai. If anyone could come away from this at least almost intact, it would be Elian."

She took a deep breath. "I'm starting to understand how he felt when I volunteered to go with Devilan. Feeling but not knowing specifics is making me crazy."

"Yes. It drove him close to insanity, especially when Devilan, or one of them, slapped you in the face. I thought he was going to break someone in half."

"That was Devilan."

"Yes, we figured it was."

Cassai adjusted her satchel and stood up straight. "I'm ready. Let's keep moving."

Hollis nodded, gave her shoulders a final squeeze and started down the trail. His squeeze reminded her of something she could do to communicate with Elian. She pinched the back of her hand, just hard enough to feel it, and then followed the companions down the trail. She had taken two steps when she felt the pressure on the same hand. She managed a small smile.

SACHA WAITED for Collin to sit before placing the mug of tea before him. He sat opposite and, for the first time, he looked uneasy. "You probably hate me already, don't you?" he blurted.

"Why would I hate you? I just met you five minutes ago, and you put extra sugar in my tea." Collin took a sip in a vain attempt to hide his discomfort. His mug trembled as he set it down.

"Marc told me what happened to you. Well, some of it. Some, he said, was none of his business to talk about. But I know enough to know I'm Fontre; of course you hate me."

Collin looked at the boy and his eyes wandered to the door that led outside. Even if he sprinted, he doubted he'd reach it before this boy outran and overpowered him. He took a deep breath and tried to stop his hands shaking. "I don't hate you for what they did. The … particular skill set of your people makes me nervous to sit alone with you."

Sacha nodded. His eyes were so sharply blue Collin felt they were stabbing him. "You think we're infiltrating the Light Ones. Like the Fontre did in the Inner Kingdom."

Collin's eyebrows rose at Sacha's bluntly honest speech. "Yes. The thought crossed my mind."

Sacha's eyebrows drew together. He sighed and his fingers drummed his mug. "I figured. You don't have to worry about me. I'm not a killer. I'm actually a lousy fighter. That's why Da volunteered to come here; getting me out so they wouldn't notice. There's no place in the Fontre ranks for someone who'd rather cook. They don't even care about good food; think it's a waste of time and energy." Sacha shook his head, befuddled, and took a slurp of his sweet tea.

Collin smiled at him. It was dangerously easy to like this boy. "Do you usually hang out with Elle and Marc and everyone?"

"I do when I'm not working. I'm paid to be here, so I prioritize. I haven't been coming around while you were here. They told me you're trying to start a fight with the Fontre in the Inner Kingdom. Figured making friends with Da and me probably wasn't on your wish list."

"Sorry. Trust me, they're not like you. I guess you already know that."

"It's okay. I know what they are. I know they did horrible things to you and your village."

Collin ran his fingernail over a chip in the wooden table. "So, what's it like living here?"

Sacha smiled. "It's brilliant! They love food, and sports, and theater...all things the Fontre think are useless. Do you play any sports?"

Collin laughed. "I used to run through town while local boys chased me and tried to shove my head into foul things no sane person would want their head in. Does that count?" Sacha laughed with him.

"Well, it's one way to get exercise I suppose."

"I herded sheep though, with a friend. His sheep, not mine, but I enjoyed that."

"Sheep? Nice. I love animals. Chickens are my favorite, but sheep are good. Any goats there? Ever milk a goat?"

Collin shook his head. "We used to have some, but they were taken for taxes. I never milked them."

Sacha stood up and drained his mug. "Come with me. You, Collin of the Borderlands, are going to milk a goat."

Collin smiled and for the second time, willingly followed the strange Fontre boy out of the room.

DAHLIA WATCHED Elian's reaction with hungry eyes. Through the fog settling in his brain, he wondered if injecting the Draught directly into his veins would have permanent side effects. He fervently hoped not. Before long the wave of nausea hit him.

The Queen stood in front of him, a hand outstretched. "Come, lie down. I'll make you as comfortable as I can." He looked up at her, wondering for a second if the liquid in the vial was something else; something that would force him to comply with her other desires. However, it took less than a minute for him to recognize the all-too-familiar symptoms of the Draught.

He accepted her hand without a word, standing to his feet. She led him into the next room, where a fire blazed cheerfully. A large bed in the center was shaped like a lily. "This was my sister's room before she decided she wanted separate quarters. Cassai stayed here." Her voice trailed off in a longing way that would have made Elian sick even without the Draught.

Elian fought against the nausea long enough to see thousands of twinkling fairy lights in the ceiling and the furniture fashioned from living, flowering vines. He felt a pinch on the back of his right hand. His heart leaped in his chest. How could Cassai have known he was thinking of her at just that moment, and longing for her? He let go of Dahlia's hand long enough to pinch his own hand. She looked at him, mystified for a moment.

"What was that about?"

"Nothing."

Her eyes narrowed, but finally she sniffed and took his hand again. She led him to the bed, and he sank into it moments before memory engulfed him.

He was seven. They hadn't reached the Inner Kingdom yet, and were training in a giant clearing Devilan called the Training Fields. Elian was wearing nothing but an undergarment and his shield, which he held in front of his body as still as possible.

The Field was dotted with boys, some his age, some older. All of them had been ordered to remain still and to hold their shields off the ground as long as possible. Their trainers circled, trying to make them flinch.

There were many things that could make a boy move when they were supposed to be still. Devilan had tried them all on him regularly, but Elian's older brother was in no mood for feinting attack, or smacking his shield. Devilan held a riding whip and, as he circled Elian, he cracked the whip across his shoulders, back or ribs, but Elian ignored him. He could put pain off at least another hour or so and Devilan knew it.

Elian also knew that whoever was first to fall would receive lashes from his trainer and be at the mercy of the ten strongest boys after the day's training. There were no rules about what the boys could do to the loser and, since the raid on the Kiatri, they'd been in particularly brutal mood, all feeding off the frenzy of blood drunk by their swords. The boy who fell first the previous week was killed in the following beating by his peers.

Elian had participated in that beating because he'd been the last left standing, but he'd only dealt the number of blows necessary to do his duty. Some older boys were not so lenient.

Elian watched the field, wondering who would crack this time. Devilan dealt him a blow that cut the back of his calf. It was hard to ignore the pain, but not hard to control his reaction.

He squinted into the sunlight and saw one of the boys, Paxton, shift his shield slightly. He wondered if Paxton was already tiring. He was big. Paxton stood a good chance tonight, if he should fall now.

Someone caught Elian's eye and broke his concentration. A large Fontre, unmistakable because of a vivid scar down his cheek, Lord Ffastian, was crossing the field toward him. The pains from each welt began to burn and Elian tried to shift his focus.

Ffastian stopped a few yards away and beckoned Devilan, who left Elian for a few moments and spoke to his father in a low voice. Elian wondered what they were saying, which was as good a distraction as any against the pain. It looked like Devilan was agreeing, but unhappy. He strode back to Elian, his forehead deeply creased.

The whip cracked across Elian's right arm this time. "Fall, Elian," he said quietly.

Elian's heart jumped into his throat. "What? I can outlast any of these boys."

"Father wishes you to be first to fall today."

Elian took a deep breath. "Why?"

"Because he feels you will grow stronger in failure than in constant success. Just fall and get it over." Elian could tell by his tone that Devilan didn't want to be overheard, didn't want the field of boys to know Elian was being ordered to show weakness.

"No."

The whip cracked again, across a welt created earlier. Elian gasped at the searing pain. "Tell me no again, and it's the last thing you'll do," Devilan growled.

Elian looked at Ffastian standing in the distance, waiting for him to obey. He set his jaw and lowered to one knee, holding his heavy shield a few inches off the ground. It wasn't a fall, but it was failure.

The field master, an ominous Fontre named Kirkus walked over. "Elian?" he said, surprised.

"He is first down," Devilan stated.

"Right. First to fall: Elian," Kirkus shouted out. A few of the older boys swiveled their heads in disbelief, each earning a strike from their trainer. Kirkus marched back to his post.

"What if they kill me tonight? Am I supposed to lie down and take that as well?" asked the little boy, trying to control his anger.

"No. Fight with all your strength tonight," Devilan answered in a whisper, making Elian think he didn't want Ffastian to hear him. "If you can't fight them off, use this to signal me. I'll not allow them to kill you." Elian felt a small smooth rock slipped into his free hand. He clenched it so Ffastian wouldn't see. "Stand, Elian!" Devilan roared for the benefit of the field. Elian stood.

Ffastian approached him. The boys all straightened their backs. It was highly unusual for Ffastian to approach any boy at a routine exercise. "Why did you not do as you were instructed?" Ffastian demanded.

"I yielded, sir, just as Devilan ordered." Even if Elian had seen Ffastian's fist swinging toward him, he wouldn't have ducked. The fist struck his right cheek so hard he went sprawling. His heavy shield wrenched his arm and sent spikes of pain through his elbow and shoulder.

Ffastian knelt beside him and lowered his mouth to Elian's ear. "I told you to fall, not kneel, holding your shield aloft as if you're some bloody god. Your defiance will cost you dearly."

Elian lay still and forced himself not to respond. When Ffastian stood, he pulled Elian up with him. "Give me your whip, Devilan." Devilan handed his step-father the riding crop. "Steady your shield and hold on to it." Elian didn't need to be told this procedure. He'd seen enough boys punished on this field, and others, to know exactly what to do. He propped the shield in the grass and held the top. "Don't you have a better whip than this?" Ffastian demanded.

"I do, sir, back in our tent."

"Never mind, this will do; it'll just take longer. In fact, that's perfect."

Ffastian brought the whip down on Elian's back and legs over and over again while the other boys stood still, pretending not to watch. Elian concentrated on the ground, the green blades of grass sticking to his shield and the tiny furrow of dirt he'd pushed up when he planted it. When the welts began to cross each other, creating fine cuts through his skin, the boy could no longer ignore the pain. He pressed his forehead against his shield to keep standing and curled his toes into the dirt, but he didn't cry out. Ffastian finally stopped and made him lie on top of his shield, where he stayed until the last boy had left the field. Only then was he allowed to pull himself painfully to his feet and go back to his tent to await his fate.

It was dark and the last ten boys had been rewarded for their strength with a hearty meal of venison stew and bread. Elian sat in his tent, elbows on his knees, waiting for them.

"Can you believe it? Last to fall all those times and then first today? I wonder what's thrown him off his game." A boy was talking about him outside the tent amidst loud shuffling of feet.

"I don't think he had a choice. Did you see Lord Devilan whispering to him?"

Elian double-checked his pocket for Devilan's stone.

"Get up, brainless. We get you tonight." A boy named Mattius strutted into the tent while the other nine waited outside.

Elian didn't move. He stared at the boy as if inspecting a particularly interesting insect.

"I said, get up," the boy growled, approaching Elian's cot.

"I don't care what you said. I don't take orders from you," answered the smaller boy coldly.

Mattius crossed the tent in three long strides, stopping an inch from Elian's face. "You do now," he growled. Elian punched him in the face as hard as he could.

Mattius jerked away in surprise. He dabbed his hand on his lip and saw blood. "Oh, like that, is it?" he advanced again and Elian swung his leg out, hooking Mattius behind the knee and knocking him off his feet. The boy fell hard to the ground.

"Come at me again, Mattius."

"I'll break that leg if you do that again."

"Not from down there, you won't."

Mattius sprang to his feet and Elian launched from his cot, ramming his head into the boy's abdomen, bringing his shoulder up into his ribs. He felt one of them crack and Mattius cried out. He retreated, clutching his side. "Get in here! I can't get him to come out."

The other boys began to fill the tent. Mattius hunched in one corner, holding his side. "Get him," he groaned. The boys tried to encircle Elian.

"You must come with us, Elian. You were first to fall. It's the rules," Curt tried to reason with him.

"Make me come. Just try it." Elian stood in the middle, feet apart, ready to take them all on if he had to.

"We can't fight you in your tent. If we smash something, Lord Devilan will kill us," said a boy named Racalf.

Elian laughed. "He definitely will. So you should think about your next move."

"This is hardly fair. You're supposed to come if you fall," said Curt again, trying to find a way to approach Elian.

"Are you saying you ten can't remove one boy from his tent, and the first to fall at that?" Elian asked.

Curt looked at Mattius. "Fine. We'll carry you out."

"Try it!" screamed Elian, clenching both fists, but not raising them.

"What's going on?" Devilan came through the flap. The boys snapped to attention.

"L-lord Devilan. I – we were trying to take Elian for his punishment, but we can't get him to come with us."

Devilan looked at his little brother and something flickered into his eyes that Elian thought was pride. "Then take him by force," he suggested. "But if you carry on fighting here, I will relieve you of your will to live."

"We've been trying, sir," Mattius said. "He won't let us near him."

Devilan laughed. "Do none of you trained warriors know the meaning of the word, force? Elian, show them what I mean. Force Curt to kneel."

Curt had no time to react before Elian had knocked him to his knees and stood over him, one hand wrenching his head back, and the other fist cocked and aimed at Curt's face. "Shall I force his nose to bleed, sir?"

"That'll do for demonstration purposes." Devilan crossed the tent to his own cot and unbuckled his belt. "Boys, whatever your plans are, I suggest you get on with them. I've had a long day. I'm full of venison and I don't feel like listening to childish squabbles."

Elian released Curt and stepped back. His blue eyes snapped with rage, daring one of them to be the first to approach.

"What is this?" Ffastian's voice invaded Elian's senses like a kick from a horse.

Devilan jumped to his feet and every boy stood at attention again.

"Sir," began Devilan, but Ffastian was glaring at Elian.

"You tell me," he demanded.

Elian clenched his teeth. "They were trying to take me, sir. Devilan said I could fight back."

"Did you fight back?"

"Yes, sir."

"Good. You may take him now, gentlemen. I swear he won't struggle. Will you, Elian?"

Elian swallowed hard and looked at the ground. "No, sir."

"Because you learn more from losing than from winning, and you are eager to learn aren't you?"

"Yes, sir."

Mattius limped up to Elian and gripped his arm. "Thank you, Lord Ffastian." Mattius said quietly, propelling Elian toward the door. The others followed, all looking at the floor. Elian glanced over his shoulder and saw Ffastian stop Curt before he left.

"Deliver him to me when you've finished. Don't break anything vital."

"Yes, my lord," Curt muttered.

The boys took Elian into the woods; to the same clearing they'd taken their last victim.

"Remember this spot, Elian?" sneered Mattius.

"I remember you kicking Eustace to death right there. Very brave of you, nine boys to back you up while you killed the youngest and smallest."

"You gave him a pretty good beating yourself."

"I used a belt and caution. You apes tore him apart for sport."

"Sport is what the first to fall is for," yelled Curt, two inches from Elian's face. "And speaking of that —" Curt threw his fist into Elian's stomach, doubling him over.

"Get on the ground, Elian," said Antone. Elian straightened up.

"No."

"Lord Ffastian told you not to fight us." Curt warned him.

Elian laughed. "You're counting on that, aren't you? If I do fight, you'll barely get a punch in, even if you keep me here all night. I'll do what he says, because I fear him, not you. I won't fight. But if you want me on the ground, you'll have to put me there."

Elian blocked out the pain for as long as possible, but the day had been long and it was hard to ignore it for more than a few minutes. The boys tried to maximize the pain, but minimize the damage. There was some advantage to being Lord Ffastian's son: no one dared disobey and break something that wouldn't mend.

At first, Elian distracted himself by counting the belt strokes, then two or three boys started on him at once, and he wasn't able to count accurately. His back was so deeply inflamed from Ffastian's first whipping, he struggled to stay still and let them continue.

"Let off on the belts," said Curt. "He's starting to bleed."

"So? They always bleed. It's allowed," said Mattius.

"Lord Ffastian said no permanent damage, and I'd rather not find out exactly what qualifies. So the next to draw blood, delivers him to Lord Ffastian in person, and they can answer for it. Turn him on his back." Elian felt hands under his shoulders, pulling him up and letting him fall. He felt the dirt and sticks against his broken skin, and pressed his lips together tightly.

"Elian, do you need someone to hold you down?" asked Curt. Elian glared. "Good. Gather round, boys. We can smack him for a good long while with our palms and practically light him on fire without doing any long-term harm."

About half an hour later, when the boys were tired out, Racalf and Curt dragged Elian to his step-father's tent, one on each side, propping him up. They dropped him at the tent flap and left without a word. Elian fell through the flap onto the tent floor, curled into a tight ball.

He heard Ffastian moving toward him. The man spoke softly, but it was hard to make out because Elian's ears were ringing. He felt Ffastian's hands around him and tried not to cry out as he touched his raw skin, but his body betrayed him and an involuntary gasp escaped his lips. His step-father lifted him much more gently than he expected, and carried him to Ffastian's cot. He stayed still, hoping he wouldn't be punished for the sound he'd made.

Ffastian raised Elian's bloodstained shirt to inspect the boy's wounds and Elian heard him swear. Thinking the anger was directed at him, the *little boy shrank away, but didn't dare ask for mercy. He closed his eyes tight and wrapped his arms over his head, waiting for the blows to start again, or the bite of a whip, but none came. Instead something cooling dripped on his shredded skin.*

"I told them not to take it so far," Ffastian muttered. "Elian, can you hear me?"

"Yes, sir," whispered the boy.

"Turn onto your stomach so I can dress the wounds. Did you struggle?"

Elian moved as slowly as he dared, trying to control the pain so he wouldn't make more noise. "No, sir."

Ffastian shifted him. "Then why did they do so much damage?"

Elian swallowed the tears searing the back of his throat. "They were angry that I wouldn't go with them until you told me to."

"Well, they certainly got their revenge," said Ffastian, dripping more of the cooling liquid into the sores, but not touching Elian's back with the cloth. Elian couldn't believe the relief it gave him, or that any relief was being given. "Lift yourself enough to swallow this."

The little boy felt a bottle pressed against his lips and rose on his elbow so he could swallow. Instant fogginess fell over him: a blissful, sleepy sort of fog. He lowered himself carefully down again, closed his eyes and fell into deep, painless sleep.

ELIAN CAME TO, lying in the fairy bed. He could tell from the pain in his back that the Draught had done what the Queen hoped: the memory lived out before her eyes. She looked delighted.

"It really is fascinating to watch. You go through so many changes, but none of it makes sense until your body reacts to the blows. How long can you take a beating like that before you cry out?"

Elian glared and tried not to make sudden movements. Lying

against the sheets was painful enough to make him shudder. "A long while," he muttered. "Do you have any water?"

"I do, let me get some." The Queen fluttered up from the chair she'd dragged to the bedside.

Elian felt nausea hit him again, and he cringed when he realized he would be in another memory before she returned with the glass.

14

THE NIGHTMARE

E lian awoke the morning after being first to fall, not wanting to move a muscle. At some point he'd have to get up; have to leave his step-father's tent. When that happened, it would be under his own steam. He wouldn't show the other daanai how deeply they'd hurt him. He wondered how long he could keep his eyes closed and pretend to still be under the effects of the drops from last night.

He heard Ffastian moving around the tent, putting on his armor. A lighter set of footprints skittered past the cot where Elian lay. Elian assumed Gabriel, his father's servant, was helping Ffastian dress.

"Is he up yet?" Devilan's voice.

"No, still sleeping, or feigning it," replied Ffastian.

"I'll rouse him." Elian heard Devilan's footsteps coming toward him.

"Let him be. He can rest here today."

Elian's stomach felt ill at this offer. He didn't want to spend the day lying on this cot. He opened his eyes and stirred.

"There's no need for you to give the boy your cot, Father. I'll take him to our tent. No doubt nursing him will soon grow wearisome. Elian, are you awake?"

"Yes sir," Elian muttered as he tried to sit up. He realized his error instantly. Pain cut through him and he froze, his eyes watering at the intensity.

"Don't move quickly, boy. You'll tear your stripes open," Ffastian admonished. "Thank you, Gabriel. That's all I require at the moment." Gabriel nodded and left the tent, practically at a sprint. Elian had no doubt the boy headed straight for the others to give word on his condition.

"I want to get up. I want to train today."

"You won't do any training today, Elian," Devilan said quietly.

"I have to. If I don't —"

"They'll know they got you down?" Devilan's voice was filled with unusual understanding. "Well, move around in here a bit and you can come to breakfast with me. Keeping a couple of eggs down may be as much training as your body is up to for today. We'll start with that anyway."

"The boy stays here," Ffastian repeated. "He does not train today. I have medicine here to mend the stripes quickly. He'll be back in the fields tomorrow or the next day."

Elian looked at Devilan. He knew Devilan wouldn't disobey a direct order, but he wished fervently for his brother to argue the point. "You'll paint a target on his back if he isn't seen soon."

"A target which can be removed in one fight. They couldn't even take him from your tent last night. He hardly stands to lose much ground in their sight or in training."

"Of course, Father. I'll bring him some breakfast."

"I'll see to his breakfast. You go see to the other daanai. I want them sword fighting in triplets today." Elian clenched his fists. He loved sword-fighting in triplets

Devilan nodded. "Elian, lie down." Ffastian, satisfied with his argument, turned back to his trunk. Devilan got as near as he could to Elian's ear and breathed, "Do you still have the stone?"

Elian nodded, slipping his hand into his pocket. Devilan put a hand on his arm to stop him, glancing at Ffastian to see if he was still occupied with the contents of his trunk.

"Keep it hidden, but tap it three times if you need me. I'll get here as *quickly as I can." His whisper was so quiet Elian was sure he didn't hear him properly. But he nodded and Devilan vacated the tent.*

"Here it is," said Ffastian, holding up a bottle. "It stings, but its healing properties are well above average." Elian lay still as Ffastian approached him. "Let's just take this filthy shirt off, shall we?" He removed the shirt and lowered Elian onto the cot. His heart raced and his skin burned wherever Ffastian touched him. Elian thought this had less to do with his injuries and more to do with his hatred of the man.

The medicine did sting, but Elian barely noticed. He wondered if Devilan would come back with breakfast in spite of what Ffastian said. He wasn't hungry, but he'd eat anyway, just to keep his step-father away for a while.

"You're a strange boy indeed. Most boys are thrilled to have a day off training. Especially after the day you had yesterday."

"I like to train. I don't like lying in bed, and I don't want the boys to think me a weakling."

"As I said, a reputation so easily put off, it hardly seems worth worrying over. You're an extraordinary warrior for any age, but certainly as a recently qualified daanai." The rag Ffastian had been using to mop his back had stopped, and Elian thought his heart stopped with it. Ffastian's hand stroked the boy's cheek and Elian jumped as if it were a whip stroke. "Did that hurt?" asked Ffastian, inspecting Elian's face for cuts.

"No, sir. It surprised me."

"Ah, you didn't think me capable of gentleness, did you? I, who ordered you to fall yesterday and then beat you for it. I will never forget how you looked kneeling there, holding up your shield to prove you hadn't fallen from lack of strength." The man's voice had gone smooth. Elian's stomach churned and he tried to slip his hand into his pocket without being noticed. "What are you reaching for?"

"Nothing sir...there's a lump in my pocket. It hurts to lie on." Ffastian's hand went into Elian's pocket and withdrew the stone.

"Ah, I've found the culprit." Elian's mouth went dry. He reached his hand out, but his step-father cast the stone to a corner of the tent. "Nothing to worry over. Probably worked its way into your pants last night when the boys had you in the woods."

Elian licked his cracked lips. "Yes, it must have."

Ffastian smiled and rested his hand on Elian's head. "These blond curls are such a mystery. They do make you beautiful though," he said. "I don't mind telling you, my boy, that I hate the start we've had. I know you resent me for ordering Heyman to die with honor, but I had to uphold the laws of our people. That wasn't my decision. It was made long before my time. It's one of the reasons I took you and Devilan when the choice arose."

Elian wondered if Ffastian believed this speech would somehow endear him. He wished the man would move his hand. He fiddled idly with one of Elian's curls and Elian had to bite the inside of his cheek to stop himself from screaming. A deep, ill-feeling washed over him at Ffastian's touch, and he decided he'd much rather be beaten than treated gently by this man.

"I've brought porridge, Elian. Thought it might be easier to keep down," Devilan announced loudly, startling both father and son. The sound of his brother's voice filled Elian with relief.

Ffastian glowered. "Ask leave before entering my private tent, boy," he growled. Devilan looked fearful; the first time Elian had seen him afraid.

"I beg your pardon, my lord. I told the boy I'd bring his breakfast. I wasn't thinking when I burst in."

Ffastian's chest rose and fell in several deep breaths and Elian waited and wondered what he would do. Such a move could get another man in this camp killed. But Devilan wasn't just any man.

"Take him back to your tent, Devilan." His voice was low and harsh. Elian needed no further prompting to push himself up and go to Devilan's side. The stabs of pain and nausea following these movements made his legs shake, but he didn't care.

Devilan put a hand on the boy's shoulder, nodded once to his father and ducked them both from the tent, propelling Elian along fast.

～

ELIAN WAS eight and they were in the Inner Kingdom. He was lying on his cot in the tiny room he and Devilan shared off the stables. Gabriel stood at the doorway, hugging himself against the chilly night air. Gabriel was still

Ffastian's personal servant, although to the Lashain's, he was presented as a stable boy.

"What is it?" Devilan growled. "It's two o'clock in the morning."

"Your father wishes Elian to come to him."

Elian rose from the warmth of his blanket. "What could he want with me in the middle of the night?" he grumbled and started to pull on his boots.

"No." Devilan's insistence startled him. "I'll go. Go back to sleep. I'll send Gabriel for you if I can't...if I'm not sufficient." Elian's eyes narrowed. Something in his brother's tone tripled the younger boy's heart rate.

"Do you know what he wants?"

"I think so. Go to sleep."

Devilan left the room with Gabriel and Elian lay in his cot, his blue eyes staring out the window into the inky black sky. It took a long time before he heard the soft scraping of the door being pushed open. Elian glanced at his brother's dark form limping back to his cot. "What happened? Did he hurt you?"

"Nothing. It was just — something went wrong with a horse. He has to correct things in darkness, so the Namarielle don't see, you know." Devilan's whisper was hoarse and his breathing too hard.

"Did I mess up the horses? Why would he punish you for that?"

"It was nothing. Just go to sleep, or are you anxious to taste the whip yourself? It's been too long perhaps?" Devilan snapped.

Elian turned his face to the wall and said no more.

The scene changed and Elian stood before his father, his expression stoic. Ffastian sat on his rough-hewn bed. He wore the plain clothes of a palace equestrian, which Elian knew he was less comfortable in than his usual Fontre armor. The red scar across his left cheek stood out in contrast to his dark skin.

"I called for you last night and Devilan came instead. Said he couldn't rouse you."

"Yes, Father." The word "Father" still made Elian's tongue stick to the roof of his mouth. He swallowed again. "Whatever I messed up with the horses, I deserved the punishment, not Devilan."

"Messed up the horses?"

"Yes. Devilan said something was amiss, or left out. I'll take the punishment now and, if you tell me what was wrong, I promise I won't make the same mistake again." He was twisting his fingers nervously as he spoke. Ffastian smiled at his unease.

"You never make the same mistake twice. It is something I admire deeply about you," Ffastian said. He stood and started to circle Elian. He ran his fingers lightly over the boy's shoulders and across his chest as he spoke. Elian felt the familiar sick feeling in the pit of his stomach. "You've always been my favorite, you know, even before you were mine. So swift in a fight; so resourceful. Always one step ahead of the rest. That, combined with your hair and eyes, it was almost impossible not to become... obsessed with you. Devilan is brilliant and brutal, useful in so many ways; but you, I will make you a king, or Genraal Majure, or anything you wish to be. Anything."

Ffastian stopped, a hand on each of Elian's shoulders. He knelt to look the boy straight in the eyes. Elian smelled something odd on his breath; a smell he'd only experienced once when a Lashaian stable boy sneaked a bottle of wine into his room and tried to talk Elian into drinking some. He'd politely refused. He was shocked to smell it now. He'd never seen a Fontre drink anything but water.

He forced himself to stand still; not to react to the man's words or closeness. His hands started shaking. He could feel Ffastian's breath in his hair.

"I punish you now for not coming when you were called. When I call for you next time, I don't expect Devilan to answer."

"Yes, sir."

"Remove your shirt."

"Yes, sir." Elian didn't fear the whipping he was about to get nearly as much as he feared the covetous gleam that had flashed into Ffastian's eyes.

DAHLIA WATCHED EXCITEDLY as the memory held Elian in its grip. He had turned his back to her and muttered under his breath, but she couldn't make out the words. When he flinched, she jumped to her feet and came closer. He jerked repeatedly, and she realized that, in his memory, he was being whipped. She gingerly lifted his shirt. Long angry welts were already criss-crossed on his inflamed back and she wondered how long the whipping had gone on before he reacted. He jerked again, and another welt joined the others. This one cut his skin. He stiffened and more cuts followed.

He thrashed in the bed, so she stepped back, unsure if he would attack her in the throes of the nightmare. He lay on his side facing her, his face contorted in pain, and something else she couldn't understand. For the first time in over two hundred years she felt her curiosity was indecent. She shouldn't be watching this moment, yet she couldn't look away. The thrill in her chest rose to fever-pitch, and her head felt hot and light. It had worked. Her reproduction of the Fontre Draught was a success at last. If he didn't die at the end, her triumph would be complete.

Elian arched his back and cried out. She went to him automatically, putting a cool hand on his arm. "Elian?" she whispered. He didn't return to the present. His chest heaved and tears streamed down his cheeks. This startled her. So he was telling the truth. He couldn't be a true Fontre; no Fontre ever cried.

Her mind went back years to a dingy room at the Elythium. A small girl with dark, braided hair.

"THIS IS A BAD IDEA, *Erik. You know she shouldn't be here. What race are you exploiting now?" A much younger version of Hollis protested. Dahlia was sitting on the bed, smiling, enjoying the scene. Hollis was always trying unsuccessfully to rein in his best friend. Dahlia wondered why he bothered.*

"She volunteered," said Erik coldly, pulling a clear green serum into a large syringe. "Hold her."

"I'm not going to hold a child still while you inject her with that thing."

"She's Fontre," Erik said quietly.

"I don't care."

"Then you don't know the Fontre. This serum is to find out if it's possible to counteract the poisons they give their offspring."

"Why would the Fontre poison their offspring?"

"To train them as soldiers from infancy."

"Rubbish! The Fontre are intellectuals and doctors. Elihed told me they're some of the most intelligent people in Dukai."

"Elihed doesn't know what they really are. Ivy," Erik addressed the girl with the braids. "Tell Hollis the truth." Ivy shook her head. "Tell him the truth, or I'll beat you."

"What?" Hollis yelped. The little girl's small shoulders rose and fell.

"So?" The mechanical nature of the girl's retort intrigued Dahlia.

Erik knelt in front of the girl, trying to look stern. Dahlia could tell he was bluffing. She wondered if the girl could too. "I'll beat you hard, Ivy. You must tell him the truth."

"I don't care if you beat me. I am Fontre. I do not feel pain. I am Fontre, I do not feel fear —"

Elian's eyes flew open and he sprawled onto his back, gulping air. His chest heaved and his entire body was soaked with sweat and blood.

Dahlia stood over him, attempting to catch a glimpse of his eyes. "Are you back?"

"Water," Elian pleaded through cracked, bleeding lips.

"I'll bring some." Dahlia walked to the table by the fireplace and snatched the glass she'd poured before the second memory took him. She muttered a hasty enchantment over it. The outside of the glass frosted and the water inside chilled. She walked back to Elian and offered the glass.

He pushed himself up slowly, his limbs shaking. "Thank you," he managed before raising the frosted glass to his mouth. His eyes slid shut as the cool water filled his mouth. She watched his Adams apple rise and fall with every swallow.

Her sapphire eyes glowed with desire. Elian lowered the glass and regarded her, his eyes bloodshot. His bottom lip was swollen and bleeding. A dark bruise bloomed below his left cheekbone. "Tell me what just happened."

"Too much to tell ... mostly Ffastian." He said, lifting the glass again.

"Your father did this to you?" she asked.

"Not my true father, but yes. Sort of. And boys from the Fontre encampment."

"Please elaborate, and feel free to add as many details as possible." Her smile was so eager, fire flashed into Elian's eyes and she thought he might refuse. That was fine. She had strategies for that too. "I'll give you something in return. Something you desperately want."

Elian breathed slowly again. "You don't have anything that I desperately want."

"I think I do. I know why you are what you are. I know the secret of the anomaly."

Elian glared at her. She wanted him to ask her how she knew this. She trembled she wanted to be asked so badly, but he didn't. "I'll inject your Krispen with the Fontre Draught and force you to watch him suffer and die."

Elian's eyes turned dark and deadly, but he didn't lash out, as she secretly hoped he would. He took another drink of water. His voice still rasped when he began to speak. "There were more memories, but the worst of it was the last. We were already in the Inner Kingdom, but Ffastian was still pretending the Fontre were peaceful. Any training or punishment was carried out at night, so the Namarielle wouldn't see. This particular desire was something he didn't even want the Fontre to see.

"He'd always wanted Devilan and me. I'm relatively sure it's the real reason our blood father died − to get him out of the way. I was Ffastian's favorite, so he tortured me more than Devilan, trying to gain my respect. Devilan's devotion to him was obvious, until that one night he called me to his chamber, but Devilan wouldn't let me go. He went instead. He thought he was sparing me, but Ffastian wouldn't allow the substitution for long. The next night —" Elian focused on the glass in his hand. "He got what he'd always wanted."

Dahlia's eyes widened in shock. "You?"

"Yes." The simple word, forced through his teeth, seemed to cost Elian all his remaining strength. He sagged against the bed frame and closed his eyes. He'd sat in the same position so long she thought he went to sleep. He finally pushed himself up and set his glass on the bedside table, fully aware of his surroundings. "Where's Krispen, may I go to him?"

"I'll take you to him in a moment. Don't you want the information I offered?"

Elian tried to stand. The effort was so painful he was forced to sit down again and summon more strength. The second attempt was successful and Dahlia was again overwhelmed by how tall and broad he was. "I don't really care why I'm what I am. But thank you for offering. All I want at the moment is Krispen."

The Queen took a deep breath and swallowed her disappointment. But after all, they had fourteen days together. That was plenty of time for her to feed his curiosity. She would make him care about it one way or another.

She reached for his hand. A look crossed his face that delighted her in spite of his lack of curiosity. He glared at her hand like she was torturing him, and he was beautiful when he was tortured. She smiled as his large rough hand slid into hers and she led him slowly from the room and up the stairs.

Dahlia didn't release him as they made their way out of the throne room and into the courtyard.

"Is Goliard at the stables?" she asked her guards at the gate. Finnis took in Elian's injured face before responding.

"He is, Your Majesty." He threw Elian a look of pity, and the Queen made a note to have Goliard punish him thoroughly for it. How dare he show sympathy to a mortal?

"Good." She sniffed and passed through the gate to a

grandiose, beautifully built stable. As they walked through the open doors they saw a group of fey guards surrounding someone kneeling in the hay, enjoying the show.

One of them called out: "Fire, Goliard. Do the fire one."

Another countered: "No, the knives are worse."

"Is that Krispen?" Elian demanded. Before she could answer, the Fontre released her hand and pushed his way through the crowd of gauze-clad soldiers. She followed.

Goliard towered over the shepherd boy, his face split in a grin, enjoying his audience. Krispen knelt with both arms over his face, as if that would protect him from Goliard's torment.

"Stop!" Elian roared.

Goliard looked up in surprise, and the break in concentration released Krispen from his grip. Goliard laughed at Elian's dishevelled appearance. "Abuse, or passion?" he sneered.

Elian advanced on the Captain of the Guard, and the Queen's heart pounded in surprise when he punched the fairy in the face.

Goliard flew back against a beam, smacking the back of his head. He sank to the ground, his face a picture of shock and agony. Elian went to the fallen fairy and wrenched him up by his shirt front. Goliard's feet hovered over the ground and he grimaced in fear when Elian pulled him against his own face. "Hurt him again, and I will end your miserable life."

"Enough, Elian," said Dahlia reluctantly. Elian turned his burning glare to the Queen. It took all her self-control not to fling herself on him. He was even more beautiful when he was furious.

Elian lowered Goliard slowly to the ground. "Krispen," he said hoarsely. "Are you alright?"

Krispen straightened up painfully. "Yes."

"Where are our quarters?" Elian demanded.

"The room off the stables, around the corner." Dahlia pointed toward the back of the stalls.

"Fine," he said, crossed to Krispen, wrapped an arm around the boy's shoulders and helped him toward the room.

Goliard watched them go, his eyes burning with hatred. When his face came into full view, Dahlia saw his nose was crooked and bleeding and he sported two spectacular black eyes. She smiled. "Is this the second time he's gotten the better of you?"

He pinched his nose to try to stop the bleeding. "Get me a towel," he barked at a guard. "How many days is he here?" he asked the Queen.

"A fortnight." She waved her hand at the eastern sky where the sun was sinking low beneath the mountains. "Not to worry, my dear Captain, you will have your turn with him. But, fair warning, I will not handicap him beforehand. If you want a fight with him, you'll be on your own."

"Good," he muttered. "I don't want him any other way."

～

HOLLIS LED the companions south through the Forest. He made little attempt to control the noise they were making since the effort seemed pointless. There were so many of them and no discernible paths through this part of Fondair.

"We could take one of Krispen's excellent tunnels, eh, Hollis?" Theoris said, leaning on his crutch and wiping his brow with an already wet handkerchief. "It would be a great deal easier, and think of the time we'd save."

"We can't do that, because we will no doubt encounter Edge-water and his remaining pack along the way. Also, once we got down there, I would have no sense of which direction we were heading. We need to head southwest, and the only way I can tell is if I'm above ground." Hollis didn't want to admit it, but the very idea of travelling in a dark, enclosed space terrified him. He felt suffocated underground.

"Just a suggestion."

"Just a bad suggestion," Hollis amended and increased the pace. Theoris tripped over an exposed root and uttered a fey curse word. "Really, watch your language around the ladies, Theoris." In the moment he turned his head to chide the fairy, Hollis' own shin collided with a thorny bramble that seemed to appear out of nowhere. Thorns ripped through Hollis' pant leg and dug into his shin. He swore so loudly, Sophie grinned and mockingly reached to cover her ears. Hollis ripped his leg free of the offending bush.

"Thank you for being sensitive to our femininity, Hollis," Cassai laughed. "Let me see that."

Hollis burned red and took more careful steps. "Leave it. There's a better path in a mile or so. Until then, everyone watch your step."

The smile died on Cassai's lips and her eyes shifted out of focus for a moment.

"Cassai?" Theoris said timidly, touching the girl's arm. "I say, are you alright?"

Her face screwed up in pain and she released a quiet, choked sound that made Hollis rush to her side. "Is it Elian?" he whispered.

"Yes, but it's...different. I don't know why. It's like, his body is so sore he can barely move. I think he was whipped or something, but I never felt the whipping. I think he hurts constantly, but I'm getting it in spurts." She cried out again.

"Do you think it's his past?"

"If so, whatever's been done to him is so severe that I'm feeling the effects. That's never happened before," Cassai whimpered, hugging herself against the pain.

"What can we do for her?" Sophie asked.

"Nothing. There's nothing to be done but let it pass." Hollis' mouth was set in a grim line.

Cassai gave him a brave smile. "Hard not to think about it," she said.

"Yes." Hollis reached into his bag and pulled out a water skin. "Drink a little. Maybe it'll pass soon."

"But not for him," she observed sadly. She took a drink and

handed it back. "I don't think this is the sort of thing that just fades away. Let's keep moving."

She was right. All day long, Hollis watched her face change from determined to deeply pained and back to determined. He finally realized his constant vigilance was annoying her and tried to keep his attention on the path.

They travelled as many miles that afternoon as Hollis could push them through. He found a clearing he was familiar with and called a halt just as the sun began to sink into the thick treetops of Fondair.

The companions gathered stones and firewood. Hollis built a ring with the stones, and Cassai begged to build the fire and try her hand at the flint and tinder strike. Hollis handed over both responsibilities and set a few traps on the outskirts of their camp, hoping to catch any unfriendly creatures who might get curious. At the very least, possibly a rabbit might stray into one and make a good breakfast.

15

THE CHEF

C ollin and Sacha were joined in the milking pen by Marcole and Jacque.

"Well, what do you think of this little surprise?" Jacque asked, rumpling Collin's curls affectionately.

"I think you're all jerks for not warning me ahead of time you knew a good Fontre," Collin mumbled, squeezing the goat's teat slightly harder than necessary.

"If we warned you, it wouldn't be a surprise." Marc grinned and kicked the stool Collin was perched on, knocking it, and Collin, to the floor.

"Hey, don't! You'll spook Ginger." Sacha protested, rushing to help Collin. Collin wiped his pants and rubbed his backside.

"Right, poor Ginger. Your turn," he told Sacha. "My hands hurt. I never realized milking was so hard." Collin pretended to be bending over to pick something up, but instead, he head-butted the unsuspecting Marcole in the stomach.

Marcole caught Collin's head in the crook of his arm and the two wrestled each other to the ground.

"Oy! Get out if you're going to act like that," shouted Sacha over the scuffling. The two boys surfaced, red-faced and laughing.

"Do you have to work all day, Sacha? We're taking Collin on a tour of the city." Jacque leaned his elbow on the penned goat and gave Sacha a pathetic look.

The goat pulled away and kicked at the boards of the pen in protest. "I can get off quicker if you'd stop spooking my goats," Sacha snapped, patting the offended animal and crooning softly into her ear.

"Right. Getting out of the way now. We're taking Collin though. Sorry, mate." Jacque pulled Collin up by the arm and walked him toward the door. Collin twisted his arm away and punched Jacque in the side.

"We'll be at the square," Marc called over his shoulder.

"Yeah, fine. See you in a bit," Sacha said distractedly, sitting back on the milking stool. Collin stopped at the doorway and watched in fascination as the Fontre boy whispered to his goat and stroked her sides affectionately.

"I've never seen anything like his gentle nature," he muttered. "And I grew up with Elian."

"Who's Elian?" Jacque asked, steering Collin toward the street.

"The only other peaceful Fontre in Lashai. He was calm and kind, but not so gentle and cheerful."

Marc laughed. "Sacha's brilliant, for sure. We wanted to introduce you sooner, but we weren't sure how you'd take it."

"I don't know what my uncle will say about it."

"Kirkus is still kinda scary. I don't know what he did before, but Sacha says he's always been a good father. He's still got that look, though," said Jacque, running his fingers through his red hair.

Collin nodded. "Where's Elle?"

Jacque rested his elbow on the shorter boy's shoulder. "Waiting for us at Askelpos' Healing Lounge."

"Healing Lounge? What on earth is that?"

"We're going to see if they can do anything about the unhealed stripes on your back. They're magic with their concoctions,"

Jacque explained, turning down another stone-paved street. "And then, shopping!" He wiggled his eyebrows and Collin burst into laughter.

"Shopping? For what?"

"For everything. Elle said you don't like the sandals. I thought we'd find you some moccasins for starters."

"I didn't bring any money with me." Collin didn't add that he'd never had any money.

"Don't be daft. We're buying with my dad's credit, idiot." Jacque grinned at him.

Collin protested this futilely all the way to the Healing Lounge. Laurelle ran out to greet them with a kiss on the cheek, and Collin's mouth went so dry he couldn't have spoken if he wanted to.

"He said he thinks there's something that will help!" she bubbled, taking his hand lead him into a large open air room filled with cushions as all other rooms in Halanah seemed to be.

"Is this our patient?" a man asked, looking at Collin through large round spectacles.

"Our what?" Collin asked, looking at Laurelle.

"He means you're the one he needs to see," explained Laurelle.

Collin looked at the kindly, bespectacled gentlemen, dressed in a white draped gown, tied at the shoulder and belted at the waist with a brown strip of leather. The man had long silver hair interrupted by several thick red and purple strands. Upon closer inspection, Collin saw they were tiny braids wrapped in colorful silk thread. His silvery beard hung past his stomach.

"This is Collin. Show him your back." Marc said.

Collin looked around at the open market and all the people milling around. "I don't really want —"

"It's nothing, mate. Askelpos is a healer." Jacque added quickly, "Like your apothecary you were telling us about."

"You would prefer some privacy," the man said.

"Yes." Collin practically shouted with relief. He'd had no

privacy since his arrival in the North, and this strangely attired man recognizing the need made Collin like him instantly.

Askelpos smiled and gestured to a bed behind a tall screen. "Gentlemen and my dear girl, if you'd be so kind as to wait here." He led Collin behind the screen, leaving the others watching, speechless.

~

ELIAN SAT on a stool in the tiny room off the stables, impatient for Krispen to finish with him so he could lie down. In silence, Krispen mopped the blood oozing from the stripes on his back. Elian sucked in a breath as the soft rag touched a particularly raw spot.

"Sorry," Krispen whispered.

"It's alright, Krispen. I've had worse. You don't really have to fuss over the stripes, you know? They'll just be doubled tomorrow."

"So this was the Queen's intent after all? I hoped you were wrong."

Elian sighed. "There was no mistaking that look, I've seen it too often."

"What look?"

"The look of someone who hurts people just to watch them suffer."

Krispen shuddered and focused on his work. "These cuts are deep. She's stronger than she looks."

"She didn't make them, although I've no doubt she could if she'd wanted."

"Oh. I thought it was just the two of you."

Elian sat up and turned to his shepherd boy. "Do you remember that night in the woods when I woke up screaming? That trance I went into and I shook Cassai?"

"Yes. The bad dream."

"Right. Sort of. The medicine the Fontre used to make that happen was used on me again today."

"But I thought it was gone. Hollis told me at the Hermit's house that he'd broken it all to bits."

"Don't worry about that, just listen to me. It's poison to you, Krispen. I won't die from it, but you will. If she comes near you with it, if she tries to trap you or comes at you with a needle...just run. Leave me wherever I am and run."

The rag hadn't touched his back in a while. Elian turned to look at Krispen, who was staring at the bloody rag deep in thought. "I can't do that."

"You have to. Whatever they're doing to me, I'll survive it, but you will not survive the Draught. I'll never forgive myself if you lose your life trying to spare me. Promise."

The boy's voice hardened. "No."

Elian sighed and turned his back again. "When did you get so stubborn? It's going to get you killed."

"Would you leave me, if I was being tortured, to save your neck?" To Elian's surprise, Krispen sounded annoyed.

He grinned. "No."

"Right. So there's your answer. Your back is clean, but I've not much to wrap it. Cassai sent bandages, but not enough for your whole body."

Elian smiled. "It's alright. We'll let it air dry. Mostly, I just want to rest."

"Food?" Krispen asked, grabbing his bag.

"Maybe a little. Just a roll or something."

The boy produced two more of the cheese-filled rolls they had eaten on the way to the palace and two strips of jerky. The roll tasted different to Elian than earlier in the day and the jerky was inedible. He clenched his jaw and pushed it back into Krispen's hand. "Not as hungry as I thought."

Krispen's brow wrinkled. "Did you eat her food? I thought we weren't supposed to eat it."

"I'm going to bed," Elian said. "If you notice anything unusual in my behavior while I sleep, strike me hard as you can."

"Strike you?"

"It's the only thing to bring me out of it. Please."

Krispen nodded and wrapped the jerky. "You have my word."

～

CASSAI STARED into the dancing flames of the campfire, brushing through her hair absentmindedly. Devilan's stinging words about her lack of care for her appearance burned her even now.

"That's quite a scowl. Worrying about Elian?" She hadn't even heard Sophie approach; the girl had inherited her uncle's ability to move silently.

"No, something Devilan said to me." Cassai blushed as if she'd been caught doing something wrong.

"Devilan? Something about your hair? Because it looks like that section's about to give up and let loose soon." Sophie took Cassai's brush, and knelt behind her, easing it through her hair without the slightest reservation. "What did he say?"

"Nothing nice," Cassai replied, grinning.

"I assumed that much. It was Devilan."

Cassai took a deep breath and tried to focus on a smouldering log and not the pain settling in her chest. "That I should care more about my appearance because of my lineage and...I don't know. It shouldn't have mattered what he said. But then he... brushed my hair and braided it."

The brush paused mid-stroke. "Oh my word. Did you tell Elian he did that?"

"Yes or partly. It's not like he was torturing me, he was just... b-brushing my hair." Cassai bit her lip and balled her fists. She wished she could punch something.

"Sounds like torture to me, but maybe we have different definitions," Sophie said, finishing the brushing and coming to sit next to Cassai.

Cassai noticed she still wore the fingerless leather gloves she'd used on the battlefield.

"Did you make those?"

"The fairies gave them to me. They outfitted us all with armor and stuff. These are particularly fine for archery."

At the mention of fairies, Cassai wrapped her arms around her knees and felt her mind shutting down again.

"Elian was brilliant, you know? He was always going to do whatever it took to get you back. He, Theoris and Uncle Hollis landed in the dungeon. I landed in a field, but they took me for leverage. Elian never allowed it and forced them to let me go: let us out of that hole in the ground. He faced the Queen all alone. I didn't know the bargain they'd struck, but she saw we were given weapons and her armies were sent to free you. They didn't like Elian, but it was clear they respected him." Sophie's spoke into the dancing flames, but her words washed over Cassai like healing rain.

"Thank you."

"I know if anyone can take her on, it's him. He'll get out. He'll come back to you."

"What do you think she's doing to him?" Cassai's body wasn't hurting now, but she'd been in pain all day.

"Nothing that hasn't been done to him before. He's Fontre. He can take it."

"I just wish he didn't always have to," Cassai murmured.

"He doesn't. He didn't have to. He could have let you go and saved you some other way later. He loves you, Cassai. What did you expect him to do? It was no more or less than you did for him, and for all of us. Thank you for that, by the way. I haven't said that. I'm not scared often, honestly. I kind of like being in danger, but being taken by those thugs wasn't a danger I enjoyed. I don't know what they would've done if not for you."

Cassai smiled at her. "I didn't mind doing it. Not for a second."

Sophie nodded. "Neither does he."

"No, I guess he doesn't. He never liked the side-lines."

COLLIN RELATED the events of the day to his uncle that night. Julius kept his face expressionless until the boy was finished.

"We need to leave here now. Possibly tonight," he muttered at last.

"No, that's what I'm trying to tell you. They're safe. They're good people, Uncle. Especially Sacha. He's been friends with Laurelle and everyone for years."

"Collin, the Fontre are cunning. This is what they do. They lived in the Inner Kingdom for almost two years before anyone beside King Patrice and Queen Annabelle suspected anything."

"Right, I know that, and I'm not dismissing the possibility. I'm just saying...trust me. Sacha is different. Even his eyes are different. His father moved him here because he doesn't want to fight. He called his father Da. Have you ever heard of a Fontre using a term of endearment?"

"Just one."

"Yes. What about Elian? We trust Elian is good. Why can't we trust them?"

"Collin," Julius took his shoulders and met Collin's eye line. "Elian lived in our village for over a decade. He grew up there."

Collin pulled away from his uncle. "No he didn't. He was already grown up. He was raised by them and he's good. I want you to meet Sacha at least, before you decide we have to go."

"We have to go because it's time. We're supposed to be at the Westerling Field in less than a fortnight and, unfortunately, we've persuaded no one to come with us. Sounds more like they've been recruiting you." Julius' voice rose with each word of his final sentence and Collin backed away from him. He'd never seen his uncle so agitated.

"Okay. I just...I guess I've been taken in by him. I'm sorry."

Julius looked utterly deflated at this reaction. "Yes, of course I'll meet him. Don't...please don't look at me like that. I've failed you so many times in the few years you've been with me. It makes me more protective than I'd like to be."

Collin looked at Julius, looked at the solidness of him. He'd always thought of his uncle as the most stable thing in his life besides his own father. The one thing that didn't crumble. The one thing that didn't fail. "You've never failed me, uncle. You can't help the things that have happened to me, any more than you can help distrusting the Fontre."

"Is he working in the kitchens tonight?"

"No, he's just outside the door."

Julius sighed and his head drooped. "Perfect. Let's go meet another harmless Fontre."

Collin led the way from their guestroom and into the palatial hall. "Hey, Sacha," he greeted his friend who was leaning casually against the wall just outside their room, grinning.

"Hey, Collin. So this is your uncle?" Sacha had changed into the usual clothing of Lightling boys, short tunic and brown linen pants. He looked even younger and more harmless without the bandana hiding his curls.

"Julius." The man extended his hand and Sacha shook it cheerfully.

"I really like your nephew. Sorry about the ...Fontre thing."

"Right. Well, you never can tell about people just from their ancestry. Collin says I'm to give you the benefit of the doubt."

Sacha grinned at Collin. "Thanks, mate. If you're up for a walk, my Da would like to meet you too. He's cleaning up from supper, but he'll be done before we get there probably. His kitchen staff's really good."

Julius smiled graciously and gestured for Sacha to lead the way. "I'm definitely up for a walk."

The evening was cool and there was just enough breeze to ruffle their hair as they took the short walk to the Elythium. Collin's chest tightened at the thought of leaving this place. He'd felt more at home here than he ever had in Plahn. He couldn't bring himself to picture the faces of Jacque, or Marcole … he sighed as Laurelle's smile drifted unbidden before his mind's eye.

"We can go around back. There's a kitchen door," Sacha said as they approached the University grounds. They circled the building containing The Eatery and Sacha led them to a wooden door around the side. It was one of the only rectangular doors he'd seen in Halanah; most were arches. "Da! I'm here with Collin," Sacha called as they entered.

Two girls with dark brown skin and glossy black hair were wiping the large prep table in the middle of the room. They smiled at Sacha, showing the dimples in their cheeks. "He's out in the Eatery. I can fetch him if you like, sir," said one of the girls.

Sacha cocked his head to one side and raised an eyebrow at them. "What did we say about calling me sir?"

The girl's smile brightened and her companion giggled. "I forgot. I'll call your father, Sacha." She glanced at the giggler as she said his name and they clapped hands over their mouths as they hurried toward the Eatery.

Sacha looked embarrassed at the girls' reactions. "Sorry, we work together a lot. I don't like them to treat me like I'm their master. I guess it's just what they do with everyone, but … still."

Collin grinned and elbowed him in the ribs. "I think they're fine with you being their master."

"Shut up." Sacha flushed and pinned his gaze on the door as though willing his father to materialize.

Julius rolled his eyes and shook his head. His smile vanished and Collin saw him stiffen when Kirkus walked through the archway. Looking significantly less menacing in a large stained apron and with flour on his nose, he was still undoubtedly Fontre. He smiled, and Julius looked like he wanted to bolt. Collin put a hand on his uncle's arm and propelled him forward.

"Uncle Julius, this is Kirkus. He's a chef here."

Kirkus wiped his hands on his apron and thrust his right out. Hesitantly, Julius took a step toward him and accepted the handshake.

"You've met my boy I guess." Kirkus voice echoed off the shiny surfaces of the kitchen and Collin winced, wondering at his uncle's reaction.

Julius just nodded. "He's a good lad."

Collin looked sideways at Sacha, who grinned and mouthed the words, "you're such a good lad". Sacha rolled his eyes. Collin looked back at the two men.

"Collin says you aren't here on the usual errand of the Fontre." Julius cut right to the chase.

"Oh, it's usual enough I suppose. That is, we were sent for the usual. We aren't good at being Fontre, unfortunately."

"And how exactly does that come about? Two Fontre, father and son, willing to disobey orders and assimilate into the Northern culture rather than spy for their own people? Isn't that...well, treason?"

Collin watched Kirkus uneasily. It occurred to him again how much danger he and his uncle might be in at this moment. And they were here at his insistence.

"Aye, I suppose it is. But, there was this woman..." Kirkus' voice trailed off and he grinned at Julius as though they had some sort of mutual understanding. Collin looked at Sacha, relieved to see he also looked confused.

Julius' eyes slid shut and he shook his head. "Isn't there always a woman?" he muttered.

Kirkus nodded sheepishly. "Right you are. So, anyway, there was a woman in the temples who didn't do as she was told. No one knew until they'd slept with her. But she had a strange power over us. She had our babies, but didn't follow procedure."

Julius' eyes narrowed suspiciously. "From what I've heard, that's impossible. Pregnant Fontre women are guarded day and night, aren't they? Treated like precious commodities, but definitely prisoners."

"I don't know how she did it, but as far as I know she's the only one ever managed it. She had a couple boys before mine. You mighta' heard of one, he's the *Genraal Majure*."

It was Collin's turn to stiffen. Julius put a bracing hand on the boy's shoulder.

"Yes, we know who Devilan is."

"But her other boy wasn't the same as the first. He came out blond-haired and eyes like periwinkles. His brother gave him special training and he was a warrior to end all warriors. Stronger, faster and smarter than any kid I'd ever seen. Their father never let on they were blood brothers. I only know because of their mother. And she only knew because she'd cheated on the pills; she knew which ones did what. Managed to take only the ones she needed. Maybe she managed to make her guard fall for her; I wouldn't be surprised. She was quite a woman." Kirkus eyes softened and he shook his head at the memory.

Collin tried to sort out this information.

"Elian? He was the other boy, right?" Sacha asked, clearly excited for the story to continue. Collin wondered how much he'd never heard before. The part about Sacha's mother seemed to come as a surprise.

"Yes. Couldn't believe the boy died in the Midnight Revolution. Really, I didn't think he was capable of doing anything as ordinary as dying. He was legend. Anyway, as you can guess, I didn't know any of this until I lay with the girl myself. She had some way of changing a man, you know? Can't explain it."

"Love," said Julius. "I can explain it. She made you fall in love with her."

232

Kirkus shook his head again. "Maybe. I'd never felt anything like it. I'd never actually felt anything, you know? I didn't think we were capable of it. It was like that girl had hold of my brain and my body. She changed me completely and I can't say I didn't like it. When she figured out how I felt, she told me how to trick the lottery so I could end up with my own son. She said she'd gone from taking only a few pills to taking none. That my son could just be ordinary but, of course, I'd have to get him away. So... he was born." Kirkus nodded toward Sacha. "I did what she said to get him. Sure enough, the only thing Fontre about him were his high cheekbones and black hair. Those eyes. He caught the High King's attention with the blue eyes. He'd already lost Elian, and I think he was eager to replace him."

"I don't know no specifics about that man, and I don't want to. But his relationship with Elian was not right I didn't think. There was just rumors and stuff of course. But still. He wasn't getting my boy, for sure. Sacha never ranked high in fights or tracking, or...anything. He hated the plain food. That was one of his more distinguishing characteristics." Kirkus gave his son a smile of such deep affection that Sacha blushed and punched his arm. "So when they looked for volunteers to infiltrate the North Country, I made sure we were on the list. Most of the men went deeper into the North, but we stopped here in Halanah, where we could perhaps have a few years of peace."

"It won't last, though," observed Julius. "They'll come here eventually."

"Aye, true enough. So, now you see why I'm asking, what I'm about to ask."

Julius and Collin exchanged a look of surprise. "What are you asking?"

"Take me and my boy with you. There's no such thing as a peaceful place to live while the Fontre rule. If you're heading anywhere to stop them, I'm in."

"What?" Sacha gasped, staring at his father in disbelief.

"You want to come with us to fight against your own people?" Julius demanded. "How can I possibly convince my townsmen of that? Your son isn't as obvious, but you are certainly a trained Fontre. They won't let you in."

"Let me worry about that. We'll get in."

"And what happens if you aren't who you claim to be? Or you stab one of my friends or my nephew in the back? What do I tell my people then?" For the second time tonight, Julius' voice was rising.

"I'll do anything I can to keep my boy out of the hands of the Fontre. Anything. You and your militia are my best chance. Sacha may not fight, but he can make himself useful, and I'm what you say I am: a Fontre-trained warrior. You'll not have a better man fighting at your side. And to be honest with you, Julius. If I wanted to do you or your nephew harm, there'd be no need to stab you in the back. I could kill you here and now with my bare hands and there's naught you could do to stop me. I don't want to harm anyone anymore. You can see how she's ruined me for bein' Fontre?"

Collin was shocked when Julius turned to him. "Do you believe him?"

The boy looked from Kirkus to his uncle. "I don't know how he could invent such a story. We know at least part of it's true – Elian."

"How could you know Elian? He died long before you'd have seen him." Kirkus looked so surprised that Collin felt hope rising even in Julius.

"Elian escaped that night," Julius said quietly.

"No! You can't mean that." Kirkus' face lit up. "I knew no boy that extraordinary would just up and die during a silly thing like a revolution." He roared with laughter and clapped Sacha on the shoulder. "How'd he get out?"

Julius couldn't help but crack a smile at Kirkus' delight. "If you like that, you'll love what comes next. I think he might have even rescued a Namarielle."

Collin stared at his uncle in shock. "What? Who?"

Kirkus' eyes widened. "He did not. A Namarielle still lives?" He laughed again and smacked Julius on the arm. The man winced and Collin couldn't imagine how the blow must have hurt. "Ha-ha! So there's still a chance for us after all, eh? We can give the boy back his kingdom and send the Fontre back to Sheol where they came from."

"*Her* kingdom," Julius corrected him. "Elian saved a girl."

Kirkus nodded and his grin broadened. "Even better. You can't think how happy I'd be to beat those mongrels and hand Lashai over to a woman. Imagine the looks on their faces. Which one did he save? Cassai, wasn't it? Had to be. He was always with that little girl."

"Cassai?" Collin spluttered. "No she isn't. She grew up with us." Collin stared at Julius who was shaking his head.

"Think about it, Collin. Of course she's Namarielle. They all showed up together. Nanna, and Elian and Cassai. Just look at Kirkus. He'll tell you."

If Kirkus was only acting delighted, Collin thought he had to be the best actor he'd ever seen. The man's face was aglow. "Brilliant! Just bloody brilliant. We'll be ready to leave in the morning. Thanks for this. I can't tell you how thrilled I am to hear it."

Julius chuckled and patted the man's shoulder. "Yes, I think we're getting the idea."

16

THE KATEVO

Elian rose slowly the next morning. Krispen helped him pull a shirt over his wounded back and tried to talk him into eating something. Elian took it, just to make the boy happy. He nibbled the roll which tasted like the cheese had soured overnight, which hadn't happened.

He smiled at Krispen. "Stay in here today. If they come and take you out by force, go with them, but otherwise, stay out of sight."

Krispen nodded.

Elian opened the door and stepped into the stables. The fey steeds fascinated him. Two horses were almost ordinary, except for the spiraling horns sticking from their foreheads, and one had wings.

The other creatures varied considerably. Some sported the heads of birds and the bodies of giant cats, or the body of a man with eight wings, four on each side, and an eagle's tale. The one in the farthest stall from their bedroom lay curled up like a serpent, but had thick arms and legs and a body covered in green scales. It had tucked its shiny head under one arm. Elian saw smoke coming from its nostrils. He smiled in spite of himself, hating to admit how much he'd enjoy riding a dragon.

He passed the two guards at the gate and both glowered at him. He grinned and put two fingers to his forehead in mock salute. "'Morning," he said. Neither guard responded, but he heard one growl as he passed.

The reason for their malice was obvious the moment Elian stepped into the courtyard. Goliard stood with two more men. His nose was purple and swollen, and both his eyes had dark red and black smudges beneath them. Elian wiggled his fingers at the Captain of the Guard.

"I'm going to kill you, Fontre," Goliard shouted.

"I'm afraid you'll have to get in line. Your Queen may save you the trouble." And feeling considerably lighter, Elian left the court-yard and entered the throne room.

Dahlia stood on the dais in front of her golden throne, another fairy faced her. Elian recognized Lily and his mood spiraled down-ward. The sisters looked like they were in an intense argument, which silenced when they saw Elian.

"You're earlier than I expected," said Dahlia, smiling her sugary smile.

"I've always been an early riser; I blame it on being a shepherd. Sheep aren't notorious for sleeping in. Hello, Lily."

Lily gave him a smile as sad as her sister's was gleeful. "Good morning, Elian."

Elian took the younger fairy's hand and kissed it lightly. "You look beautiful today."

"Thank you."

"She always has that effect on men," Dahlia observed coolly.

Elian turned to her and bowed respectfully. "You look beautiful as well, Your Majesty. But I'm sure you don't need me to tell you that."

Dahlia continued to smile, but the room grew darker. "Are you toying with me?"

Elian shrugged. "It's my turn."

"You seem to be in a good mood," Dahlia observed.

"I ran into Goliard in the courtyard. He's looking well."

Dahlia's eyes twinkled. "He was quite upset with your outburst last night. He wants a rematch, which I told him he could have when I'm finished with you."

Elian grinned. "My pleasure." At the look on Lily's face his smile faltered. "Sorry, Lily. I always forget the two of you are together."

"Shall we go down?" Dahlia held out her arms, which sparkled with several diamond studded bangles. Elian nodded to Lily and accepted the Queen's hand graciously. "Did you sleep?" she asked as they descended the steps.

"Not well."

"Another memory?"

"Two more."

"As bad as yesterday's?" she asked conversationally.

Elian looked at her. They had reached her chamber which, although it was filled with light and luxury, was taking on the feeling of a stone dungeon to Elian. His light mood was evaporating. "They would have been, but Krispen managed to stop them from taking hold."

"Really? I didn't know you could stop them. How is that done?"

Elian rolled his eyes to the fairy-lit ceiling. "You have to hit me really hard. Sharp pain in the present pulls me out of the past."

"Interesting." Dahlia sounded genuine for the first time all day.

"Not information needed for your purposes though," he said.

"No. No I don't need that information at all. However, it's a pity I wasn't there to observe it."

"A great pity indeed."

"Breakfast? I had one of everything made up this morning. I want you to have lots of options." She gave him a glittery smile and led him to the table. It groaned under every breakfast food imaginable. His heart sank at the sight of it, but his stomach roared.

"Thank you, but I'm not hungry," he lied.

The Queen laughed. "Of course you are. In fact, I would be very surprised if the words, 'not hungry' ever applied to you again." She fluttered to the table and tossed a bright red strawberry into her mouth. "People are mistaken about fey food, you know. It doesn't bind you to our realm in the literal sense. It just makes you long for it...for eternity." She popped another berry in her mouth and perched on a chair to pour a cup of tea.

Elian swallowed hard and looked at the food. "Good to know the truth."

"Isn't it? What is that old saying from the Book of the Ancients? 'The truth will set you free.' Not really applicable in this case. Sugar?"

"Do you have any coffee?" he asked quietly.

The Queen smiled brightly. "I do. How do you take it?" She clasped a small glass canister in the center of the table, added a few scoops of grounds and poured hot water from a kettle over it. Elian's mouth watered at the aroma.

"Black."

"Of course." She placed a lid on top and pushed a plunger down. "When can we expect another memory to strike?"

"Sometime soon, I imagine. Although I don't know the exact effects of injecting it." Elian piled a plate with fluffy biscuits, bacon and eggs and three kinds of fruit. He figured he might as well enjoy the food while he could.

"Does the Draught heal you from the memories as well?"

"I doubt it. Its healing properties are for immediate, life-threatening injury. The injury it inflicts afterwards is a side-effect."

"While we wait, let's chat a little, shall we? Tell me about Cassai."

Though the food tasted like paradise, he felt a strong urge to spit it out. Telling this evil fairy about Cassai felt wrong. "What do you want to know?"

"When did you meet?" The Queen asked, handing him a steaming mug of coffee. "We'll start there."

Elian took a long drink before answering. "I met her in the Inner Kingdom. I guess it's sixteen years ago now. She was two-years-old at the time."

"You fell in love with a two-year-old?" asked Dahlia, her eyes gleaming in a way that made Elian's stomach churn.

"I was a child myself. I loved her, but only as children love each other and want to play and be near one another. Obviously I didn't love her as I do now." He was angry at himself for defending his feelings, knowing how much she enjoyed it.

"She came to the stables with her brother, Patrice. When she saw me, she ran to me with her arms outstretched, so I would pick her up. I had no experience with small children, especially not girls, so I didn't understand. Patrice explained that she liked me and wanted me to hold her. I did. The moment she was in my arms, she wrapped her own tiny arms around me and laid her head on my shoulder. I'd never been touched like that. Never been hugged or had someone trust me enough to lean against me. I was lost, forever. From that moment on, we were barely separated."

"How sweet. And then the Midnight Revolution. You got her out?"

"Yes. I knew the plans because Ffastian had given me a list of people I was to eliminate. The moment the slaughter began I ignored my list and ran to find Cassai. My brother was in her room, also looking for her. He was tasked with killing the family. I hid behind the door, ready to attack him if he pulled her out of hiding and tried to hurt her, but she wasn't there. He moved on. I knew he would find Patrice and the others. I didn't have time to save them. All I could do was find her. I got to Nanna's room, but they'd left there too. I checked corridors and halls I knew she

240

loved to play in. Then I remembered our secret passageway. I ran down it and found her and Nanna already cornered by Devilan. I tried to talk him out of hurting them at first, but he ignored me. We fought. I won. Then we ran." Elian paused to take another bite of biscuit.

"And you hid in the Borderlands. How did you manage to keep her a secret?"

"Many people fled the Inner Kingdom and filtered into the Borderlands after that night. We simply went in around the middle, where Devilan wouldn't think we'd be, and settled in. A man in the village helped me build a cottage. He only knew we'd escaped. He had no idea she was Namarielle, but she said something to him while we were building. Something about playing in the palace toy room. He thought she was a friend of one of the princesses. It scared me and I knew we had to do what I was dreading. We altered her memories so she couldn't tell anyone who she was. We wrote down everything we did because Nanna has a terrible short-term memory and, if something happened to me, we had to be able to reverse the spell when she was old enough to know the danger she was in."

"But you didn't reverse it, did you? She knew almost nothing of herself when she came here."

Elian sighed. "She knows now."

"Does she still love you, now she knows?"

"She does."

"But she hasn't forgiven you. I can tell from the tone in your voice. I wonder if she'll ever fully forgive you for that." The Queen looked triumphant and Elian looked away and took another bite.

He chewed slowly and started to reply, but a wave of nausea hit him. He cringed and buried his face in his hands, knowing what was coming. Dahlia watched eagerly. He knew she would be careful to do nothing that might bring him back before it had concluded.

WHEN ELIAN CAME BACK to the present, he was on the floor. He couldn't remember where he was. He heard a woman's voice, but couldn't untangle the fog of what had happened. His back was raw, and bleeding again. His mouth felt like parchment.

"Water," he murmured, hoping the woman might hear him. He heard someone very light moving toward him. "Cassai?"

"Dahlia," said the woman. Elian flinched as the present flooded back. Stronger hands than he expected helped him sit up. "Here's water." He took the cold glass and brought it to his lips. The water filled his mouth and cooled him to his core.

"Thank you," he whispered.

A tinkling laugh. "You're most welcome. Tell me about the memory. It looked different from yesterday."

Elian looked up, wishing he could reach up and break Dahlia's tiny neck. It would be easy as snapping a chicken bone. Instead, he drained his water glass and pushed himself up. Every inch of skin on his back protested, but he ground his teeth through the pain and stood.

"Let me take your glass. Would you like more?" She set the cup on the table which, he noticed, was cleared of breakfast. He wondered how long he'd been out.

"No. I just need to find..." His voice trailed off as dizziness overwhelmed him. He caught himself on a chair just in time. He tried to settle comfortably, but couldn't rest on a spot that didn't burn or stab when touched. He finally drew a deep breath and sank into the cushioned chair anyway. He shook all over, which annoyed him. Dahlia sat across from him.

"Are you alright?" she asked.

"Yes."

"Is there anything I can do to make you more comfortable?"

"You could leave me alone," he muttered. His lip was bleeding again, and he felt like one of his ribs was broken.

Dahlia took a dainty sip of something pink from a glass cup. "Anything besides that? Tell me what happened."

He rubbed his temples. "It was the same memory, but a different time, or maybe it was two or three different times. I fought him in the first memory, made him beat me until I couldn't fight any more." Elian pulled up one side of his shirt slowly, showing where a whip had wrapped around his ribs and cut repeatedly into his skin.

There were dark bruises not made by a whip. Dahlia's eyes widened.

"He let me heal before he sent for me again, so I figured I'd fight every time and at least have a break in between. I think the second memory came from a time after all the fighting."

"You stopped fighting him?"

He nodded. "It was odd, he'd waited so long before revealing his true nature, but once the door was opened, he couldn't control himself longer than a few days. I found out that, between calling for me, he was abusing Gabriel instead."

"Gabriel? Another brother?"

"His servant boy."

"A friend of yours?"

"Not really. But, a boy who didn't deserve to be hurt any more than I did. Anyway, whether he meant to or not, he'd found his way to make me more cooperative. What else do you want?" This last question came out in a growl.

Dahlia rested her chin on her fist and stared at him, mesmerized. "You're bleeding again. Would you like me to dress your wounds?"

"Actually, I'd rather be boiled in oil," Elian replied.

~

"COLLIN, COLLIN, WAKE UP." Collin woke to someone shaking him in his bed.

243

"Whattimeisit?" he mumbled. He tried to bring the intruder into focus, but all he could see was a halo of curls and blue eyes.

"It's the middle of the night. Don't wake your uncle."

"Sacha, what in the −?" Sacha pulled him to the edge of the bed and padded softly through his room, looking around for something that turned out to be his shoes.

"I said, be quiet. Don't wake him up. Oh, thank the Weaver, you have moccasins. If I had to figure out those sandals in the dark, I think I'd jump off a cliff." The soft shoes Jacque had purchased for Collin that afternoon were forced onto his feet. "Get up, they're waiting for us outside."

"I don't think −" Collin began, but Sacha's large hand clamped over his mouth. He pulled the smaller boy up and walked him to the door. Collin was coming to full consciousness and his heart started pounding. If Sacha meant to do him harm, what could he do to stop him? But surely that wasn't it. He couldn't have misread him so badly.

"Did you get him?" A hissed whisper came out of the darkness of the Welcome Hall.

"Yeah, but he's still half asleep. Are the others already there?"

"Marc's trying to nick more wine from the Elythium kitchen," said the other voice. Collin relaxed, recognizing the voice at last: Jacque.

"Don't do that. Da needs that wine for the sauce tomorrow night."

"You won't even *be* here tomorrow night," Jacque hissed.

"Right, but still... If I take my hand off, swear to be quiet?" Sacha whispered in Collin's ear. Collin nodded. The hand was removed and Collin pulled away from his abductors.

"What is going on?" he demanded in a voice that echoed off the ceiling. Both boys cringed.

"You said you'd be quiet!" Sacha protested, covering his mouth again and pulling him up against his chest. "Let's just get him there." Jacque led them out of the hall on tiptoe.

The boys forced Collin down the street and through a dark alleyway. Collin squirmed, trying to loosen Sacha's grip, but unfortunately it had the opposite effect. His grip tightened to the point Collin was practically carried down a set of basement stairs and through a warped wooden door.

"Surprise!" Laurelle called out cheerfully from the corner of a candlelit room. Her face fell. "What did you do to him?"

"It's his fault. He tried to wake everyone up." Sacha released his captive onto the cozy rug and went to shut the heavy door. "There. Yell all you want down here. We should be okay."

Collin stood in the middle of the room, trying to bring his situation into focus. Cushions in various states of shabbiness lined the room and stacked against the walls. Marc, Nihl and two girls Collin hadn't met, lounged on a pile of cushions next to a squat table covered with half melted candles, bits of food and three partially empty wine bottles.

Laurelle stood in front of him, eyes shining with excitement, and possibly too much wine. "It's a *katevo*," she said taking his arm and leading him to a large cushion on the other side of the table.

"I'm guessing *katevo* is the Lightling word for kidnapping?"

"What's kidnapping? Sounds fun. Does it have to do with baby goats?" She bubbled. Collin looked sideways at her and she laughed. "A *katevo* is a send-off. We do it when someone is of age and going to University."

"Or getting married," said Marc.

"Or heading to war," said Jacque cheerfully plopping down on his other side and ruffling his hair. "It's a friend thing."

Collin finally grinned. "Oh, okay. Because in my town, when a Fontre snatches you from your bed in the middle of the night, it usually means your friends and family will never see you alive again."

"So basically the same thing," Sacha said with a grin, snatching a bottle of wine from the table and taking a swig.

Collin rolled his eyes. "Right."

"This is Bria and Natty. They like Nihl and Marc for inexplicable reasons known only to them," Jacque pointed to the girls Collin hadn't met.

"Hi. Nice to meet you," Collin said shyly.

"Oh, my word!" one of the girls squealed with delight. "He's so adorable!"

Collin's eyes widened and he looked at Jacque. The taller boy shook his head and wagged a finger at the girl. "Company manners, remember Bria? We *just* talked about this."

"Are you packed and ready for tomorrow?" Laurelle asked. She'd snagged a plate and was filling it with cheeses and bread. "Do you like grapes? Have you even had them? They're like... berries? I don't know. They're really sweet and good and full of juice. I'll just get you some."

"Oh, is that plate for me? I like grapes, but I don't like the cheese with the blue stuff in it," Collin said. Sacha shouted in protest.

"That's gorgonzola, you savage! It's imported all the way from the Troikord!"

Collin shrugged. "I still don't like it."

"Give that here." Sacha snatched the plate from Laurelle and scooped the crumbled rejects onto his own plate. "You have no taste whatsoever." He shoved the plate back toward Collin. "You don't deserve this."

The younger boy rolled his eyes and took a bite of bread. "I'm all packed, Elle. Timothy got me set before I got back from dinner."

"Timothy?" Laurelle asked.

"My *malderone*."

The girl smiled and wrapped an arm around his shoulders. "I love you for learning his name."

Collin's heart pounded in his ears and he felt hot. Her closeness would have triggered the reaction alone, but the fact that the words "I love you" had just come from her lips made him dizzy. "I'm going to miss you," he said, wrapping his own arm around her waist.

"No you won't."

"Of course I will."

"She means, you won't have a chance to miss her," said Marc helpfully.

"What does that mean?"

"We're coming with you, mate," Jacque informed him. He picked an olive off Collin's plate and popped it in his mouth. Collin barely noticed.

"But you can't come. It's too dangerous."

Jacque punched his arm. "Ha! You think a little armrest like you is going to stop us? We're already packed. This is our party too. I didn't swipe the bread my mother made for breakfast in the morning just for you. You think a lot of yourself."

"How long have you been planning this? How can you just leave everything and come with me?"

Jacque settled back against the cushions and folded his hands over his chest. "I have to now. Mum'll kill me when she wakes up and finds her bread missing. I'll blame it on Nihl of course, but she'll never believe me."

Nihl shrugged. "I've always been her favorite. It's my winning personality." Natty snorted with laughter at this, and he grabbed her, tickling her until she collapsed in a fit of breathless giggles. Collin had never seen Nihl enjoying himself.

"What did your parents think about this?" Collin asked. Laurelle looked sideways at Marcole.

"They weren't thrilled about it, but they were alright."

"Both of you? Really?" he looked at Laurelle.

"Of course both of us. You think I can sit at home and wait for news?" she demanded.

He chewed his lip and shook his head. "No, I know you couldn't do that. But I just meant – "

"I know what you meant." She squeezed his hand. His stomach unknotted slightly when he saw she wasn't angry.

"I wish I could keep you safe from all this," he whispered.

"No one is safe with the Fontre in charge. Isn't that what you said?"

He nodded mutely and looked at Jacque. "What about your mum and dad? Are they upset at you?"

"Not sure. They probably would be if we'd told them."

Collin gaped at him. "Wait, you're kidding right? You are going to tell your parents you're leaving?"

Jacque shrugged. "It's complicated."

"It's not. You have to tell them. We're going to fight a war, Jacque. You may never see them again."

Nihl glared at him. "If we tell them, they'll never let us go."

"If you don't tell them, you'll never forgive yourselves. You know what the last thing was I said to my mum before she died in that fire?" Everyone had gone very sober. "I said I wished I was old enough to be on my own...and the next day, I was." Collin focused on his bread so he didn't have to make eye contact with them. "You should let them know you're going, that's all."

Laurelle had put a comforting hand on his arm, and Sacha pressed a wine bottle into his hand. "Sorry, Collin."

Jacque looked at his brother. "We'll tell them, mate. It's alright. We'll wake them in the morning before we leave."

"Good." Collin took a sip of wine and coughed. "Ugh! How can you drink that stuff?" he spluttered.

Sacha looked shocked and snatched back his bottle. Collin heard him whisper, "savage" under his breath.

Jacque just laughed. "It's an acquired taste."

"But why would you bother?" Collin muttered and took another bite of cheese, trying to chase the bitterness from his mouth.

"I don't know. People say it numbs the pain."

"The pain from what?" Collin asked, mystified that these strange children in the cushioned life of Halanah would seek such a refuge.

"Drinking too much," Jacque replied, grabbing the bottle from Sacha and taking a long swig.

17

THE GIFTS

Elian walked back to the stable that night, his body stiff with pain. The Draught had claimed him three more times, The Queen had again offered to treat his wounds, but he couldn't bear the thought of her touching him. He resolved to hold out as long as possible. If the Draught didn't let up soon, he would have to accept more help than a wet rag and herbs.

"Hello, Krispen," he said entering their tiny room.

Krispen's face screwed up at the sight of him. The boy sprang to his side and practically carried him to the bed in the corner. "Just lie down. I'll get the stuff."

"Thank you. Sorry to ask so much of you."

Krispen lowered him onto the soft mattress. "I want to help. I wish I could stay with you during the day."

"There would be nothing for you to do except watch it happen. That would be much harder on me than letting you dress my back afterwards."

Krispen lifted his bloodstained shirt as gently as possible. "How many times?"

"Five or six. They run together after a while."

"How many more horrible memories can there be?"

Elian chuckled bitterly. "A few." The cool rag touched his back, and the antiseptic burned like fire against his broken skin. He ground his teeth together and tried not to react and make Krispen' job more difficult. Eventually, the medicine took effect and he felt the angry welts begin to cool. "That actually feels almost bearable, Krispen. Would you mind doing the back of my legs as well?"

"Of course I will." Krispen helped him peel off the rest of his clothing and Elian lay on his stomach on the bed, buried his face in his arms, grateful beyond belief that he hadn't refused the boy's offer to come in the first place.

"Thank you, Krispen. For everything," he muttered.

Krispen was silent for a few moments while he worked. "I found something today to read to you. Maybe it'll help. Before we left the Hermit, Cassai loaned me her copy of The Book of the Ancients. She said to read you the Songs of the Shepherd if you needed comfort."

Elian smiled. "She's always done that for me. There's something healing in his words."

"I read different places today, but none that I liked so much as those songs. Can I read some to you?"

"Yes." Elian closed his eyes against the pain wracking his body and let the songs of the ancient shepherd wash over him.

Krispen read verse after verse. Elian felt a peaceful fog blanket his mind. He drifted into a dreamless sleep while his faithful shepherd boy read to him and kept vigil late into the night.

~

COLLIN WOKE EARLY the next morning. Despite the late night, his anxious thoughts wouldn't allow him to go back to sleep. Julius must have had the same problem, because Collin heard him get up shortly afterwards.

He finally surrendered and got up to finish packing. Even this was useless, because Timothy had packed his things neatly away the night before. Collin sat on his bed, staring at the sturdy leather bag Jacque had bought him the afternoon before. Julius worked his way through their room, checking and double-checking they weren't leaving anything behind. Collin shifted from one foot to the other impatiently.

"Haven't left anything then?" he asked finally on his uncle's third trip through the room.

"It seems we've got it all."

"Are you nervous about the trip, Uncle?" asked Collin, suspecting the delay had nothing to do with a stray sock or memento.

"Yes." Julius didn't hesitate a moment before admitting the truth. "I'm worried what our reception will be when we get to the others. We were trying to muster some sort of army, and we're arriving with a Fontre, his son and a few rebellious youths. Not exactly what Elian hoped for, or needed."

"I hope the others have had better luck," muttered Collin. "I'm sorry I couldn't persuade them. I shouldn't have volunteered for this. Surely Simeon or Altaskith could have done a better job recruiting."

"You did as well, or possibly better, than anyone could have with the Light Ones. You've made friends among them and warned them of the darkness coming. I fear that, until the fight is at their doorstep, they won't see the reality of the danger."

"What if Kirkus and Sacha are honestly fantastic actors? What if they're really lying and I'm leading them straight to our friends?"

Julius stood from looking under the bed and stared at Collin for a long moment. "Elian will know. He'll be able to tell if they mean us harm. They gain nothing from attacking us before we get to the Westerling Field, so let's hold a steady course until then, eh? If we notice anything suspicious we can always lead them off in the wrong direction or something."

"Deal." Collin grinned at Timothy. "Thank you for everything.

I wish we could get you out of here too. I suppose you could always hide in my luggage."

Timothy smiled his gleaming white smile. "Thank you, sir. It's been my pleasure. Let me get those for you. I'm to walk with you as far as the gate." He lifted Collin's bags easily, and Collin could see that, although his arms looked skinny, they were roped with muscles.

The three left the room and came into the main hall to see the rest of Collin's new friends gathered and ready to go. To Collin's surprise, each was armed to some degree.

Nihl and Jacque both carried leather breastplates with a scarlet lion worked into the front. Two Lightlings Collin hadn't met stood behind Laurelle and Marc. The man was older, darker and clearly a Kiatri from his average stature and agelessness. The woman, their mother, stood erect and tall as the Lightlings, beautiful, although her eyes were red and puffy.

Laurelle ran to Collin. In addition to the white linen dress she always wore, she wore a soft leather jacket lined with sheep's fleece and leather boots that came up to her knees. Around her waist was a belt with a short-bladed sword and a pouch of something that smelled of lavender. She threw her arms around him and kissed him on the cheek.

"Ready to go?" she asked, her voice sounding gravelly.

"I am. Are you alright with your parents?"

"Oh, fine. Just … harder than I thought." She carried a satchel designed to strap over her shoulders, loop under her arms and rest on her back. "What do you think? It's a backpack. Marc made it for me ages ago to carry books. Perfect for packing other things too."

"So, you all have a cache of weaponry at the ready?" Collin asked, fingering the ornately gilded sword.

"Most of them belonged to father and mother from the old times. They fought in the Dukain Wars."

"I didn't know. That's a beautiful sword."

"I've brought something for you too," said Laurelle turning to Marc, who, in addition to his own trappings and weapons, carried a sword wrought from a metal that looked almost white.

"It's called Dukain steel, supposed to be the strongest of all metals. Layered over a thousand times by their enchanted sword-smiths and hammered to perfection. My father's gift to you," Marcole explained, handing Collin the sword in a ceremonial way. It was lightweight and balanced in Collin's hands nicely. On one side of the handle an image of a mouse was beaten in gold, on the other side, a lion.

"I had a local man modify it a bit. Have Marc tell you the tale one day of the lion and the mouse, eh," said their father kindly.

Collin looked up in disbelief at the man who stood behind his daughter with tears in his eyes. "Why should you give me a gift? I'm the reason they're leaving."

"It's an honor to gift you my father's sword, Collin of the Borderlands. My children have shown more purpose and strength of character in this last week than they have all their lives. I pray they will be a help to you in your war. May Zeno watch over and guide you and bring you all back to us safely." Zeno was a Lightling Deity, but Collin couldn't remember which of the hundreds he was.

"Here, you're supposed to have it girded on you by a fair maiden," Laurelle smiled at him and held up a leather belt with a sheath on it. She wrapped the belt around his waist and fastened it. He smiled at her and, for the first time ever, sheathed his own sword. "Collin of the Borderlands, I hereby present thee with *Lionpontari*. May it serve you well in battle."

Collin touched her cheek and looked up to her father. "Thank you, sir. I can never thank you enough for this," Collin nodded toward the sword. "Thank you for letting them come with me. It's not too late for you."

At this, the man smiled and his boyish face wrinkled in all the right places. Collin thought he must spend a lot of his life smiling.

"War is a young man's game...or young woman's," he added, winking at Laurelle. She turned and hugged him and then hugged her mother too.

"Be safe, my dear ones. Come back to me," she whispered, wrapping both her children in a fierce embrace.

"Love you, Mama," Marc said.

"We'll bring you back something from the Inner Kingdom," said Laurelle as if they were heading out on a shopping trip.

Their mother reached over and put a soft hand on Collin's cheek. "Be safe, dear boy."

Not wanting the others to see how deeply this motherly gesture moved him, he nodded and pretended to need something from his sack. Julius shook hands with the parents and they turned and started toward the gate.

Jacque walked beside him as they went, but didn't speak. Collin had noticed his parents didn't see them off, but resisted the urge to ask about them. When Collin glanced over at Nihl, he noticed one of the tall boy's cheeks looked very red and slightly swollen. Collin's chest tightened. He was glad when they reached the gate.

Lady Ella, and two male senators Collin didn't know, waited for them there. "You are off on a dangerous quest, my friends. May it bring peace and enlightenment to our world." Lady Ella pressed her palms together and bowed and the other senators followed suit. Collin, taking his cue from the others, mirrored the bow.

"To the gentle Lady Laurelle, we present a golden necklace." The first man said, holding up a gold chain, twisted into tiny rope. A black pendant hung from it. "Its powers have already been tested in battle many years ago. Now, may it serve you to its fullest capacity. Speak *patoret* to the jewel and you will fly above your enemies and land on your feet ready to fight once more."

They presented Jacque and Nihl with two identical silver rings, which had the ability to call one to the other's side with one full turn on the finger. They gave Marcole a dagger, which would be invisible to anyone but himself. They gave Julius a spear: the head mined from the mountains of the Kiatri. "Similar to Fontre blades, but without the cruel histories and bloodlust," said the second senator in an airy, affected accent.

"To our dear Kirkus, a watch that, if you set it on your oven, nothing you cook can burn. And to Sacha, a pouch of spices. Each spice is in a separate compartment." The senator opened the pouch so Sacha could look inside. "No matter how much you use, as long as you leave a pinch at the bottom, the spice will replenish itself." Sacha's eyes glowed with excitement as he tied the pouch to his belt.

"Thanks," he exclaimed with as much awe as any had shown for their gleaming weapons.

Lady Ella approached Collin and handed him a leather breast-plate, similar to Nihl and Jacque's, with a blue eagle engraved at its center and a cuff of a white metal he'd never seen before.

"The eagle represents the freedom from oppression which you so desperately seek. The cuff, if struck in battle, will not yield to any sword, even the blades of the Fontre." Lady Ella smiled and handed the cuff to Laurelle. Laurelle locked the cuff into place for Collin.

"One more gift I bestow upon you, Collin of the Borderlands," Lady Ella continued. "You have spoken many times in your short stay against the enslavement of the Riverfolk." She patted Timothy on the head. Kindly meant, Collin told himself, though it reminded him of a dog and its master. "I promise you I will consider legislation on their behalf, if you promise me that you will come back and study here at the Elythium when you have won your war." The Lady smiled warmly at him, and Julius' face lit up.

"Well, what about that, Collin?" said Sacha, clapping the smaller boy on the back.

Collin's heart jumped into his throat. "I would be honored, my Lady."

"May all the gods of the heavens protect you."

Julius dipped his head. "And may the Weaver protect the North Country from foes."

Collin looked over his shoulder one last time, and waved goodbye to Timothy. Timothy's face lit up with a smile and he waved as if his arm was hinged in the middle.

ELIAN MET the Queen the next morning and couldn't muster even a little false bravado. Krispen had woken him twice in the night, pulling him back to the present. Elian was starting to wonder if the memories would kill him after all.

He ate in silence on the softest couch in the Queen's sitting room and still it felt as if hot irons were being pressed against every inch of his back. The Queen watched him, but barely said a word. When he'd finished breakfast, she went to the cupboard where she kept the replicated Fontre Draught.

Elian realized what she might be planning and stood, determined to fight her off should she intend to inject him again. When Dahlia turned and saw his posture, her eyes grew wide. She smiled and fluttered back to her seat carrying a markedly different bottle: a small silver vial similar to the one Cassai had strung at her neck.

"Are you going to fight me, Elian?" she asked.

"Perhaps," he replied in a threadbare voice.

She crossed her legs and propped her chin on her fist. She looked thrilled. "How does that fall under the agreement of full cooperation?"

"Full cooperation, but not to death," Elian clarified.

She smirked at him and nudged the vial. "Do you know what this is?"

"Another poison?"

"It's the antidote to what I gave you a few days ago. It stops the memories haunting you, begins to heal your body."

Elian looked skeptical. "There's no antidote to the Fontre Draught. The only cure is to outlive its effects."

"To the one you gave me, yes. To the one I made, no. I know it works quite effectively. I tried the Draught on one of my own kin and administered the antidote just before the poison killed her."

Elian sank into the cushions but couldn't relax. "Who?"

Dahlia smiled. "Lily."

Elian scowled. "You poisoned your sister?"

The Queen shrugged her tiny shoulders. "I had the cure handy just in case it went as you said it would. And it did."

"Did you know the antidote worked before you gave it?" Elian demanded.

"Oh I didn't care one way or the other. Goliard was the one who insisted I give it at the last moment. He crashed in on us. Poor Goliard. He's sure he can make her happy one day."

"Goliard saved Lily from you?" Elian tried to rectify this information with what he'd seen of the Queen's Captain of the Guard.

"Surely a Fontre who's learned to feel has also learned that people are not just one thing or another. Goliard is a brute, but he's lived a long time. Longer than either Lily or I put together, and he's loved her over two hundred years. This isn't the first time he's saved her life. I'm sure it won't be the last."

Elian frowned and shook his head. "So what do you want for the antidote? I assume something I cannot give."

"It's certainly something you can give. It's only a matter of willingness."

"I won't go to bed with you. If that's the price, then no."

"What if it was that, or poison?"

"I would rather die."

The Queen's red lips pursed. "Think carefully about your words, Elian. There's more at stake than you realize. If your life ends, so does the life of the woman you love. All that you've suffered will be for nothing – less than nothing. Lashai will be destroyed in an apocalypse unlike any since the foundations of our world."

"What is wrong with you?" Elian asked.

"Cassai," she growled.

"What about Cassai?"

"I want her, but cannot have her. That was your choice. So I want to destroy her and her precious little perfect world." The queen began to breathe deeply; the room grew dark. "I'm always at the cusp of getting exactly what I want...and finding it corrupted. Do you understand?"

"I – not really," said Elian nervously.

"Think of this; you want an apple. It sounds delicious. It looks delicious. You crave it for a long time. Finally, you're allowed to have it, and you find it's rotten inside, ruined by worms. This is always the way of things for me. I am Namarielle. Did you know that? Actually Namarielle, just as much as I am fey. I could have that throne. I could have you. Cassai is my cousin by blood."

Elian gaped at her. Of all the things she could have confessed to him, this had never entered his mind. "You want the throne?"

"I want everything she has. Think what I could do. Think what we could do as rulers of Lashai. We could easily remove the Fontre from power." Her eyes shone with wild intensity. "I know their weaknesses. I have the power to bind them where they would never harm another soul."

"Do that, won't you? It would save us all a lot of trouble," said Elian dryly.

The Queen shrieked with mad laughter that Elian felt in his spine. "Oh Elian, you mock when you should beg for mercy. You make light when you should see the gravity of your situation."

Dahlia's eyes had grown too large to be normal and their color had gone from blue to bright purple. Her cheeks flushed and her chest rose and fell too fast.

"You think you ever had an upper hand on me? Your little antics in my dungeon, your bravado with my Captain, they are all allowed because I enjoy them. You think your powers as a Fontre or a man ever really stood a chance against The Queen of the Fey?" Her voice and body had risen and she stood arms flung out. A red light glowed all around her and Elian was afraid of her for the first time.

He sat as still as possible and made no noise, waiting for her next move.

"Tell me about her now, Elian. Tell me about the power of Cassai." She advanced on him and pushed a hand against his chest, pressing him against the couch. It burned where she touched him. "You are so deeply devoted to her. Surely she has something more impressive than the ability to fling her arms around you and cling to you as a child." Her voice mocked him, burning him worse than the hand on his chest.

"Alright," he said quietly, "I can tell you whatever you wish to know about Cassai. Dahlia, I will need to be able to breathe."

Her eyes faded back to emerald blue and she removed her hand. "Very well," she said in a voice still poisonous but softer. "I'll sit here then. You breathe, and you tell me what binds you to her so."

Elian pushed himself back up and drew a ragged breath. "Cassai's powers as a Namarielle are not important to me. I don't care if she rules, or if we're shepherds, or if we live in the bottom of a well. I just want to be with her. Cassai is filled with kindness and light. There is so much good in her, and she pulls the good out of me. That is not an easy feat when one considers that I was raised by Fontre. She not only sees it herself, she makes me see it too. I – I've loved her so long, I can't remember exactly why, but that is probably the foremost reason."

"More," said the queen in a hoarse whisper. Elian felt an icy blast in the air and shivered.

"She mends what is broken in body and soul. Not just in me,

in everyone and everything. If something can be fixed by loving it, she will see it fixed. Her mind is brilliant and open to everything. She drinks in new information and experiences as if they are life itself. But, home and familiarity renew her spirits. It'll be a long time before I can give her those things again." He said this last part to himself, as if he'd forgotten Dahlia altogether.

He saw her shift on the couch. The red haze still burned around her and he wondered when it would diffuse.

"Touching. So, what on earth does she see in you? Does she know all these things about your past? Have you shared what is darkest and most damaged about you, Fontre? Or, do you only let her see the light she draws from absolute thin air?"

Something sharp seemed to be working its way between Elian's breastbones. He was having trouble making his lungs draw in air and each time he tried was a little more painful. "I'm-."

"It seems to me that someone so light, so good, so full of all that is pure and holy would find it rather hard to deal with, much less accept, the deep pit of blackness that resides in the innermost being of any Fontre. Especially the constantly abused son of Ffastian the High King."

Elian wished a memory would take him, or that Dahlia would physically attack him in some way. If she had stabbed him, or whipped him, or broken a bone, it would have hurt less than these words. He looked at the floor and clenched his hands into fists, refusing to comment.

Her voice was smooth as glass when she spoke again. "Your past haunts you, Elian. It always will. It will attack you at the worst possible moments, and you'll need someone who understands what you're going through. Someone who won't be shocked or mortified, but someone who lets you be who you are in your darkest and your lightest moments. Don't you see? I'm offering you another life. A life better suited to your needs."

"I love her," he said at last.

"Then you should let her be with a better man. Her innocence, her light, her purity deserve that. If you love her, let her go."

He glared at her, wished he could strike her back. "She loves me. And I cannot give you an explanation for that, if you're hoping for one," was all he could think to say.

"What does a child like her know about love?" Dahlia scoffed.

"Enough to know that it cannot be bought, or coerced or tortured out of someone. I know what you want, and I know there's truth in what you say. But, since Cassai and I love each other, we'll figure it out. And if she doesn't want me in the end, she doesn't have to have me. I will spend my dying breath protecting her, nevertheless. Because damage and broken pieces and darkness and all, I love her."

Dahlia's eyes were glazed with tears when he finished. He was shocked to realize that she actually felt something from what he'd said.

"I envy her," she said in a small voice, the red haze lifting at last.

Elian felt calmness creep over him. He wondered if Dahlia had the ability to manipulate feelings as well as atmosphere. "She would be sorry to hear you say that. She loved being here, loved being with you. No matter what you wish for her, she doesn't want you to be unhappy."

"I believe you. I could sense how sweet she was. I wish I could have her to keep in my pocket, honestly. I'm sure I would find a way to ruin her though, so I suppose it's just as well."

Elian couldn't believe that he had it in him to feel pity for such a creature, but he felt a deep sorrow, in that moment, for the fairy. She had curled her legs up against her chest and wrapped her arms around them as Cassai did sometimes when she was upset and just wanted to block out the pain. "I'm sorry, Dahlia."

"Will you ask me a question?" she said.

His eyebrows raised. "What question?"

"Any question. For once in my life, I want someone to be curious toward me."

Elian nodded, thinking this was the least painful of the things she could ask. "Alright. You wanted to tell me a few days ago why I'm different than my fellow Fontre. I know some of the reason. Do you know the full story?"

Dahlia's eyes lit up. "I do. I was there at its origin." She refilled his cup and sat back to get comfortable. "There was a Lightling named Erik. A brilliant and ridiculous boy. The only person I've ever met whose curiosity rivaled my own. He immersed himself in the study of the races of men and tried to isolate the substances that made them what they were.

"He started with the Lightlings' abilities to process and memorize information. Then he moved on to the Kiatri's impossibly long life spans. He wanted to determine the properties of the werewolf, but he hit a snag when his closest friend protested some of his more dangerous schemes.

"Then he discovered the Fontre. They were sufficiently different to occupy his mind for a while. They were mortal, the mirror image of their relatives in Dukai, yet they found a way to alter themselves. No other race did this. Every twenty years or so, a Fontre would attempt to alter their blood, or their genes, trying to ensure there were no mishaps; no cases such as yours. These attempts proved futile and fatal to the recipients.

"Erik developed a serum to reconnect the parts of the brain shut off by the Fontre's pills. He tried it on a Fontre child he'd discovered in the dwellings of the Riverfolk. She'd strayed from her parents that morning to gather berries and got caught in one of his traps."

"He set traps for them?"

The room grew pleasantly brighter the more interest Elian showed in Dahlia's story. "Not for Fontre, actually. He set them trying to capture one of the Riverfolk. He had an experiment he wanted to try on them, but was hesitant to use a slave. The Riverfolk are handpicked to be sold in the land of the Light Ones. Did you know that?"

"Yes, I'd heard."

"The slaves are modified slightly. Humans have such a strong instincts to fight enslavement."

"Oddly enough," Elian interjected, rolling his eyes.

Dahlia grinned and nodded. "Anyway, Erik wanted an unaltered specimen, but what he caught was a Fontre child."

"Were the Fontre infiltrating the Riverfolk?"

The Queen laughed. "The Fontre considered overtaking their small villages for a short time, but the Riverfolk were too content to be turned. All they really care about is fishing in the river, weaving nets and baskets and making a good enough living to enjoy their leisure. You can see how the Fontre would quickly give up acquiring such a worthless race."

"Indeed, they sound despicable," said Elian.

It was Dahlia's turn to roll her eyes. "Erik asked the Fontre girl if she would come with him. She was sufficiently curious to come without duress. Erik was civilized enough not to force people to participate in his experiments. Also, I don't think he could have qualified for the grant he was getting should he be discovered forcing victims into taking medicines and serums. At last he had his chance to try the serum on the one gender he hoped to help. He always felt the Fontre women got an unfair lot, always used one way or other, with no hope of any chosen profession.

"The girl reacted to the first serum differently than he'd expected. Her change wasn't immediate enough to help with his research. The only thing it ignited in her brain was deeper hostility. She went back to her people and became famous as one of the most brutal of the Fontre's female warriors, a leader in the Crimson Army. When she retired, however, she did something no one expected. She moved into the temples. She had only one child, your mother."

Elian sat up straighter at this and instantly regretted it. Pain wracked his body and he sucked in a breath.

The Queen stopped in surprise. "Is another memory taking you?"

"No. I moved without thinking."

A look of pity mixed with curiosity crossed her face. "I can give you something for the pain," she offered, almost kindly.

Elian breathed rapidly, trying to wait it out. "What else will it do to me?" he asked through his teeth.

"Nothing. It's not that sort of medicine." Dahlia flitted back to her cabinet and brought a handful of small red pills. She tipped them into Elian's hand. "Take only one every few hours. They numb it for a while."

Elian looked at the pills suspiciously. Feeling he had almost nothing to lose, he finally put it into his mouth and took a sip of his now cold tea to swallow it. "Thank you."

"Certainly. Where was I? Your mother. Erik's serum had hijacked your grandmother's nervous system to the point where she threw up some of the daily pills. So much so that she unknowingly bore a child whose mind and emotions were almost intact. Your mother was brilliant. She was so beautiful and highly sought after, even as a small girl. It's against Fontre Law to move a girl to the temples before her eighteenth birthday, but they made an exception with your mother and moved her at sixteen. It took her no time to figure out how to circumvent the system of pills that created the ice cold warriors. Devilan was her first to try eliminating certain ones. You were the first to be born when she seemed to have a grasp on which pills to take and which to grind to powder.

"She did some tinkering of her own and tried some of her concoctions on the men who came to her. Your father responded positively to her experimental treatments. He started out obsessed with her, but gradually grew to love her. She probably tried the same with others. I'm not sure how successful she was. I stopped following her progress after you were born."

"You've been spying on me since my birth?" Elian asked quietly.

"Yes, you and Devilan. You see, I was there the night your grandmother received Erik's serum."

"You and Erik were...together?"

"No. I was deeply in love with Erik's best friend." She stared hungrily at Elian, begging him to ask her the next question. He smiled. These were the least unpleasant moments he'd experienced since entering her chambers days ago.

"Who was Erik's best friend?" He knew instantly he'd asked the right thing. She wriggled with uncontrollable excitement to answer. The light in the room grew so bright it made Elian's eyes water.

"Hollis Ferrell. They'd been like brothers since they came to the Elythium."

Elian reacted with genuine surprise. "Really? I knew you and Hollis had a history. I never realized how far back."

"Yes. We got very close, but Hollis never cared for me as I cared for him. At first, I thought perhaps it was Erik he was more interested in, but then he met Lily and his preferences became obvious." The bitterness in her voice chilled Elian to the bone. The reason for her cruel treatment of her sister grew increasingly clear. Dahlia stared at him, as though trying to read his thoughts. "Do you have any other questions?"

Elian wracked his brain, knowing that the longer he asked questions, the less pain he would endure today. "I have one, but it has nothing to do with the current topic."

"Oh, please ask."

"I was wondering about your father. What happened to him?"

"Ah well, he certainly wasn't around to raise me. There's a reason the Namarielle are called 'the Forbidden Race'. Few blood-lines are allowed to mingle with theirs, and only under very specific circumstances."

"Marriage by a Lashaian priest."

The Queen giggled and Elian couldn't think of any sound more obnoxious. Surely she was thinking, as he was, that the possibility of his ever marrying Cassai under those perfect circumstances was slim to non-existent. "Yes, it's all very orderly. Specific wording to the vows, binding oaths; that sort of thing. Namarielle men and women can't really have what any other mortal would consider a fling without the most severe consequences. This particular Namarielle didn't have a choice."

"He was captive?"

"And heavily drugged. Mother's curiosity was even more sinister than mine."

Elian felt her building the tension purposefully. A wave of nausea came over him and he knew he didn't have much more time in the present. "Just tell me," he asked quietly, fighting the memory off long enough to hear her gleeful response.

"Oh, he did what she was hoping for, but not the *way* she hoped because she wanted to conduct more experiments. He got to the point of impregnating her, then had a horrible seizure...and died."

Crushing reality hit Elian seconds before the painful past engulfed him. He sank into the couch cushions and surrendered to it almost gratefully.

18

THE MATCH

"Where are we headed, Uncle? Why so far off the road?" Collin had drawn up to Julius as he and the Lightlings followed Julius and Kirkus off the road and onto a well-hidden path in a wheat field. "Nihl's struggling with the wagon."

"Kirkus heard about random patrols of Southern Guard and even some Fontre searching villages this far north of the Borderlands. There's one place where they haven't bothered."

"Another village?"

"Another entire race," said Julius.

Collin squinted up at the sky, trying to get his bearings from the position of the sun. "We're heading farther west. The Riverfolk?"

"Ah, you remember your geography lessons well."

"Why don't the Fontre bother the Riverfolk?"

"They went to them once, long ago. Found them too primitive and poor to trouble with. Didn't even ransack them, just left and never returned."

"Wow," Collin murmured. "Who knew that being destitute would have such benefits?"

Julius smiled and Collin fell back to Jacque and Sacha. "Did you find out?" Sacha asked quietly.

"We're going to follow the river," Collin replied.

Jacque went stiff. "Wait, are we going toward – "

"The Riverfolk? Yes." Collin finished for him.

"But they're savages. Actual savages, not just people who don't like the weird food Sacha likes, but people who ... I don't know, might eat their own young or whatever."

"Where did you hear that?" Collin asked.

"My father."

Collin and Sacha both started laughing at the same time. "Incredible!" Sacha exclaimed breathlessly.

"What's incredible?"

"What people will tell themselves to justify enslaving their fellowman," Sacha said.

Jacque scowled and dropped an arm on Collin's shoulder absentmindedly. "I'll remember you said that when you wake in the night and they're standing over you with a knife and fork."

Collin rolled his eyes. "Ridiculous. If they're as savage as you say, surely they won't bother with knives and forks."

THE NEXT FEW days passed for Elian in a haze of interrogations by the Queen, painful memories from the past and nights with Krispen dressing his wounds and reading him the Songs of the Shepherd. Agonizing memories had started to recycle. He had been revisited multiple times by Devilan's brutal training sessions and the days his arm was broken by both his blood father and Ffastian. Elian set the bones himself at first, but by the time he had lived out both memories twice, his arm was too swollen and inflamed to set the bones properly.

The short walk from the stables to the palace the next morning was only possible with his shepherd boy's support. Dahlia snapped her fingers and two fairies fluttered in to assist Elian into the room as well.

"I want to stay with him today," Krispen said when they'd lowered Elian onto the couch.

Dahlia looked at him with an equal mixture of malice and fascination. "Why? What could you do for him that I could not?"

"I just...I'm not sure he'll be able to walk back."

"No, Krispen," Elian managed to mutter. "I'll be alright."

"I'll send for you when you're needed," Dahlia snipped.

"Please fix his arm." Krispen pointed to the heavily bandaged arm. "He couldn't get it to set."

"I'll mend his bones, if he'll allow it."

The distraught shepherd boy turned to his master. "Please allow it. I know it's horrible, but if you could manage to ... Just let her help you." He slumped back to the stairs and out of sight.

Dahlia watched Elian nervously. The man refused to make eye contact but glared straight ahead.

Dahlia sat next to him and held out a hand. "Give me your arm."

"Let me be," he growled.

"Your match with Goliard is set for tomorrow. You cannot hope to win in your present condition. For Cassai's sake, give me your arm."

"Why tomorrow? There are still four days before Nuelletide's Eve."

"Your shattered arm among other things. He wants to fight you before you are too damaged to give any sport at all."

Elian still refused to look at her, but painfully lifted his arm and let it drop into her waiting hand. She caught it deftly and began to unwrap the bandages. She gasped at the swelling and broken splints. "How many times did you say he broke your arm?"

"If you're going to mend it, get on with it."

Dahlia arranged his arm in her lap, palm down, looking miffed. "I don't know why you're so angry with me. It isn't as though these injuries are recent. You could have avoided them altogether. You brought this on yourself, you know −" In a flash, Elian's undamaged hand was around her neck, the ball of his palm pressing hard against her windpipe.

Flames of rage leapt into his eyes as he drew his face within an inch of her nose. "Say another word, fairy, and it'll be the last you ever speak."

Dahlia's mouth snapped shut, her eyes wide with shock. Somewhere in the back of Elian's mind he knew she could call on some power or other to throw him off, but for now she pressed her lips together. He felt her neck contract as she swallowed nervously. His hand relaxed slightly, but he didn't release her.

"My reflexes. You may add that to the list you've been making of ways I'm still like my kin. Except...I'm quicker." She nodded slowly. He thrust her away. "If you wish to mend my arm, feel free. If not, I assure you I will still meet your Captain of the Guard tomorrow and do what I can against him."

The Queen massaged her neck, trembling with actual fear for the first time. She drew a shaky breath and sat herself next to him. "May I speak?"

"If you must."

"I can see you told the truth when you said you could stand a great deal of physical punishment. I think we'll draw the line at presenting you with one useless arm tomorrow. I assured Goliard you wouldn't be badly handicapped for the fight." She reached for his right arm once more and continued to unwrap it, this time not daring to speak. Even her gentlest movement filled Elian with so much pain he shut his eyes tight and ground his teeth. When she'd finished unwrapping, she pressed two fingers into his palm. His hand was on fire. His arm was on fire.

Cassai lay at his feet, dead, stabbed to death. Goliard stood over her, mocking Elian with a sneer. "Too late, Fontre. You got here too late."

The room swirled, and it was Sophie, an arrow through her heart.

Krispen, beaten to death.

Collin, whipped, bleeding out while Elian tried to stem the flow. "It's alright, Elian," he gasped. "Just let me go home to Anaya."

Hollis, his throat ripped out by Edgewater...

At last the room solidified again. At last the fire faded.

Dahlia watched his face eagerly. He finally released his breath and sat panting on the couch, shaking again. She laid his arm carefully across his lap. "Would you like to eat something?"

"No." Elian's stomach growled so loudly Dahlia started. He couldn't imagine the self-control she mustered to keep from smiling. "Fine. I'll eat whatever you've got."

"Pain killers?" she asked and jumped away from him at the look he gave her. "Right. I'll have some breakfast sent down."

"Coffee."

"Yes. I'll be sure there's coffee."

She returned in moments, followed by three fey children bearing trays of food. They all ogled Elian as they set down their burden. One particular female gave him a curious smile, which wasn't returned. They fluttered from the room and the Queen perched opposite him looking tentative.

Elian didn't bother with the plates set out for his use. He grabbed a large plum and ate it in two bites. He took the plate piled high with eggs and bacon, added two muffins, and devoured it with such appetite that half the plate was cleared before Dahlia had poured his coffee. He drained the mug in five swallows and handed it back.

"I see you've thrown caution to the wind with regard to the food," she quipped.

Elian swallowed a bite of muffin before responding. "The match tomorrow. What are the stakes?"

"Stakes?"

"I don't fight for the sick entertainment of the fey. I'm no gladiator," he assured her.

"The glory of victory?" Dahlia said.

"There's no glory in bloodshed."

"Says the leader of a revolution."

"Freedom."

"Freedom what?"

"I fight for freedom. Always. Freedom is the only spoil of war I consider worthy of the cost."

"There are still four days until I have to release you. What if the memories continue and I'm not there to mend your bones? What will you do back in the mortal world?"

"Cassai is there. She'll sort me out. If I fight Goliard tomorrow and win, my man and I leave early. You give us our freedom. If I lose, we stay until the fortnight is complete."

"If you lose, I release Krispen at the Westerling Field and bind you here for eternity," she countered.

"There were no conditions under which I stay forever."

"There were no conditions about you bringing Krispen either, yet I've allowed him to stay. I've even ordered my men off him, not that any of them were particularly inclined to trifle with him after —"

"I threatened to kill Goliard if they didn't let him be," Elian finished.

"You don't have many options, Fontre. Your brand of magic won't release you from this land, as no doubt Cassai's would have, had I attempted to keep her. Perhaps I could allow for a rematch in the future. Or a visit to the mortal world should you wish to attend Cassai's wedding to a qualified suitor."

Elian flinched. The Queen's evil smile returned. She held out her small hand. "You should lie down. You look as if you could fall over at any moment."

"If you're upping the stakes, so am I," Elian said.

"Please do. What would you like? An elixir for eternal life? Seeds to grow your own fairy garden?"

"I want your pet."

"My pet?"

Elian pointed to glass case next to the Queen's bed.

"My dandelion fairy? What use could you have for her?"

"I have no use for her. I just want her freed."

Dahlia snorted. "She's been in my care so long she won't have a clue what to do in the mortal world. It's likely her own kin won't remember her."

Elian glared at her. "Her freedom and mine. Those are my terms."

"Fine." The Queen stared at him for a long time, then, slowly her lips curved upward. "The reward for victory is freedom."

❦

"ARE WE TAKING THE ROAD?" asked Theoris, peering over Cassai's shoulder at the map she was tracing.

"No. It's too dangerous. I don't know where Devilan is, but I know they'll probably take the road. The damage we did may have slowed them down enough not to be far ahead." Cassai led the group down an old deer path.

"The trees are dangerous too," said Theoris nervously. He'd taken the guard every night that week, convinced that Edgewater and his men were close. Hollis shared this concern and he slept only two or three hours, keeping vigil with the fairy most of the night.

There were no signs of the pack yet, however, and they all fervently hoped it stayed that way.

Cassai spent much of her time trying to ignore the throbbing pains that lingered in her back and legs. Occasionally a sharp stab she couldn't ignore would shoot through her. She tried hard not to react. The look on her companions' faces when she suddenly gasped or grabbed at her side were harder to bear than the second-hand pain. She could now add throbbing in her right arm to the list.

Theoris' spirits, heightened by their stay in the Hermit's Valley, had begun to spiral downward. He'd taken to playing his flute at

274

night, and true improvement made these impulses much more enjoyable for everyone. However, the crutch he carried, his constant reminder of his brokenness, weighed on him and he couldn't seem to help occasionally mentioning that they would all have been better off had he stayed behind. Hollis, in these moments, seemed unable to disagree, which annoyed Cassai.

"Let's camp here tonight, Cassai. We won't see another clearing this good for a while," Hollis suggested, coming up behind her.

Cassai looked around them and smiled. The dapplenut trees now surrounding them still bore clusters of the hazel-colored nuts. "We can roast those and have a good supper."

Hollis grinned and gave her arm a friendly squeeze. "We'll comb the trees if you'd like to start a fire."

Cassai worked on the fire while Sophie and Hollis climbed the dapplenut trees to retrieve fresh nuts. Theoris collapsed next to Cassai and laid down his crutch. "Did you feel anything from Elian?"

Cassai tried not to make eye contact with Theoris at this question. "I feel things occasionally, but not as bad as it was when he was with Edgewater." At the name of the pack leader, Theoris jumped and scanned the outlying trees. Cassai saw no reason to explain further. She took a deep breath and concentrated on the fire.

"The spoils of the hunt, my lady," said Hollis gallantly, as he dumped a tunic-full of nuts beside her just as the fire began to blaze.

"We should let it die down a bit. It'll just burn them now."

"Get up then. Let's do another lesson while we wait." He pulled her up and fetched her sword from her satchel.

She sighed and rubbed her sore legs. She wished Hollis didn't always have to be so efficient with time. She just wanted to rest. He and Sophie had been taking turns teaching her with their weapons of choice each night. Sophie's lessons had greatly improved her technique with bow and arrows, and Hollis practiced swordplay with her.

He grinned and handed her the Fontre blade. "Tired?"

"Not a bit," she returned, raising the sword and taking her stance.

"Good." He raised his fairy blade and took his stance as well. "We'll work extra hard tonight."

~

COLLIN and his friends followed Julius and Kirkus on to the hut-lined shores of the Greater Kai. His companions hung back, filled with uncertainty at walking into such an alien culture. Sacha had no difficulty striding in beside Collin, grinning at some girls sitting in the low waters of the shoreline weaving baskets from long reeds growing over their heads. The girls smiled back and waved at the strangers.

A short, skinny Riverman exited his hut and spotted the men. He backed into his doorway slowly, until Julius smiled and waved him out. The man stepped cautiously toward the group.

"They don't trust anyone who travels with Lightlings," Sacha whispered to Collin.

"Yeah, I wonder why that is," he said under his breath.

He heard his uncle talking to the man, but the man didn't speak either of the languages Julius tried. Kirkus looked back at Sacha. "Come here, Sacha. Talk to this fellow. Let him know what we're about."

Sacha trotted up to the threesome and gave the man a huge grin. He started speaking rapidly in the man's language, gesturing toward the group of young adults and then back to the men. Collin didn't understand him, but the man he spoke to finally nodded and indicated that Sacha should follow him into the village. Sacha nodded to his group.

"They can take us for the night," he said.

Collin noticed Jacque and Nihl still looked leery, but Elle and Marc moved to join Sacha, so the brothers followed.

They walked down dirt paths well worn by the barefoot River-folk. The basket-weaving girls abandoned their task and ran up to greet them.

Sacha spoke in their native tongue for a moment and then turned to his friends. "They're excited to see outsiders and want to wash our feet."

A painful knot formed in the pit of Collin's stomach. "Um, tell them thanks, but no thanks. They aren't our servants."

"It's a gesture of welcome in their culture. If you refuse, you'll insult them."

Collin looked at the girls and swallowed hard. They stared back at him with glowing brown eyes. Collin wondered how their coppery skin always shone so. He'd thought it was only the Lightling slaves. "Right. Okay, that's fine."

A girl a few inches shorter than him slipped a hand into his and pulled him toward the Greater Kai. The entire group followed to the water, including Julius and Kirkus. After their feet were washed, they sat on the bank and let them dry before heading back to the village on the dusty road. One of the girls talked to Sacha the entire time and he tried to translate for his friends.

"She says they're preparing our accommodation and a feast. She wants to take us to the bonfire and dance for us."

Collin's internal knot began to untie slightly. "What did you say to that?"

"Oh, we're honored that they would treat us so kindly. I mean, I guess we should be honored they didn't shoot us the moment we walked in with them." Sacha nodded toward Jacque and Nihl. "It's not like we've earned any trust."

"That's for sure," Collin said.

"Seriously? Some of them appreciate the life we've offered in the Land of the Enlightened," Nihl protested.

"Appreciate you enslaving them?" Collin asked.

"Shut up, Collin. You don't know anything about our culture, or theirs, so don't pretend you understand our relationship."

"I know they haven't come at us with forks or knives yet," Collin snapped. "Or do you think washing our feet is meant to keep us clean so they don't get grit in their food?"

The girls looked at the two boys and back at Sacha for an explanation of their angry exchange. Sacha said something and they burst into peals of laughter that echoed around and filled the riverside.

"What did you say?" Nihl demanded.

Sacha stood as the girls gestured it was time to leave. "They were wondering why you were growling at each other. I just told them you both have corn mush for brains." He offered Collin a hand and Collin laughed and accepted.

"Fine criticism coming from a Fontre," he said. Sacha punched his arm and turned to help Laurelle up as well. She accepted his hand graciously and threw Nihl a disapproving look.

"Could you stop chomping his head off every time he opens his mouth?" she asked.

"I would if he'd stop being an ignorant git every time he does," Nihl answered.

Collin put a hand on Laurelle's arm. "Hey, let's go. They're leaving without us."

"Why do you always say stuff like that?" she fumed at Nihl, ignoring Collin.

"Elle, it doesn't matter what he says. I don't care; why should you?" Collin whispered.

Nihl glared at him, but Jacque stepped between them. "Easy. Let's follow the girls, okay? I think I may have a chance with that taller one," he joked with his brother.

Nihl rolled his eyes and put his hands up. "Fine, I give. Sorry." They started down the path, Collin trying to ignore the hostility he felt emanating from behind him. "And by the way, I don't think you've got a chance in the world with the taller one," he jabbed Jacque with an elbow.

The girls led them into the center of the community, which Collin figured was their gathering place. Large tables lined one side of the giant square. At least fifty women stood around cook fires with enormous black pots filled with food that sizzled and smelled of spices. The women were wrapped in brightly colored scarves and togas that reminded him of the Light One's fashions except, instead of gauzy white, they were red, blue, pink and purple, with flowers woven into every inch. Ropes of heavy clay beads hung from their necks and arms.

"Come, sit," said the girl who had been speaking only with Sacha.

"She speaks the common tongue?" Collin asked, surprised.

"Just a few words," Sacha said. "She said supper will be ready soon. The men had a good catch today, so the whole village will feast tonight."

The smell of spices, fish and crispy fried batter filled the air. Collin noticed that in spite of the common assumption in Halanah that Riverfolk were starving, none of them looked underfed. "Wow, they really seem to be languishing, right?" he said to Sacha.

"Mm...I think we're going to eat well here. I'm going to see if I can get some of those spices to take with us. There's one particular scent I can't place." Sacha began talking to their guide again, who giggled and led him over to the cook pots. The ladies greeted him and all started speaking at once.

With no one there to interpret, the girls and the Lightlings shared an uneasy silence. Finally, the tallest of the girls tugged on Laurelle's arm and gestured to several seats hewn from large felled trees. "Come," the girl said sweetly. Julius and Kirkus were still talking to the Riverman who'd greeted them at the entrance of the village.

"They want us to sit down." Laurelle followed the girl, grabbing Collin's arm so he would come with her. The group gathered around the fire and settled on the logs. Rivergirls joined them, fitting in between them easily, as if there was no barrier at all between them, language or otherwise.

Jacque smiled at the tallest girl and patted the seat beside him. She gave him a dazzling smile and sat. Collin and Nihl rolled their eyes in unison.

The men came to sit with them. The Riverman's white teeth gleamed in his gaping smile.

"It smells delicious," Julius said, taking a seat on the other side of Collin.

"Do you trust them?" Collin asked, feeling uneasy at their overwhelming hospitality.

"I would say that if they're hiding something sinister, they're very good actors. Even Kirkus suspects no foul play. The man's name is Lotus. He knows a wide enough path through the Forest of Fondair to accommodate our wagons. It will get us through quicker than if we stick to the road...which is good, since we can't stick to the road."

"Do they go into Fondair often?"

"Lotus did. He used to run a trade route all the way to Dukai. There was another village of Riverfolk on the other side of Lashai for many years. Fontre wiped out most of his kin there. He wasn't as excited to meet Kirkus, but Sacha seems to be getting along fine." Julius smiled toward the boy who was now surrounded by chattering women, all trying to press bags of spices into his hands and explaining their uses loudly.

"Yeah, he seems to do fine wherever he is," Collin chuckled. "I hope he fares as well with the Keepers."

"He will. He'll get Elian's trust, and the Keepers will welcome him for sure. Or, he'll cook something and they'll have no choice but to love him." Sacha now held one of the large wooden cooking paddles, moving sizzling battered fish in the vats of boiling oil.

"Well, we know it'll taste good now. Sacha touched it," Laurelle said.

"Wish they had some wine though." Jacque already had an arm wrapped around the girl beside him, who looked tiny against his tall, broad frame.

Collin grinned happily around him. He enjoyed the meal of fried fish and vegetables roasted with just enough spice to slowly burn on his tongue. He wasn't aware just how much until he stopped eating. He downed two glasses of the sweet, iced, milky drink he'd been offered. He wondered drowsily what was in it as the dancing and music began.

Rivermen sat around the fire, pounding drums made from hollow logs with animal hide stretched across them. There were stringed instruments Collin couldn't put a name to. Then the girls jumped from their seats and started to dance. Their bare feet moved so gracefully they seemed to float above the dusty ground. They twirled and sang to the music. Then the girl Jacque liked grabbed a flute, and others grabbed Laurelle and pulled her into the middle, teaching her their beautiful dance. She laughed and moved smoothly into the group, picking up the footwork and sweeping her arms through the air.

Collin felt all the worries of the mortal world melt away as they danced; as Laurelle's feet twirled through the dust and her skirts swirled around her. The Rivergirls wrapped ropes of beads around her neck and wrists and put two intricately woven scarves around her waist and head.

They laughed and danced until the fires died to embers. Then a Riverman stood and told stories in a low drawling voice that made Collin's head feel even heavier with blissful sleepiness. Sacha sat cross-legged on the ground in the middle of the group, translating softly as the man wove his language into a tapestry of words that made Collin feel the danger of the hero and the despair of the father and mother whose daughter was kidnapped by the evil villain.

"And the hero rushed to the palace where he saw the kidnapped girl's face in the topmost tower. He scaled the wall to get to her, only to discover the evil prince standing over her, stabbing her through the heart.

"The hero fought the evil man valiantly, though he couldn't save the girl. The hero felt such a man didn't deserve to continue living and so he defeated him. He returned to his village, victorious, but vanquished for eternity. He wandered the forest from thenceforth, a lock of the girl's black hair clutched to his breast."

Collin sighed. It seemed all fairy tales ended with dead damsels and heroes clutching something to their breast. He wished someone would tell a story that ended happily. With this heavy yet contented feeling, he laid his head on Laurelle's shoulder and fell into a deep sleep.

Elian stood on the edge of an arena the fey had grown in a distant paddock. Dahlia had told him enthusiastically over breakfast that several of her *jairdeneites* (which she had told Elian was the fairy name for growers and weavers of flora and fauna,) had been up all night preparing it. The stands were made of living tree branches, on which all the fairies perched themselves awaiting the show.

On one side of the arena Goliard and his men gathered in a semi-circle, talking to their captain of the guard and jeering across the field at Elian and Krispen.

Elian had only caught a few hours of broken sleep. Krispen was so vigilant to bring Elian out of any memory that might cause him more injury that he woke Elian several times when the man had only moved in his sleep.

"Did you take a red pill?" Krispen asked as he glared across at the fey guards.

"No," said Elian. He straightened up and grinned, forcing

himself not to react to the pain that shot through him even now. "I wanted it to be a fair fight."

Krispen, apparently in no mood to be mollified, turned a glower on his master. "This would have been a fair fight a week ago," he grumbled.

"We've been here ten days," Elian reminded him.

"I know."

Elian grinned. "Krispen, I promise you I'll live through this. We'll both get out of this realm alive, hopefully today."

Krispen put both hands on Elian's shoulders, forcing the Fontre to look him in the eyes. "The Weaver be with you, Elian."

"Thank you. I'll see you soon, my friend." He clapped his shepherd boy on the shoulder and leapt over the waist-high wall surrounding the arena.

Dahlia and Lily floated out to the center, followed by a small fairy boy bearing a cushion on which he had balanced the weapons of the match. Both Elian and Goliard started toward them. When they reached the middle of the field, Dahlia smiled. "Fair fighting, gentlemen. Remember, everyone is here to enjoy the match, so be sure to give them a good show."

"What are the terms of victory?" asked Goliard.

"Victory goes to the one who draws surrender from the other." Then she looked pointedly at her Captain of the Guard. "You may not take his life. He may have only an ounce of strength left, but you may not kill him. He's mine."

Goliard's eyes glowed with delight. "Trust me; I'd rather leave him alive."

She smiled and turned to Elian. "Of course, if you can manage it, you're welcome to dispatch him."

Lily's face had its usual stamp of misery, but she attempted to smile as she presented Elian with his own sword and silver dagger. "Good luck, Elian," she murmured.

Elian bowed his head. "Thank you, Lily." Their fingers brushed briefly as he took his weapons. She blushed deep crimson, stood on tiptoe and kissed him on the cheek.

She then plucked the other sword from the silk pillow and turned to her fiancé, who was frowning at her. She held out the sword, the blade of which showed no seam or hammer mark, the glittering weapon was woven from a fine, strong metal, with a gold-plated flowering vine from the handle to the tip of the blade. "Good luck, my love," Lily whispered. Goliard took the blade in his right hand, wrapped his left around her tiny waist and pulled her up to kiss her.

The two women and the fey boy went to the stands. Elian crouched to tuck the dagger into his boot. The familiar coolness against his ankle lifted his spirits slightly. He stood and faced Goliard for the first time. The fairy Captain winked. Blood pounded in Elian's ears.

"On my mark!" cried the Queen.

Before Elian could draw his sword, scorching pain surged through his bones. He forced himself to stay upright and slowly, painfully, raised his weapon. The pain increased, this time knives stabbed him in a dozen places. "You can't even fight without your little parlor trick?" he asked through gritted teeth.

Goliard's face transformed into the ugliest smile Elian had ever seen outside of Ffastian. "Maybe the Queen will grant me a weekly visit to your cell."

The pain temporarily lifted, Elian took a swing, which Goliard countered easily. "Aw, don't flirt with me, Captain. I thought you loved Lily."

The sword was in his other hand in a flash, adrenaline drowning out the agony more than a week of torture had visited on his body. This blow caught Goliard off balance and he stumbled back, but didn't fall.

The pain was back. Razors shredded every nerve in his spine. His eyes filled with water, making the fairy swim in a wobbly stance before him. Elian continued to fight with every ounce of strength he could muster.

Goliard managed to knock Elian's blade aside and drive his fairy blade into the man's right shoulder. Elian jerked away before it pierced too deeply and returned the blow so powerfully, he almost knocked the fairy from his feet. Goliard stumbled back and he glared, sending another dose of pain through Elian's spine.

Elian felt his energy waning. He hadn't had a meal since the night before, although Krispen had plied him with fruit and meat from their stores that morning, the food had done nothing to fortify him. Dread began to settle into his chest, growing rapidly each time Goliard lowered his sword to engage his most powerful weapon.

On the next wave, Elian sank to his knees, his chin in his chest, immobilized by the onslaught. When he managed to raise his head a fraction he saw, not Goliard's sandaled feet, but the muddy, booted feet of the Hermit. He swallowed and turned his bleary eyes upward in disbelief.

"Let go, Elian," said the Hermit softly.

"I can't. Cassai. What will happen to her if I'm trapped here?" he whispered.

The Hermit smiled. "I have a message for you from the Weaver. It's not Goliard who holds you down. Goliard's power only works with pain and bitterness already working within his victims. Let go."

The pain crashed back over him, a different sort of agony that originated from deep inside. Elian bowed his head and ground his teeth against it.

"Let it go, Elian. Forgive and be healed."

Elian shut his eyes. Tears flowed freely from his eyes. "I can't," he said softly. Visions swirled in his brain: his father towering over him, demanding Elian's arm; Devilan beating him; Ffastian … Elian screamed.

He felt the Hermit's hand on his stooped shoulder, felt the

weight and darkness drawing upwards through his body. "You can. Won't you trust me?"

The pain deepened. He thought the blackness would consume him. His whole body shuddered uncontrollably. A word rushed to his lips and he blurted it out before he had a chance to reconsider. "Yes!" He knew he'd shouted because the fairy crowd reacted immediately. Goliard looked startled, but not enough to break his focus. Elian felt warmth glowing in his chest, and then it grew, fighting against the blackness and cold.

The Hermit knelt before him now, his voice directly in Elian's ear. "Then you are free, my boy. Free of the darkness of your past. Free to live in your present world. Rise, my son." The light grew and glowed brighter. Elian looked straight into Goliard's eyes. He got slowly to his feet. "That's it, Elian. Now, stand and see the salvation of the Weaver," the Hermit whispered.

The Hermit smiled before he vanished, and Elian stood alone. Goliard's forehead now glistened with perspiration, his face burning red as he focused every ounce of his strength on disabling his opponent.

But Elian felt nothing.

He raised his sword and took a step toward his enemy. Goliard's eyes grew wider, as he tried again to focus his power.

Elian took another step toward him. Goliard lowered his head and his shoulders rose and fell in deep, calculated breaths. Elian grinned and winked at him. "Ready for the real fight, Goliard?"

"I'll kill you, Fontre. I'll kill you anyway," the fairy shrieked. He lunged at Elian, his sword raised. Elian parried the blow easily and turned to swing his own blade. Renewed strength coursed through his body and he smiled as his sword clashed with his opponent's over and over again.

Goliard's fury drove him madly into each swing, but Elian countered every lunge and began to gain ground. The fairy was a skilled warrior but it soon became obvious he was no match for Elian.

As the fey's strength began to ebb, he paused and glared at Elian once more, seeming to concentrate all his efforts on disabling the Fontre with his usual method. Elian threw himself at the fey and knocked him to the grassy floor. Before Goliard could rise, Elian kicked him onto his back. He pushed a heavy boot into the fairy's chest and pressed his cold black blade against Goliard's throat.

"Would you like to be my first kill, Captain?" he murmured, his voice hoarse.

"No! Elian, please!" Lily's distant scream made him draw a deep breath. He turned back to the stands. Tears streamed down Lily's beautiful face. Dahlia was pale as her frothy dress. Her mouth hung open in mute disbelief.

"I have your permission, do I not?" Elian called out to the Queen.

Dahlia's eyes widened, but she nodded.

Elian turned back to Goliard. Every vein and tendon in the fairy's neck stood out as he tried to stretch away from Elian's sword tip.

He felt the Captain's chest push fruitlessly against Elian's boot. "Don't bother trying to get up, unless you'd like me to ensure that Lily never has to endure bringing your offspring into this world." He drew the tip of his blade down Goliard's body with only enough pressure to slice through his thin tunic. It stopped at the area Elian threatened. Goliard froze, every muscle of his body tense, his face screwed up in terror.

"Surrender," Elian growled.

"I'll kill you, Fon —"

"Surrender!" Elian shouted pushing the point of the blade a fraction of an inch.

"I surrender!" Goliard lifted his hands above his head.

Elian waited to be released from the realm, but when nothing happened, he glared at the stands of fairies. Dahlia stood with hands clasped to her breast, drinking in the scene, craving more violence from him.

"He surrendered. Release me." Elian's voice was hoarse. He could already feel the temporary strength of the fight draining away.

"You must draw blood, Elian. We came to watch a fight," shouted Dahlia.

Elian looked back at the fairy who lay beneath his sword. Goliard hadn't moved, but his eyes had narrowed and focused again. Elian felt a twinge of pain, and knew Goliard was trying to engage his usual torment again. This gave the Fontre an idea: an idea that turned his stomach.

"I bear you no ill will, Captain, but if there's no other way she'll let me go, at least I can release others from your torments." Elian lifted his sword and Goliard looked surprised, as if he thought Elian was going to kill him after all.

Elian took a deep breath, and in a blink dug the tip of his sword into the fairy's right eye. Goliard screamed. "No!"

"Will that break your powers, or need I do the other as well?" Elian asked.

"Please, I'll do anything. Please don't."

"Tell her to release me," he growled.

Goliard held a tight grasp over his remaining eye and turned his face to the stands. "Let him go. He's won. Please let him go."

Elian kept his sword directly over Goliard, but his eyes cut to Dahlia. Her mouth twitched and contorted as though she was experiencing an internal struggle. She finally sighed and nodded at Elian. "Citizens of the Fairy Realm," said Dahlia, her voice carrying magically into the branches full of breathless fey. "I give you, Elian, son of the Fontre, leader of the armies of Lashai. The clear victor."

Elian lifted his boot from the Captain of the Guard. She gave him one last longing look, and melted away before his eyes.

19

THE FONTRE FREED

C assai sat on a fallen branch, nibbling a roll and sipping
water from a water skin. The group had halted for
Sophie to loosen a pebble from her boot. Hollis rolled
his eyes, clearly annoyed at stopping so early in the day.

"You should go without shoes as I've done for years. The soles
of your feet would thicken and nothing would cause you
discomfort."

"Ha!" Sophie threw her black hair back as she hooted. "Exactly
what I'm hoping for, uncle, feet so calloused nothing will ever
penetrate them. Very attractive."

Cassai started to laugh, but it turned to a gasp. Fire shot
through every vein, burned through her skin. Through bleary eyes
she saw her skin wasn't ablaze.

"Cassai?" Hollis appeared at her side. She wondered if she'd
screamed without realizing. Her mind was a haze of pain. She had
a moment's break before a dozen knives sliced into her. She
wrapped her arms around her chest and clenched her teeth. "Cassai, what's happening? Is it Elian?"

"Someone is torturing him," she whimpered. Another respite.
She tried to breathe.

Hollis touched her back just in time for her to scream and arch it. Razors this time. "It's alright. It's alright," Hollis murmured over and over, sounding more helpless each time. She grabbed her shoulder and gasped. The tip of a sword had been pushed in, but not all the way through.

"I – I think he's fighting with swords or something. But –" She clutched her sides frantically as if trying to hold her skin together. "But there's so many pains attacking him."

Hollis sent Theoris a painful look. "Goliard or Melkana?"

Theoris nodded. "Goliard, most likely. Melkana tends to stick to one thing or the other."

Hollis held Cassai tight, rubbing her arm more vigorously than was comfortable. "Hang on. It'll stop soon. I promise, it'll stop." Cassai wasn't sure if he was reassuring himself or her. Either way, he turned out to be right, the pain was lifting. She looked up at the worried faces surrounding her.

"It's gone. Hopefully, he's winning." Her voice sounded weak, even to her own ears. She leaned against Hollis and took several slow, deep breaths.

"Let's sit here a few more moments and rest," said Hollis. Cassai felt keenly how much this kindness cost him, but didn't feel she could force her wobbly legs to begin the hike yet.

"Yes," she whispered, sinking against a tree trunk. "Rest sounds good, for a moment."

～

WHEN THE SCENERY came back into focus, Elian and Krispen stood together in the middle of a clearing. Surrounding them stood, not a crowd of fairies, but the people Elian longed to see more than all others.

Cassai made an unintelligible noise of delight and threw herself into him with such force it almost knocked him off his feet. He wrapped his arms tightly around her and squeezed, shaking with laughter of sheer elation. He'd never felt so light. He knew she was crying because light, warm rain began to sprinkle around them.

"Oh, my Taiya. How I missed you," he murmured into her hair.

The rest of the group closed around them before he relaxed his grip enough to notice.

"You're alive! You're okay!" Sophie exclaimed, wrapping her arms around as many of them as she could.

Elian looked up from the joyous throng of bodies to see Hollis grinning at him and Theoris crying freely on the Kiatri's shoulder. "Welcome back, Fontre. It's about time."

Theoris looked up and wiped his eyes. "I say, dear boy, you do have a habit of turning up unexpectedly." He sniffled happily. "What in this mortal world —?" Theoris cried, pointing over Elian's shoulder.

Elian turned to see a tiny, blinking creature floating beside his face. She flickered her tiny purple eyes at him. Miniscule tears flowed down her cheeks. Elian smiled and reached out a hand for the dandelion fairy to rest in. "So she let you go after all. I can't believe it."

"Is that a dandelion fairy? Oh my word!" said Sophie. "How did you —? You have to tell us everything right this second."

"Everything is a bit much for this particular second." He already felt his strength leaching away. His back burned and his shoulder wound had started to bleed again.

"Do please tell me that's the fairy I think it is. The one at her bedside table?" Theoris demanded, too focused on the fluffy-skirted fairy to notice Elian's pallor.

"It is. Her nightlight." The tiny fairy landed on Elian's finger and he looked into her eyes. "You're free now, my friend. Go home to your family." The fairy blinked, but gave no sign of understanding.

Hollis stepped up and held out a hand. Elian tipped the fairy gently toward Hollis. "*Isilinoth eire*," Hollis whispered. The fairy landed lightly on Hollis' hand and sang something in the same language. Hollis replied something Elian didn't understand and the fairy buried her face in her tiny hands, her shoulders shaking with sobs. "Believe it or not, she's very happy. She asked me to thank you."

Elian nodded. "My pleasure. Can she find her way back to her people?"

"Of course she can. No fairy can forget the way home." Hollis whispered something else to the dandelion fairy, who reached up, wiped her eyes and nodded.

Turning to give Elian one last, sad smile, the fairy raised her arms, singing a high, haunting tune of her people. She lifted into the air as she sang, spinning so quickly she appeared as a blur for a fraction of a second, and vanished into the air.

Cassai let out a delighted gasp. "I'm so glad you rescued her."

"Look what else the Queen sent," Krispen said, holding out a bag clearly not made from mortals' materials. It was blue and shimmered ostentatiously against the dull backdrop of trees and earth. Krispen opened it curiously, but Elian laid a hand on his.

"It's from her, Krispen. Be careful."

Krispen withdrew his hand slowly. "What's this silver thing?"

A silver chain dangled from his fingers and from it hung a vial that filled Elian with relief. "By the Weaver," he breathed, "she sent me the antidote."

"The antidote?" asked Cassai.

"To her version of the Fontre Draught," answered Elian. A shadow crossed his face for the first time. He took the vial from Krispen, unstopped it and brought it to his lips. When he'd taken two sips, he replaced the stopper and dropped the chain over his head so that the vial came to rest on his breast. "I don't know how much is needed to break the symptoms, but we'll start with that." He smiled at Cassai, but she didn't smile back.

"She had the Fontre Draught? How? I thought it was destroyed."

"She took a sample from me before lending me her help with the Koninjka. Part of our deal."

"I get the feeling you got the very raw end of that deal."

Elian cradled her face in his battle-worn hands. He drank in every detail of her sparkling grey eyes and the freckles on her nose and ached to kiss her lips. "I would say I underpaid."

Cassai smiled, and kissed one of his palms. The trees trembled, but she ignored them. She took his other hand in hers and kissed that too. The feeling of her lips pressed against his skin, coupled with adrenaline from the fight wearing off, made Elian light-headed. He swayed and Krispen rushed to catch him.

"He needs medicine — more than just that stuff." He nodded to the silver vial.

The flurry of people and voices surrounded Elian, but he couldn't discern them individually.

"Hold him up a moment and we'll make a pallet."

"Here, let me get this side."

"Someone hand me that water skin."

"Get my satchel and Hollis'. I need everything we've got." That last was Cassai. Elian was being lowered onto soft blankets. Gentle hands began to unwrap him from his clothing. He knew, deep down, that he should feel embarrassed to be undressed in front of everyone, but he couldn't summon the energy.

"Why's he shaking like that?" cried out Sophie in alarm.

"He's just fought with Goliard for our freedom, and he was already tired out," Krispen said, his voice trembling.

"He'll be alright, Krispen. Someone get Krispen some water, he's been through a horrible ordeal," Cassai ordered. "Elian, I'm giving you something to help you rest. Hold your head up a bit. Perfect. Swallow and lie back down. You're going to sleep now."

"I don't want to sl —" Elian couldn't finish his thought because a thick, velvety blackness dropped over him.

CASSAI SAT ON THE GROUND, working in almost total silence. Everyone stood quietly around her. She only spoke to ask someone to lift Elian's body or hand her a clean rag. When they had him stripped of his clothes, she gasped and clapped her hands to her mouth at the state of him. Hollis put a comforting hand on her shoulder, but she couldn't help noticing he was shaking. She determined that she wouldn't cry no matter how bad it was, but a few angry tears fell anyway. The back of his body was raw, cut and bleeding from the nape of his neck to his knees. She barely saw one inch of skin untouched by whoever had been torturing him.

Krispen sat at Elian's head, anxiety etched into every feature.

"Krispen, what on earth did this?" Cassai demanded.

The boy bowed his head. "They made him take that stuff the first day. I wasn't there. I couldn't stop them." Krispen's voice cracked, but he took a deep breath and continued. "It was terrible. Every bad thing his folks ever did to him happened again, and again, and again. They only let him go at night. I stayed up to bring him out of the memories if they struck him." Krispen buried his face in his arms and started to sob.

"Nothing they did to him was your fault, Krispen," Hollis said. Uncharacteristic softness had crept into his voice. "You couldn't have stopped her and Elian wouldn't have wanted you to try."

"No, he certainly wouldn't have. You would've been hurt, and that would've been more torturous to him than this," Cassai assured the poor boy. "Come on, I'll need your help. Let's get him cleaned up. I have something to fight off infection and ease the pain."

Krispen had a haunted look in his eyes. "She watched it happen all day long. She loved it, I swear."

Cassai's stomach roiled. She gripped her rag a little tighter, but tried desperately not to let the image get to her. "Of course she did. She's insane. The blue bottle, Krispen. I need almeris...and some cold water from my water skin."

She busied herself cleansing the wounds and then treating

them. All around her the companions had begun milling restlessly. They'd only planned to stop for a few minutes and were over an hour off-schedule. She hoped no one would mention this. Elian would insist on not holding them up and probably damage his body further.

"Goliard stabbed his shoulder too," Krispen informed her when she had worked her way down his legs.

"Oh, right. I felt it only a few minutes before you two reappeared." Cassai rubbed her shoulder absentmindedly. "I'm almost finished here then we'll bandage him up and turn him."

"What can I do?" Hollis was over her shoulder again.

"We need to turn him in a minute. Let me finish the bandages first."

"I can help with the bandages. Hand me a stack." Hollis began at the shoulders, while Cassai worked on his legs. She wrapped bandage after bandage around his hips. Hollis managed to make a large pad to cover his back and only had to secure it with a few wraps around Elian's torso. He had woken enough to groan in pain each time they lifted him.

"Try his other side," Cassai suggested after they had done this twice. She felt his right ribcage and knew why he was groaning in pain. "He's cut up and bruised badly on his right side, and I missed it."

Hollis swore and moved to Elian's other side, made difficult by the tree trunks the pallet lay against. "Let's move the bedding so we can get to him. Krispen, grab that end." Elian cried out as his bed pivoted away from the obstructions.

"I'm so sorry," Cassai murmured at his ear. "That's all done now. Let's get this side of you patched up, shall we?" She tried to keep her voice light, but her anger at the fey was growing darker with every newly discovered injury. "I'm going to kill her, Hollis."

"Yes," he agreed grimly. "I'll add her to the list I'm making. We'll have to get him on his back for the shoulder wound. He can't lie on that side."

"He can't lie on his back either," she muttered. "I guess it's the lesser of two evils."

"Cassai?" Elian whispered.

Her heart raced at the sound of his voice. "Yes, I'm right here."

"Oh, thank the Weaver. I thought it was a dream..." His voice trailed off and he reached out his hand for her. She slipped hers into it. "Could I have a drink of that?" He nodded toward the water skin next to his head.

"Absolutely. Can you lift yourself a bit? Sorry," she added when he pushed up and grimaced in pain.

"No problem. I feel better now. Thank you." He sounded out of breath.

"Can you roll onto your back? We've got to see to your shoulder," said Hollis.

Elian took a swallow of the water Cassai had lifted to his lips. He closed his eyes tightly and nodded. "Yes. It may take me a minute." He held his breath and inched himself over slowly. Cassai caught him and lowered him down as gently as possible. He lay against his damaged back, panting with the effort and pain.

"Here's the wound. About three inches across, but it's pretty deep and bleeding so much. I should have staunched it right away." Cassai assessed the stab-wound clinically. "Krispen, hold this against it hard. I need a needle and thread." Krispen obediently applied pressure, and Cassai dug through her satchel for the sewing kit the Hermit had given her. "We can't move him today, Hollis," she said, not looking at the Kiatri.

Hollis, looking into Krispen's bag, simply nodded. "No. We can't." His easy compliance to this request struck her in a way that none of her nursing had done. Her eyes welled up and she couldn't hold back the tears. Dropping the sewing kit, she pushed herself up and fled into the trees.

She found one with a wide, sturdy trunk and sank to the ground at its roots. She heard the rain hitting the leaves, breaking through, felt them on her shoulders and falling into her hair. She heard soft footfalls and assumed someone had followed her. Long cold fingers touched her shoulder. When she looked up, it was into the sad, purple eyes of Theoris.

"Will he make it?" he asked hoarsely.

"I think he will. He's so strong...it's just going to take a while," she choked out between sobs. He lowered himself awkwardly by his crutch to sit beside her.

"I'm sure I'm not who you wish to see, but Hollis is stitching up Elian and asked me to make sure you were safe."

"Why would I not wish to see you?"

Theoris ran his fingers distractedly through his spiky yellow hair. "Because I am fey," he admitted.

"I don't hold this against all the fey, Theoris. There's no way this could possibly be your fault. You've been with me this entire time."

"I'm pretty sure Hollis won't see it that way."

She choked out a laugh. "No, probably not. But he'll live. He knows what she is better than anyone."

"Indeed. He does know...that doesn't mean he understands. He looks at me like he wants to run me through." Theoris shuddered. Cassai felt a pang when she noticed how soaked he was. She shrugged and put an arm across his sodden shoulder.

"He's always looked at you that way. He's probably trying to decide which of you he's more upset at, Elian for being Fontre or you for being a fairy." She smiled and he rolled his eyes.

"It's a close contest." Hollis' voice made them both jump.

"Oh hello, Hollis. We were just talking about how much we love you." Cassai gave him a smile and he winked at her.

"He could use you, if you're feeling up to it."

"Yes. Sorry, I just..."

"I know. Don't worry about it." He held out a hand to help her up. Theoris shrank away from him. "I don't know why you're flinching, fairy," Hollis growled. "It's not like she'll let me hurt you." Then he held out a hand and helped Theoris up as well making Cassai smile to herself.

Cassai walked slowly back into the clearing, trying to swallow her guilt that everything, including Elian and his bedding, was now rain-soaked. Someone had propped his head on a rolled-up blanket. Probably Krispen, she decided, feeling warm all over for the boy.

Elian's eyes were open. She noticed heavy bruising on his face, and his lips were cracked. "Krispen, could you give us a minute?" Elian asked.

Krispen nodded and pushed himself up. He threw one more apologetic look toward Cassai and disappeared into the trees.

Elian beamed at her and she dropped down next to him. "That was refreshing," he teased.

"Shut up. Did Hollis stitch you correctly?" She pretended to need to check his stitches. He caught her hand and pressed it against his stubbly cheek.

"I can't believe it's really you. I didn't think I'd ever leave that place. I almost didn't," he breathed.

"Thank you for making it back to me."

The look he gave her was so intense it made her insides turn from warm to blazing hot. "I love you so much, my darling girl."

"Don't. You're going to make everything wet again," she warned him as more tears welled up in her eyes and threatened to spill over. "I love you too, you know. A little," she added, trying to lighten the mood. He laughed softly and closed his eyes, still holding her hand against his face.

20

THE ASHES

E lian woke lying on his stomach the next morning, stiff
and feeling as if his whole body had been pressed against
a red-hot iron. Cassai lay curled up against his undamaged side. He smiled and stroked her face softly, trying not to
wake her. Her lips curled upwards in her sleep, but she didn't stir
when he pushed himself up slowly and painfully.

No new injuries this morning, he thought with relief. Perhaps
the antidote had worked. When his blanket fell off, he realized he
was naked. He tried to remember details from the previous day,
but it was a haze of pain and drug-induced sleep.

Krispen sat against a tree trunk above where Elian's head had
lain. His arms rested on his knees with his head buried in them.
The way his shoulders rose and fell, Elian assumed he had fallen
asleep keeping watch. He looked around for his clothes and saw
them strung up close to the fire along with other articles of clothing. Rain. He remembered now. Cassai had cried while trying to
mend his shoulder. He snagged his clothes from the line and
ducked into the trees to dress. He didn't see Hollis until he almost
tripped over him.

"Morning," said the Kiatri, without looking up. "How are you feeling?"

"Slightly flayed... but good." Elian pulled his clothes on slowly, bearing the searing pain in silence. Finally dressed, he lowered himself next to Hollis.

Hollis held out a roll. Elian shook his head. "Not hungry?"

"Not really."

A muscle jumped in Hollis' jaw. "She made you eat the food."

"Yes."

The Kiatri sighed. "It wears off eventually."

"Good to know."

"Never completely though. Sorry."

Elian shrugged. "It's not the worst that could have happened."

Hollis shook his head. "No, there, it certainly wasn't. How are you otherwise?"

"Free." Elian smiled and picked up the roll from Hollis' bag. "I'm sore from head to foot, but honestly, I've never been better."

Hollis' eyes widened. "Really? I'm glad to hear that torturous experience was so positive for you."

Elian laughed and took a bite of the roll. It tasted like sawdust, but he ate it anyway, his body needed the nutrition. The two men sat in silence, eating rolls and cured meat and watching the trees.

"At the risk of sounding like Cassai, do you want to talk about it or just sit there grinning like an idiot?" Hollis asked finally.

"You sound exactly like Cassai. The resemblance is uncanny." Hollis glared at him. "The Queen was...herself. I was her toy and for a while she enjoyed ripping me to shreds. The Fontre Draught is even worse when reformulated by fairies and injected into your bloodstream. So I relived everything from my past over and over again. Then Goliard wanted a go at me. Happy as I was to fight him, by the time Dahlia had her fun I could barely stand, much less fight. At first it went as you'd expect. He had me pinned to the ground, but he didn't realize who he'd picked a fight with."

"You defeated Goliard?" asked Hollis in disbelief.

"With some help. The Hermit showed up." Elian watched Hollis' face, but he showed no surprise. "At least, I think he was really there. No one else seemed to see him. He talked to me; talked me into letting go of all the past I'd held on to so tightly for so long. And that was all. I couldn't feel the pain. All I felt was freedom. I stood up and looked straight at Goliard. He was so angry."

"His power was broken?"

"The Hermit said Goliard only had his victim's own pain and bitterness to work with. So, I couldn't feel the pain anymore. It was a more even match after that. Sort of. No disrespect to fey warriors, but Goliard wasn't exactly trained by Devilan. I didn't kill him. I didn't have to. He surrendered. I...gouged one of his eyes out."

Hollis' head swivelled toward Elian, his mouth gaped. "You did what?"

Elian frowned and avoided eye-contact. "I knew he'd carry on torturing people as before, and Dahlia didn't release me when he gave his surrender, so I gave them a little nudge in the right direction."

"Well," said Hollis shaking his head. "You are Fontre after all."

Elian shrugged.

Hollis smiled. "That shouldn't make me as happy as it does, should it?"

"No, probably not. Doesn't matter though. I'm happy about everything at the moment."

"Well, nothing like a good war to keep your spirits up. When we get to the Westerling Field, lead out with that."

Elian chuckled, shook his head, and stood. "I'll break camp. We should travel as far as we can today."

Hollis nodded. "If we make good time, we should be there tomorrow or, at the latest, the next day. Hopefully, Marcus will be ready with the Kiatri by then. I can't imagine they'll be much good

301

though. One month is nothing when it comes to training an army."

Elian looked down at him. "Maybe we can buy him more time. I have an idea."

"Go on."

"It isn't a full plan yet, but I'm thinking we might do to them what they did to us. Infiltrate and win this war from the inside out."

"How can we get in? There are a few of us I think they'll recognize," Hollis pointed out.

"The tunnels."

"Edgewater's tunnels?"

"Edgewater's tunnels."

"What if we should encounter Edgewater while trying to use them? How many battles are you planning here?"

"We're going to use them with Edgewater's permission."

Hollis shook his head in total disbelief. "There's no way Edge will agree to that. Those tunnels are supposed to be secret."

Elian nodded. "Exactly, supposed to be secret, but we know about them. Might put Edgewater into a bargaining mood."

"Or, into a shredding us to bits sort of mood," mumbled Hollis, but Elian ignored him.

CASSAI WOKE to the sound of the campfire sizzling as it was doused. "Elian," she said hoarsely, pushing herself up. "What are you doing?"

"Good morning, beautiful," he replied softly.

"Good morning. Are you packing up? Where's everyone else?"

"Hollis is patrolling, Theoris is there," Elian pointed to the fairy rolling up blankets. "Sophie's hunting."

Cassai saw that Krispen was just waking and stretching out from the long night sleeping upright.

"How are you this morning?" Elian asked.

Cassai ran her fingers through her tangled curls and scowled at him. "How are *you* is the better question. Why are you up and moving around? You should be resting."

"I can't sit still. Sorry. I haven't ruined any of your doctoring."

Cassai got up and pointed to the blankets she had vacated. "Lie down. I'm reapplying everything before we leave."

Elian rolled his eyes. "We can do that later." Cassai fixed him with a withering glare. "Or we could do it now." He peeled his shirt off slowly.

"Pants too," Cassai ordered.

Elian finally stopped smiling. "I just got them back on."

"Pants too!" she barked.

Elian held up his hands in surrender. "Pants too, got it."

"Is Sophie back yet?" Hollis asked, coming into the clearing. Elian's fingers froze on his belt.

"Not yet," he said embarrassed.

Hollis' eyebrows shot up. "Have I interrupted something?"

"I'm going to put more ointment on his wounds and change his bandages. I could use your help," said Cassai. Elian sighed and unfastened his belt.

"I'll help," said Krispen groggily.

Elian lowered himself onto his stomach and felt Hollis at his shoulders.

Hollis patted his shoulder cheerfully. "Remind me about that eternal happiness business."

Elian winced as the rag touched his raw skin. "Shut up, Hollis."

WHEN THEY STARTED OFF, Elian was glad of Cassai's fussing. His back felt cooler and, while his shoulder throbbed painfully, he was able to carry his own gear and sling Cassai's satchel over his uninjured shoulder. She protested, but, since he'd given in earlier, he felt he'd earned the right to ignore her. She and Sophie walked on either side of him, chattering about their journey. He smiled and nodded enough to keep them both going.

By midday, Cassai called for a halt. His legs and back were on fire again, and he stifled a groan when he sat down.

"I wonder if we should —" said Cassai.

"I'm not undressing right now," he stopped her.

"I have something that'll help." Krispen dug through his bag and produced a small red pill. Elian's stomach lurched at the sight of it, more from the memory it inspired than the pill itself.

"What's that?" Cassai demanded.

"It's medicine the Fairy Queen gave him. It doesn't do anything bad. Just numbs the pain for a while," Krispen said.

"If it doesn't do anything bad why would she give it to him?" she asked, her eyes narrowing.

"She was strange that way." Elian held out a hand and Krispen dropped the small red pill into it. He popped it into his mouth and washed it down with a swallow of water from Cassai's water skin. "I took it a few times while I was there. She wanted me to be able to carry on conversations when I wasn't — well, anyway, I had to take something to be able to think straight." Cassai bit her lip, and Elian pulled her up against his good side. "It's alright."

"She drugged you to make you suffer, then watched you suffer, then drugged you so you could suffer some more," she whispered.

"That makes it sound worse than it was," Elian tried to reassure her.

Krispen huffed out a breath. "Sounds *better* than it really was."

Elian sighed. Hollis took a long drink of water and shook his head. "Never mind them, Krispen. This is what they do." Elian was surprised at the lack of venom in the Kiatri's voice. "Shall we discuss this later? When that pill kicks in, we should get moving again."

"We're almost walking parallel to Plahn," Cassai remarked, not budging from Elian's side. "Could we risk a peak into town, Hollis? If we stick to the woods and just look through the trees?"

Hollis looked at Elian, who shrugged. "Your choice, Cassai. If we can stay out of sight it won't be much of a delay," Hollis said.

"We'll keep off the road. I just want to see it again, even from a distance," said Cassai. Elian gave her a final squeeze and unwrapped himself from her.

"The pill is working. We can head that way," Elian said. Krispen extended a hand, and Elian took it to pull himself up. He tried ignoring the pain that lanced through his shoulder, but there was no misreading his eyes.

"The pill isn't actually working yet is it?" Cassai demanded quietly. Elian smiled and squeezed her shoulder.

"Working well enough. I'm ready to see my village again."

Krispen frowned, but instead of protesting, he lifted the satchels from Elian's shoulder and slipped them on top of his own.

They made their way down the path as quietly as they could. The closer they got to the outskirts of town, the quieter they grew, not wanting to alert anyone to their presence. Elian judged they were about a mile outside of town when he smelled the smoke. Cassai noticed it at the same time. His heart sank at the comprehending look on her face and they broke into a run.

He heard the others trying to keep up behind him, but didn't slow down to accommodate them. Wounded as he was, he outstripped Cassai and managed to throw out an arm to stop her from tearing through the underbrush into the smoldering ruin that had been Plahn.

"Don't. There may be Fontre here," he muttered, and moved slowly out of the trees, wanting to assess the damage without being spotted by lingering soldiers.

Every building had been torched. Most were razed to the ground, but he could make out the charred skeletal remains of the Apothecary. One wall of the building where they held Hermordes still remained. He looked around for signs of life, but his senses detected nothing.

"No one is there," he assured the companions following him slowly out of the trees. Cassai slipped her hand into his, and they drew comfort from each other as they moved toward their beloved village's remains.

"It's my fault," she breathed. He squeezed her hand.

"No. It's the fault of those who set it ablaze."

"It must have been your brother. He did it because I escaped rather than keeping my word to return with him."

Elian's eyes narrowed. He put both hands on Cassai's shoulders and turned her to face him. "The Fontre did this because of who they are, not because of you. Devilan's a monster, and that's final."

Her shoulders moved up and down and he felt the muscles start to relax. "Okay."

"Okay. Let's comb the rubble for survivors." He pulled her into a quick hug, drawing comfort from her before plunging in to what was sure to be a devastating search.

The others had caught up. "Holy dragons-breath! What a mess!" Theoris exclaimed, totally winded, but supported between his crutch and Hollis' shoulder. "Was this your town?"

"Devilan?" Hollis asked.

Elian nodded. "We're going to see if anyone survived."

The group moved soberly and silently into the smoke-palled streets.

Elian raked his fingers through ash heaps looking for human remains, but finding only ashes and blackened stones. He was sifting carefully through the Butcher's shop, when Hollis called out.

"Elian, over here." Hollis stood in the middle of what had been the Hermordes building. Elian watched the one remaining wall carefully, wondering how likely it was to fall. "See the door?"

The door had collapsed inward and lay almost intact, the

outside of it facing up. "It was bolted," Elian said. "From the outside."

"Yes. But I don't see any —" Hollis paused and glanced around for Cassai. She was several feet away, looking into the tiny schoolhouse. "Bodies." Hollis finished in a whisper. "If they locked them in, where are their bones?"

Elian chewed his lip and tried to allow himself a flicker of hope. "Maybe they got out some other way."

"Maybe they were taken." Sophie had come up from behind the men.

"That seems likely," Elian admitted. "But then, why lock the door?"

She shrugged. "Why burn everything? They're Fontre, right? Maybe there was something else in here they thought the people wouldn't want destroyed."

"Trust me, of any building in this town these people didn't want destroyed, this building was least likely to inspire despair." Elian rubbed his forehead and looked at Cassai. She made eye contact and started toward him.

"I don't see signs of...anyone," she said.

"No. Everything is empty. I don't know if that's a hopeful sign or not." The lightness Elian had enjoyed that morning started to desert him.

"They could've seen the Fontre coming and found some clever place to hide," Theoris offered. "They don't exactly blend into the landscape. Or, well, in this blackened landscape they would perhaps, but a cheerful little town —" He let the thought trail off and Elian tried to smile as if encouraged.

Cassai's eyes were filling with tears. He saw her fighting hard against them and resisted the urge to go to her, knowing his touch would break her tenuous control. "I want to see our valley again." Her voice trembled.

Hollis shook his head. "We should move on."

"It's on the way and there's plenty of tree cover," said Elian.

Hollis sighed and nodded reluctantly, looking up at the sky. "We'll camp there tonight. It's as good a clearing as any."

Elian nodded silently and closed the gap between himself and Cassai. Her eyes were set, controlling emotion. She laced her arm around his waist and he rested his on her shoulders. They walked back into the tree line that led to their valley. Elian's throat hurt and despair sank into his chest. All the pain he'd displaced on the journey started to push in on him.

"Am I hurting you? Your back just went all stiff," Cassai said.

"I'm hurting, but it's not you. I'd rather have you near."

She pressed in closer. "I missed you so much."

He drew her up and kissed her head. The surrounding woods rumbled, but not dangerously. "I can't even describe how much I missed you. I thought I'd never see you again."

"I would've come and taken you back by force if I had to," Cassai assured him.

Elian grinned and gave her another squeeze. "I believe you, but I'm glad you didn't have to. Could you feel the torture?" he asked.

"Not the whippings. Presumably because they happened in your past. But I felt the soreness. Right before you came back to me, I think maybe Goliard had you. It felt like burning and stabbing and all of that. I felt it all until it lifted, not just the momentary pang as usual. And then you were here. I can't believe she let you go early."

"I guess we can thank Goliard for that. He wanted a go at me before I was too injured to fight. The Draught she'd concocted was even harder on me than the original. I experienced my past over and over and over until I could barely walk. In the end, Krispen was helping me up and down. Thank the Weaver for that boy. I'm pretty sure he kept me alive." Elian's voice trailed off as his thoughts went dark and cold. He shivered. A painful spasm hit him and he had to pause and wait for it to pass.

"Krispen!" Cassai called. The boy was at Elian's side in a moment. "We need another pill."

He produced the red pill and the water skin. "I should have had it for him sooner. I'm sorry," Krispen lamented, waiting for the agony to pass enough for Elian to hold the water skin.

"No, don't apologize. He was just saying how very helpful you were in the Fairy Realm. I'm so grateful."

Krispen's features darkened and he looked away. Elian wished there was something he could say to ease the agony from his shepherd boy's eyes. "That's better. Thanks." He straightened again and rested his arm on Cassai's shoulder again, though perhaps heavier than before. She bore him up without a word.

"Everything alright?" Hollis asked impatiently.

"He needs a moment," Krispen said.

"No, I'm ready now," Elian assured them.

"I can help him; we're coming." Cassai stood up even taller and propelled them both forward.

Elian tried hard not to lean too heavily on her while the pill started to work.

"Tell me more about your time there."

"They have a dragon," said Elian, grinning.

"A dragon?"

"And a cherubim, caged, sadly. I wish I could have ridden the dragon. She probably would have let me, but it wasn't safe. I was taken at such unpredictable times by the memories."

"The same as before?"

Elian took a deep breath. "I went to more of the ones with Ffastian, unfortunately." He felt her stiffen again. "I'm doing better now than I ever did," he assured her. "I let it all go at the end. I just forgave him." When his voice broke she stopped in the path to look at him.

"Really?"

He smiled and stroked her face, following the freckle line down her nose on to her cheek. "Really. Finally."

Her face lit with relief. "I'm so happy for you. What a weight off your shoulders."

"Yes, possibly to be replaced by more," he said, glancing back toward their ruined village.

"At least it's not one thing on top of another," Cassai noted, replacing his arm on her shoulder.

"Agreed. How many times have we walked this path? Remember when we used to go into town and buy sugar and cloth?"

"Ah! The good old days. I miss them. I miss Nanna. I miss our sheep."

"Me too. All of that."

The trees had started to thin and the companions ahead slowed as they approached their destination.

"Should we circle around and check it out first?" asked Hollis.

Elian nodded. "The Koninjka know where it is."

Hollis and Sophie started in one direction and Theoris and Krispen went in the other, staying in the trees.

Elian and Cassai approached the last of the tree line and peered through where they used to be able to spot their cottage. Cassai gasped. Elian jumped and followed her gaze.

No Koninjka were in sight, but clusters of people dotted the whole valley. Townspeople. Their people. Elian and Cassai looked at each other, shocked.

"Do you think it's a trap?" Cassai asked.

Elian drew his sword. "Stay here."

For once she didn't argue, but ducked behind the shrubbery where she'd hidden the day he sent her to the *Lozere*. He paused to make sure she couldn't be seen and then stepped through the trees and into the valley.

A cry of recognition sounded.

"Elian!" shouted a voice that made Elian's grip on his sword tighten and his body tense. Cobbs, his face smeared with grime and soot, was walking toward him, his sword also drawn.

21

THE BEAUTY

"Elian, I'm sorry." Cobbs spoke first. Elian noticed that the blade of Cobbs' sword trembled as he spoke.

Elian scowled and raised his own sword an inch higher. "Cobbs, what is this? Are the Fontre here?"

Cobbs shook his head as he sheathed his sword. He raised both hands in surrender, looking weary to his bones. "It's just us here. They searched for us, but in the wrong direction. We hid ourselves really good."

Elian heard cries of recognition coming from clumps of townspeople, but he kept his gaze pinned on Cobbs. Behind him, his companions had started to gather round him cautiously.

"Elian? Is he friend or foe?" Hollis asked.

"Foe," said Elian.

"Friend," said Cobbs at the same time. Elian heard a rustle and both Sophie and Hollis had arrows aimed at Cobbs' heart. Cassai joined them, her sword raised. "I swear, I'm a friend," Cobbs shrank back.

"Explain," Elian growled. "Quickly."

"Yes, I will. Do you want to sit? It's a kinda' long story and you look a bit ... used up."

Elian glanced at his companions for an answer. "Do you trust them?" Hollis asked quietly.

"I don't trust Cobbs not to lead us into an ambush."

"If there are Fontre here, they've hidden well. I saw no sign of horse or boot prints anywhere in the woods," Sophie said.

Elian looked into Cassai's eyes. "What do you make of it?"

She scowled at Cobbs, "Collin," she said quietly.

Cobbs flinched. "I — I screwed that up."

Elian turned back to him slowly. "Screwed that up? Is that really the best you can do?"

Cobbs shook his head again. "There ain't nothin' I can say about that to make it right."

"As I recall, you smiled while they whipped him and then threatened Elian with the same. Or did you think I'd conveniently forget that moment?" Cassai demanded, taking another step towards him.

"Cassai, I swear I didn't know what they did after. I didn't know...'bout Naya." His voice broke, but Cassai looked far from convinced of his contrition.

Her eyes filled with rage and she pushed the tip of her blade against his chest. "I wouldn't bring up Anaya if I were you."

"I saved them. As many as I could —" Cobbs stammered instead of answering. He made no move to protect himself from Cassai's sword.

Elian lowered his weapon and put a hand on Cassai's shoulder. "I think he's telling the truth," he whispered.

"What if he's just saying what he thinks we want to hear to let him live?"

Elian sighed and shrugged his shoulders. "Then we'll kill him."

Cassai turned back to Cobbs. "Give up your sword. Remove it slowly with your thumb and forefinger."

Cobbs looked surprised, but pinched the handle of his sword and withdrew it as ordered. He held it out to Cassai, offering her the handle.

Elian glared at his old enemy. "Don't make any sudden movement or any attempt to signal anyone, or you will find yourself missing appendages ... or the ability to draw breath. We'll hear you out."

Cobbs nodded and turned to lead them down into the valley. A flurry of excited townsfolk greeted them. Elian's elation that they were alive and not captives or burnt to ashes overwhelmed his suspicion of Cobbs. He and Cassai hugged and kissed the cheeks of their old friends while Elian attempted to convince himself that all was well.

He noticed a great change in the way they treated Cobbs, as if they not only trusted, but respected him. Elian took this as a hopeful sign. Steaming mugs of tea were passed to the group. They sat around a blazing fire in the old stone fireplace, which now stood alone in the rubble of their cottage.

Elian's insides warmed at the friendly reception. Krispen helped Theoris over the rubble and lowered him carefully to the floor. Sophie had slung her bow across her body and sheathed the arrow. Krispen sat at one side of Elian, Cassai pressed against his other side, holding her tea and staring around in joy and disbelief that their friends were still alive. Hollis stood alone at what had once been their doorway, his arrow still aimed at Cobbs' head.

"Tell us," Elian said quietly.

Cobbs swallowed hard and looked into the fire rather than meet Elian's gaze. "I – I had a creekstone from Lord Devilan. They left it with me when they went off to the Forest. The Fontre could send messages through it. Anyway, I had it in my pocket and yesterday it started to deliver somethin'. It said: *Gather everyone for Hermordes. Bolt door outside.* Made me go all cold, it did. What could they want me to do that for? I could only think o' one reason. They wanted to gather 'em all up to kill 'em. I hate myself, but I was gonna' do it.

"I went into the blacksmith's shop to tell Frederick's wife there was a special Hermordes meeting. Cinda and her girls was there.

Olivia looked at me and smiled, jus' like that. Smiled at me like I was welcome. Said: 'Hey Cobbs. What can we do for ya?' And... and I jus' couldn't do it."

Tears filled the man's eyes and he searched the crowd for the girl. Elian spotted Olivia sitting next to her mother, smiling at Cobbs even now. Cobbs returned her smile and took a deep breath. "'Run', I says. 'We gotta' run and there's no time to lose. Where can we hide from 'em?' I took a second to explain the message and we all spread out, getting to everyone we could, sendin' them out to get others. When we thought we had everyone, someone says: 'There ain't no place big enough to hide us all.' Then I remembered this valley. I knew the Fontre knew where it was, but there's lots o' trees to hide in if they came, and I don't know – we jus' got lucky I guess.

"I thought to lock the door of the Hermordes building before we all took out. We was careful to stay on the road and not leave no footprints comin' from the building. I led 'em all here, then went back to watch from the trees.

"The Fontre marched in: Lord Devilan, and a few of his black soldiers. Didn't see Dershom nowhere. I got another message tha' said: 'Is it done?', so I messaged back, 'yes'. They went straight to that big building and spilled some kind of liquid stuff all around, checked windows to make sure they was secure, then torched it. It took 'em a while to realize there weren't no screams of fear or pain or nothin'. Then they went through and burned the whole town, every building, lookin' for us everywhere. Devilan sent me another message tha' said: 'You are dead.'" Cobbs held up the stone, which still blazed blood red with the threat. "They took the road toward the next town. I guess they're gonna' look for us there."

Elian stared at him. "You really did save them," he said, his voice filled with awe. "Cobbs, you actually did the right thing."

Cobbs looked sheepishly across at Olivia again. "Guess there's a first time for everything."

Elian grinned and gave Cassai a squeeze. "My thoughts exactly."

"So what is your plan now? The Fontre will be back," Cassai pointed out, taking a sip of tea.

"I don't know what to do now. We been tryin' to plan it out. Cinda said you and your Keepers was plannin' to go to the Westerling Field. Thought we should prolly head there."

"So why didn't you?" Elian asked.

"She jus' now said somethin' about it. Took her this long to trust me enough."

Elian nodded at Cinda appreciatively. "Not a bad idea," he assured her. "We should all leave tonight, as much as I'd like to rest. The Fontre certainly won't let a little darkness stop them." A low buzzing started as the townspeople reacted to this pronouncement.

Cobbs nodded and put his cup down, wiping his mouth. "Will you take me with you?"

Elian considered for a long moment. "Possibly. On one condition."

"Anything," answered Cobbs.

"Collin gets the final say on what happens to you." Elian stood painfully and helped Cassai to her feet. "Agreed?" he asked Cassai.

"I think that's more than fair," Cassai answered.

Cobbs nodded too. "Alright."

"Understand, if he says you should be whipped, or imprisoned or sent back to the Fontre, you will be. No questions asked. I'll tell him the good you did. But he gets the choice."

Cobbs paled, but nodded again. "Sounds about right. Where's he gone?"

"He's meeting us at the field. We'll discuss it there." Elian turned to the group of townspeople who had all started to mill around awaiting instructions. "We have to move quickly and quietly, and we can't use the road. We'll split into three groups.

Cobbs will take one group, I'll take one, and Cinda, will you lead the third?" Frederick's wife nodded heartily.

Elian divided the townsfolk by family. Very few men were present – most had gone to recruit for the Keepers. Elian tried to get an even number of the remaining men in each group and told men and women to grab anything they could use as a weapon. He sent Hollis with Cinda's group ahead of them into the woods that ran parallel to the road. "Do you know how to get there?" he asked Cinda.

She nodded. "We used to sometimes take the girls there to camp."

"Good. Hollis has eyes like a hawk, and he's very good in the woods. Listen to him if he tells you he senses danger." Cinda nodded and smiled at Hollis, who dipped his head but didn't smile.

"Let's get a move on, folks." Cinda raised her hand. The group assigned to her followed in a clump only breaking up at the woods to filter through the trees. When the last of them disappeared into the semi-darkness, Elian turned to Cobbs.

"Take your group next. Sophie, you and Theoris keep close watch on either side. Stick with them tightly. If you see any sign of Fontre, get them to hide in the trees and send Sophie straight back. You'll find us coming after you."

Sophie nodded soberly and she and Theoris circled round to the front of the group.

The sensation of Cobbs nodding agreement and heading off into the trees leading a group of his fellow townsfolk was so strange to Elian that he shook his head as he watched them go.

"I hope this is right," he murmured to Cassai.

"He did save their lives. Why would he do that just to massacre them in the woods?" Cassai reasoned. "Oh, wait! Cobbs, stop!" she called out. Cobbs halted and pivoted to face her. "Your sword," Cassai said, handing him his weapon. Cobbs smiled and sheathed it again. "Take care of them," she whispered earnestly.

Cobbs looked more sober than he had ever looked. "I promise."

Elian smiled at her as she trotted back. "Ready?"

She drew her sword and looked at him with fire in her grey eyes. "Yep."

He resisted the urge to pull her close and kiss her, no doubt destroying whatever was left of their childhood home. "Alright, Krispen?" The boy nodded. "Then let's get going."

COLLIN and the Lightlings followed Julius and Kirkus from a short distance, talking and teasing each other as though they were out for an evening stroll through the woods. Jacque and Nihl spent half the journey standing next to brambles or tree trunks and twisting their rings to see if they could call their brother into the middle of a bush or tree.

"You two need to stop it," Laurelle admonished them. "That is not why Lady Ella gave you those."

"You should try yours, Elle. Come on. Give it a go." Jacque urged her as he dislodged himself from a particularly spiky bush.

"This is childish." But Laurelle was lifting the necklace. "*Patoret*," she whispered. She gasped and threw her arms over her head as she shot high into the air, and landed fifteen feet down the path. Though the necklace slowed her down before she landed, she couldn't catch her feet under her and tripped hitting hard on her bottom.

"Elle!" The boys yelled half concerned half trying to conceal their laughter.

"Oh my word, are you alright?" Collin gasped, grabbing her arm to help her up.

"Oh you bunch of idiots!" she yelped. "Let go of me." She jerked her arm away from Collin and brushed the dirt and leaves from her dress.

"I'm sorry, Elle. I had no idea it would –" Jacque's explanation died at the black look she gave him.

"What are you kids playing at?" Kirkus demanded, rounding on the group. "D'you think we're out here having some sort of holiday?"

"Collin?" Julius said quietly but in a tone Collin could not mistake for anything but trouble.

"Sorry, they were trying out their gifts from Lady Ella and we got a bit carried away," Collin said quickly. "I'm so sorry."

"You realize, boy, this forest is full of werewolves, skorpelaks, molrats, poisonous insects of every variety and that's before the Koninjka get to you?" Kirkus roared.

Collin stood frozen to the spot.

"Where's Sacha?" Kirkus fumed.

"He's pulling the wagon," Nihl mumbled.

"Well maybe it's time you and your brother took a turn at that, eh? Maybe give you something better to do with your time than try and break each other's limbs against tree trunks."

"Yessir," both boys said in unison and fell back to relieve Sacha.

"Collin, get up here and walk with us." Julius said, his voice as soft as before, and still as terrifying to his nephew.

"Yes sir." Collin slunk to his uncle's side, glancing over his shoulder at Laurelle who made a face at him.

Sacha trotted up to join them, having not gotten in any trouble, hugged his father and chatted excitedly about what sort of food they ate in Border towns.

"So, Collin? What's the food like?"

"It's pretty plain, Sacha," Collin said shrugging. "Just bread and a bit of meat sometimes if you can get it. Greens if you grow them. My mom was pretty good at growing things but -." He glanced uncomfortably at his uncle.

"I was rubbish at gardening and we couldn't afford the Fontre's tariff on vegetables anyway." Julius shoved his hands in his pockets and Collin could tell he was embarrassed.

"Hey, you know what's fun to talk about?" Collin said, elbowing Sacha's ribs. "Flour rationing. Now that's a subject I discuss all day."

Sacha looked sideways at him but before he could ask Collin if he'd lost his mind, his head jerked up and he sniffed the air. "Do you smell that?"

Collin took a deep breath and his stomach felt instantly sick. The acrid smell of burning stone and wood filled his sinuses.

Julius and Kirkus darted through the trees, peering down toward Plahn. "Leave the wagon and get out of sight," hissed Kirkus to the youths. They scattered into the trees and waited as the older men made their way cautiously toward the road.

"What's wrong?" Sacha whispered loudly.

"Smoke. Lots of it. Something bad's happened," Marc hissed back.

They waited in a tense silence until they heard the men returning. Julius looked sober and pale. Kirkus was scowling.

"What is it?" Collin asked.

"Collin, come here, son," Julius said. Something in his tone made Collin want to run from him and into his arms at the same time.

"What's happened?" Collin asked, hearing his heartbeat pounding in his ears.

"Come here." Julius pulled Collin into his chest with one arm. Collin tried to breathe, now listening to his uncle's heart pound as well. "Plahn is...burned to the ground," choked Julius.

Collin started shaking, but Julius was holding him so tightly he couldn't fall even if his legs gave out.

He heard Laurelle gasp. "Oh, Collin!"

"Are they all dead?" Collin asked into Julius' shirt, bracing himself for the answer.

Julius' heart beat for a long time before he answered. "Worse. I think they've been taken captive. No bodies anywhere."

"Maybe they escaped. Some may have anyway." Collin pressed his face into his uncle's shoulder, but resisted the tears until he thought he would retch from the strain. Julius gripped him harder and Collin felt him shaking, felt something falling into his hair, then dripping onto his forehead.

Nobody spoke or moved until the two broke apart. Julius took a deep breath and walked into the trees a little ways off.

"Um...it's okay we're just..." Collin let the sentence drop and wiped his uncle's tears from his face.

Kirkus looked up at the companions. "Let's move. We should get to the rendezvous as quickly as we can. If the Fontre are about it's a bad idea to linger."

Sober and silent, each of the Lightlings followed Kirkus. Collin looked at Julius who turned at last, shoulders rising and falling evenly now, and joined the group.

Collin's throat had stopped burning, the tears had given up trying. He sighed, grabbed the abandoned cart handle and heaved it down the path.

"I've got it, Armrest." Jacque ruffled his hair and took the handle from him. "Just go be with your uncle."

HOLLIS' group walked late into the night until he felt they'd put enough distance between themselves and the potential invasion of the Fontre.

"I think we can stop here and get some sleep," he said to Cinda. The woman had trudged tirelessly along after him.

"Let's stop for a bit," she called out to the townspeople. Groans of relief rose from the group. They broke up into smaller huddles and began to lie down on blankets, or dropped onto the most comfortable patch of ground they could find.

"I'll be back," Hollis said to Cinda and started back to signal to the other groups about the halt. Cobbs' group had caught up and also stopped when they saw the families gathering to sleep.

"Give them a few hours' rest. We'll be at the Westerling Field in another few hours," said Hollis to Sophie and Theoris.

"Thank goodness! I'm collapsing where I stand," Theoris said. Hollis glared at him.

"Not you, idiot. You have to keep watch. If the Fontre come through these trees, your whole group will be slaughtered where you lie."

"I'll stay up," Cobbs said wearily. "I can't sleep anyway."

"Yes. Take that corner of the wood, and face outwards. Theoris, you take that tree. Sophie —"

"I've got the back," she replied.

"Yes." Hollis touched her face gently for a moment, searching her dark brown eyes for signs of exhaustion. She looked tired, but not worn out completely. "I'll come back through in a moment." He dropped his voice to a whisper. "Make Theoris get off that leg for a while, won't you? Make it sound like it was your idea."

He moved on to find Elian and Cassai's group. They were close behind and he saw them in only a few minutes.

"We think we're far enough from the valley to get some rest. There are a few children in my group who simply can't carry on." Hollis explained as he approached.

"Yes, mine as well," agreed Elian, looking back at the weary travelers. "Take some rest here, my friends. We should be out of danger." Even as Elian reassured them, Hollis' skin prickled, he grabbed an arrow and pivoted toward the trees.

"Shh," he whispered to the group. They quieted at once and froze.

"Hollis Farrell?" The familiar voice made Hollis' fingers tense on his bowstring.

"I've got an arrow pointed straight at you. Don't come any closer."

To Hollis' shock, Elian put a hand on his arm. "It's alright, Hollis, I knew he would come."

"You brought the pack here?" Hollis demanded.

"Krispen's scent brought them. Remember, we need to talk."

"We can smell you've got the kid. We jus' wanna' work somethin' out," said Edgewater.

"This is a mistake." Hollis shook his head.

Elian squinted into the darkness and gave a resigned sigh. "Come out. Let's talk."

Krispen pressed himself against Elian. "I don't wanna' see them."

"We won't let them hurt you, Krispen," Elian assured him.

"I guarantee it," Hollis growled, keeping his arrow trained at where Edgewater's voice came from.

Hollis turned to look at Elian and the man nodded.

"Fine, we'll talk," Hollis said, glaring as the pack stepped into the light of the torches.

Elian approached confidently. "Krispen, are they safe?" he asked the boy. Krispen bit his lip. It looked odd now, tall and broad as he had grown, for him to show a sign of nerves.

"I don't know, but I think so," he answered. Elian smiled at him and gave his arm a reassuring thump.

"Come and sit. We're taking rest just now." Elian turned Krispen toward the companions and they entered the circle together. Edgewater followed cautiously, keeping an eye on Hollis. Hollis looked around for more of the pack, and realized with a shock that these four were all that remained.

"You can put tha' down, Hollis Farrell. I mean ye no harm." Edgewater glowered at the arrow.

"If you mean no harm the arrow will do no harm to you. If you try anything, I can assure you it will take me less than the blink of an eye to run it through your heart."

"Me heart's not soft enough to be a good target. Ye' might wanna aim elsewhere." Edgewater grinned and, pushing the arrow aside, approached Hollis and patted him on the head. It was the friendliest gesture Hollis had had from the man in many long years, and it made his mouth feel dusty.

"Don't do that, Edge," Hollis warned quietly. He was keenly aware that every eye in the circle was trained on him and Edgewater. Elian's hand rested casually on his sword hilt.

"Shall we talk?" asked Elian.

"Yeah," answered Edgewater, not taking his eyes off Hollis' face. "Talkin's why we came." Hollis' glare didn't waver from Edgewater's yellowed eyes.

"Do you mind if I speak first?" Elian gestured to a spot on the ground big enough for the pack to sit.

Hollis sat down next to Elian with Krispen the other side of his master. Cassai sat on Hollis' other side, eyeing Edgewater with a venom rivaled only by his own.

"A small group of us need to use your tunnels," Elian whispered.

"Ha! You gotta' be kiddin' me! I knew the kid would give us up the minute he found ya'. Them tunnels ain't made for yer use. They're secret and I mean them to stay that way." Edgewater crossed his beefy arms across his chest and glared at Krispen. The boy shrank away from him.

"They'll stay secret to all but a few," Elian assured him.

Edgewater bared his teeth. "They'll stay that way, period." Hollis' bow slowly rose again, but Elian put up his hands for calm.

"I hope to have an intelligent discussion, Edgewater. I know you're capable of carrying on such a discourse. I don't mean to threaten or alarm you, and you're free to go any moment you wish."

Edgewater looked surprised at the diplomacy. Hollis swallowed hard and lowered his arrow again. He knew Elian's strategy was well thought out. He must keep from ruining it by spooking Edgewater before he heard the full plan.

"We need to infiltrate the Inner Kingdom, but a few of us are too…recognizable to go in at any gate. We want to go under the walls using your network."

"And what'll you give us in exchange? We don' give somethin for nothin'."

"Of course not. What do you want?"

"Fresh meat," said Edgewater.

Elian's eyes narrowed. "To eat?"

"No."

Elian shook his head. "Then, no. I won't give you innocent victims to grow your pack."

"Nothin' else we want."

"Would you prefer to continue as you do now? With a Namarielle on the throne there's a chance for the land to regenerate. Possibly, you and your men won't starve to death in Fondair. If the Fontre stay in power, within a year or two there'll be nothing left of Lashai."

"I thought you didn't mean to threaten me."

"I mean to tell you the truth. Perhaps you'd prefer a lie?"

"Have you got anything to drink?" Edgewater grumbled.

"We do. Tea or water?"

"Booze," Edgewater snarled.

"Sorry, none at the moment. I suppose I could add a little mud to the water and come nearer to the hospitality you showed me."

Edgewater roared with laughter and a few of the townsfolk who had settled down for the night startled awake. "I guess that's true enough, eh, sheepherder?"

"Sh!" admonished one particularly harassed looking mother who had just gotten her two children to sleep.

Edgewater started from his seat toward the woman, but Elian stood first. "Don't. And keep your voice down. These people have had a long day. I can offer you money from the coffers of the Fontre, should we manage to overthrow them. I can offer you sanctuary in this Forest, if we're in control. I can offer you many things that will make you considerably more comfortable. I cannot give you human sacrifice."

Edgewater sat down again. He looked at Hollis. "What abou' him? What's he say abou' all this?"

"I'm sitting right here. It isn't as though you've actually lowered your voice, so why speak about me as if I can't hear?" Hollis snarled.

"Alrigh' Hollis Farrell. I'll speak to you direct-like. What d'you think of this sheepherder's plan?"

"I think if anyone knows how to defeat the Fontre it's Elian. I think you're a traitor and a villain and more than likely planning even now how you will double-cross him. I'm also thinking you're in for a surprise if you think you can pull it off. He's good-hearted, but smart and more than willing to defend these people with his life... taking yours if necessary."

"Can I have him?" asked Edgewater in an offhanded way. Elian chuckled quietly, glancing at the exhausted mother.

"No. Sorry. I need him too badly."

Edgewater shook his head at Hollis. "Never thought I'd see a day you'd take up with a Fontre."

"He's hardly 'taken up' with him," Cassai spoke for the first time. Edgewater jumped as if he'd forgotten she was there.

"Hasn't he now, girlie? Don' suppose you're lookin' to take up with a real man and leave these posers to get themselves kilt on their own?"

Hollis put a hand on Cassai's shaking arm. "Not worth it," he whispered in her ear.

"I don't want to use his tunnels. I don't want to owe him anything ever," Cassai said sounding very close to losing control.

Elian's gaze met hers. "We'll think of something else."

"Now wait a momen'! How come she gets to decide?"

"She's the queen of this realm, or hadn't you heard?" Elian said, finally sounding hostile. Hollis felt it was about time. "The army, the forest, all of the Inner Kingdom belongs to her. If she says you get nothing, you get nothing."

"Queen of this realm, is she? This little girlie? What d'you know abou' that, eh' boys?" Their raucous laughter filled the woods and many more eyes turned to them in disapproval.

Elian glared pointedly at him as his hand slipped into his boot. "You're treading on dangerously thin ice, man."

Edgewater's gaze went to Elian's boot. He quieted instantly, remembering all too well the silver dagger hidden within. "I fergot. She's yer's ain't she? Young lovers and all that? Alrigh', yer Majesty. Alrigh', here it is. You may use my tunnels. You may have 'em fer free, and no hard feelin's fer that one time in the forest, eh?"

"Right," answered Cassai darkly. "No hard feelings."

"So here's a real offer. We don' want gold or nothin'. Tha' won' do my kind no good anyhow. Where would we spend it, eh? We want fer the Queen to do away with the old huntin' parties."

"Hunting parties?" Cassai repeated. Hollis' jaw went stiff.

Edgewater's eyes were completely devoid of mirth now. "That's right, girlie. There was huntin' parties fer those like us. Yer father set 'em up his own self. I seen more than one man strung up a tree jus' fer bein' bitten. Nothin' else. Not fer fightin' nor killin', jus' for bein'. What'd'ye say abou' that, now girlie? You think tha's right?"

Cassai looked at Hollis. "Is that true?"

Hollis twisted uncomfortably and nodded. "It used to be."

"I assure you, Edgewater Monse, there will be no such hunting parties under my rule. I'll make laws against them."

"I'll also say," Hollis hissed, "barbaric as those sanctioned hunting parties were, it isn't as though your kind did anything to ingratiate yourselves to mortals. I remember more than one raid by werewolves in the mountains and even more when I lived among the Borderlings."

"Well, what'd'ye expect us to do, eh? We can't earn a livin' or nothin'. We do what we gotta do to survive."

"We can help you in whatever way you need," Cassai assured him. "But you cannot raid villages in search of humans to bite. When the moon is upon you, you must remove yourself from humanity as far as possible. If you promise me that, I promise you we can find you jobs and resources. We can even try to find you a cure if you want it."

Edgewater chewed his lip for a long while. The clumps of people who had roused at his loud voice had all started settling when he finally spoke. "There ain't no cure fer this, girlie."

"There might be."

"I looked. I looked an' looked, and that man there looked with me." Edgewater nodded toward Hollis, who felt a knot of emotion forming in his abdomen. "We never found nothin' that'd take it away. But we like you. Like yer thoughts. You seem fair enough. Who knows wha' you'll be like when you get to tha' throne, but we'll see." Edgewater pushed his hands against his knees and stood with the rest of the pack.

Elian and his companions rose with them. For the first time, Hollis felt no inclination to aim an arrow.

Elian put out a hand. "Thank you for your co-operation."

Elian's hand disappeared in the man's giant grip. "There's a tunnel jus' on the other side of Plahn, should lead you under tha' wall and close to the castle. 'Course, there's spots everywhere and we can always dig more."

Elian nodded. "We'll start there."

Edgewater turned to Hollis. "Guess we'll be seein' ye then, eh?"

Hollis swallowed hard. "Yes. I'm sure we'll encounter each other again."

"Been a long time since I thought about them old days —" Edgewater's voice cracked. Hollis nodded. "Well then," Edgewater patted Hollis on the shoulder.

He turned to Krispen. "I'll give ye a minute boy. Say yer goodbyes."

"What?" Cassai said.

"Krispen stays with us," Elian said.

"Tha's not yer choice. He's one of us. He should be with us."

Krispen's face screwed up with tears. "I don't want to go."

"We'll keep comin'. Next time, we won't be so nice about it." Edgewater looked genuinely sad, but didn't yield.

"Edge, leave him be. He's happy here with us," Hollis said.

"He belongs with 'is own kind, Hollis Farrell. An' what're you gonna do with him, eh? Gonna tie him up at full moon? Keep him as a pet?"

"Keep him as a pet?" Cassai's voice went shrill. "He's not an animal!"

"No, he ain't. An' I'm real glad you see it that way. Hopefully, you'll keep it in mind if you take back this wretched land." Edgewater nodded to Krispen and he and his pack faded into the darkness.

"Krispen! Don't leave. We can protect you. We can do anything." Cassai was trying desperately not to cry, which Hollis was grateful for.

Krispen wiped his eyes with the back of his hand. "They'll hurt you if I don't. I can tell by his eyes he will."

Elian's hand was on Krispen's muscled forearm. "You don't have to go if you don't want. We can figure something out with Edgewater."

"You'll keep them safe for me, won't you?" Krispen looked at Hollis, who nodded. Krispen grabbed Cassai into a hug. It wasn't a deep, affectionate hug of a grown man leaving a woman he loved, but the clinging, tearful hug of a small boy wanting his mother. "Goodbye." He released her and pelted into the woods after the pack.

Cassai stood still for a long while, staring after him, her chest rising and falling as she tried to calm herself.

Elian went to her side, but didn't touch her. "It's my fault. I shouldn't have engaged Edgewater. I knew he would come for Krispen, and I just let him because of my plans. I'm so sorry."

Cassai's turned away. "If one more person sacrifices himself for me, I swear..." But there was nothing to swear. Hollis knew the men surrounding Cassai would die to keep her safe. He certainly would.

Elian slipped his arm around her shoulder and led her away from the group where, Hollis assumed, they could mourn their lost shepherd boy in private.

22

THE WESTERLING FIELD

The next afternoon, Elian led his group into the Westerling Field. Cinda and Cobbs had halted their groups before coming out of the trees, waiting for Elian's group to join them before they all trudged into the giant field together. There were already several large tents dotting the fields. Borderlings, some they recognized and some not, milled around, stoking fires and sharpening farm tools into weapons.

Cassai walked beside Elian and looked up at him. "Ready to meet your army?" she asked.

He smiled. "I think these men belong to the Queen's army, actually." He gave her a squeeze and motioned everyone to follow him into the camp.

"Elian!" cried Altaskith, running across the field to greet them.

"Al!" Elian greeted the man with a bone rattling hug.

"Cassai! Are we ever glad to see you two? Weren't sure you'd make it. Where's Marcus and Frederick, that old rascal? He owes me a card match."

"Coming with the Kiatri."

"And Julius?"

Elian shook his head. "No word yet. Hopefully coming. How did you fare, my friend?"

"The Eastern Borderlands are feeling about the same as us. Got quite a few recruits, but nowhere near enough for a war. Just pockets here and there."

Elian smiled. "It's alright. Little things add up. We'll see how we stand when the rest have gathered. Have you any food or water? This group is famished and exhausted."

"Ay, a bit. What the blazes? You brought the whole village?" the butcher yelped, having at last torn his eyes from Elian and Cassai.

"We had no choice. The Fontre burned it to the ground."

Altaskith gaped at him. "You can't mean that? Who'd they kill?"

"Almost no one, thanks to Cobbs of all people." Elian scanned the group for Cobbs.

"Cobbs? That simpering *Nordian?*" The butcher's eyes had fallen on the unfortunate Cobbs, who'd been hidden by the crowd. "Here, boy, you get over here and explain," shouted Altaskith.

Cobbs came forward, his face downcast.

"Easy, Al. He's done a good thing."

"That don't undo all the bad things he's done," growled the butcher.

"I know it don't," Cobbs said quietly.

"Shut yer mouth, boy!" Altaskith roared. "Now tell me what happened."

Cobbs looked uncertainly to Elian. "Shut my mouth, or tell what happened?" he asked quietly.

Elian grinned. "Tell him what happened, Cobbs. I'll get people to start setting up camp. Hear him out, Al. Leave something for Collin to chew on when he gets here."

"Yeah! What about Collin, Cobbs? You start there, why don't ya?"

Elian caught Cassai's eye and he tried not to laugh. "Shall we leave Cobbs to his doom and see to our people?"

"Yes. I'm tired just looking at them."

The afternoon was occupied with getting families set up in the center of camp so they would be surrounded by fighters on every side in case the field was invaded. They got as much food as they could find and fed the women and children.

"There's not enough," Cassai said quietly as they took a single loaf of bread to the last family.

"I know," Elian muttered.

"What can we do about that?"

"We'll meet the men tonight and find out what they know. The Southern Guard has a stockpile somewhere. They keep the provisions they've stolen in taxes until Devilan sends for them."

Cassai smiled. "How fun would it be to find their stockpiles and feed our townspeople with food Devilan stole from them in the first place?"

Elian laughed. "Stealing anything from Devilan sounds pretty good at the moment."

A disturbance on the wooded side of the Field caught their attention. A small knot of people had emerged from the woods in almost the same place they had. Their welcome seemed to be turning hostile.

Elian glanced at Cassai and they sprinted toward the spot. Collin and Julius stood between a fed-up Altaskith and a large group of his followers from the west. Collin had his arms thrown wide, protecting the people behind him. Elian could see that two of the younger men were Lightlings, and two others looked like a mix of Lightling Blood and something else. All had drawn weapons and looked apprehensive at this hostile greeting. But the boy Collin's body was blocking sent a spear of ice up Elian's spine. Undoubtedly Fontre, and he recognized the man next to the boy.

He drew his sword and saw Cassai do the same. "Collin!" called Elian to draw the attention of the group.

"Elian, I need you," Collin said in a strained voice.

"Elian! They've betrayed us," yelled Altaskith, his face red with fury.

"Everyone calm down," Cassai said, walking between Altaskith's men and Collin. Altaskith's eyes grew huge, but he swiftly lowered his butcher's knife. The other men followed his lead.

"Collin, you can explain this, right?" Cassai pleaded with him.

"I can, if that bloody fool doesn't kill me first," Collin replied.

"Right, I know it's been a long day, Altaskith."

"Aye, it has. First that bumbling oaf and now Fontre. Actually bringing Fontre here." Altaskith shook his head.

"They're not Fontre," Collin shouted. "Me, Al? Remember what they did to me? Do you think I'd bring the enemy here? Let Elian talk to them. He'll know. He can verify." Collin's eyes pleaded with Elian. Elian approached, but kept his sword drawn.

"Elian!" exclaimed the Fontre Elian knew very well.

"Kirkus," he said quietly, tipping his head to the man.

"I never would have believed it. You really got out, you miraculous boy! And who's this? Is this the girl we've heard so much about?"

Elian wedged himself between Cassai and Kirkus. "She's none of your concern. Collin, this man is a Fontre: an actual, highly-trained, brutal Fontre warrior. What is he doing here?" Elian's sword seemed to have risen of its own accord, for Elian couldn't remember raising it, but Kirkus stepped closer, not put off in the least.

"I can tell you what happened, Elian. And it's not the boy's fault one way or the other."

"Drop your sword," Elian growled.

"Eh? Oh, right." Kirkus drew his sword with two fingers and dropped it to the ground.

"What else have you got on you?"

"That's my only weapon, I swear."

"What is that in your belt?"

"Oh, that? That's a spatula. I always bring it with me because…you just can't find really good ones outside of Halanah." Kirkus lifted out the spatula as the group behind him stifled laughter. Kirkus held the utensil out to Elian. "You can check it all over, son. It's just a spatula."

"Collin?" Elian asked.

"He's good, Elian. Your mum —"

"My what?"

"Your mum ch-changed him. I swear I would never have brought him if I really thought he was dangerous."

Elian turned to Julius. "My mother changed him?" He spoke each word slowly, feeling his self-control slip. "Do you know how many training sessions I endured while this man looked on? How many boys he beat, tortured or killed in fights that meant no more than a lesson in sparring or hand-to-hand combat?"

Kirkus' eyes went cloudy. "Yes, there were a lot of those. That's true enough," he admitted apologetically to Julius and Collin. "I know it, boy. I know."

"You know?" Elian repeated in disbelief. Kirkus' voice had gone fatherly and comforting. He looked like he wanted to pat Elian's shoulder in reassurance. Elian swore to himself he would lob Kirkus' hand off should he approach him.

"I do know. I knew I would come as a shock. This is… this is my boy, Sacha. He's…well, he's sort of your brother, by half-blood anyway."

Elian's gaze traveled from Kirkus to the Fontre boy. Sacha, stood up straighter, as though trying to make a good impression, tension etched in every feature from his booted feet to his curly black head. His eyes were confusing: large and blue and very unlike a normal Fontre's eyes. They were his, Elian's eyes, staring back at him as if he was looking in a mirror.

"Hi," said the boy, stepping out from behind Collin and extending his hand. "I can't believe you're Elian. I can't believe

I'm actually meeting you, and – and I know you don't like me, and that's okay. I just – I'm so excited to finally meet you."

"It's nice to meet you, Sacha," Cassai stepped out as well. "Thank you for coming. You must all be exhausted."

"Cassai," Elian said in warning.

"We can't stand here staring at each other all day."

"You are Cassai. By the Weaver, you're beautiful. The spitting image of your mother," Kirkus whispered.

Elian's arm went protectively across Cassai's chest. "Do not speak to her about her mother." Cassai put a soft hand on his arm.

"It's alright, Elian. It's the kindest any Fontre has spoken to me about her."

"Is that Cinda and the girls?" Julius asked, finally seeing beyond the group.

"Yes. Did you go to Plahn first? There were survivors. A lot of them, thanks to...well ..." Cassai's eyes cut nervously to Elian, whose eyes rolled heavenward.

He sighed heavily. "Bring them in, Al. But don't give him back that sword and check him for other weapons." The butcher nodded and stepped forward, clearly nervous to approach a Fontre. Kirkus smiled and nodded at the man.

"There's no problem with that. I don't need to be armed."

"No, you certainly don't. Take him to that tent and I'll deal with him shortly. Julius, you can join him in a moment. First, there's another matter to sort out. Sorry, Collin, we've got an unpleasant surprise for you too," said Elian, feeling weary to his bones.

"Do you want to meet the others?" Collin asked nervously.

"Right. Yes. Who did you bring?"

"This is Laurelle and Marcole, brother and sister from Halanah. These are brothers, Nihl's got dark hair and Jacque's got the ginger. The Light Ones wouldn't come and join a war, but – but these are my friends, so they came anyway."

Elian tried to look gracious. "Thank you for coming. If you're hungry or thirsty, there's a little food in that tent there."

Sacha watched eagerly as he pointed to the makeshift kitchen tent. "We brought a lot of food with us. We'll add it to your stores and I can cook. I actually like it very much."

This eager statement drew a genuine smile from Elian; his first in a while. "If you're Collin's friends, you're welcome here. Please come with him. He'll be badly in need of moral support in a moment." Elian turned and started back toward the camp and the last place he'd seen Cobbs.

Collin and his friends chattered excitedly behind him, pointing out different people and asking Collin for everyone's names. Collin was thrilled to see the clusters of families from Plahn, and Elian prayed it would be enough to help him keep his head.

"What's the surprise, Elian? I can't believe they all made it. We were sure everyone was dead. Wait, who is that?" Cobbs had emerged from a tent carrying an empty bucket. He saw Elian approaching and froze when he saw who followed. "Elian?" Collin had stopped dead.

"Collin, he saved them. He got them all out. That's the only reason I let him stay," Elian assured the boy quietly. Jacque and Sacha had moved to stand on either side of Collin.

"Who is he, Collin?" Jacque asked, holding Collin's shoulder protectively.

"Cobbs." Collin said. He had started to shake.

"What is this? Why?" shouted Jacque, drawing his sword. Cobbs took a step backward, though he was nowhere near the small group. Elian noted that Sacha carried no weapons at all. He couldn't decide what to think of the boy.

Elian gestured Cobbs to approach. He obeyed hesitantly. "All I will tell you is he saved the people of Plahn from dying in the Hermordes building. He was ordered to lock them in, and he didn't. He got them out instead. His fate is up to you. Only I won't let you kill him yourself. Should you wish him executed or whipped, or sent back to the Fontre, it will be arranged, but not by you." Elian's hand closed around Jacque's sword and he lowered the blade.

"His future is up to me?" Collin asked in a small voice.

"Yes. Your decision is final. That was our agreement. Please consider everything before you make your call though."

"I'm sorry, Collin." Cobbs had come within a few feet and stopped, both hands up in surrender.

Angry tears poured down Collin's cheeks, and his face was so red he looked ready to explode. The Lightling group formed a single line now, with Collin in the middle. Laurelle and Nihl had drawn swords.

"You're sorry?" Collin croaked. "Right. Thanks for that."

"I didn't know what they were gonna' do." Cobbs started and realized his error in an instant. Collin threw his sword to the ground and lunged. Cobbs didn't fight back as the smaller boy pummeled him as hard as he could.

"They killed her, you *Nordian*! They killed Anaya. How dare you make any excuse for that? I'll kill you!" Each scream was punctuated with a punch which Cobbs made no attempt to block.

The larger man's eyes went to Elian. "What do I say?" he yelled over Collin's tirade.

But Elian shook his head. "Don't say anything. Just let him be."

Collin's fist caught Cobbs between the legs, and he groaned and doubled over.

Elian flinched, but forced himself to stand silently while Collin beat Cobbs until he'd worn himself out. The shattered boy finally sank to his knees and buried his face in his bleeding hands, his shoulders shaking with sobs. Cobbs knelt in front of him and put a hand on the boy's heaving shoulder.

"I can't make it right, Collin. I can't. I swear I would if I could. You d-don't have to forgive me." Cobbs' own eyes were red and swollen. Elian had never seen the man show any emotion. "I can't make it right," he repeated, laying his head on Collin's shoulder and joining him in his sobs.

Elian looked at the Lightling group. "How could you let that brute come here?" Jacque spat at him.

Elian shook his head. "All Collin has to do is say it, and he's gone. I just wanted to give him a chance to have his say. He did save my townspeople from being burned to death." Elian's chest had knotted so tight he felt it would never untangle.

Collin's tears had turned to gulps for air, and Cobbs sat back on his heels, waiting for the boy to pronounce his fate. Collin looked up. "Please go. Not – you don't have to leave the camp or whatever, but...please just let me be. I can't say what you want to hear right now."

Cobbs looked shocked. "Yes. I'll leave you alone. Sorry." He pushed himself up and bowed his head.

"We'll talk later, Cobbs. Just get the water, or whatever you were doing," Elian said.

Cobbs nodded, picked up his bucket and walked away, wiping his nose on his shirt as he went.

Jacque and Laurelle rushed to Collin and helped him to his feet. He looked into Elian's face, still breathing hard, more from emotion than his encounter with Cobbs' torso. "Why?"

"I'll make him leave," Elian repeated.

"Why do I have to decide what becomes of him? What did I ever do to you to deserve that?"

"It's not what you did to me; it's what he did to you. He's wronged us all, almost everyone in town, but he cut you deepest, so he's yours to do with what you will. I'm sorry. I think it is the only just way to deal with him. Do you want me to have him flogged?"

Collin's looked away from Elian, off into the trees, looking desperate to run into them and disappear. "I don't want him flogged."

"Do you want me to send him away?"

"No. But I don't want to be near him. Can you keep him off me?"

"I can."

"Thank you. I want to go now if that's alright."

"Yes, you and your friends set up wherever you like. You seem fairly well armed, so pick a perimeter and keep an eye out for anything or anyone harmful." The Lightlings turned and started toward the tree line. "Sacha, come with me. I'm going to interview your father. I'd like you there."

Sacha looked nervously at his friends, who looked nervous in return. "Yes sir," he said almost in a whisper.

"We'll see you soon," said Marcole, thumping him on the back. "We'll set up our camp over by those trees. Come find us."

Sacha nodded and looked back at Elian. "Will I get to come back to them?"

"I think so," he said. He saw the boy swallow hard and turned toward the tent where they had taken Kirkus. "Let's go." Sacha followed obediently.

23

THE MEETING

lian and Sacha ducked into a large tent filled with bedding and pieces of armor. "We're working with the supplies we've got. It's not much." Altaskith apologized, following Elian's gaze.

"This is fine, my friend. As long as the people have been under the Fontre's thumb, I'm surprised to find we have any armor at all."

Elian's gaze fell on Kirkus, tied with rope to a wooden chair in the middle of the tent. Elian assumed the two sober-looking men standing at attention on either side intended to guard him. Elian knew if Kirkus felt like breaking the chair to bits and using the bits to kill them, he was certainly capable.

"D'you want us to truss up the boy as well, Elian?" Al asked.

"No. He'll be alright," Elian assured him.

Julius stood by Altaskith, looking agitated. "There's no reason to treat him like a criminal, Al. He's not done anything wrong."

"He's Fontre," Altaskith growled. Elian noticed the man held his butcher's knife too close to Kirkus. Ropes or not, he knew the Fontre could have pulled free, grabbed the blade and dispatched the butcher at any moment.

"Give us a few moments in private," Elian ordered. The men nodded and began filtering out of the tent. "Al?"

"I'm staying."

"Then step back from him with that knife. It would take him less than a second to take it from you and gut you into the bargain." Kirkus grinned at this, but Altaskith's eyes bulged and he backed away from the Fontre. Sacha settled himself crossed-legged by the armor and started sifting through it.

Elian snagged a chair from the pile of supplies and sat in front of Kirkus. He leaned toward the man, elbows on his knees. "What in the name of the Weaver do you think you're doing here?" he demanded.

Kirkus shook his head, looking awed. "I never thought I'd see you again, boy."

"No, neither did I. In fact, I hoped for it quite fervently."

"That's fair enough."

"So you have a son...your actual son, I assume?" Elian looked at Sacha, who pretended to be studying a large metal gauntlet, but he'd frozen, clearly listening in.

"Indeed he is. Your mother told me how to cheat the lottery and land with my own boy."

"And how exactly is that done?"

"You ought to know. Your father did the same."

"Shall we leave my father out of it for the moment?"

"If you like."

"So, my mother showed you how to cheat. But why? Why did you care if you got your own son or another? You killed your first boy in a training exercise and your second, Antille, was slaughtered almost immediately in the Dapaal Dahk. You expect me to believe your own flesh and blood would fare better? All sons of the Fontre are children of their lord. Or did you forget that?"

A look of intense pain crossed Kirkus' face and he looked at Sacha. Sacha's eyes had widened in horror and he stared at his father as if he'd never seen him before. "Sacha," Kirkus groaned. "Please let me explain."

Elian recognized Sacha's agony. He stood, walked deliberately across the tent and grabbed a second chair. He clunked it next to his own so hard Kirkus jumped. "Have a seat, Sacha. He owes us both this story."

Sacha looked at Elian as if he were torturing him. "I – yes, sir." He put down the gauntlet and went to the chair, his eyes already clouding.

"Right...so, the Revolution was over. The Fontre turned the Inner Kingdom to suit their ways. You know how they do. They took over one particularly beautiful church and turned it into one of their –" he swallowed and looked away from Sacha's face, "temples. Your mother was there, working as always. She was a high priestess by this time, so it was a great privilege to go into her chambers. I was given the opportunity because –" His voice faltered.

"Because of all the innocent people you'd killed in the Revolution. Yes. I'm familiar with the reward system," Elian finished for him coldly.

Kirkus blushed and kept his gaze pinned to the floor. "Yes. So, she gave me tea beforehand. I didn't know it, but she started all her sessions with tea and conversation. There wasn't a lot of conversation with the men, so I enjoyed talking with her for a time. I didn't know what was in the tea, but it was something she'd given your father too. I learned that later. For the moment, it just made me light-headed and very happy. I'd never felt happy before. It was wonderful.

"I got a message from her a few days later. She was inviting me personally. That was hard to get...a personal invitation from a high priestess. So, of course, I went. But meanwhile, something strange was going on. I had started to feel wrong. I whipped our stable boy and it left a sick feeling in me. I couldn't figure out why.

I'd whipped enough boys in my time. I whipped you pretty well that time, do you remember?"

Elian's jaw set hard. "I do. That's not helping your cause."

"Of course you do. You can't forget," Kirkus said, sounding flustered. "So anyway, besides feeling bad about doing wrong to folks, I also couldn't get your mother off my mind. Her beauty and wit. Her deep questions and philosophical thoughts. Brilliant, she was. I guess your mother figured out that what she'd tried had worked on me as it had on Heyman. She'd tried a couple times after him and it didn't work, so she was thrilled. She got me to admit I loved her. I can't believe I said those words. She was quite a woman." Kirkus' eyes had gone soft, lost in his memories. Elian looked from him to Sacha, who also looked deep in thought.

Elian massaged his temples. He hated to admit he was starving for a tea cake from the Fairy Realm. His mouth watered just thinking about them. "So you fell for my mother and had Sacha. How did you keep him alive?"

"That was tricky, but not as tricky as before we got to Lashai. We couldn't follow the same procedures as before, in the kingdom. We could have, I guess, but the High King had done his best to convince the people they were safe under his rule, so it wasn't quite as bad. He didn't just kill boys for screwing up a fight or such. Sacha took his fair share of beatings — took them like a Fontre, if I may say so. But it was clear he'd no love for training. He was put to work in the kitchens. I put in to go to Halanah and infiltrate the city. A few years ago, the High King finally let us. By the Weaver, we loved that city. So much good food. Sacha had friends for the first time, real friends who liked him. It was a miracle. We were happy there."

Elian studied him. "Then why come here?"

"Ah! Collin messed it all up, you see? Came and gave us hope that maybe the Fontre could be overcome. Maybe we could, someday, have a good life. That boy is quite a wonder himself." Kirkus smiled and shook his head. "Accepted our story and enjoyed our cooking. I like any boy who knows how to eat."

"He doesn't like gorgonzola though," Sacha said.

"Don't he? Ah well, I guess nobody's perfect."

Elian looked from father to son in disbelief. "You're telling the truth. I can't believe I'm saying it. You actually love this boy and love...cooking?"

Kirkus smiled. "I'm real glad to see you're alright, son. They told us you'd been killed in the Revolution. I never could quite believe it, special boy like you. And here you were the whole time. Saved that Namarielle girl and saved all our lives to boot. Well done, Elian. Really well done."

Elian took a shaky breath, trying not to react to Kirkus' kindness. He looked up at Altaskith and then to Julius.

"A Namarielle?" breathed the butcher. "Not Cassai? She's Namarielle?" Elian nodded. "You saved a Namarielle in the Revolution?"

"Sorry, old friend. I couldn't tell anyone. I even made it so she didn't remember her bloodline herself for a while. I had to keep her safe."

"You succeeded so far, Elian," said Julius with a smile. "You've done what needed doing. Nobody blames you for not telling of the girl's lineage, not with folks like Cobbs about. Where's Collin, anyway?"

"He and the Lightlings are setting up camp at the northern perimeter. I'll bring him here if you like."

"No, let him get set. We'll have them at the meeting tonight, though?"

"Yes."

"What did he say about Cobbs?" asked Julius quietly.

"Only that he wants Cobbs to stay away from him. He doesn't have to leave." Altaskith grunted disapprovingly. Elian smiled at him. "Mercy is allowed, Al. I know I'm always glad when I don't get what I deserve."

"Is he going to let me flog him at least?"

"No. No flogging's been ordered yet."

"You agree with that? You trust Cobbs?" Altaskith demanded.

"Cobbs is from Plahn. He's our people: he saved our people. That's good enough for me. And I always agree with a decision not to flog someone."

"Huh! Saved 'em because he was cavorting with the enemy."

Elian nodded. "True enough. I'll take it however it comes. I'm just glad they're still alive."

Altaskith teared up at that. "Ay. I'm glad they are too. I just want to die I'm so glad." Altaskith mopped his eyes and beard.

Elian looked at Kirkus. "There's a meeting at sundown to plan the next step. I expect you there."

Kirkus smiled. "Yes, sir. I wonder if maybe..." His gaze wandered to his son.

Elian nodded understanding. He reached into his satchel and pulled out the spatula Kirkus had given him earlier. He handed it to Sacha. "You won't be able to attend the meeting, Sacha. You'll be needed in the kitchen tent."

Sacha's eyes danced. "Oh, I don't need that one. I've got one of my own, and it's much better than Da's."

Kirkus roared with laughter and stood up. "You see what your mother did to me, Elian? See what I have to put up with?"

Elian grinned. "Indeed. She's doomed you forever."

ELIAN'S FEELINGS of disquiet grew as the sun dipped in the western sky. This field had been named centuries ago as the westernmost point on the map. Trees surrounded the enormous clearing on three sides, The River Kai formed the fourth border. The Southern Borderland began only a few miles from where they stood, but the trees provided perfect cover.

Elian's mind wandered to Marcus, Frederick and the Kiatri. He worried that rather than return to the Inner Kingdom, Devilan planned another surprise attack on the Troikord. If he caught the Kiatri before Marcus was able to train them ... Elian tried to rein in his thoughts before spiralling into despair. He had to focus on what he could control.

"Have you had any supper?" Cassai's voice made him jump.

"No. I should."

"I know food isn't your main concern since you got back from...but anyway, Sacha made you this plate specially. He really wants you to like him."

Elian smiled. "I do like him. I'm just not sure how to reconcile what I know about his father's past with what I saw of them today. I think he genuinely loves Sacha, but I knew Kirkus. I saw him do unspeakable things to others and to his assigned sons. It's hard to let that go. I thought I'd let go of everything." He sighed, and accepted the plate from Cassai. A stuffed bird as big as his fist and a roll that smelled so good it made his stomach grumble.

"He tried to get me to bring you wine as well, but I told him that was a waste of time. He seemed disappointed and said the stuffed *filber* was to be served with a good red. Whatever that means."

"Red wine. There's red and white and that's about all I know."

Cassai smiled at him and held out a water skin. "Shall we sit?" They found a spot of grass and settled next to each other. "Have you seen Hollis today?"

"He's walking the boundary nearest the mountains." As Elian said it, his gaze turned to the west.

"Is he coming to the meeting tonight?"

"Yes."

"Am I coming to the meeting?"

Elian looked at her, surprised. "Of course. You're the Queen; at least to us you are. Besides, I need your mind in there. You have a knack of finding a way round things when I can only see in black and white." He took a bite of the bird and real flavors burst in his

346

mouth for the first time since the Fey. He closed his eyes and savored the sensation.

"Good isn't it?"

"Ah! Bless that boy. I thought I'd never care for the taste of mortal food again. Does he have some sort of fairy powder he's sprinkling in?"

Cassai laughed. "Not that I saw."

Elian took another bite, smiling. "Well, he stays one way or the other."

"Nanna always told me the way to a man's heart was through his stomach. I just figured I was doomed."

Elian shrugged and chewed another bite before saying: "That's not the only way to our hearts."

Cassai elbowed him hard in the ribs. "I can't believe you just said that to a lady...and a queen."

He grinned and looked off into the sunset. "I've said worse things to a queen."

"Really?" Cassai asked coyly. "Do tell."

"Well, there was this one really bad day when I might have offered to wring the neck of our favorite Fairy Queen for her...politely."

Cassai laughed. "That's fantastic. Did she believe you?"

He shrugged. "Oh yes. She definitely believed me. I was telling the truth."

"Wow. What did she do?"

He chilled at the memory. "We should get going. I told everyone sundown." Cassai looked disappointed, but nodded. "Sorry. I'll tell you more, I promise. It's a long story though; one you've earned the right to hear. You're the one, after all, who had to doctor me back to standing on my own."

"By the way, we haven't checked those bandages in two days."

"I'm sure they're fine," he said dismissively, and then withered at the glare she pinned on him. "After the meeting."

THE TENT they'd chosen for their strategy meeting was larger than the one he'd met Kirkus in earlier and it was bursting with men and women from across the Borderlands. Some of the townspeople had crowded in as well. Elian took in the throng and wished he'd been more specific about who was invited. Planning strategy would be difficult in such a crowd.

The people parted for the couple as they made their way to the center pole holding up the canvas. "Good evening," said Elian when they'd stopped.

He spotted Hollis and Theoris at one side and motioned them to come closer. Hollis dipped his head wrapped an arm around Theoris and the two threaded their way through the bodies. Theoris, made constant apologies to everyone as they moved aside for them and he tried not to catch anyone's foot with his crutch.

"I'm Elian, a shepherd by trade from the town of Plahn and, obviously, I was born a Fontre. This lady is Cassai. She is the last living Namarielle, and true heir to the throne of Lashai." Elian turned to Cassai, went slowly to one knee and bowed his head. Hollis followed his lead, and there was a great scuffling as everyone in the crowded tent bowed.

Cassai looked at each of them. Elian could see she trembled with emotion, but her small chest rose and fell and she tipped her chin up. "Thank you all. Please, make yourselves as comfortable as you can." The people shifted back to sitting or standing as before.

"Is there anything you'd like to say, Your Majesty, before we begin?" Elian asked as formally as possible. To his surprise, Cassai nodded and turned back to the room.

"Lashai belongs to us. It's a terrible thing to go to war, but in this case, it's a more terrible thing not to. The Fontre are not good or caring rulers, and they've practically taxed us all to death. If we complain or demand things be made right we're killed for our efforts. And so we will fight them and take back Lashai. If we win this war, and you make me your Queen, I promise you, I will give you back your land and your freedom." The room had gone silent. No one moved or spoke. Cassai looked back at Elian, who stared at her in wonder. "That's all. You can start the meeting."

He smiled. "I think you just did that."

Applause started in one corner of the tent and soon exploded through the entire room. Cassai smiled and sat on the floor, no doubt hoping they would settle down.

Elian raised his hand for silence and the applause died out. "This meeting is to determine leaders for our armies. Besides our Queen, we will need people who can strategize, organize troops and lead them into battle."

"I thought you were the leader, Elian," shouted Julius from a far end of the room. Elian saw the group of Lightlings and Collin gathered around him. They all started clapping and nodding. Elian was glad Cobbs was in the opposite corner of the tent.

"Yes. This was your plan in the first place," Altaskith agreed. "You're fit to lead us into battle against these barbarians if anyone is."

"I'm not sure I'm the one who —" he started.

"Shut up, Fontre, and just accept so we can move on," Hollis said loudly enough to cut him off.

Elian grinned and nodded politely. "Thank you. I'm honored. I nominate Hollis Farrell as my second in command."

Hollis glowered at him as the nomination was accepted by virtue of Cassai nodding vigorously. "Honored," he growled.

"Very well. Let's get on with it, shall we?" Elian jerked his head, indicating Hollis should join him at the center. Hollis pushed himself up and walked to Elian's side, arms crossed, scowling at everyone.

They charged Julius with leading a small team into the Southern Borderlands the next day, to find the provisions of the Southern Guard. Altaskith volunteered to fit fighters with weapons. To the great surprise of many men, Elian charged Cinda and Sophie with their own commands. Cinda was to take charge of the Borderling fighters from the West. Sophie to command a troupe of Kiatri militia whenever they arrived.

"Under Namarielle rule, you would be captains and colonels. We shall call you the same. Those in command should meet us in this tent at first light. We'll organize all other camp needs at that time." People started to shift around, finding ways to stand.

Elian held out a hand to help Cassai to her feet. As soon as she stood he held her hand up high and yelled: "Long live the Queen!"

"Long live the Queen!" echoed the group of rebels. Cassai blushed, but smiled at them all in acknowledgement.

"Long live Lashai." She added quietly.

"Yes," said Elian and Hollis together. "Long live Lashai."

24

THE SCOUTS

E lian lay on his stomach in a small tent near the western boundary of the Field. He had come crashing down from the adrenaline of the meeting with just a few words from Cassai.

"I need to see to your bandages."

He'd sighed and made a show of protesting, but the moment she mentioned his back, the pain resurfaced and made itself impossible to ignore.

"It's looking better, but a few of these deeper cuts keep opening up again. I may have to stitch them. I'm going to leave the wrappings off it so it will get air tonight. How does it feel?"

"Fantastic," Elian muttered into his pillow.

"Oh, stop it. Is it hot and burning? Does it stab or prick, or is it a low, throbbing pain? Details matter, you know? It tells me a lot."

Elian raised himself slowly on one elbow. "It's usually low throbbing, but when people remind me of it, like for example, make me strip down and describe it to them, it slices through me like Al's butcher knife."

"Ignoring it won't make it go away," Cassai said.

"It might."

Cassai sighed heavily and pressed a cloth into a sore harder than she normally would. Elian cringed, lowered back into his pillow, but said nothing. "I'm putting more almeris on, and letting it air out. That's the best I can do now. On that subject, we're going to have to set up some sort of surgery tent for the wounded. I wonder how I can get medical supplies in large quantities."

"We're working on the supply raid now. Julius is choosing a team for reconnaissance in Pyrene-Valla. I considered going along."

"You can't go along. You're leader of this army now, remember? Besides, you're wanted by the Fontre. The Southern Guard will recognize you if you show your face."

"You're starting to get on my nerves," said Elian.

"I can't understand you in that pillow," Cassai said in a tone that told him she most definitely understood. Her cool hands turned his head so she could look at him. He smiled because her tired, freckle-covered face made the pain melt away.

"Hello."

"Hello," she answered softly. Concern etched the corners of her gray eyes. "You've never really told me about these memories you relived. I know Devilan was a monster in your training sessions and Ffastian was brutal."

Elian's heart pounded uncomfortably in his ears. He wasn't prepared for this question now. "It's as hard to hear as it is to talk about. I want to tell you for many reasons, not the least being I don't want another woman out there to know more about my past than you do. Especially not ... her." Elian's thoughts churned. The hand that gripped Cassai's started to tremble.

Cassai kept her features clear of emotion. "If you're ready to tell me, I can bear it."

Elian was fascinated by how much she had changed in the last few weeks. He rolled to his good side to look at her more closely. "I can tell you that the Fontre Draught should be drunk, not injected. Injection makes its effects infinitely less pleasant, and it was bad enough to begin with."

"I'm sorry."

He stroked her small, soft fingers as he spoke. "I relived the memories, just as I had before. More of them, unfortunately, and much closer together. After a few days they started to recycle. That hadn't happened before."

"All those years of torture in the space of a few days. Despicable," Cassai whispered.

Elian nodded. "Devilan's training sessions were painful, but they were nothing next to reliving the moments with Ffastian. He – he wasn't usual for a Fontre. Didn't like the temples and hardly ever visited them. Devilan and I were the only boys he'd had any interest in. He never participated in the lottery."

"I always thought, because of the way you hated him, he must have killed your father purposely."

"Yes, I think he did. That wasn't the only reason I hated him." He heard his voice go quiet. The pain in his chest was deep, but not unbearable. Not how it used to be. "He wanted us, especially me. We didn't know why for a long while, though Devilan figured it out before I did. He actually s-spared me once. Maybe more, but once I know about. And then he got what he wanted at last."

He watched Cassai closely, wondering what her innocent mind would make of this information. He noticed she bit the inside of her lip repeatedly, and guessed she was trying to deal with her emotions without soaking the camp. "Oh, I see," she finally said stonily. "I would have thought such behavior is forbidden by the Fontre."

"It is. Ffastian kept quiet about it, told me no one would believe me and I'd be killed if I said anything. Which was probably true. I'm sorry to tell you like this. Sorry I never told you before." Elian realized he was squeezing her hand so hard her fingertips had turned white. He took a breath and loosened his grip.

Cassai looked at their hands intently. "When you told me

you'd managed to forgive Ffastian for everything, I had no idea you meant *that*. Was he doing this to you in Lashai? Was it when we knew each other and played together?"

"Yes." Elian smiled, the heaviness deep inside him reflected back to him in her eyes. A stab of panic hit him, but he tried to keep his words measured and calm. "Are you – do you still want to be with me?"

Her lips parted slightly in surprise. "Oh Elian, is that something that's been plaguing you? I wish I had the perfect words to say to you, but I don't. The only thing can I think to say is that it wasn't your fault. Ever. It was Ffastian's doing. You are who I want, now and always."

Elian felt his eyes cloud over and unshed tears seared his throat. "Thank you. There's...something else to tell you before you decide."

Cassai's grip tightened. "Alright."

"Dahlia told me something about her father that –" Elian swallowed hard and focused on her fingers instead of her face, "that might affect your choice."

"Nothing Dahlia had to say will affect my choice." Cassai's voice had gone hard and cold.

"Her father was Namarielle; I think she told you that." Cassai nodded. "He was an unwilling participant in one of her mother's experiments. She wanted to get pregnant by him, but shortly after...or maybe even that moment, I don't know the details, he died. The Namarielle can't just be with someone. They must follow the rules to the letter, and we don't even know what all the rules are."

He looked at her face, but she was glaring at his arm. "We can find out."

"I think the ones who knew, the Lashaian priests, have been wiped out. That's what Devilan said. He's been hunting for one."

Cassai shook her head, her mouth set in a tight line. "Right. Because he was going to marry me."

"Banaker."

"What?"

"The Hermit told me there's a man called Banaker who knows a priest, or has information that'll help us. He lives in hiding."

"So we find him, or we get the Lost Book back from Devilan. One way or the other, we'll figure it out."

Elian gave her a ghost of a smile. "Okay."

Cassai ran her fingers up and down his arm. "Didn't you tell me there was a day Ffastian broke all the bones in your right arm?"

"There was."

"Not broken now." Cassai looked upset, and Elian couldn't figure out where her mind was going.

"No. She healed it before she pitted me against Goliard."

Her chin tipped up. "Well, how thoughtful," she said in a tight voice. "And then you had to fight with her Captain of the Guard after all that?"

"It was strongly implied that if I didn't, Krispen might be freed, but I would never set foot in the mortal world again. I don't know if she would have kept to that or not. Thankfully, I didn't have to find out."

Cassai's chest rose and fell. Outside, Elian could hear the wind picking up at the corners of the tent. "What a wretch."

Elian chuckled softly. "Agreed. She liked talking about you. I'm sorry to say I did it quite a bit. Nothing damaging, just...talking. Thinking about you eased the pain. She also wanted —" Elian's mouth had gone too dry to continue.

"You." Cassai finished for him.

He met her eyes and nodded. "It was a long week."

Elian wondered if he'd pushed too much information on her for one evening. The swirling wind had loosened the ties of the tent door and it flapped freely, letting in the chill. He shivered and hoped she was finished so he could pull up a blanket. Cassai

355

noticed and grabbed the blanket herself, laying it gently on top of him.

"I'm so sorry. And thank you." A single tear traced down her cheek and he reached up to catch it.

"You are most welcome, your Majesty." His eyes twinkled and his one dimple barely showed on his scruffy cheek.

She laughed, welcoming the relief of tension. "Oh, for goodness sake. I had no idea you were going to make such a show of all that."

"I had to. These people must see you as their Queen. I heard the women arranging to make you a special tent and everything."

Cassai rolled her eyes. "Ridiculous. We're preparing for war. The last thing we need to worry about is making a fuss over one little nobody."

"I'm sorry to disagree, but you were never a nobody and you never will be. They do need to fuss a bit for their Queen. They need to see you as someone they wish to rule over them, and you will allow them to do so. Things will get very difficult before this is over. If they've no-one to fight for, they'll give up and we'll be in a worse state than before."

Cassai opened his hand, and laid her cheek on his palm. "I really liked keeping sheep."

He ran his fingers through her curls. "So did I." He brought a lock of her hair to his lips and kissed it. "I love you."

She straightened up and looked business-like again. "I love you too. Now roll over so I can tend the rest of your back."

ELIAN AND HOLLIS STOOD WITH JULIUS' group at the southern edge of the Westerling Field just as the sun started to rise. Sophie clutched a fur-lined coat close to her body, and Laurelle wore her fleece lined jacket, but the other Lightlings had no heavy clothes to keep out the chill.

Elian frowned as they shivered. "Do we have any winter clothes to spare?" he asked Simon, who he'd put in charge of provisions.

"There are blankets, sir. Nothing more. I'm afraid."

"Blankets will do. Collin and Sacha, run and fetch some. We're past Nuelletide, it only gets colder from now."

"Yes sir," the boys said and hurried off to the supply tent.

"Why are you going along?" Hollis asked Sophie while they waited. "Can't stand another guard duty?"

"No, I like guard duty. But I like moving better. I want to see the Southern Border. I've heard it's quite a melting pot."

"A witches' brew, more like," muttered Elian. "Boiling den of thieves and scum. Watch your backs in there, all of you. Don't be caught anywhere alone. Stay clear of anything with even a whiff of trouble about it. If you get caught by the Southern Guard, co-operate; if you get caught by the Fontre, escape or die trying." Elian dropped a small, smooth stone into Julius' hand. "It's a creekstone. If there's trouble and you need me, whisper *'eveille'* into the stone. Speak your location. There's no need to say more."

Julius nodded and pocketed the creekstone.

"You Lightlings will draw attention – probably not negative. Sophie is correct, Pyrene-Valla is a melting pot of races, so you won't be the only ones of your kind. Just don't engage, don't purposely stir anything up. We need the location of the stores of the Southern Guard. From what I understand, they're scattered throughout the city. When you've located them, contact me, and we'll plan our attack."

Julius grinned. "Yes, Lord Elian."

Elian's brow furrowed. "Don't even think of starting that Lord nonsense with me unless you'd like to be run through here and now." Julius laughed at that and opened his arms as though inviting Elian's sword.

Before he could think of a good retort, Collin and Sacha arrived with a stack of blankets and the companions wrapped themselves against the chill.

"Lord Elian." Elian cringed as a man approached who he had not formally met. He was from the Eastern Border. "I want to join this team."

"Don't call me, Lord. Do you have experience in reconnaissance?" Elian asked.

The man stood an inch shorter than Julius. Under his white tunic and brown coat, Elian could see a powerful body, thin enough to fit into small spaces, too large to be trifled with. "Sort of. I'm good at finding things and people without causing a fuss. Altaskith found me in Minoth, in the East. If you've got questions ask him about the Goat and Bridge Pub incident. He'll vouch for me. I also have other skills that may come handy." The man held up a brown pouch. He seemed to be enjoying himself without smiling. Elian thought his plain brown hair and eyes would help him blend into any crowd. Nothing about the man stood out.

"Hey! That's mine," yelped Marcole, snatching the pouch.

"Indeed it is. I got it off you without you noticing. What does that tell you?"

"I don't believe we've been introduced," Elian said.

"Malcolm Hopps. At your service, my lord."

"Please, don't call me lord. Sir or Elian is good enough."

"Yes, sir. Whatever you say."

"Very well. I'll definitely be double-checking your credentials with Al. Julius has command of this group, if you go, you follow orders." Elian nodded to the group of Lightlings. "You should get a move on. Say your goodbyes and stay safe." They all turned and bid farewell to Sacha, who hugged everyone with tears in his eyes. Sophie hugged the boy, and tried to make a joke about how much more fun he would have staying behind.

Elian turned back to Malcolm and lowered his voice. "How good are you at finding people?" Elian asked. He found a scrap of parchment in his pocket.

"Very." Malcolm smiled.

"This man. He's a merchant now, I believe. I need to get in contact with him. Find me everything you can."

Malcolm nodded, read the name silently, mouthing the word, 'Banaker'. "I'll do what I can."

"Thank you. It's a private matter. My greatest thanks to you all for taking on this dangerous mission. May the Weaver go before you and make you successful on your quest."

Hollis grabbed Sophie into a hug and kissed her cheek. "Be safe," he whispered in her ear.

"Is it alright to ask the Weaver for help on a quest to steal things?" asked Sophie, her eyes dancing.

Elian rolled his eyes. "I don't know. I'll ask him one day. Good luck."

They walked off into the morning mist, Malcolm explaining to Sophie the morally gray area of stealing goods that were stolen to begin with.

Hollis turned to Elian when they were out of earshot. "So, the quest for Banaker begins, eh? Do you think Devilan already knows where he is?"

Elian shrugged. "I don't think so. Last time we spoke about it, he didn't. Well, Sacha, what do you say to some breakfast?" He clapped the boy on the shoulder.

Sacha grinned. "I need better ingredients, but I have something planned for you, sir."

"You're my brother, Sacha. You don't have to call me sir."

"You can be sure I never will, and I'm not related to him by even a drop of blood," added Hollis helpfully.

THE SCOUTS ENTERED a filthy outlying district of Pyrene-Valla that evening. Pyrene-Valla was a significantly wealthier city than the surrounding Borderland towns. Julius fairly boiled over at the obvious misuse of taxes the Southern Guard beat out of the poorer towns to fill their coffers.

Deciding his group fit in better in the seedier areas surrounding the main city, Julius had ordered them to find a room for the night. Mostly populated by laborers from the city, farmers and thieves, this area, known to locals as the Silo, boasted multiple inns inexpensive enough to house them for a few days.

They found one that looked accommodating and rented one of the largest rooms, making the brown-toothed proprietor happy enough to dance.

The wooden floors were coated in a fine layer of filth and the stone walls were chipped so badly in places they had to stuff rags into some of the larger cracks to keep the wind from whistling in.

"Ye'll be stayin' how long?" the proprietor asked when he unlocked the door and handed Julius two keys.

"Seven days, if it's available." Julius dropped two gold coins into the man's hand. His eyes shone greedily.

"Ay, this is enough for seven days." The man's voice made Collin suspect it was enough for more than that, but he said nothing.

There was only one large bed in the middle of the room, and Malcolm walked straight to it and dropped his bag in the center. "Find a soft spot of floor, kids. The grown-ups get the bed."

Collin frowned at him. "I think the girls should get the bed."

"Here's the problem with that, son," Malcolm began with a smirk. "Women these days, they like to be treated as equals, see? So, we men just give 'em what they want. They want the right to sleep on the floor? Who am I to argue?"

Jacque rolled his eyes. "That's a pretty weak argument just so you don't have to sleep on the floor."

"Ha! And what if I decide I'll sleep wherever I like and I'm not going to let a man tell me I'm sleeping on the floor. What do you say to that?" Sophie demanded, dropping her own bag on the other side of the bed.

Malcolm raised one eyebrow and opened his mouth, then shut it again.

Julius walked wearily to a corner of the room and dropped his travel bag. A cloud of dust raised from the floor. "Malcolm, there's not a chance in this world I'm sharing a bed with you. Now move your bloody bag and give the bed to the girls."

~

"OKAY, here's what I could find from that stall in the square," Sophie piled clothes into Collin's arms. "All the latest fashions, if you believe overfed, under-bathed salesmen in pink boots."

"They'll be fine," Julius said.

"Fine? I gave seventeen denaris for this stuff!"

"That Malcolm pickpocketed from that guy we met earlier," Collin mumbled.

"Excuse me, if you have a problem with our methods, you traipse out there in the middle of the Southern Guard and those Fontre men who look at you like they needn't bother with daggers, just run you through with their eyes."

"Sophie, these are perfect!" beamed Laurelle, holding up a bright, heavily beaded scarf and blue cotton shirt.

"They'll go with your brown skirt. We'll do up your hair and make you look the part. We can sneak you into the more posh areas. Collin will have to pretend to be comfortable in a nicer suit, which may prove the more difficult task."

"I can do whatever I need to," Collin grumbled.

"I wonder where the boys are with the food," said Marc, nervously watching the window. He hadn't been able to settle down in the dingy room.

"There they are," Collin announced, spotting Jacque and Nihl striding back into view. Their height and looks drew the attention of a group of women gathered across the street. The women didn't seem to Collin to have dressed properly for the cold. They wore coats and gloves, but all their clothing revealed a great deal of their bodies. "Uncle, those women over there are talking with the boys. What do you think they want? They must be freezing."

"Ah, well yes. Probably," said Julius, peering out the window at the ladies in question. "Steer clear of them while we're here, alright? Their attentions are the last thing we need at present." He looked pointedly at Marc, who grinned, but nodded.

Jacque and Nihl had stopped briefly, nodded politely at the women's shouted comments and headed into the inn.

"Ugh!" Sophie exclaimed, also looking out the window. "Men are pigs. I guarantee you there's a man making them do that."

"Making them do what?" Collin asked. "Dress so poorly for the cold?"

Sophie and Laurelle exchanged a smile. "Yes. It's a dastardly deed for sure," Sophie said, ruffling the boy's hair. Collin wished she wouldn't. It made him feel like a small child, and Sophie wasn't even a full year older than him.

The door opened and the two Lightlings entered, hefting bulging paper bags. "Rubbishy food is certainly cheap here," Jacque said excitedly as they handed round greasy packets of fried fish and potato slices. "They call them chips. You put this red sauce on them," Jacque explained, handing Collin a packet. "I'd wager they'd give Sacha a fit if he were here."

"Oh, my word! They taste like paradise," Laurelle exclaimed.

Nihl laughed. "And might send you there sooner, if you eat too much of them."

"What did the ladies across the street want?" Collin asked, his mouth full of salty, crispy fish.

Jacque flopped down next to him and took one of his fries. "Money. Apparently they're very hard up." He winked, but Collin didn't get the joke. Jacque ruffled his hair, and Collin glared at him.

"Can you all please stop doing that?"

"They're harlots, Collin," Laurelle said, finally taking pity on him. Collin flushed red and looked at the floor.

"Right. That makes sense then, about their clothes."

"Or lack thereof," Nihl added, falling onto the bed, the rusty springs squeaking so loudly it made Collin's ears ring.

25

THE CITY

Collin and Laurelle walked arm in arm down the street, chatting and enjoying Julius' assignment to get the lay of the city. The previous three days, they'd taken a carriage from their inn and been dropped off in different parts of town.

Today they started in a district full of shops, directly in the center of Pyrene-Valla. The street was paved with tar and lined with carefully manicured sidewalks. The trees planted periodically down the streets no longer had leaves, and Collin struggled to recall if he'd seen anything like them before. Their smooth slender trunks were trimmed to perfection, and the rounded limbs, which reached only about fifteen feet in the air, formed a delicate lace pattern against the frozen gray sky.

The buildings in this area were costly-looking and well maintained. Unlike the Silo, where buildings were mostly chipped mortar and broken bricks, these buildings were magnificent structures of stone with glass windows that showed no sign of age or decay.

"Look at that shop," Collin said, pointing to a large, windowed storefront. "The dresses are all made of silk. What would you do with such a delicate dress?"

Laurelle giggled. "Wear it to a party?"

"In the freezing cold?"

"Look how many layers are in that skirt! It would be warm enough, especially with that fur and those pretty boots." Laurelle pointed to a pair of shapely black boots positioned next to the frothy dresses.

He rolled his eyes. "Hey, look. I think that's a Guard Building. Let's try out our act."

They ducked into an alleyway. "Muss up your hair so it looks like you've been running," Laurelle suggested.

"Okay, we'll approach the building at a run. Ready?"

Laurelle's eyes brightened. "Definitely."

The building they darted toward was taller than most on this street and much less appealing. No picture windows or brightly colored curtains graced its front. Instead, a heavy iron door was surrounded by thick stone and two small windows on either side. The building was well kept, with ivy creeping up its walls and around the door. Three men in the red garb of the Southern Guard milled around the front, talking and drinking from mugs.

"Sir, may I beg a favor of you?" Collin asked breathlessly. "My companion has had her purse snatched on the street back there. I saw her attacker, but he fled so quickly I couldn't catch him."

"Eh? Purse snatched you say?" The guard gave Laurelle his full attention and she flushed, which Collin hoped the guard would take for exertion.

"Yes, sir. He hurt my arm he wrenched so hard. We saw him run between the buildings, but the alleyway looked ominous so we thought we'd leave it to bigger and stronger men." Laurelle stamped a look of admiration on her face and Collin bit his lip to stop laughing.

"A good idea, lass. You don't want to meddle with criminals if you can call on us to do it for you. I bet it was that fiend, Thompson. He's been spotted hereabout the last couple of days. You go inside out of the cold, and get yourselves a hot drink, eh?" The guard placed a gentle hand on Laurelle's back and led her to the door. Collin followed, his heart hammering in his chest. He couldn't believe they'd made it inside.

They were led into a large open entryway with a wooden desk in the middle.

"Adelaide," the guard addressed a broad-faced woman sitting at the desk. "Get these two some coffee or tea, won't you? This lady's been robbed and we're seeing to it."

"Ay, Bramus, bring them 'round here. I'll get something to warm them, bless their frozen heads. Over here, youngun's, no need for shyness." Adelaide opened a small wooden half door that led to the other side of the desk. "I'll get ye' some hot grog, shall I?"

"Thank you," both Collin and Laurelle responded, looking all over, trying casually to take in as much information as possible.

Bramus left, closing the iron door behind him with a tooth-rattling clang. Adelaide shook her head at the noise and bustled around gathering mugs and fixing drinks from a little cart crammed into one corner.

"I've never been in an official building before," Laurelle gushed. "It feels very...secure."

Collin rolled his eyes. "How long have you worked here, Miss? They were speaking very highly of you outside."

"Ay, and they better speak highly," Adelaide turned her beaming face to Collin. "Guess it's been about fourteen years or so. Good lord, how the time flies. I keep my boys well stocked in hot grog and pastries. They each have a hollow leg to fit all their sweeties in. I also keep up with all their dadgum paperwork, them and all over this district. I deserve a medal for that alone."

Collin gave her a warm smile as she pressed the mug into his hand. "Thank you so much." A round, sticky pastry with a hole in the middle was handed to him in a napkin. "You oversee everything then?"

"Ay, laddie, I do, and it's no joke keeping these grubbers in line. Thirteen outposts and one dame. I need a raise in pay and that's a fact." The woman pointed to a map on the wall upon which each station was marked with a red-tipped pin.

"You've certainly earned a raise, just for uplifting us on such a wretched afternoon," commented Collin as he studied the map.

"You just take a bite o' that donut, lad. It'll improve your outlook leaps and bounds."

He cut his eyes to Laurelle, who shrugged and nibbled. "Oh, that is delicious. Even better than the chips," she whispered to him.

"Have you never tried one? Where did you two say you were from?" The genuine surprise on the woman's face rattled Collin's nerves.

"The north part of the city. Both our mums are strict about what we eat; at least mine used to be. She's gone now," Collin said, giving Adelaide a pitiful look.

"Oh, bless your sweet head, that's too sad." Adelaide gave him a maternal stroke on the cheek and returned to her chair.

Collin liked the woman immensely, in spite of her position with the Southern Guard. She didn't participate in the fleecing of the surrounding towns. He could like her if he wanted. He looked at Laurelle, trying to think of some way to get them into other rooms in this building. He took a sip of grog, which tasted like apples, cinnamon, and something strong and biting at the end. His insides filled with warmth.

"Do you have a room where I could relieve myself?" asked Laurelle suddenly. "I'm sorry to be a bother."

"Indeed we do, it's no bother. I've my own private privy just so I don't have to go where the men do. Men are disgusting creatures, bless them. I'd take ye, but I'm supposed to man the desk.

Through that door, down the hallway, last door on yer right. There's no missing it. There's a lass painted on the door."

"I'll take her. I don't want her wandering about alone, if you don't mind. And I could use a privy myself."

"Ay, yours is on the left. Don't you be using mine." She looked very stern about this last point and he nodded soberly.

"No ma'am, I swear I won't." Collin put a hand on Laurelle's arm and deliberately led her to the wrong door, opening it and looking inside quickly. It led to a stairwell and what looked like a stone-lined basement.

"Not that one, silly boy. The next door. You almost toppled down those stairs!" cried Adelaide. Collin feigned surprise, though he'd been nowhere near. "You'd'a given Horace quite a start."

Collin laughed uneasily. "Sorry, I'm not good with directions."

"No, he certainly isn't," Laurelle laughed. "You should've seen him trying to get to the milliner's earlier. Oh, poor man!" Laurelle said with compassion, peering down the stairs herself. "Does he work alone down there?"

"Ay, for the most part. He's not used to folks falling in on him, as it were. That room's only really good for storage and such, no sane person would want to be in the dark all day. I suppose someone's got to guard it though. All the men go down there on pay day to get what's owed 'em. I always make Bramus carry my wages up for me. Them stairs are too steep for me, and I don't trust 'em."

"Aw! Does he have to work down in the dark night and day?" Laurelle asked sweetly. Collin marveled at her ability to get vital information with such harmless questions.

"He locks up at night, of course. None but two guards stay the night, and they stay up here. Don't fancy sleeping in a tomb I reckon. That's all that room is, one giant, underground crypt."

"It's this door, then, is it?" Collin asked, going to the door Adelaide had pointed out before. Adelaide nodded and Collin opened it for Laurelle. "You're bloody brilliant, you know that?" he murmured in her ear as she passed. She pranced past, giving him an overwhelming urge to grab her and kiss her. He took a deep breath and closed the door behind them.

They came into a long hallway lined with doors on each side. They peered in the dark windows set in each door.

"Look as much as you can, as quick as you can," Collin whispered. Laurelle took one side and Collin the other as they walked to the privies.

"This one looks official. Look, there's a Dep. Dir. before his name. What do you think that means?"

"I'll bet Dir stands for director. No idea about Dep."

"What are you two doing back here?" demanded a deep voice from the opposite end of the hall.

Laurelle jumped. "Sorry, sir. We were looking for the privy. Miss. Adelaide said it was down here." Laurelle gave the man her biggest eyes, and Collin swallowed and tried to look innocent.

"She has to go pretty badly."

"It's down here," barked the man, his features softening only a fraction at Laurelle's charms. He led them to the end of the hall, motioning to a door with a stick figure of a woman painted on it.

"Thank you so much," Laurelle gushed and went through the door.

The guard didn't leave, so Collin stayed frozen outside the privy.

"What are you two here for?"

"Elle's purse was stolen. A couple of your men went to find the man who snatched it." He tried to keep his voice steady, but the man eyed him so suspiciously it was hard not to shake.

"Her purse, you say? Was there something of value in it?"

"Not very. Just some pocket money. Sh–she was hoping to buy a hat downtown."

"Right. And what were you along for? You like shopping for women's clothes?"

"Her father won't let her shop alone. It's safer if I'm with her."

"Didn't do much of a job protecting her though, did you?"

"I'm sorry, what? Surely someone in your line of work knows that it's a bad idea for a young girl to be alone in this city. I believe the man snatched the bag and ran without molesting her because I was at her side." Anger increased Collin's boldness and covered for the fact that he could no longer hide his shaking voice.

"All done!" announced Laurelle shrilly as she opened the door and found the two men glaring at each other.

"Good. Get back to the clerk's desk before I find need to ask further questions."

"Of course, sir," Laurelle replied, looking mortified. Collin deliberately wrapped an arm around her waist and led her down the hall.

When they returned to Adelaide, both breathed a sigh of relief.

"You two look like you've seen a ghost. Did ye get to take care of your business?" asked the lady sharply.

"Yes, thank you. We met a guard in the hall and he wasn't very nice." Laurelle sank into a chair.

"Oh, that'll be Fritz. A fine guard, but not very sociable. Sorry, lambs, if he scared ye'."

"He didn't scare me," Collin said untruthfully and sat back down to his grog. He had barely taken two sips when the giant front door opened and three guards came crashing through with a protesting man between them.

"I don't know what you're talking about! I've done no thievery today," their captive huffed between trying to yank himself free. "Let me go! I swear I ain't done it."

"Alright then, lads. Let him go as he says," said Bramus. The other two shoved their captive into the room with such force he ran headlong into the wooden desk and crumpled to the floor clutching his head. Bramus kicked the man onto his back and Collin saw him wrestling something from his grip.

When Bramus straightened, three purses dangled from his

wrist. "No thieving today eh, Thompson? I suppose all these match your shoes?!" Bramus kicked the hapless Thompson in the side. He doubled over, groaning.

Laurelle threw Collin a terrified look, surmising that this man had been arrested on their false testimony. Collin reminded himself the man on the floor was not innocent if he was carrying three stolen purses.

"Which one of these is yours, miss?" Bramus chunked the purses down on the counter and Laurelle approached cautiously.

"I b-believe it was...yes. This one is mine." She held up a large black bag.

"Good, that's settled. Ada, my dear, keep these other two safe, will you? No doubt their owners will come in and make a complaint at some point. Anything missing?" he asked Laurelle.

She rummaged through quickly and said, "I think there was more money."

Bramus frisked Thompson roughly and resurfaced with a bag of coins. "Must be this here." He tossed the bag to Laurelle, whose eyes grew huge. Collin stood up, hoping to remove her before she lost her nerve. "You want to make official charges?"

"Oh, that's not necessary. I'm sure he's learned his lesson," Laurelle said hastily.

"He will have when these lads get through with him. Got a few denaris to spare, for our trouble?"

"Of course," Laurelle dug through the bag, dropped a few coins on the counter and blushed. "Go easy on him. I'm sure he meant no harm."

The three guards laughed. "Oh, we'll go easy on him, don't worry your pretty little head, miss. Get her home, boy. You both stay out of trouble, ye' hear?"

"We will, sir, thank you," Collin muttered and took Laurelle by the elbow. "Let's get home, Elle, before I have to explain to your mother why you're late to dinner."

The two hurried from the scene. As the door closed with its

uproarious clang, they heard another kick and another groan from Thompson.

Laurelle was shaking, and Collin kept an arm around her waist more for support than anything. By the time they found a carriage heading toward the Silo, he was propping her up.

"Are you alright?" he asked when they started on the bumpy carriage ride.

"I guess so. What do you think they'll do to Thompson?"

"I don't know. I hope nothing too bad; maybe just kick him around a bit more. They seemed to know him as a regular; maybe they're fond of him. Without men like him they have nothing to do. I don't suppose they want to injure him permanently. You've got the nerve of a Fontre in a sticky situation," he said, shaking his head. "How did you even think to say there was more money?" Collin pulled a piece of blank parchment from his bag and hastily scribbled.

"I don't know. I just looked in the bag and figured the thief probably had more on him and we need money badly. Otherwise, it would have gone to those thugs, wouldn't it?"

"Or into that storage room we found," he said. "I feel weird, though. Bad, actually. I've never stolen anything before."

"Oh I know. I remember the first time I stole something my stomach didn't stop hurting for hours."

"Why would you steal anything? You and your family didn't need money."

"Oh, it wasn't money. I stole some sweets from a shop. Mother wouldn't let me get any, so while she was busy picking fabric for her next frock, I snatched some. I didn't know it was wrong until afterwards. I confessed to Marc, and he told Mother and Father. They made me go back and tell the shop owner and pay out of my pocket money."

"I'm pretty sure I would have been beaten for that."

"Well, Marc probably would have been too. Mother and Father

were never much for beatings, especially not their precious baby girl."

Collin rolled his eyes at the innocent look on her face. "Right, poor lamb."

"I can't wait to tell everyone what we found out."

"Yeah," breathed Collin as they bumped down the street and past the shop full of dresses. He held up the parchment, on which he had copied the map pinned up in the Guard building, marking every station. "I can't wait either."

Laurelle gasped in excitement. "Oh, my word! You're bloody brilliant!"

"YOU WON'T BELIEVE what we found today!" Laurelle announced as they burst through the door of the boarding house room.

"Something useful, I hope," said Julius, who was drinking something dark red directly from a long-necked bottle. "I found a stockpile of food in a broken-down warehouse in the Silo, but have no idea how to get at it."

"Where are the boys?" Laurelle asked.

"Coming along soon no doubt. Don't know what I was thinking, having them scout the Silo again. They don't fit in well down here. Too tall and too...pretty, for lack of a better word. I should put them with you two in the upper district tomorrow. Mal may be our best man for the job of the food store warehouse; he's got no conscience at all. I can barely deal with these scumbags."

"This'll cheer you up then," Collin announced, dropping the map he'd sketched into his uncle's lap. "We also got more money, though neither of us were excited about the method."

"What's this? Is this a map?"

"It is. We found a central hub today, at least I think it was. Met a few Southern Guards and found out these dots mark other stations. There was a basement where they keep money at least and I don't know what else, but there may be weapons down there as well. We didn't actually see inside the storeroom. But there's only a couple of guards on at night."

"You miraculous children! This is like finding gold. I'll message Elian tonight. Surely this is something to work with as a plan of attack."

"What are you drinking?" Laurelle asked, picking up the bottle and sniffing it.

"Don't ask and don't drink it," Julius responded. He rummaged through his bag and pulled out the creekstone. "Hopefully, this will make their day at the Field. I wonder if they've seen anything of Marcus and the Kiatri yet."

Marcole, Nihl and Jacque came into the room then. The brothers looked exhilarated, but Marcole's face was white.

"What happened to you?" Laurelle asked.

"They chased us," Nihl boomed. "All the way from the edge of the Silo, to a few blocks from here. We managed to lose them."

Julius' brow furrowed. "Who chased you?"

"Couple of distinguished homeless gentlemen near that warehouse. They weren't security or anything. They saw us snooping around and wanted to chat." Nihl grinned and grabbed Laurelle into a headlock, rubbing his knuckles on her scalp and then kissing her when she squealed.

"Get off me!" She ducked away from him and hid behind Collin.

"You wouldn't be so cheerful if they'd caught us. Two of them had clubs and one wore a glove with spikes on the knuckles," Marc said.

Collin shuddered. "Yikes. Glad you didn't get caught."

Julius shook his head. "I knew you two were too much for that area. We'll send a less conspicuous team tomorrow. By that I mean Mal and Sophie. Anyone spotted them yet?"

Jacque flushed. "I saw Mal. He uh...went inside the boarding house across the street as we were walking up."

"Into the brothel?" Julius demanded, turning purple. He swore under his breath and grabbed his jacket. "Collin, you and Jacque get us some food. I'll be back in a minute." He fumed and slammed the door as he left.

Collin stared at the door, which was still vibrating. Jacque grinned. "Got any money? We spent what we had left trying to get info on the local muscle."

"Yeah, we got some money today. Or stole it, more like." Collin grabbed the bag Laurelle had put on the bed and rummaged until his hand hit what he thought was a bag of money.

"What's this?"

"That's not the money. It's a facial bag," Laurelle said, snagging the purse from him and looking into its depths.

"Facial bag?"

"You know, like her lip rouge and stuff...here's the money."

"What on earth is lip rouge?"

Laurelle rolled her eyes. "Pigments that make your lips redder. The pressed pink powder goes on the cheeks and the black paint is for around the eyes."

Collin shook his head and turned over the facial bag. "Completely mental, girls are. What a waste of money."

"Give me those. It's not a waste of money; it makes us feel pretty."

"But you're pretty as you are! Why make your lips red when lips aren't even supposed to be red?"

"Oh, go find some food," Laurelle huffed. "Not everything women do is for men, you know. Some things are just fun and fashionable. Bring back more of those chips you found last night."

As the two were heading out, Mal shoved the door open noisily. He limped in, clutching a dark spot in his right side, a heavy bag heaved over his shoulder. His right eye was black and swollen, and a smear of blood on one of his stubbly cheeks made Jacque's jaw drop.

"What the —?" Jacque started, but Mal silenced him with a look and dropped his bag with a thud onto the dirty floor.

"Julius just took off after you. Did he see you?" Collin asked.

Mal ignored him. "Look through them things and see if any of it's useful." He aimed this at Laurelle.

"Don't order her around. You're not in charge," Collin growled. Mal's eyes narrowed and he took a step toward Collin.

"Let me get my belt off, boy. I'll give you a thrashing and then we'll talk about who's in charge." Mal fumbled to unbuckle his belt. Collin glared and took a step toward him.

"Easy." He felt a firm, gentle hand on his shoulder. Jacque. "Back off, mate," Jacque warned Mal.

"Oh stop it, all of you. What happened?" Laurelle asked, holding up her hands between the younger boys and Mal. "Are you hurt? Your side is bleeding."

"Nothing. Just a stab wound. Not deep, and I already got it stitched up by them fine girls across the street." Mal shrugged and winked at Collin, who took a deep breath and buried the urge to lunge at him. Jacque still hadn't slackened his grip on the smaller boy's shoulder.

Laurelle went to the bundle and pulled out one piece of black leather gear after another. Collin caught his breath. They were unmistakably Fontre. "Where did you get these?" asked Laurelle.

"Sophie and I hit an outpost station near that warehouse. Couple of Southern Guards, couple of Fontre." Mal grinned. "They never saw us coming. That girl's a whiz with that bow. Dropped two of them before I had a chance to get in on the fun."

"You killed them?" Laurelle paled.

"I did. It was a great rush, let me tell you. Still in high spirits from the whole thing."

"Where's Sophie?" Nihl asked.

"We separated on the way back. A couple others saw the action and took off after us. We decided splitting up was our best chance of losing them."

"So you don't know where she is?" Nihl clarified.

"She don't need looking after, trust me. She's coming. Anybody got a drink stronger than water?"

"There's a bottle of wine on the table there." Julius had returned, and his voice made Collin jump in surprise. Julius looked at Collin and Jacque and then back to Mal suspiciously. "You two go. We're all hungry."

Collin and Jacque grabbed the heaviest jackets they could and escaped into the cold night.

"Alright?" Jacque asked as they started down the street.

"Fine. Mal gets on my nerves is all. No honor among thieves, I guess. I'm no better." Collin shoved his hands deep into his pockets. "What do you think Elian will do next?"

"Don't know. Probably plan more recon. We should scout out more locations on that map and make sure the layout is similar. What were the Southern Guards like?"

"A lot nicer when they're trying to get your money back for you than pulling it out of your father's work-raw hands for taxes," Collin answered with a bitter laugh.

Jacque frowned and rested his arm on Collin's shoulder as he had in Halanah. The taller boy ruffled Collin's curls. "You need a hat. It's too cold out here in just the jacket. We spotted a shop not far from here with heavier winter clothes. Let's go and see about getting some," Jacque suggested.

"I didn't bring enough money. I thought we were just getting food."

Jacque shrugged. "Maybe they'll give us good deal." Something about the way his friend's eyes sparked with excitement made Collin's throat constrict.

"Let's just get food and go back. I'm fine in this jacket if I keep my hands in my pockets."

"You're chattering. Come on. It's this way."

Collin hadn't thought the lighting on the streets could get poorer until they rounded the corner. They weren't on a proper street, but a narrow alleyway. The backs of aging stone buildings loomed on each side. The combined closeness of the buildings and the rubbish piled against the walls made Collin feel pressed in too tight, though there was plenty of room for two people to walk side by side. The alley was poorly paved, with a mixture of broken brick and grayish mortar Collin had seen used in poorer sections. The street sagged slightly in the middle, darkened by something wet. The stench forced them to breathe through their mouths.

"It hasn't rained, has it?" Collin asked, avoiding the dark center.

"Nope. That's definitely not water," Jacque observed. "There's the shop ahead. Watch your back and stay close. There are some interesting characters around here." Jacque steered him to a rotting wooden door, painted green some years before and then painted red over the green. Jacque tried the doorknob, but it resisted.

"Why are we coming in through the back alley? Is it locked up for the night?" Collin asked, growing more uncomfortable by the moment.

"Nah, the door's stuck. Hang on." Jacque leaned his shoulder against the door, took a step back and heaved himself into the wood. The door gave with a loud groan of protest. Light filtered through the opening and Collin realized the shop was open for business.

They entered a small, dingy hallway and through another doorway blocked with a dirty red curtain. With one hand, Jacque pulled back the curtain and let Collin go first.

Collin squinted in the dim candlelight at a room wider than it was long, with three huge tables taking up almost all the space. Piled high on the tables were heavy woolen clothes of every variety and color.

A boy several years younger than Collin stepped out from behind one the tables. "May I help you, sirs?"

Collin jerked back in surprise. "Sorry, I didn't see you."

The boy grinned and Collin saw his two top front teeth were missing. "Yes sir. We're hard to see."

Collin now realized that the shop was full of small children. He guessed this boy was one of the oldest.

"Hey, Whit," Jacque said cordially. "We're looking for some warm stuff. We'd uh... like to send you home early tonight." Jacque held up the bag of coins, jingling it enticingly.

Whit's muddy brown eyes grew twice as large. "How much is in there?"

"Enough. Line up and you can all have some, but then you gotta leave for the night. Lock up the front. We'll go out the back."

"If you take enough for it to show, we'll catch it from the Missus," Whit warned him.

"We won't get you in trouble," Jacque promised solemnly.

"Hey, y'all come on and line up. We're goin' home in a minute." Whit waved over his fellow workers who joined him, some reluctantly. One tiny girl withdrew into a darkened corner where she practically disappeared.

Collin dug in the bag Jacque was holding and grabbed two heavy coins. He moved slowly toward the frightened girl. "We won't hurt you. We have money. Look." He held out the coins in an open palm. Tears streaked down her dirty cheeks and she covered her face with blistered hands.

"No, go 'way. Leave me 'lone," she whimpered.

Collin's chest tightened. He stooped, laid the coins on the filthy floor and backed up. "You can take them and go home now, if you want," he whispered. Children were already rushing for the door, clutching their treasure, not looking back. Collin watched them scurry out into the cold like a colony of mice released from a cage.

The little girl grabbed the coins, snatching them up so quickly Collin almost missed it. She darted to the door, taking the hand of one of the older boys as they ran into the night.

Collin looked at Jacque, who watched them leave with a grim expression. "I wonder if we just paid them more than they make in a week," Collin said, his voice very hoarse.

"Yeah, or a fortnight more like. I saw their 'missus' this morning, a giant hag of a woman. She slapped that littlest girl's ear so hard it bled. Take what we need. Just one or two things from different piles. I don't want them to get in trouble."

Collin smiled at his friend. "Next time, warn me in advance about your plans. I thought you were holding some sort of heist, not a prison break."

Jacque grinned. "I like the look on your face when you figure out what's going on." He threw Collin a heavy-knit gray cap from one of the piles. Thick gloves followed, pelting Collin one after the other. "Grab one of those scarves and get me a pair of gloves from that stack nearest you. These are all too small for me."

Collin grabbed a pair from the largest stack and noticed the tiny knitting needles with a half-finished cap lying nearby. His chest gave another pinch. "Basically, just slaves."

"Yup. I knew you'd enjoy this little stunt."

"I do, yeah. I wish we could get them out of here permanently."

"Well, they're heading home early with a little extra. Maybe it'll buy them dinner tonight."

"Do we have any money left? We'd better get out of here and get some chips for Elle. She'll be ready to scalp us when we get back."

"Scalp *you*, more like. I don't take orders from Elle. I gave them everything we brought, so she'll just have to deal."

Collin shrugged. "Well worth a night of hunger."

The boys blew out the candles and slipped out through the back door as promised.

26

THE WAREHOUSE

E
lian gripped the creekstone and rushed to tell Cassai his news. He found her in the tent the people had prepared for her use. Situated in the center of the camp, it was the tallest and newest of the canvas they'd acquired. Hollis and Theoris stood sentry outside the opening. Elian jerked his head for them to enter with him.

The three men found Cassai bandaging the hand of a small boy from Plahn named Peter. "He helped build the cook fires this morning and got too near the hot pans." She kissed the bandage and the boy grinned and ran from the tent.

Cassai straightened up. She wore a long gown of blue and purple striped silk. Elian recognized it as having belonged to one of the more well-off women in Plahn.

"You do look beautiful this morning, Your Majesty," exclaimed Theoris, gripping his crutch to bow. She stood and dusted off her skirt.

"Thank you, Theoris. You don't need to bow when we're alone."

"Morning," Elian said, smiling. "I like your dress. Wasn't that Rosella's?"

She rolled her eyes. "She gave me four of her fancier things. Said they were more fitting for a queen than brown pants and tunic." Cassai beamed at them. "You look like you have news."

"I do, from Julius. They think they've found some of the stockpiles, but they need a plan."

"How many did they find?" Hollis asked.

"I'm not sure." Elian held up the creekstone on which the words, "Found stockpiles, need plan" were etched.

"So we meet and discuss it?" Hollis asked.

"Good! I'm bored out of my mind," Cassai said.

Elian's eyes narrowed. "I'm not sure it's wise for you to leave the camp."

"It really isn't," Theoris piped in eagerly. "Any manner of things may accost us on such a journey. I should probably stay behind with her. Don't you think that the safer course of action... for her, I mean." Hollis' glower silenced him.

"If you're going, I'm going," Cassai declared.

Elian sighed. "I should've counted on that."

"Yes, you should've. How long have you known me?"

He smiled at her. "Not nearly long enough."

"So signal back to Julius we'll meet him today."

"Yes, your Majesty. Anything else I can do for you?" Elian asked, taking her hand and bowing deeply.

She glared at his sarcasm. "Talk the women into giving me back my clothes. I can barely move in this get-up."

"Agreed, it doesn't suit you at all," Hollis muttered.

ELIAN, Cassai, Hollis and Theoris waited at the outskirts of town in an abandoned barn they'd picked to meet in. Elian looked down and saw Cassai twisting her fingers nervously while they waited. He dropped a comforting arm around her shoulders. "I'm hungry," she whispered.

Elian pulled her up against him. "Sorry. Maybe Julius will have found some food."

"I hope so. The Lightling stores are running low. If we don't find some soon, all of us will be too weak to think, much less fight."

Hollis reached into his pocket and pulled out a few dried leaves. "Chew them. They help."

Cassai smelled the peppermint and popped them into her mouth gratefully.

Theoris withdrew a small silver flask from his overcoat pocket. "This will also lift your spirits, my lady."

"Thank you, Theoris, but I'm alright."

"Is that a fairy brew?" Elian snapped at him.

"Oh, indeed not. Sacha supplied it. He brought it from the North Country. I'll be jiggered if it isn't the best rum I've tasted in this barbaric mortal world."

Hollis snatched the flask and glared at him. "You're guarding the Queen, idiot!" he spat at Theoris. "No alcohol."

Elian grinned and held out a hand for the flask. Hollis gave it to him, and he pushed it into the pocket of his fleece-lined coat. "You need to keep your wits about you, Theoris. You're welcome to have it back when you're off duty."

"Which will be never," Hollis assured him.

"Namarielle." The whisper outside the barn silenced them.

"We're here," Elian said.

Julius, Collin, Laurelle, Sophie, Jacque and Nihl materialized in the doorway.

Julius bowed his head at the sight of Cassai, which made her push harder against Elian's side. Seeing the bow, the rest of his group did the same. She twisted her lips into a gracious smile, but Elian knew she was finding everyone's deference difficult to get used to.

"I'm so glad you're all safe," she said. "Where are the others?"

"Mal's scouting a warehouse we found; full of food, we

383

suspect. And we always leave at least one in our room, so Marc stayed today. We have quite a few things in there we aren't anxious to part with," Julius explained.

"Understood. How many stockpiles?" Elian asked.

"Thirteen, though we haven't looked into all of them individually. Collin found and recreated a map of the city and the markers."

Collin pulled a folded piece of parchment from his coat and handed it to Cassai. She smiled. "This is perfect. What is this little symbol at the top?" Cassai studied what looked a bit like the Namarielle seal, only instead of an oak tree in the center was a large K, encircled with three stars over the top.

"It's nothing. A symbol I was working on. You know how all those runes and symbols for the races? I thought the Keepers of the Kingdom needed one," Collin said.

"I like it." Elian looked over Cassai's shoulder and nodded. "We'll have to check each marker to be sure. How many guards are at each do you guess?"

"We know this one," Collin put his finger on the central marker, "has only two guards at night...for now. If they get wind they're in danger, I suspect that'll change."

"So we'll plan it so they don't get wind of it," Hollis replied.

"Or," said Cassai, "we don't. We need food more than weapons right now. What if we hit the warehouse first, but don't take it all, and leave a calling card." She smiled and pointed to the symbol Collin had created. "Then we let it leak that we're planning to hit again another night. If they're busy guarding the warehouse, maybe they'll leave the other stockpiles less guarded."

Elian looked at the rest of the group, who all seemed to be considering this idea. "Sometimes the safest way to get a target off your back is to give the enemy another target to aim at."

"What if the Southern Guard calls the Fontre in? How quickly can they get troops in here?" Julius speculated.

"They don't like the Fontre any more than we do. I guess they never get paid as much after the Fontre have been through, especially the Koninjka," Laurelle said.

"And they're scared of them. What would the Fontre do if they found the guard failed to keep the warehouse safe?" Collin added.

"They certainly wouldn't be happy," Elian said. "Maybe they would prefer to handle it themselves. Good point."

Cassai felt a thrill. It was one of the first times she felt she was making a decision, not as a mere rebel, but as a queen. "We should take stock of the warehouse sooner than later. Tonight even."

"How much food is there?" Elian asked Julius.

"We haven't been inside. I only got a view of the place from the road. It's just a rundown building from outside; you'd never guess there was anything useful, unless you already knew. Some of the locals told me about it. They've found ways to sneak in and steal from it sometimes, but not so much the Guards would notice."

Elian looked at Cassai. "If we're seen by anyone in the Fontre —"

"We're dead," Cassai agreed. "If we're described by the Guards to the Fontre we're dead."

"What if you didn't look like yourselves?" Laurelle asked. Her face lit with a smile as she held up a bag.

"What's this?" Cassai asked, opening it.

"Make-up. And I know how to use it." Laurelle shot Collin a look that made him flush.

Cassai grinned at Elian. He sighed but nodded. "Might work."

"If you're coming with us into the city, you should put your disguise on here. There are plenty of unfriendly eyes on the streets in the Silo. Jacque and Nihl draw enough attention as it is," Julius said.

Jacque grinned and Nihl wiggled his eyebrows. "Happy to be of service," Jacque said.

"You should probably also hide your hair," Laurelle suggested to them both. "It's pretty distinctive. I also have two Guard uniforms. I think one will fit Julius, and the other may fit you. Sorry, I don't remember your name."

"Theoris," said the fairy as he reached for the uniform. "I must say, red is not a good color on me." Everyone ignored this.

"Theoris can't go this time," Hollis said bluntly.

"Yes," Cassai nodded. "There's no way he can go in his condition."

"I was only kidding about the color," Theoris protested.

"Your leg, man. You can't go into any sort of fight with your leg as it is, and this could definitely turn into a fight."

Theoris looked hurt, but Elian put a hand on his shoulder, and Cassai wrapped an arm around his waist. "We'll come back and get you as soon as it's over. That leg is healing fast. The next fight has your name written all over it."

Sophie tilted her head thoughtfully. "What about Elian? Speaking of distinctive —"

Laurelle bit her lip. "I have an idea, but I have a feeling you're not going to like it. Mal stripped these off two Fontre guards at an outpost in the Silo. I — I think he killed them just for the fun of it. He's not very shy about hating them." Laurelle withdrew a black bundle from her bag. "Do you think any of it will fit you? I can darken your hair without much trouble, but you'll have to look a bit more the part."

"The disguise may fool a Southern Guard, but if a Fontre is anywhere in the area, they'll know instantly. The Fontre cannot forget things that happened in their infancy, they certainly won't forget who's posted where."

"So if a Fontre shows up, run," Sophie suggested, shrugging.

"What about his blue eyes?" Cassai asked.

Laurelle held up a scarf. "I can hide one, but...the other..." Laurelle looked around the group and nervously chewed her bottom lip. "Can someone punch him really hard? Like, hard enough to almost swell it shut, but not enough that he can't see?"

"I suppose I could," Hollis volunteered. He grinned at Elian and took off his jacket. "But only because it's for a good cause."

Laurelle's eyes widened at them. "Okay." she took a step back.

"Sure you're up to it, old man?" Elian chided him.

"I'll do my best."

"I punch back."

"That's actually fine." Laurelle added, her voice a bit uneven. "It'll sell better if it looks like the two of you got into a legitimate fight. Because we're going in with him like he's – um – like we're his prisoners."

"They're not actually going to fight," Cassai said firmly. She looked from Elian to Hollis and rolled her eyes. "Your injuries –"

"Oh, that's right," said Elian kissing her head and backing away. "I'd forgotten about my injuries." He smirked at Hollis and the Kiatri threw a punch which Elian deflected and took in his shoulder. Elian lunged for his mid-section, feeling more alive than he had in days. Hollis gave beneath his weight and both men fell to the floor of the barn.

They tussled for a few minutes before Elian got in a punch that sent Hollis rolling away, clutching his lip. "I'll kill you for that, Fontre," Hollis swore, spitting out a mouthful of blood. His lip swelled and a gash oozed blood, but his eyes sparkled as if he was having the time of his life.

"Just his eye," yelled Laurelle. "I need you to punch him in the eye and stop it."

Elian pushed himself up, invigorated, but wracked with pain. Of course, Cassai was right that he shouldn't be fighting. His back and legs screamed with every movement. "That was brilliant. Thank you, Hollis. I believe we should get on with the lady's plan."

"Hold still then, idiot." Hollis approached him, drew back a fist, and landed it directly into the shepherd's right eye. Bursts of white light exploded across Elian's vision and the room swirled. He staggered back and then righted himself, nodding manfully at

Hollis. All the women looked horrified. Elian saw Jacque pass Nihl something that looked like a gold coin. He smiled.

"What was the bet?"

"That you'd never let him get the last punch in," Jacque said.

"You bet against that?" Elian asked Nihl. "You've never met a real Fontre, have you?" Elian grinned at Hollis, who rolled his eyes and raised his fists.

"Did I go too easy on you, Fontre? Eager for more?"

"Don't! You're both being ridiculous!" Cassai protested as Elian flew across the room, knocking Hollis onto his back and pinning him to the floor. Elian raised both Hollis' arms over his head and held them in one hand while he made a fist of the other.

"Surrender, Kiatri," he ordered with a smirk.

Hollis scowled at him. "Never. It's against my creed to surrender to a Fontre."

Elian clacked his tongue. "I'm afraid that'll cost you. Nose or cheek?"

"Cheek. I want to keep my nose pretty," Hollis quipped. He turned his face and grimaced, awaiting the blow. Elian laughed and patted Hollis' cheek patronizingly.

"You can get up now, Hollis. I accept your surrender." He stood and offered the Kiatri a hand which was smacked away.

"I'm definitely going to kill you," Hollis growled, wiping his hand over the pardoned cheek.

"I look forward to it."

Nihl and Jacque exchanged a look, and Nihl rolled his eyes and dropped Jacque's money back into his brother's outstretched hand.

"I would consider that more like a draw," Nihl grumbled.

AN HOUR LATER, Elian emerged from the barn followed by the rest of his group. Cassai limped out, her head wrapped in a long scarf, and her face carefully lined to look like a much older woman. Collin found her a stick to lean on. She tapped the ground with it. Three shawls wrapped around her concealed the Fontre blade in her belt.

Hollis had altered his clothing and hidden his bow and arrows. His lip was still bloody from the brawl, as Cassai called it, and he was in higher spirits than he had been in days.

Elian felt least comfortable of all. He'd glanced in Laurelle's hand mirror before they vacated the barn and instantly regretted it. He wore the black leather fighting gear of a Fontre guard, his face artfully mangled by Laurelle's make-up. He couldn't believe how much he resembled Devilan, but the thing that made him feel he'd swallowed broken glass was a long red scar she'd painted down his left cheek. She couldn't have known that Ffastian's face swam into his head at the sight of it, so he said nothing as he wiped it off, careful to leave the rest of her artistry untouched.

Laurelle had wrapped the black scarf around his head and over one eye. Under the cloth was a blood-red gash, as if he had recently lost an eye in battle. The other eye was almost swollen shut, courtesy of Hollis. He squinted at the job she'd done darkening his hair with a powder.

"If it rains, we're made, but otherwise the powder will keep you looking just right."

"I think we're safe from rain at the moment," he assured her. He smiled at Cassai, who still looked miffed. "It was for the authenticity of the mission," he said innocently.

"You two have been aching to have it out for ages. Feel better?"

"I do. Thanks for asking. I didn't realize how badly I needed to trounce someone."

Cassai limped away, leaning on her cane and muttering something under her breath about all men being idiots.

~

THE HORIZON WAS streaked blood red when they reached the outskirts of the Silo. Collin hoped the darkness would hide his knees knocking together under his gear.

Julius turned to the group. "I'm going to stop by our room and see if Mal is back. He'd be a valuable asset for this kind of thing. Anything you kids need from the room?"

"My cuff and my sword," Collin said. "I didn't realize we were heading to raid the warehouse straight away."

"Alright. I'll grab it. Laurelle, you're good?"

"Fine, I've got my sword. Tell Marc I – I love him and I'll see him soon." She took a deep breath and let it out slowly.

Collin rubbed her back. "Sure you wouldn't rather wait with him? He could probably use an extra person just in case anything were to –"

"Stop it. I'm going. You think I can just sit in the room and hope these get-ups actually work?"

Collin worked a pebble loose with the toe of his boot. "It was worth a try."

"We'll meet you there," Elian said, motioning for the group to follow. They kept to the woods surrounding Pyrene-Valla as long as possible and only emerged into the darkening street when the warehouse was in sight.

The building was tall as it was wide and looked as if abandoned for years. This didn't fool Collin. Every building in the Silo had black mold climbing its sides and bricks crumbling around the edges. Collin expected it to be more secluded, but it was sandwiched between two other buildings, both looking even more neglected. A group of men dressed in filthy coats and scarves that looked passed down through several vagrant generations, lounged outside, drinking from brown bottles.

The companions heard them laughing, but couldn't distinguish the conversation from where they stood.

Elian ducked into the recessed entrance of the building next door and the rest of the group joined him. "Are we waiting for Uncle Julius?" Collin whispered.

"Yes. He shouldn't be far behind."

Julius appeared within five minutes. He'd almost passed their hideout when Elian gave a low whistle and Julius jerked his head around. Collin waved him silently to the spot, noticing two greasy paper bags in his hands.

"Any trouble?" Elian asked in a whisper.

"None. Marc is guarding the room, but unfortunately Malcolm was still out. You never know what that man is up to. I also brought some of these." He held out the bags. Collin grinned at Laurelle, recognizing the aroma of fried fish and chips. "I heard the Queen was hungry, and we can't have that." Julius touched Cassai's cheek affectionately and she rewarded him with a delighted smile.

"Oh, thank you, Julius. You're fantastic," Cassai said, tearing into a piece of fish without waiting for the others.

The companions passed around the warm, crunchy food and ate in silence for a few moments. Nothing remained of the meal but empty bags and one packet of red sauce, which Nihl pocketed.

"It's so good, I can't throw it out. I'll find something to put it on," he explained to Jacque's look of incredulity.

Elian grinned at the brothers. "Hollis, take Sophie and Nihl and circle round the back. Tell me how many guards you see behind the building and try to find something to transport the goods in once we have them. Anything with wheels. The rest of you, stay with me; remember you're my prisoners. The Guards are under my command. I'll play the part of an inspector here to report back to the Fontre."

Collin peered down the street at the men in rags. "Who are you going to act like this with? It's just a bunch of homeless men."

"I assure you; they're guards for this facility and well paid, which probably means they can fight. Everyone stay alert; keep your weapons hidden but ready."

"I almost forgot," Julius whispered, throwing his cloak aside to reveal Collin's sword. "You'll need this."

Collin took the sword and sheath, weaving it into his belt. Then he took the cuff, which Julius had worn on his own arm hidden beneath a sleeve.

"Boys, you've got your rings on?" Julius looked at Jacque and Nihl, who nodded and showed their fingers. "Don't forget to use them if you have to. And Elle ..." The man gave Laurelle a pained look like her father had the morning she left. "Please be careful. Stay behind us and —"

"I'm not going to get killed, Julius. Don't worry about me." Laurelle smiled and waved off the concern. Julius kissed her forehead.

"I wish girls weren't quite so courageous," he whispered.

"Agreed," Elian muttered, casting Cassai a look which she pointedly ignored.

"So looking for more filthy vagrants round the other side of the building then — got it?" Sophie said, rolling her eyes. Hollis glared at her and motioned to Nihl to follow and they crept out into the street and ducked into the alleyway on the opposite side.

"What about once we're inside?" Cassai whispered.

"Follow my lead. We'll figure it out. There are only eight I can count. Probably more inside. Got your sword?"

Cassai opened the front of her piled-on shawls, revealing the sword already in her right hand.

"Good girl. Keep it hidden. Let's go." Elian straightened and marched into the street. Laurelle reached for Collin's hand. Her own was freezing cold and she was trembling. Collin squeezed it.

"Don't worry. Just look like you're a prisoner. Looking scared would be normal," he whispered as they approached the building.

The men stopped laughing at the sight of Elian. They straightened, and one stood, his eyes wide with terror. "Is that L-Lord Devilan?"

"Do you really think the *Genraal Majure* concerns himself with local matters?" Elian barked. "I'm an inspector from Pyrene-Valla. Who is the head guard here?"

"I am, my lord," stammered the man, running his fingers nervously through his coarse black hair. "My name is Grint. And I —"

"I don't care what your name is. I heard there was a group of rebels asking about this warehouse. Is that true?"

"M — my Lord, if they asked about it, they wouldnt'a heard much. Just that it's abandoned." Grint bowed low. Collin saw that, though it appeared they were drinking alcohol, not even one gave the slightest appearance of drunkenness. So Elian was correct — definitely Guards in disguise.

"Are the goods still in order?" Elian asked.

"Indeed sir. Very much in order. Would you like to —"

"Of course, we're going inside. What do you think, man?" Elian growled, making the black-haired man jump. "I caught this group sneaking about and took them into custody. I think they're with the rebels, but we'll soon find out. I've called for these Southern Guards to transport them to prison. There is one in particular," Elian gave Collin an unexpectedly hard shove in the middle of his back, sending him to his knees, "seems to be leading them. I'll question him inside." Collin's eyes watered as he caught himself on his palms, rubbing them raw on the pavement, but he kept his face stoic.

"This is the rebels?" asked a man with two missing front teeth. "An old woman, one bloke and a bunch of kids?"

"Are you questioning my authority to apprehend criminals, sir?" Elian demanded.

The men paled and one even dared give Collin a sympathetic look. "Of course not, my Lord. I just thought maybe the kids stumbled upon something by accident or —"

"How dare you look at one of the prisoners of the Fontre?" Elian raised his sword and bashed it against the man's skull. He dropped like a stone. Collin's stomach lurched and he pushed himself to his feet. His knees ached. Julius bowed his head, looking defeated. "Open the door," Elian growled at Grint, who bowed hastily and withdrew a ring of keys from his pocket. Elian snatched them.

"I'll do it. Show me which one opens it."

"Th—this one is for the front door."

"And the others?"

"They open everything else. The round headed keys open storage rooms. The two square ones open guards' quarters and the kitchen." Grint glanced nervously at his fallen friend, who hadn't moved. None of the men dared to check on him.

"I can take you through, my lord. I know where the goods is kept." The man in the hat rose, brushing off his frayed brown coat. He lifted the hat's brim and Collin glimpsed his face for the first time: Malcolm.

Elian showed no sign of recognition, but inserted the key and twisted it hard. The door swung inward. "Very good. Lead on. The rest of you, wait here. I'll see to you after I've finished my inspection." The men glanced nervously at each other, no doubt wondering what Elian meant by "see to you".

Elian's boots thudded against the hard stone floor as he marched through the hallway. "You said there were Guards' quarters?" Elian's voice had dropped down to his usual tone.

"Yes, down this hallway," Malcolm said, bowing and leading the way.

"Are there any weapons here?"

"From what I've seen so far, and that ain't much, just food. But each of those men outside is heavily armed and trained to fight. We may not get away with this ruse for long. Where's Sophie?"

"I sent her with Hollis and Nihl to look around out back. Hopefully, they can find a way to transport the food back to the

394

Westerling Field." Elian replied as they rushed down the hallway. "Do you have any weapons on you?" Malcolm opened his coat, revealing something tucked into his belt.

"What is that thing?"

"It's a pistol. They've all got one. Shoots lead balls with a bit of fire behind it. I guess the Fontre's been developing them for a while."

Elian nodded. "So they've finally done it, have they? Those are supposed to be more accurate and more deadly than arrows. If one is aimed at any of you, duck and run. Alright, we're going to the guards' quarters first. I'll give them a scare and then lock them in so I can begin my private inspection. Who's okay with being manhandled?"

"You've already started with me. No need to switch up," Collin offered bleakly, rubbing his raw palms on his pants.

"No, don't do him. I'll take −" Jacque's voice cut off as Collin elbowed him in the ribs.

"No need to worry, Jacque. I won't hurt him badly. Collin, absorb the blows and react as if they're much more painful than they are. Cry out and show them that beaten look you gave the men outside. If we can scare them sufficiently, this could be easy." Elian straightened up to resume his role. "The rest of you, keep up the looks of horror. You're convincingly terrified of me." A nervous chuckle rumbled through the group.

"Yes. We're really good actors," Laurelle mumbled, shrinking away from Elian.

Elian grinned, chucking her under the chin. "Keep up the act. It's working."

27

THE RAID

Before they entered the guards' quarters, Elian told Malcolm to pretend to be knocked out. The man drooped between Jacque and Julius. They dragged him through the doorway. "This man interfered in the affairs of the Fontre. Would any of the rest of you maggots care to join him?" Elian pulled Malcolm's head back by his hair for the benefit of the shocked guards. They'd woken everyone when Elian stormed through the door. They now sat on the edges of their wooden bunks staring at Malcolm in terror.

"N-no my lord," one of them stammered. "How can we help you?"

"I need to inspect your inventory. I have it on good authority that this group of miscreants is part of a larger rebel group looking to rob this facility." Elian released Malcolm's head and it lolled forward. "You, lead us to the storage area." Elian pointed to one groggy man. "The rest of you – I'm locking you in. I'll be making a full report on your cooperation. Cause one moment's trouble, and this will look like a holiday." Elian grabbed Collin and rammed his fist into the boy's side. Collin cried out and gripped his side, staggering away.

Laurelle, whimpering, rushed to him, but Elian grabbed the sleeve of his jacket and pulled him back. "This boy was leading the rebels. By the end of tonight, he'll not only wish he'd never dared challenge the Fontre, he'll wish he'd never been born. I'm taking my prisoners with me, and you, let's go." Elian barked at the guard he'd picked.

"I – yes my lord." The guard Elian had pointed to stumbled to his feet. "I'm sorry. I'll lead you to the storerooms straightaway." Nobody spoke as Elian marched back through the door, followed by the terrified guard and his companions. He locked the other guards in.

The guard hastily led them down one of the long corridors. "There are many storerooms here, sir. Where would you like to begin taking inventory? Can I lock any of these rebels away for you? We have holding cells here."

"I'll keep them with me for now and use them to help me load a shipment."

"A shipment, my lord?"

"Indeed. We're to deliver a shipment to the Koninjka immediately. Apparently, they ran into trouble in the Western Borderlands and need supplies."

"Ah, yes. The Western lands are almost dried up of goods. I've been there myself in the last month. Had to knock a few men around just to get rightful taxes from them. Killed one shepherd who claimed his whole family would starve if we took our allotment of sheep. There wasn't much left of them to defend. Stupid blighter. He's better off dead anyway."

Elian's uncovered eye cut to his companions, who all looked furious. "Right. I think some of these rebels are from villages to the Northwest. Said they wanted to bring down the Southern Guard for joining with the Fontre. Despicable creatures." He cuffed Collin in the face. The boy gazed at the floor.

The Guard looked nervous at Elian's statement and carefully smoothed his features into a look of indifference. "Indeed. Here's the room with the freshest goods. Only the best for the Fontre, eh?" The guard had set his jaw and Elian caught a flash of pure hatred. "I can unlock it for you if –"

"I have a key," Elian growled. "I'll take your weapon though, if you don't mind."

"I beg your pardon, my lord."

"Your sword and pistol, sir. If you have it on you."

"Oh, yes, sir. I always have it on me." The guard looked abashed as he lifted his dressing gown to reveal the weapon tucked into his pants.

"Not a very wise place to keep it, is it?" Elian asked grimly.

"I – um, no, my lord. I sleep lightly and on my left side, so the sword always stays at my right."

"Remind me to have a few of the Koninjka visit this facility and give you a lesson in weapon safety. They manage to sleep in full armor." Elian held out his hand. The guard drew the sword and pistol from his waist and handed them to the Fontre. "Very good," Elian said, pretending to inspect it and, before the guard could react, he brought the hilt down hard into the guard's temple. He fell to the ground to gasps from Cassai and Laurelle.

"Elian! You could have killed him," Cassai dropped to her knees and grabbed the guard's wrist, feeling for his pulse.

"I didn't kill him. I know how hard to hit a temple to kill a man. Give me some credit." Elian tasted bile when he saw the slack face of the unconscious guard. "Get inside, all of you. Let's see what this storeroom holds. Collin, you alright?"

Collin grinned. "Of course I'm alright. I've been hit harder than that by Elle when she's mad at me." Laurelle glared and punched his arm.

"Bring the light in, Jacque. Mal, you can wake up now." At Elian's instructions, Malcolm shook himself and stood up straight again. The companions filed into the large room and Cassai let out another gasp.

"There's enough food here to feed all of Plahn for six

months." Cassai moved to a tower of grain sacks marked 'wheat', and then to another, stacked equally high, marked 'barley'.

"By the Weaver," breathed Malcolm, who'd bypassed the grain. "Apples!"

"It can't be. Where in the Borderlands are they able to grow apples?" Collin asked and rushed to pillars of barrels stacked four high and eight deep.

There was the sound of scuffling on the other side of the door, as though a fight had broken out in the hallway. Elian drew his sword with his left hand, still holding the guard's sword in his right. "Get the door!" he bellowed. The group pulled arms from various places in their garments and Julius rushed to open the door.

"On your right, Uncle!" Elian heard Sophie shout. He ran into the hallway and found Sophie, Hollis and Nihl grappling with four guards they had encountered outside the warehouse.

Elian plunged into the fray, surprising them enough to catch a man in his side before he had a chance to respond to the fresh onslaught. Nihl's sword clanged against the blade of another. Sophie was holding her own against the man with missing teeth. Her skill with a blade wasn't as impressive as her archery. Grint had recovered from his blow to the head. He and Hollis were grappling hand to hand, both having lost their weapons.

Elian lunged at Grint and ran his sword into the man's back between his shoulder blades. Grint let out a gurgling sound and Elian felt his full weight as he dropped, the sword still lodged in his ribcage.

"Good one, Elian," Hollis said breathlessly. "Dropped my sword back in the entryway. I'll get it."

"Use this one, it's extra. If the rest of the guards break through before we get the supplies we'll have a much stronger fight to deal with." Elian could already hear the guards he'd locked up pounding the door, shouting for their friends.

"Sophie, hold on. We're coming," shouted Malcolm behind him.

Sophie heard him, connected with the guard's sword and wrenched it up, dancing out of the way while Malcolm ran him through the heart.

"I surrender!" shouted the last guard standing, dropping his sword and holding up his arms. "Please, don't kill me. I'll come quietly," the man begged. Nihl held the tip of his sword against the man's throat and backed him to the wall.

"Elian?" Nihl asked.

"Let him live, but bind him. Bring him to the second store-room on your left. There's more food in just the one than we can haul away tonight." Elian looked for Cassai and found her standing at the edge of the hallway, sword drawn. His heart lifted. "What happened?" he asked Hollis.

"We circled the perimeter, but couldn't find any entrance but the front door. When we rounded the corner, the guards, who were already on high alert, came alive. Two of them dropped with my arrows in their chests before they could do more than yell. Sophie got another on the way in. That left these four. They were in such a frenzy, they put up a very good fight, just not good enough." Hollis toed the man Elian had stabbed. Elian felt as if a lump of lead was sinking through his insides. He sighed and yanked his blade from the man's back. Hollis sighed. "First kill?"

"Yes." Elian's tongue felt too big for his mouth. He tried to swallow, but thought he might gag. "Devilan taught me that maneuver years ago. I always thought it a petty trick, to stab a man when his back was turned." He felt a soft hand slipping into his. Cassai had come to his side. Her costume of shawls and blankets were shed in the storeroom, and she was herself in her tunic, pants and plain brown jacket.

"Are you alright?" she asked quietly.

"I'm fine. We need to find some way to transport that food or these men died for nothing."

They dragged their captive back to the storeroom and shut the door, locking it behind them. Nihl dropped the man against the wall and Elian knelt in front of him. "How do you transport shipments back and forth? Are there carts or wagons here?"

The man shifted uncomfortably. "You should know, my lord," he muttered.

"You really aren't that quick at the uptake, are you?" Elian said, pulling the wrapping off his eye. "I'm not with the Fontre. I'm with the rebels."

Understanding dawned on the man's face. "Elian...did one of them call you Elian?"

"They did. Where are your carts?"

The man's eyes grew twice as large as normal and his feet scuffled as he pressed hard into the wall. "L-Lord Devilan's brother?"

"Yes."

"I can't...you don't. Please sir! Take me with you!"

It was Elian's turn to look surprised. "What?"

"Please, I'll do anything for you, I promise. Please don't send me to Lord Devilan." The man was screaming now, he had shuffled to the side, but caught himself off balance and fell sideways to the floor, his hands bound and nothing to break his fall.

"Right. Stop it. It's alright," Elian rushed to assure him. He put a firm hand on the man's forearm. "We'll take you with us, alright? Trust me – I'm not inclined to send anyone into the hands of my brother. What's your name?"

The man stopped thrashing and lay panting on the floor looking exhausted. "Peter."

"Peter, how can we move these supplies to our camp? Our army is starving."

"The supplies. Yes, sir, I can help you with that. They're on wheels you see? All the stacks have wheels at the bottom so we can attach them to horses or donkeys and move them through the city." Peter pointed to the bottoms of the pillars of food and Elian saw they were two or three inches from the ground, on top of wheeled platforms.

"Brilliant. Alright, let's move. We have to get as much of this out as we can. Collin, do you have anything to draw with?"

"Draw?"

"Yes. I think the Keeper's symbol should be on that wall, right where the wheat was."

Laurelle reached into the pouch at her side and pulled out a tube of red lip rouge. Collin grinned. "Yes sir. I can do that."

"Bind my hands in front and I can push one of the platforms," suggested Peter eagerly.

"Stand up. I'm going to search you. If you move a muscle while I do, I will drop you and you will wake up in my brother's personal carriage. Is that clear?"

"Yes, sir. I swear, sir."

Elian patted the man down and, finding no weapons, retied his hands in front.

Each of the companions selected a stack of goods and positioned themselves to push. Elian opened the door and they filed out, two to each stack. Then he joined Peter at the last stack and they rolled their bounty down the long hallway to the cacophony of the guards still thudding against their prison door.

Elian paused beside the prone form of the man he'd killed. "What was his name?" he asked Peter.

"Dimitri," Peter replied in a hoarse voice.

Elian pushed Dimitri onto his back, crossing his arms over his body and placing the dead man's sword in his hands.

The lump of lead from earlier seemed to have settled in Elian's abdomen now. "Hurry. I think that door's starting to give," Elian said softly, standing and taking his place next to Peter.

"Are we coming back for more?" Cassai asked from behind the platform of wheat she and Hollis were pushing.

"Not tonight. This will send our message nicely." Elian was pushing a platform full of salted meats that smelled so good it made his mouth water. He smiled when he thought what Sacha could do with all this food.

~

"So, do we go back to the Westerling Field now?" Marcole asked that night while all the Lightlings tried to recount their adventures to him at once. Collin thought he took the stories rather graciously considering how disappointed Marc was at being stuck on guard duty.

"Not yet. We're meeting again tomorrow night to plan the simultaneous attack on the guard stations. That's where the wealth is, and probably weapons too." Laurelle was lying in bed and Collin sat beside her, rubbing the spaces between her fingers.

"I can't believe how full-on Fontre Elian can go when he needs to. He was terrifying," Collin said with a shudder.

"I thought he was terrifying before he went full-on Fontre," murmured Laurelle. Her first fight had drained her. She'd fallen across the bed fully clothed the moment they got to the room and hadn't moved since.

"That's because you don't know him. You'll come to find he'll do whatever has to be done even if it's hard, but mostly, he's just a giant bowl of mush inside," Collin said. A sudden pain shot across his back then and he cringed, but tried not to make any noise.

"Y'alright?" asked Jacque, passing him an apple from a bag Cassai had filled.

"Fine. My back hurts sometimes still; I think it's mental. Happens whenever I think about the Fontre, or...home," Collin said quietly. He took a bite of the apple, then closed his eyes and savored the sweet, tart juices filling his mouth.

"I thought Askelpos took care of that." Jacque said, taking a bite from his own apple.

"He did what he could. He healed the stripes that wouldn't clear up any other way. He said the muscles underneath have

some permanent damage. I'm alright. By the Weaver, this apple…"
He crunched into it again and lay back beside Laurelle.

"Tomorrow, we scope out the other guard stations on the map," Julius announced from the corner, where everyone thought he was asleep. "Lights out, my friends. Collin, get off that bed."

Collin grinned up at the ceiling, gave Laurelle a kiss on the temple and twisted from the bed. "Are Elle and I headed out in fancy clothes?" he asked as he settled on his pallet.

"Just sneaking in and out. We'll all be dressed casual. We want to blend in and disappear, not draw attention. Nihl and Jacque, I'm afraid you're sitting this one out."

Jacque let out a sound that sounded like a cross between a growl and a groan. Nihl was curled up on his pallet, fast asleep.

"Hey, I don't want to hear it," snapped Marcole. "I missed the whole dang party today."

"Lights out," said Julius again, much more firmly.

Malcolm looked up from his book, blew out the lamp, and was snoring before its last flicker died away.

Collin made his way to the pallets in the corner that he, Marc, Jacque and Nihl had made for themselves. He lay next to Jacque, staring into the darkness for a long while. His body was exhausted, but his mind filled with the events of the evening.

"Jacque? Are you awake?"

"Mffrttme," Jacque mumbled and rolled over to face him.

"I think that fellow tonight, the one Elian killed. That was the first time he'd ever killed anyone. I'm pretty sure."

"Why does this mean I can't go to sleep?" Jacque asked, his eyes still closed.

"What about when it's us? How do you think we'll act when we have to kill someone, or be killed?"

Jacque opened one eye and stared at his friend. Then he wiggled his eyebrows. "What makes you think I haven't killed already?"

"I'm being serious."

"Okay, seriously. We'll deal with it when it happens. We'll just...figure it out. Now then, in the spirit of the conversation, Julius is going to have us up at crack of dawn and *you* are going to be my first kill if you don't let me get some sleep."

~

ELIAN LEANED AGAINST A TENT POLE, arms crossed, watching Sacha with a smile. His little brother darted between each stack of food, examining, smelling and laughing with sheer happiness.

"How on earth? I mean, by the Weaver, Elian, this is brilliant! I'm going to make you the best meal you've ever tasted tonight."

"Did you look in that last barrel?"

Sacha went to the barrel he'd pointed out. "This is honey! What? How on earth?" he took out a spoon and dipped it in the golden liquid. He groaned with delight when he brought it to his mouth. "Oh, you have to taste this."

He crossed the tent to Elian, who took the spoon.

"When was the last time you tasted honey? This is the good stuff too. This is from the North Country. I guarantee it."

Elian froze, the spoon poised at his lips. "The North Country? How can that be?"

"The Fontre have a steady trade with the Light Ones. Didn't you know that?"

Elian handed back the spoon without tasting the honey. "No. I didn't. What goods does the Fontre provide?"

"All kinds of stuff. There's a quarry in the Inner Kingdom with pink granite. The Lightlings love it. They've built more than a few buildings with it. Then there are the people. The Lightlings don't have any problem with slavery, you know."

Elian sighed. "Yes, I knew. I thought their slaves came from the Riverfolk."

"The Riverfolk aren't of the highest intelligence after they've been modified with the serums Lightlings use to make them subservient. There are Kiatri women there who service some of the wealthier men; Kiatri men too. They make good...um..." Sacha looked away from Elian, his cheeks growing bright red.

"Personal slaves," Elian provided.

"Yeah, because they never look older. The North is obsessed with youth and stuff. And everyone being thin. For some reason, looking like you're starving is a sign of beauty there. Totally mental. Anyways, the Light Ones are a lot kinder to them than the Fontre. You know, a bunch of the Kiatri, especially the girls, died when they first brought them back. They just couldn't bear up under the Fontre's regime. So they're happy to be with the Light Ones and don't try to run away."

Elian shook his head and finally pushed the spoon into his mouth. "No wonder Lady Ella didn't want to join our efforts."

"She was nice about it, though." Sacha defended her.

"Right. The Light Ones are nothing if not nice," said Elian grimly and handed the utensil back to Sacha. "Do you have the right things to make teacakes?"

"Absolutely! This whole stack is of bags of sugar." Sacha glowed, eager to change the subject.

"And the honey? Can you make them taste like honey?"

The boy's eyes sparkled. "I'll make you the best honey teacakes you've ever had. They will literally melt in your mouth. They go perfectly with some of this —" He went to the back of the tent where sat the pile of supplies he'd brought from Halanah. Elian mirrored the boy's delight when he held up a bag labeled Jasmine Tea.

"You're my favorite person in Lashai right now, Sacha. Don't tell Cassai."

28

THE SIEGE

"**D**o you think your militia is ready for their first test?" Elian asked Cinda, handing her the map Collin had made of the guard stations.

"I do. I think they're dying to get moving. Why? Are these the weapons caches?"

"There are weapons at three of them at least," Elian replied, pointing them out. "Unfortunately, we're moving in with almost no weaponry ourselves, but we'll distribute what we can among your men."

"And women," Cinda said absentmindedly.

"Yes, and women. My point is, your troops will be as well armed as we can make them. But, that's not saying much."

"Two armed guards at each? Is that what I heard?"

"As far as our spies have discovered; a few are more heavily guarded. We think those may also have weapons, but they may just be in richer areas which can afford more guards. The Silo one only keeps one guard on duty at night. We're giving our people as much advantage as we can. We've spread a rumor that we're hitting that supply warehouse again on the night of the siege. We know word has reached the Southern Guard, but they're keeping it from the Fontre. As we suspected, they don't want the Fontre to get involved, because it'll mean their own men will be mistreated."

"Which night is this?"

"Tomorrow. There will be no moon tomorrow night. So have your troops train hard in the morning and then sleep through the afternoon. We need them rested as possible."

Cinda straightened up, her face set and unreadable. "Very well. They'll be ready for you, Lord Elian."

"Please, just sir. I strongly dislike being called Lord."

"Yes, sir."

"Thank you, Cinda. Let them know there are extra rations for all fighters tonight and tomorrow."

"They'll be delighted to hear that," she said, smiling for the first time.

Elian nodded and returned the smile. "I thought they would."

THE DAY PASSED SO QUICKLY that Cassai told Elian it felt like a blur. "I wish I was going with you."

"I know. But we can't risk your life again. The warehouse raid was nothing compared to what we're planning now. I'm sorry. I know it's hard."

"You don't actually know how hard it is because you're going."

"I'll leave you with a way for us to communicate." Elian held up a creekstone. "You'll know the moment we're safe."

Cassai took the creekstone and turned it over in her hand. Elian wondered if she remembered when he used to make them for her as a girl. "Do you feel nerves before a fight?"

Elian looked at her for a long moment before answering. Finally, he ran a hand down her cheek. "No. Fighting makes me think clearly. I come more alive than I ever do in normal life."

"I hate that. But I guess it's better than the huge knots that have been in my chest all day," she said.

"It comes in handy."

"But what about when there are no more fights to fight?"

He shook his head. "Let's win these particular fights first, and then revisit that question."

"Good idea."

Elian pulled her to him and held her against his chest for a long while before pressing his lips to the top of her head. They braced themselves for the rumble that followed. He held her tighter and waited for the tent to stop shaking. "Get some rest now, love. Tomorrow will be a longer day."

ELIAN AND HOLLIS, accompanied by Cassai and Theoris, made their way from Cinda's militia to their own group from the Eastern Borderlands. Men and women stood in seven lines twenty people deep, dressed in the darkest clothes they could find. Each was armed with knives, scythes and any other object that could serve as a weapon.

"Ladies and Gentlemen, we move swiftly, we wait for total darkness, we take everything we find and we get out. Kill if you must, but don't take prisoners. We barely have enough provisions for ourselves. We've nowhere to hold captives. You're already split into groups of twenty and each captain will have a particular guard station to hit."

"The Weaver go with you and keep you safe from harm," Cassai said, smiling bracingly at the lines of men and women.

Elian nodded to the leaders of each line, and they walked to the last group. This team comprised only people he knew personally. Hollis and Kirkus were preparing to leave. They would be joined by the group already stationed in the Silo.

"Everyone's said their goodbyes?"

Kirkus gave a tearful smile. "Yup."

"Do be careful, everyone. You must come back safely, especially you, or staying here guarding the Queen will have done no good," Theoris said. He rocked nervously back and forth on his crutch.

"Don't fidget, fairy," Hollis said. "And don't ever imply that guarding the Queen is a waste of your time, or I'll cut your tongue out."

"Which station are you heading to?" Cassai asked.

Elian bit his lip. "We're hitting the warehouse again."

"But...I thought the point of that rumor was to draw the most guards there and away from our people." Cassai frowned so deeply that Theoris shrank away from her.

"Yes. That's what we're hoping for," Elian admitted.

"So, your group is going where all the armed guards are stationed?" Color rose rapidly into her cheeks and Elian braced himself.

"We need that warehouse, and we need to...reduce their ranks."

Cassai shook her head and stared at him as if he was a stranger. "Why didn't you tell me you were heading on a suicide mission? How could you do that?"

"We planned to tell you, Cassai." Hollis stepped between them, his face matter-of-fact. "We were going to let you know the scope of the plan as we prepared to leave. We're at war as of a few nights ago. There's no keeping us all safe from now on. There's just war and strategy and the warehouse must be taken. That's all there is to it."

Elian saw the emotions warring within her and how she labored to master them.

"I'm well aware of the perils of war. I know I can't keep you all safe. I want the full plan from this moment forward. If you survive this night, I expect candor about the missions...in advance. Doesn't that fall in my rights as Queen?"

Elian nudged Hollis, who nodded and stepped aside. Elian looked into Cassai's eyes. "Yes. From now on, it does. And we'll survive this night and many others. You have my word."

"If you don't —"

"We will." Elian kissed two fingers and pressed them against her lips as he used to when they lived in their valley. "We have to go. I love you."

"I love you too. Please be careful."

"We will."

"If it costs all of our lives, he will survive this night," Hollis vowed. He reached out one arm and pressed her into an uncharacteristically affectionate hug. "We'll be alright," he whispered into her hair. She wrapped both arms around him and gave him a hard squeeze before breaking away.

"We're all hoping to survive, right?" asked Theoris nervously.

"I swear, Theoris, if the Fontre don't kill you soon, I may save them the trouble," Hollis growled.

Elian jerked his head and the men started toward the tree line. "Goodbye, Taiya. I'll let you know the moment we take the warehouse." He held up his creekstone.

Cassai bit her lip. "Goodbye. The Weaver go with you and keep you safe."

ELIAN MARCHED DOWN THE STREET, leading his group straight to the warehouse. He knew they would be seen as they approached. There were three brightly lit streetlamps in front of the warehouse, illuminating a force of guards. None lay feigning drunkenness tonight. All stood on high alert, dressed in the smart red uniforms of the Southern Guard. Elian counted twenty men outside and expected a much larger force inside.

He halted before they were spotted and drew his group into the shadow of a building two from their target.

"This group must be defeated quickly, before they can sound any alarm. Hollis, Sophie, take your positions at windows in the building nearest the warehouse and shoot to kill any that move toward the door to signal reinforcements. We'll move when you're in position." The two nodded and crept away, keeping in the shadows, ducking into the next building, which appeared to be a hotel.

The group on the street heard someone inside react to their sudden appearance. Then silence. Elian held his breath, watching the guards at the warehouse; waiting for them to turn toward the stifled cry. He saw one man's head swivel towards the inn, and then decide he'd misheard.

"Did they just −?" started Collin, who seemed to have realized the sudden silence meant the person in the inn was dead, but Elian raised a hand for quiet.

"We need to give them a moment to take position," he breathed. They froze. Waiting. Then glass shattered, and one of the streetlamps went out. "That's the signal. Move in."

When the second lamp shattered, one of the guards cried out, pointing to the inn's window. Before he could utter another syllable, an arrow sank into his neck. Another guard panicked, knelt beside the man and pulled the arrow out, sending twice the blood gushing from the wound.

Before the guards had time to locate the direction of the attack, Elian's men were upon them.

The moment Elian made the first slash with his sword, everything became clear, as if he was reading it in a book. Where he should strike; whom he should hit first; where he should hit them: none of it took more than a moment's thought. The surrounding guards were dispatched quickly and efficiently, and the rebels moved inside.

The warning that this particular spot was in danger reached far, for the inside of the warehouse was filled with Southern Guards, all taut as bowstrings, waiting to defend it. Kirkus took point, breaking through the lines, cutting through men with his

Fontre blade as if they were fashioned from soft clay. The rest followed. Elian intentionally staying in the rear until the narrow entryway was taken.

The men paused for a moment to take up positions at the doorway. Hollis and Sophie joined them from the inn.

"There's only one hallway leading to this room. Keep it clear," Elian ordered. Malcolm and Julius stood on either side, waiting for more Southern Guards to charge in. "Sophie, guard the front door. Collin, you're with her. Let no one enter and live. Kirkus, ready to go room to room and clear them out? Hollis, cover us. Nihl and Jacque, follow Hollis. If anyone gets past us, take them out."

Kirkus and Elian charged into the dark hallway. All lights were extinguished as they took the front of the building. Doors flew open and Southern Guards charged, but they got nowhere against the two Fontre and Hollis' arrows.

IT TOOK two hours of sweeping each room in the warehouse to satisfy Elian that every guard was killed. They pulled the fallen from the rooms and dragged them outside. Elian counted two hundred who met their demise, mostly killed by the slaughter machine that was Kirkus and him. Both surveyed the pile of bodies grimly.

"Feel anything from your sword?" Elian asked Kirkus, his voice hoarse from shouting orders.

"Nothing. Just...sorrow. Never thought I'd say that. Did you?"

Elian sighed deeply. "Never thought I'd have to say anything about my kills."

Kirkus knelt beside one of the last guards to be brought out and closed the man's eyes. "Used to be fun," he said sadly.

"There's two hundred here. I wonder how our other groups have fared."

"Do they have your clever little creekstones?"

"Yes. No word yet, except from the Silo. They killed the guards posted there. Haven't said anything since."

"What do we do with all the bodies?" asked Sophie quietly.

"Move them out of the way so we can move the supplies," Elian replied. "Each group will rendezvous here tonight. With their excellent wheeled system, everyone can take a load back. We'll clear this warehouse by morning." He felt shaky and out of sorts now the adrenaline of battle was wearing off. He went back inside to send a message to Cassai. He could only fit a few words on his stone and only said they were safe.

Collin came in and lowered himself on the cold floor beside him. "I don't know how many people I just killed," he said in a small voice.

Elian dropped an arm around the younger man's shoulders. "I'm sorry, Collin. I would have spared you this carnage if I could. Perhaps your own children will never see the pain you've endured because of what you did tonight. Hold onto that, let the rest go."

Collin drew his knees into his chest and sat, staring at the opposite wall. He let Elian's arm rest on his shoulders, but said nothing.

Elian wished he could sit there all night in total silence. He picked up his creekstone to see if any others had checked in and saw that it already blazed a message from Cassai that turned his insides to fire, "Devilan is here."

29

THE NAMARIELLE

assai paced the kitchen tent, watching Sacha in a baking frenzy. In the two hours since his father had left with Elian, the boy had prepared four giant batches of bread, boiled enough eggs to feed the entire camp breakfast, and made a small tin of something he told her were scones.

"These are for you and Elian when he returns. You can eat them with tea and celebrate."

A cry from Theoris made them jump and rush outside.

"Get back in the tent, Your Majesty!" shouted the fairy, drawing his sword and hobbling out. Cobbs had also drawn his, and they both blocked her body with theirs.

"What's going on?" Cassai demanded, trying to pry them apart to see the camp. In the small slice of daylight between them she saw women from Plahn hurrying their children toward the tents, some picking them up and sprinting for cover. She heard swords clanking in the distance. "Move!" she shouted at her two bodyguards.

"I say, Cassai, you really must get back inside!" Theoris yelped.

"I have to see that the women and children —"

"You have to get inside now!" Cobbs growled and grabbed her arm to pull her into the tent.

"Sacha! Come inside and get behind us!" Cassai screamed at the boy. He'd frozen at the tent entrance, his face white as a sheet.

"It's the Koninjka," he whimpered.

"Obey your Queen, boy!" barked Theoris, in a voice Cassai hadn't realized he could muster.

Back in the kitchen tent, Cobbs blocked the door, while Theoris stayed outside to stand guard.

"I should be out there. I'm the only Fontre left to fight them," Sacha said, pacing frantically. "Do you think they caught our groups going into the city? What if they caught Da? What can I use as a weapon?" The frantic boy's gaze fell on his cooking knives, and he snatched a long, sharp one without hesitation.

Cassai stood silent, working to overcome a deep sinking feeling of helplessness. "No. They were coming into camp from the wrong direction. I bet the guards on that side of the wood are dead." She looked up at Cobbs, her eyes filled with grief. Their fellow townsmen had been on guard at the Western border of the field.

Cobbs chewed his lower lip. "I'm so sorry, Cassai."

"It's not your fault, Cobbs. It's no one's fault."

"Not fer this. Fer everything."

Cassai looked at him and took only a second to respond. "I forgive you, Cobbs." He gave her one of the only pleasant smiles she'd ever seen from him.

"Elian," Sacha yelped. "He said he left you with a creekstone so I could see that Da was safe. But you can send messages too, can't you?"

"Yes!" Cassai said, frantically sifting through her satchel until her hand touched the smooth, flat stone. She whispered the word Elian taught her into the stone and then said clearly, "Devilan is here." She silently prayed it would reach him. Even so, Elian couldn't be back in less than two hours. They were alone.

"Where is the Namarielle?"

Her heart jumped into her throat when she heard Devilan's voice, muffled through the tent canvas.

"The Queen is under our protection," she heard Theoris reply, full of bravado.

"Move, Cobbs," Cassai couldn't make her voice louder than a whisper.

"I can't do that, Cassai." Cassai couldn't believe his dedication and resolve to protect her had held.

"Cobbs, he won't kill me. But he will kill you and everyone else if you don't let me speak with him."

Cobbs gritted his teeth and resolutely blocked the way.

"I'm going. You may guard me out there if you wish, but I'm leaving this tent." Cassai heard the wind pick up outside. Cobbs heard it too and looked at her warily. He finally nodded and turned to lead the way out. "Sacha, stay here," she barked on her way out. Sacha froze in his tracks.

"I can help. I've been trained to fight too...as a kid."

"Please stay here. I don't want them to know you're here, or your father. Okay? If they come in, run."

Sacha nodded and Cassai hoped he really understood and intended to obey.

She ducked beneath the tent flap and took in the scene. Devilan and seven Koninjka in a loose formation stood in front of the tent. Her heart throbbed painfully at the sight of Devilan's sword so close to Theoris' chest he could run him through in an instant.

The *Genraal Majure* grinned and leaned toward the fairy. "I didn't realize the Namarielle was such a close friend of the fey, and a cripple at that," Devilan mocked Theoris inches from the fairy's nose. Theoris stood arrow straight before him, his sword drawn and his chin rigid.

"Indeed, you should have guessed, my lord." Theoris' voice cracked slightly. His upper body leaned away from Devilan, but his feet remained firmly planted in front of the tent door. "You know the Fairy Queen herself is half-blooded Namarielle, and she's always had a soft spot for her own kin." The wildness of this lie almost made Cassai laugh.

"Good evening, Devilan," Cassai said.

"What the devil?" Theoris cursed, glaring at Cobbs. "I thought you were keeping her inside!"

"I was, I tried. She just ... she said she was leavin' and I believed her," Cobbs said, with a shrug. Cassai noticed he avoided eye contact with Devilan.

"Good evening, Cassai," said Devilan as if they'd just been having tea. "I knew all I'd have to do is start threatening people and you'd come."

Cassai looked at Theoris. "Yes. You always lead out with that, don't you? Predictable. You'd be disappointed if someone you'd trained became so careless."

"I suppose I could gut one of your men and let him bleed to death in front of you. That would give you a change, wouldn't it?" Devilan offered, wriggling his sword around Theoris' abdomen.

The wind swirled the dirt at Devilan's feet, but though the smile melted into a frown, he didn't take his eyes off her. "How did you know we were here?" Cassai asked.

"Did you think you could really hide from me, you stupid girl?" At these words, Theoris flushed and knocked Devilan's sword aside with his fairy blade.

"Oy! How dare you speak to her that way?" he roared.

Devilan looked at the fairy with cold amusement. Cassai stepped to Theoris' side, placing a calming hand on his arm. "Thank you, Theoris. It's alright. I assumed you'd find us at some point," she said to Devilan.

"Where is Elian? I expect him to throw himself in front of you any second, or has he lost interest?"

"I'm afraid he's causing trouble for your men in Pyrene-Valla at the moment."

Devilan grinned. "They can hold off the advances of your ragtag militia, I assure you. Cobbs, this will be a painful night for you, old friend. I fear you chose the wrong side."

"I did choose the wrong side, at first," Cobbs said, holding his sword higher than he should have, its trembling blade telling Cassai he was just at the verge of losing his nerve.

"Killing you will be my pleasure, but my men would like a few hours with you first. Just a bit of … preparation for the last moments of your miserable life." Cobbs blanched and his glance darted to the Koninjka who glared back at him grimly.

"Move aside, Cobbs. He won't be taking anyone today." Cobbs looked at Cassai, shocked at her authoritative tone.

Devilan laughed. "Do you really think I'll accept some sort of bargain with you again, Cassai? You lied last time, and I won't trust your word again. My men will slaughter everyone in this camp. You will watch me torture your two pathetic guards to death. Then I will take you to the Inner Kingdom, where you, unfortunately for both of us, will marry me."

Cassai looked down, concentrating all her energy; all her love for Elian; all her forgiveness for Cobbs; every positive thought she could muster. She put a hand out toward Devilan.

"You will take no one!" Cassai shouted, throwing her hand against the air between them.

Devilan flew back several feet and landed on his backside. There was no trace of smile or glare. He couldn't mask his shock. Cassai held both arms up in front of her, palms inward.

The silent Koninjka began to back away.

"Get out of my camp!" she said, flipping her hands outward. Four black soldiers flew one way and three the other, toppling into each other and landing in two heaps on either side of their *Genraal Majure*.

Devilan pushed himself up, his face blotched red with fury. "You will pay for that, girl," he said, raising his sword to advance on her.

"I said — get out." Her voice had lowered to a terrifying growl. She pointed a hand at one of the fallen Koninjka and found it took little concentration to draw him toward her and then thrust him back toward his master. Permanent shock stamped on his face as he slumped forward, impaled by Devilan's sword.

"I learned in the battle at the broken road, your special blades pierce even your own armor. That feels like poor planning on your part," Cassai said coldly.

"Stop!" Devilan barked, pulling his sword from the dead man's back. "We're leaving, but you are making a dangerous mis —" He cut off when Cassai raised another of his men into the air. The soldier twisted, his face full of fear, unable to fight the invisible force that held him in mid-air. "We're leaving!" Devilan shouted, sheathing his sword as a precaution.

"Yes. You are." Cassai lowered the soldier, but didn't release him. "And don't you dare come back again." She dropped the guard, who toppled to the ground and scrambled to his feet.

Devilan pressed his lips together, and his face screwed up with inward struggle. Cassai smiled, realizing he wanted desperately to deliver a parting blow, but, perhaps for the first time in his life, he was scared speechless.

ELIAN SPRINTED the remaining mile to the southern border of the Westerling Field. He pushed through the tree line and pelted toward Cassai's tent. "Cassai!" he screamed, casting about frantically as he ran. The air had gone frigid, and his heart felt frozen too.

Halfway to her tent, he saw her. She stood at the Western border. She'd heard his scream and started toward him. Elian cut the distance to less than a moment, and her arms were around him, holding him so tightly he couldn't breathe.

"You're alright?" he managed to push out of his throat. "Oh, thank the Weaver! Where is he? I'll kill him."

"Gone. He's gone. But he killed…they killed Simeon and Mayes and Haymitch." She trembled all over and finally collapsed against him. Elian caught her, and held her up, trying to see where she was wounded.

"Elian!" Theoris cried and hobbled toward them, his face an odd mixture of panic and relief.

"Theoris, how −? What happened? She says he's gone."

Theoris shook his head, clearing out cobwebs. "He's gone right enough. As to what happened, I don't know if I can explain it." His voice went quieter and quieter until it faded out entirely.

"Cassai saved our necks, is what happened," Cobbs said, coming up behind the fairy. "Took a lot out of 'er, I guess. Jus' look at 'er." He approached the couple and put a comforting hand on Cassai's back.

"She fought Devilan?" Elian croaked.

"Told him to leave, pushed him and them Koninjka around in the air, then they jus'…left. I think they had to. She'd killed one of them already." Cobbs pointed toward the kitchen tent, where a black figure lay motionless.

"He killed…they…they killed Simeon…" Cassai muttered, almost incoherent. The air around them went utterly still, and Elian looked around in alarm.

"Cassai, it's okay. It's okay. You did it. You got them to leave. You saved everyone else," he reassured her softly. He reached one arm around the back of her knees and lifted her as if she weighed no more than a child. "Hush now, my darling girl. You've saved us all."

Elian, still feeling a whirl of confusion and getting little that made sense from Theoris or Cobbs, carried Cassai to her tent. "Guard the door," he said to the pair. They nodded soberly and posted themselves on each side. He took Cassai across the threshold. The tent smelled like wildflowers.

"Elian?"

"Yes, my love?" Elian whispered, lowering her onto her bed.

"I – I can move people if I want. If I – if I feel the r-right things," she stammered, sounding very weak.

"Yes, so I've heard." Elian was filled with awe, as he stroked her cheek.

"I th-threw Devilan. He was going to hurt my people."

"I heard that, too. Unbelievable, what you did," Elian breathed. "Brilliant."

"How did your team fare?"

"Let me get you something to drink. Are you hungry? Just let me care for you a moment, and I'll tell you everything, and then you can tell me what happened here, okay?"

"Okay. I'm so tired."

"Yes, you've earned a rest. I'll be right back." Elian kissed her cheek. The ground rumbled, but he ignored it. He went to the tent door. "Cobbs, can you tell Sacha the Queen needs something to eat and drink immediately?"

Cobbs nodded. "Yes, sir."

"Cobbs is getting you something, Cassai. Are you alright?"

Cassai smiled weakly at the ceiling. "Cobbs was wonderful." A tear traced down her face. "He said he would d-die for me."

Elian shook his head. "Who would have thought?"

"Certainly not I." Cassai pulled in a deep breath and sat up, propping herself on one elbow. "I had to stop him. I had to. And I thought of you. I felt all my love for you filling me up with power. And Devilan said he'd kill everyone. And Cobbs said sorry for all the things he'd done. Feelings for him piled onto feelings for you and everything was clear as glass after that. I had the power to stop them, and I did. I –I even killed one of them. I didn't want to do that, but I d –didn't think Devilan believed I would, so I had to." Another tear followed the first, but no more fell and there was no pattering of rain on the canvas roof.

"I have food and tea." Elian heard Sacha and pushed the tent flap aside. "Hey, Elian," Sacha said, ducking into the tent, balancing a tray filled with triangular pastries, two cups brimming with tea and a milk pitcher. "Is Da —?"

"He's fine. He's a brilliant fighter, Sacha. Don't worry."

"She's so weak. Did she tell you what she did?"

Elian nodded and managed to smile. "I'd wager our brother won't lick his wounds for long, but I can't wait to spread the story that the *Genraal Majure* was defeated and sent packing by a Namarielle."

Sacha returned his smile and handed him the tray. "For the Queen, with love. Those are the scones I promised her."

"Scones? By the Weaver, kid, I love you."

ELIAN WOKE to the sound of happy shouting throughout the camp. He pushed himself off the rug next to Cassai's bed. She'd just sat up. "Do you hear that? I think someone's back." She sounded groggy.

"Let's go see," he said, holding out a hand to help her from the bed.

When they emerged from the tent, Cobbs and Theoris still stood guard outside. Elian smiled and saluted them, which they returned. "Someone's back. Can't tell who from here, though," Theoris said.

"Come find out with us," Cassai said. "And then you must both get some sleep."

Theoris yawned and made no protest. Cobbs grinned and followed them to the Southern edge of camp.

It was Kirkus' group. The man himself abandoned a pallet of food, and embraced his son, who sobbed on his shoulder. Elian wasn't sure he'd ever get used to that sight.

"What do you hear from the others?" he asked as he approached.

"Some are already back, some on the way. A couple of groups ran into trouble and a few are wounded. I think most survived the night though. Cinda wrote her group had to scatter and hide. There were more in one of the central outposts than we reckoned. They got ambushed, I think." Kirkus held up the creekstone Elian had left with him.

Cassai looked uneasily at Elian, but he put a reassuring hand on her shoulder. "That's not a bad report. We expected some resistance at the bigger guard posts."

"All of you come with me. I want to see for myself that you aren't injured," Cassai ordered the Lightling group.

~

COLLIN SAT cross-legged on the floor in the meeting tent. There was lots of room in here for Cassai to examine them, but he felt weird just sitting and waiting for her to come and look him over for injuries.

Malcolm dismissed himself from the examination before it began and Nihl followed his example. Marc and Jacque were talking over in one corner, and worst of all, Cobbs was standing just outside. As Cassai's guard, he stayed close to her most of the time and his proximity to Collin made the boy wish he had Mal's nerve.

The men had tied up a curtain on one side so the women could undress in privacy, so Laurelle was over there somewhere and Collin felt tired and agitated. He wanted to eat or sleep or punch something or run.

"You alright, Armrest?" Jacque settled down beside him and ruffled his hair. A gesture which Collin used to find annoying, now oddly calmed him down.

"I think so. You?"

"Yeah. I guess. Any injuries to report to Cassai?"

"I don't know, honestly. Things hurt and I think my arm might be bleeding somewhere. I don't know. It's hard to tell." Collin closed his eyes and tried to think about how his body felt.

Nothing felt normal since they'd left for the warehouse. Nothing felt normal since he'd stabbed the first Southern Guard in the stomach. Blood had come out everywhere: so much blood, and some of the man's insides. Collin's own stomach turned over when he thought of it.

"That doesn't sound alright. Let's have a look." Jacque sat him up straighter and started to undo the pieces of Collin's armor. The boy didn't bother protesting.

"Have you seen Uncle Julius?" Collin asked as Jacque worked.

"Yes. He was talking with Elian outside. Do you want me to get him?"

"No. I just wondered." He was vaguely aware of Jacque untying his cuff, then pulling him up so he could work on the straps of his breastplate. A sharp pain lanced his shoulder. "Jacque."

"Mmhm?"

"That hurts."

"Okay. Take a deep breath and give me one second." Jacque unbuckled the last strap and pulled the piece off in one swift, painful movement and Collin gasped. "Cassai, Collin needs you," he called to the other side of the curtain.

Cassai rushed around the curtain toward them. Collin was already shaking his head. "It's fine. Just sore. I'm sure it's nothing."

"It's his shoulder, I think. It hurt him when I unstrapped his breastplate," said Jacque.

"Probably torn muscles, hopefully not dislocated," Cassai muttered under her breath approaching Collin.

"I swear it's nothing."

"Then it's surely not dislocated or you wouldn't be able to speak without screaming, much less manage to say it's nothing. You're bleeding too. Right here. Let me get a bandage. Jacque, get his shirt off for me. I'll be right back."

Collin sighed as she whirled away and scowled at Jacque. "I said it's nothing."

"And she says you're bleeding, so I'm supposed to believe you?" Jacque was already easing his tunic off his back. "Okay, another deep breath I think. There it is. Off." He whipped the shirt off with the same smooth movement he'd removed the armor.

"Don't you have any injuries that need tending?"

"Nope, I'm impervious to injury. One of the advantages of my kind."

Collin snorted. "Shut up."

"I sliced my hand, but Nihl wrapped it up before we left Pyrene-Valla," Jacque admitted sheepishly.

Cassai returned with her bag and Laurelle and Sophie followed her. Collin rolled his eyes. "Really?"

"Are you alright? Cassai said you got injured," Laurelle asked, rushing forward to examine his shoulder.

"His arm's been mostly chopped off," Jacque said helpfully.

"I'm fine. It's barely a cut. Cassai," Collin growled. "Make her stop it."

Cassai grinned at him and moved Laurelle to his other side. "He's alright, Elle. Just give me a moment with him and then you can kiss his battle wounds."

Laurelle leaned against his left shoulder while Cassai wiped the blood off his right and Collin couldn't help but smile a little. The word "battle wounds" sizzled pleasantly in his brain.

"We'll need a cold cloth for your torn muscles, and blankets to keep the rest of your body warm. Goodness, Collin. You've worn this shoulder completely out. Let's give it a rest for a few days, okay? Jacque?"

"Cold cloth and blankets. Got it." Jacque saluted and ducked out of the tent.

"Okay, I'll give you two a minute. I'm going to salve Sophie's hands if it kills both of us," Cassai said, grabbing

Sophie's arm and dragging her to the other side of the curtain.

"I don't need salve," Sophie groaned loudly.

"I can always call Elian to come sit on you," Cassai warned.

Collin smiled and closed his eyes again, enjoying not being prodded and Laurelle's closeness. "Are you cold? There are some blankets already in here," Laurelle said softly, her cheek against his bare arm.

"Actually, could you just stay put for a moment? This feels nicer than anything has in days."

"Of course I can. I can sit here as long as you like."

"What did you do last night at the inn?"

"I sat and waited for news. The one thing I didn't want to do when I came along."

"Don't look at me. It wasn't my call."

"I think Marc put Julius up to it."

"I'm so glad you weren't there," Collin whispered. "It was so much worse than that first fight. I can't even tell you how much blood there was. We killed so many people."

Laurelle readjusted his arm, wrapping it around herself and settling her cheek against his side. There was a buzzing in his ears that had nothing to do with his injuries. "Do you want to know a secret?" she murmured.

"Sure."

"I'm glad I wasn't there too. I'm glad I didn't see it. Don't tell Elian." She was trembling with this confession, and Collin's arm tightened around her.

"That's okay, Elle. I won't tell anyone."

"I'm such a coward."

Much as he hated to move, he turned so he could see her face. "What did you just say?"

Her face was so pale her golden eyes looked dark in comparison. She wasn't crying, but her chin quivered and her whole body shook. "Why did I think I could do this? I'm such an idiot to think

I could go into battle with all of you brave people and fight like a soldier. I like make-up for Zeno's sakes!"

Collin shook his head in disbelief. "Hey, that's ridiculous. Elle, come on. You are not an idiot and certainly not a coward. Who marched into that guard station and bold as brass walked back out with someone else's purse and extra money? Who stands up to all of us stupid boys and makes us toe the line when we're acting like fools? What would we have done in that warehouse without your brilliant disguises and that make-up you love so much? We need you. Okay?"

Her cheeks flushed. He realized she believed him, and he believed himself. They needed her. He needed her. She was so pretty it hurt him on the inside.

And he kissed her.

He felt her take a sharp little breath of surprise. He felt the muscles of her lips relax, and then she melted into him and kissed him back. The buzzing from earlier grew to a roar and he couldn't hear or think or move. That didn't really matter though.

Nothing mattered.

Elle was kissing him so the rest of the world could burn to the ground as far as he cared.

CASSAI STOOD next to Elian waiting for the rest of their groups to return. Anxious as they were to hear from Cinda, last night had been a roaring victory for their little army and everyone was in a good mood.

"Do you know what we should do tonight, Elian?" Cassai asked him, beaming.

"Plan our next attack?" he guessed. She frowned. "Infiltrate further into Pyrene-Valla?" She punched his arm. "Bury all the bodies of the men we killed last night – ow!"

428

"Stop it! We should have a Nuelletide celebration," she fumed at him.

"I don't know. Do you really think Sacha would enjoy cooking all that food and having all those people fawning over him and Laurelle would have to decorate the meeting tent and she would despise that and –"

"I'm going to get my sword."

"Violence is a poor way to solve your issues with me. Especially since you will end up feeling everything too." He patted her cheek. "I think a celebration sounds just about right though." His dimple started to show. She glared at him and shook her head. Then slipped her hand into his and leaned against him.

"You're such a wretch. I guess we do have to take care of all those poor bodies though." They stood in silence for a few moments, each absorbed in their own thoughts. "We can win this, Elian. Right?" She watched his face closely. His blue eyes went very serious and determined.

"Yes. If I didn't believe we could win it, I never would have gotten you wrapped up in it in the first place."

She smiled and nudged his elbow. "Last night was good."

"Last night was very good." Light was returning to his eyes.

Kirkus approached them from behind, and Elian nodded to him. "Here comes another group, Elian. Lots of weapons in that lot," said Kirkus, grinning.

Elian gave Cassai an elated smile. "Thank the Weaver!"

"Yes."

"Any word from Cinda yet?" Cassai asked out of habit.

"Sent two words a few minutes ago that said, still alive. That's it."

Cassai cut her eyes to Elian. He just nodded. "Okay. Still alive is better than nothing. Write back asking if she needs help."

Kirkus nodded as well.

"Can you help Sacha in the kitchen today? Cassai is thinking a celebration is in order."

Kirkus' face split into a wide smile. "I'm dying to get back into the kitchen."

"Good. We're late for it, Nuelletide was a couple of days ago when we were all still coming in from everywhere, but that's alright. We're still calling it a Nuelletide celebration." Elian's eyes danced and Kirkus gave Cassai an understanding look.

"Good one, Cassai. Very good. Any traditional foods for Nuelletide?"

"Suckling pig and a special plum cake. The cake we might have the things for. I'm pretty sure the pig is out of the question," Cassai informed him.

"Sacha makes killer cakes though. I'll get him on that. We'll do what we can with what we've got. We'll make a celebration fit for our Queen." Kirkus bowed his head to her and started to walk away until he saw Cobbs running up to them from the other direction.

"Elian! You'll never guess who's here!" he shouted through gasps for air.

"Cobbs? I thought you were taking a rest," Cassai admonished him.

"I was going to. Sorry. I just couldn't settle in and then I looked out my tent flap and there they was, coming through the trees. Come on. Come see." Cobbs ran toward the northern tree line and Elian, Cassai and Kirkus all followed him. "Never seen 'im all decked out like that, but I'd bet my right hand, that's Marcus comin'."

Cassai screamed in delight and bolted toward the man Cobbs pointed to. Marcus, standing straighter and walking more steadily than Elian had ever seen him, grinned and marched into the clearing. He was followed by row after row of men and women dressed in shining armor.

The Kiatri army had arrived.

AFTERWORD

An ancient woman hobbled up the steps to the High Temple, watching for signs she'd been followed. It hadn't been hard to persuade her personal "attendants" to drink the sleeping draught she'd concocted, but she had no way of knowing how long it would last.

Her knees ached before she reached the palatial entrance. She knew this had once been a sacred church of the Lashain's, but the Fontre had taken it years ago to use for their vile sex trade.

"I wish to see the High Priestess Madeleine," she said in a rasping voice. Two months living in the drafty Castle had done her lungs no good. She handed a scrap of parchment to the guard and held her breath, unsure if the forged invitation would be received. She stared intently at the guard's black eyes, moving his mind, rearranging things so he would be more receptive.

"Yes, this seems to be in order," he growled. Pocketing the parchment, he turned on his heel and opened the giant oak door. "Follow me, Madame Nannarsette."

The woman's cane made an unnaturally loud clacking sound on the marble floors within. She was ushered into an entryway that looked very like a cathedral. The stained glass that had once told the story of the Ancients and the Weaver were now covered with heavy velvet curtains.

Women in various states of undress reclined on chaise lounges, waiting for their customers to come and claim time with them. One approached the Fontre Guard, swaying her hips provocatively as she advanced.

"This is not a regular, Namak. What brings this woman to the High Temple?" she asked in a low, husky voice.

"She has an invitation to tea from the High Priestess Madeleine."

"Very well, follow me please." The woman led the way with a much more business-like gait, through double doors opening into a round room which split into three separate hallways. They took the middle one and walked the length of the corridor, stopping at the farthest door.

"Are you sure the invitation says Madame Madeleine?" the woman paused to ask the guard.

"It does." The guard withdrew the parchment and handed it over. The old woman focused on the prostitute's eyes, making them see what she needed them to see. She finally nodded and knocked on the door, though she still seemed reluctant. Nannarsette realized this woman must be unusually keen. Her enchantments could only confuse the woman a certain amount.

Another Fontre guard opened the door and his black eyes speared the three of them. "Madame is resting. What is it?" he demanded.

"This lady, Nannarsette, has an invitation to tea. The time is set at now."

"Enter then," the guard snapped at the old lady and, as soon as she'd hobbled across the threshold, he slammed the door on the others. "Sit there. Madame always serves tea in her sitting room."

Nannarsette nodded politely and took the overstuffed chair the guard indicated. He marched from the room and it was only minutes before the lady in question appeared.

She was tall and stately, her dark skin and hair accentuating the perfect proportions of her face. Though they'd never met, the old lady recognized those large black eyes, the long straight nose. Only the slim red mouth was unfamiliar. It must have come from her mother's side. Nannarsette smiled, her hazy green eyes sparkling with anticipation.

"You're here for tea, I understand?"

"I am. Will your man be joining us?"

"No. I didn't recognize your name, and I wasn't certain what you were about, so I had him stay in my chambers so I could talk to you undisturbed. You said your name is Nannarsette?"

"That is my given name. I am an Ancient from the Old Kingdom, and most people call me Nanna."

"I'll call you whatever you wish, Nanna." The woman walked gracefully across the room and lowered herself to the couch opposite her guest. "Would you like tea?"

"Oh, I can't stay long. I would prefer to get straight to business."

"And what business is that exactly?"

"I wish to discuss something I believe you have a keen interest in: namely, the overthrow of the Fontre and the removal of the High King, Lord Ffastian."

The woman's black eyes grew enormous. She stared at Nanna, as though trying to find a lie or trap in her eyes. After a few moments, she smiled. "You are correct, Nanna. I am deeply interested in hearing your plans."

GLOSSARY AND PRONUNCIATION GUIDE

Places
Lashai (Luh-SHY)
Dukai (Doo-KY)
Dulon (Doo-LON)
Troikord (TROY-kord)
Lozere (Low-ZAIR)
Fondair (Fon-DAIR)
Garcone (Gar-sone-AY)

Characters
Cassai (Kuh-SIGH)
Elian (El-ee-uhn)
Devilan (Dev-LAN)
Theoris (Thee-OR-is)
Altaskith (Al-TAS-kith)
Rishnet (REESH-nay)
Dershom (Der-SHOM)

Races
Namarielle (Nuh-MAR-ee-ell)

Fontre (Fahn-TRAY)
Kiatri (Kee-AH-tree)
Dukains (Doo-KAINS)

Words in Dukies

Daanai (Dan-i) Unqualified Fontre seven years old or younger
Dapaal Dahk (Da-PAHL DAK) Fontre qualification day
Genraal Majure (Jen-RAHL May-JUR)
Hermordes (Air-MORD-es) Weekly religious meetings
Kolonel (Kol-NEL) The Genraal Majure's second in command
Koninjka (Koh-NINJ-kah) The most elite faction of the Fontre warriors
Nordian (Nore-dee-AN) Citizens of Lashai willingly working for the Fontre
Taiya (TIE-yuh) Life-breath
Veraador (vare-ah-DORE) Traitor

ACKNOWLEDGMENTS

The greatest thanks to my Heavenly Father, who is constantly, patiently and beautifully weaving the tapestry of my life. Thank you to my incredible husband, Jason Jamar, who has spent countless hours researching, brainstorming, plotting, editing, marketing and finding the past and present in all of my characters. The eye you have for anything out of order is amazingly helpful too, love.

Thank you to the brilliant Julia Underwood for your editing chops. This book would be total rubbish without you. Thank you to Aimee Coveney for designing a cover that is so pretty people buy it without even caring what the book is about.

Thank you to Aria Stubblefield and Rhema Stubblefield, my extraordinary nannies who love my children and clean my house and help me keep my sanity intact. Also for this book, Hannah Chandler and Kailey VanGundy, thank you for pitching in when my regulars thought they should have a life or whatever nonsense they got up to last summer.

Thank you to my brilliantly talented brother, Ryan who heard I needed a map for the book and said, "Okay, but you'll have to give me a week to draw it for you." And that was before I'd even *asked* him to draw it for me. I love you, Bubba.

And for the love, my launch team, you are all ridiculous in your wonderfulness and I can never thank you enough. But I'll try.

ABOUT THE AUTHOR

Julien was born in 1980 and spent the first few years of her life traveling through America with her family. She was raised in Dallas, TX. Her father, a prolific novelist and poet, taught her to write as a very small child. She writes dark, thrilling, fantastic tales of mortal battles and daring exploits. She also writes a helpful little blog designed to inspire a lighthearted approach to life's trials and everyday tasks. She lives with her husband and five children in Marble Falls, TX. https://www.julienjamar.com

Books by Julien Jamar

The Namarielle Chronicles of Lashai | *Book 1*
The Fontre Chronicles of Lashai | *Book 2*

- facebook.com/thenamarielle
- twitter.com/julienjamar
- instagram.com/savelashai
- bookbub.com/books/the-namarielle-chronicles-of-lashai-book-1-by-julien-jamar

Made in the USA
Lexington, KY
26 January 2019